TAKEN FROM CARINHALL

Peter J. Marzano

Swan Publishers
Durham, Connecticut

For book and story information, visit www.peterjmarzano.com.

Publisher's Note: *Taken from Carinhall* is a work of fiction. Any references to historical people, actual places, and events are fictitious. Any names, characters, places, and incidents are used solely within a product of the author's imagination. Any resemblance to actual people, living or dead, or to businesses, companies, events, institutions, or locales is entirely coincidental.

Editing and formatting: Rita M. Reali
Cover design: © 2024 Peter J. Marzano
Map of Moroccan cities: © 2024 Peter J. Marzano
Final cover Assembly: Al Esper Graphic Design
Cover Photo: Young Hermann Göring.
Cover Photo: Gold Bar with Nazi logo.
Cover Photo: Templar Crusader symbol.
Cover Photo: Camel with rider.
Cover Photo: Junker 290 airplane.
Credit for cover photos: Creative Commons - Attribution-ShareAlike 4.0 International - CC BY-SA 4.0

Ordering Information:
Special discounts are available on quantity purchases of more than 20 books by schools, book clubs, corporations, associations, and others. For details, visit www.peterjmarzano.com.

Taken from Carinhall / © 2024 Peter J. Marzano – 1st edition.

ISBNs
Paperback: 978-1-7366827-4-6
eBook: 978-1-7366827-5-3

Swan Publishers
Durham, Connecticut

Books by Peter J. Marzano

Litany of Sorrows

Search and Deception

Taken from Carinhall

Dedication

To our grandchildren…

Layla, KC, Mark, Isabelle, Brayden, Ryan, Kate, Gavin, Allie, Stella, and Matthew.
How impressive you all are, and what tremendous futures you all have!
Set goals! Follow your plan!

*****

To my dear sister, Patricia…
Thank you for so many things.

*****

To my cousin, Anthony Daly, of Cork, Ireland,
who, as a young monk, served as Pope Pius XII's
personal carpenter in the Vatican.

Anthony also helped Monsignor Hugh Flaherty
hide Jews in Rome
amid the German occupation during WWII.

Acknowledgments

Thank you to my early readers: Susan Ciani, Christine Kopyt, Pat McGarry, Bill McGrath, Al O'Leary, Denise Stemmler, and my sister, Patricia Marzano-Smith. Your feedback has been so valuable. Thank you to Rita M. Reali for editing and Al Esper for help with the cover. A special thanks to Curt Hockemeier, whose critical eye for line editing and story assessment is greatly appreciated.

Again, I want to thank my dear wife, Kathleen, whose patience and support allowed me to focus on writing my third book. I love you so much!

Donation

Ten percent of the profits from the sale of this book, *Taken from Carinhall,* will be forwarded to the **Adenoid Cystic Carcinoma Research Foundation (ACCRF)** to help in the effort to find a cure for this uncommon cancer that affects the lives of hundreds of thousands of people around the world. It will be sent on behalf of our daughter, Shawn Elizabeth George, who suffered in the past from the disease. For more information, visit **ACCRF.ORG.**

Author's Note

My writing journey has occurred during a historic time in America and abroad. Our Constitution establishes a federal democratic republic, the ideals and values of which have become a target of extremists on the edges of each political party. Congress's recent inability to pass meaningful legislation is shameful, and gerrymandering activities in states and counties aiming to diminish the value of selective blocks of voters are sadly at a high point.

Hopefully, the canyon between political parties in the United States will be bridged by the next generation of inspiring young leaders willing to listen carefully and respect divergent opinions while negotiating fair and equitable compromises. These individuals must commit to speaking truthfully and rejecting false narratives to sustain our democratic way of life.

Meanwhile, the United States of America and other democratic countries in the free world face a daunting task as Russia continues a malicious, horrific, and immoral invasion of Ukraine. Vladimir Putin's desire to expand the Russian homeland by invading Ukraine is parallel to Hitler's invasion of several countries when he desired to take back land for Germany because of the Treaty of Versailles' post-WWI terms and conditions.

May the Ukrainian people succeed in their struggle for a safe and independent country.

– Peter J. Marzano

"Cherish your dreams and your visions…
for they are the children of your soul,
the blueprints of your ultimate achievement."

– Oliver Napoleon Hill

TAKEN

FROM

CARINHALL

<u>**CHAPTER ONE**</u>

Time with Massimo

Brian had hoped today would be more relaxing, but the tension in his back hadn't eased as he turned up the gravel drive after his hour-long walk. And his sense of crushing grief from the events of the past six weeks felt more overwhelming than ever. To most of the world, Brian O'Sullivan was a respected art-history professor at Rutgers University. But for the past twenty years, he'd led a double life as an Interpol agent, and recent horrific events in the Agency had caused the deaths of the three people closest to him. Heaving a sigh of resignation as he reached the front door, Brian concluded day two of his visit to his old friend Massimo was already a bust.

Brian's frustration had begun early that morning when Massimo left him hanging during a conversation. He'd abruptly looked at his watch in the middle of a sentence and announced he needed to leave – something about attending a formal luncheon. Through the rest of the morning and into the afternoon, Brian constantly revisited the dreadful events of the last few months. He couldn't shake his grief and guilt.

As he entered the house, the elderly cleaning woman smiled at him on her way out. He barely returned the smile while tipping the brim of his baseball cap. He headed to the guest room, changed into swim trunks, and returned to the kitchen. He poured himself a glass of dry white wine and stepped through the sliding doors onto the back deck. Brian repositioned the colorful striped lounge chair to face west. He loved the heat, and his partial Italian heritage and olive-toned skin allowed him to sit comfortably in the warmth of the afternoon Sicilian sun.

Massimo had said he'd be home by three, but he sent Brian a text moments earlier, saying he'd be delayed. *"Running twenty minutes late. Need to make two calls. Home soon."*

Tonight's Siracusa Yacht Club monthly meeting would be complicated. A growing issue between two club members, whom Massimo called Big Dick One and Big Dick Two, was getting ugly. Each had made false claims against the other in recent weeks while maneuvering to become the club's next commodore. His calls would be to demand the two behave civilly at tonight's meeting. Relief surged through him as both agreed not to let their brewing debate turn ugly. But he knew boys would be boys, and just a long stare at the wrong moment could incite a nasty argument between grouchy Sicilians.

Massimo finished his call to Big Dick Two as he pulled into the driveway. He quickly moved through the kitchen, grabbing the open bottle from the refrigerator and an appropriate wine glass, hanging upside down above the island. He paused to pour the chilled Frascati, then stepped outside. Unlike Brian, he hid in the shade of a multi-colored umbrella in a teak lounge chair. Massimo sipped his wine and focused on the Mediterranean's deep blue water beyond his pristine green yard. Three lemon trees filled with fruit stood nearby, in colorful contrast to the yard and ocean. The abundant yield would soon begin its journey as a neighborhood project to become limoncello.

Massimo didn't miss a beat and amazingly picked up his conversation with Brian exactly where he'd left off that morning.

"Brian, my friend, I never understood your wife, Grace. Frankly, I'm not sure how you were able to deal with her all those years. She was an enigma, a paradox of sorts."

Brian nodded. "You're right. Our marriage was complex and never easy. I often felt like I was walking on eggshells with Grace. We were intensely attracted to each other at first sight. Her sharp mind, quick wit, and fun attitude made our lives together exciting. But as the years passed, she became snippy and moody. At times, she was a complete mystery. I wasn't sure who I'd wake up to one day or the next. Over the years, her spirit became more depressed. I couldn't put my finger on it, but something wasn't right. Sometimes, I'd see her eyes drift into the distance, and I'd ask if something was bothering her. She'd say it was nothing and change the subject. Eventually, her prolonged moodiness and indifference drove a wedge between us."

Brian sank his head into his hands. "You and my sisters are the only people I can confide in. Of course, I'm still sad. It seems like we were married forever. And when I wasn't at school or in the field working, Grace was my life. My emotions are shot, and my heart hurts. I have a $53 million inheritance in a Swiss account, but it's not making me feel any better."

"My friend, all you've been through in the last few months no doubt deeply affects your emotions," Massimo commiserated. "First the deaths of your adoptive mother and your Interpol partner, Erick… and then Grace's filing for divorce and her shocking death! It's enough to knock anyone off their feet. Then your birth mother Katrina's death three weeks ago… Brian! So much tragedy in so short a time! It's not good – it all must weigh heavily on you."

Brian nodded in grief-riddled silence.

After an uncomfortable silence, Massimo continued. "It would help if you were to talk to someone. You know, a professional shrink. Go in, lie down, talk, get things off your chest. Let it all out. You cry a little. You feel better."

Brian gave his longtime friend a wry smile. "Isn't that what my visit and discussions with you are about? Should I be in a leather recliner instead of a lounge chair? And while we're at it, can you absolve me of my sin of negligence?" He sighed deeply. "I feel so guilty."

Massimo sipped his wine as Brian wiped away a tear.

"Well, my friend, there's another way of looking at all this. Your life story is moving on. You need to turn the page and start the next chapter. An entirely new adventure is ahead of you. That's it! Your new book starts today! Chapter One begins, 'Brian's a lucky man, having an attractive young woman waiting for him in Amsterdam. She loves him dearly and is waiting to take him into her arms. But who knows what unknown adventures are ahead for the couple? Will they find more Nazi art hidden in lands far away? Will they be fighting criminals and spies? Will they—'"

"Okay, okay," Brian interrupted. "I hear what you're saying. Nina is beautiful. And I do love her… but I still feel terrible about Grace. I feel guilty for years of neglecting her during her moods and – indirectly – for her death."

"Well, that's exactly why you need a shrink. And that situation in Malta after Katrina's burial. Tell me again what happened. Maybe telling me will perk you up and keep the curious professor in you moving forward."

"Maybe. It's worth a try," Brian agreed with a shrug. "Okay, here goes. In the few days I spent with Katrina after all the murders, she shared more about her husband, Luca. She told me about how he grew up in Rome, and how his family dabbled in finance and owned a bank. Luca was caught by his sister flirting with an older woman in the theater, and his father demanded that he go live with the Friars at the Capuchin Crypt as punishment. Luca's mother then pressured him to enter the priesthood. He worked in Rome's Jewish Ghetto as a young priest and even became involved in hiding Jews during the war with an Irish priest, Monsignor Hugh Flaherty, and an Irish monk, Anthony Daly, both of whom worked in the Vatican.

"In our time together, Katrina mentioned a letter and would repeat, 'I can't find the letter from the cardinal. Do you have it?' At first, I couldn't figure out what she was talking about. I'd look around her bedroom when she was in another room but never saw anything.

"After Katrina's death, I returned to Malta for the burial, then stayed two weeks to arrange the transfer of ownership of the property into my name and deal with some other legal matters. I searched through her things but never found the missing letter. One day, I was in the library looking through a floor-to-ceiling bookcase, hoping to find the letter hidden in a book. Then, on an upper shelf, I spotted a lever. I pulled it, and the bookcase unlatched from something behind it. It took a bit of tugging before the entire bookshelf cabinet creaked and slowly swung open, revealing a wide, six-panel door with an old glass knob and a brass key in the keyhole. It gave me pause, and I wondered what could be waiting for me behind it.

"I turned the key and knob and opened the door. It revealed a rough, unfinished door frame and a wooden staircase leading to a dark cellar. Several wide boards lay slanted on the steps, as if ready to slide something down to the bottom. I carefully stayed to the side and descended fifteen steps into a cold, musty basement. About halfway down, a spider's web grabbed my entire face. It was nasty, and I needed to spit the web from my mouth and wipe it from my eyelashes.

When I reached the bottom, it took a few moments for my eyes to adjust to the dark. In front of me and to my left, I saw twelve wine barrels neatly lined up in a row, sitting lengthwise on short stands. In front of the barrels were two old chairs with cane seats. A short, wide plank spanned two upright barrels, making a small table. Atop the makeshift table was a candle shoved into a dusty old Chianti bottle. Colorful wax from old candles had dripped down the bottle's neck onto the straw wrapper, and a partially open box of wooden matches and a couple of hand tools sat beside it.

"I slowly walked past the twelve barrels and, tapping their sides, determined all were empty except the last two. Peering further into the darkness, I saw a broken bottle on the floor. I lit the candle and saw the room was twelve or fourteen feet longer than I first realized. I took the candle and walked to the end of the room, where I noticed a short door – three feet wide and four feet high. It was hidden behind two standing barrels and completely covered with spider webs. A lock looking like it was from the Middle Ages guarded whatever lay behind it.

"I returned to the makeshift table and grabbed the hammer and screwdriver. But instead of trying to pry open the lock, I set the candle down and knocked out the pins on the door's hinges. The heavy oak door, held by the lock, swung open, the lock broke, and the door landed with a huge thump, almost knocking the candle over. Dust flew everywhere, making the air feel thick and hard to breathe. But within a few moments, a sudden puff of air from nowhere arrived and blew the candle out. Honestly, it felt a bit spooky when that happened.

"After relighting the candle, I crawled through the passage. I dragged the wine jug candleholder with me. Once I was through, I spotted a string. Hoping it was attached to a light fixture, I pulled it, and an old light bulb – like a Thomas Edison original with a huge filament – lit. Just ahead were six wooden boxes or crates, five feet long, two feet wide, and two feet deep. Three sat upon the other three; the bottom boxes were on pallets and off the ground. I figured they held bottles of old wine. I set the candle down, reached for the hammer, and began opening a crate using its claw. As I did, I accidentally bumped into the lightbulb and broke it. When the filament flickered brightly before failing, the flash startled me, but the candle was still lit, and I moved it closer to see what I was doing.

"It took a few more tugs to loosen the crate's top. I lifted it off and saw straw spread across what I first thought were wine bottles. But as I pulled away the straw, I exposed two small statues, side by side, nestled in more straw. They were about four feet long and maybe twelve inches in diameter. They looked Egyptian. I thought Luca might have been interested in antiques and had started a collection. Then it crossed my mind that Paolo Luzzi might have stolen and hidden the statues sometime in the past. After all, it was the house where Luzzi grew up, and he made it his home between Interpol assignments. Regardless, I knew I'd need Nina's help to sort through and identify the items' origins.

"Just as I began to pry open the second crate, Carlo, the property care-taker, knowing I was in the house, started calling for me. I put the top back on the crate and left everything else. I crawled back out, shoved the small door back into place, and reinserted the hinge pins. I took the loose wooden planks from the stairway and stood them up behind the upright barrels in front of the door. I put the candle back on the makeshift plank table, blew it out, and climbed back up the stairs. I moved the secret door behind the bookcase back in place, dusted myself off, and went to the foyer.

"Carlo said an important visitor was waiting outside on the loggia. He was right. The person making the unexpected visit introduced himself as Tony Costa, Grand Master of the local chapter of the Knights of Malta. He was handsome, with black curly hair, a striking face, and deeply set blue eyes. He easily could have been a movie star. He began by expressing his condolences about Katrina's death, whom the locals only knew as Mrs. Luciano. He said his visit had been prompted by chapter members saying, 'The lady's other son is at the house.'

"He said he grew up in Malta and was installed as Grand Master a month before. He told me Luca had joined the Order after he purchased the house, with Carlo as his sponsor. This surprised me because Katrina had never mentioned the Order during our conversations. Costa then asked questions about Luca, which I couldn't answer. He said, 'While looking through the minutes of old chapter meetings, I saw Luca Luciano made a promise to the Order a month after he joined. The minutes of the next meeting show Luca either making the promise again or a different promise.' Costa added, 'No details of the promise were put in writing, but the secretary writing the minutes believed Luca had something significant in mind. A year later, in further meeting notes, the Grand Master asked members if they thought Luca's family would ever make good on his promise.'

"He said, 'There's reason to believe a gift was made, based on an entry in the Order's minutes two years later. It was after Luca died and after a member spoke to your now-deceased mother. But there's no record of "the gift" ever being received by the Order. Sir, I'm trying to understand the Order's assets and determine if a contribution was made, and if so, what the value might have been.'

"I told Costa I had no clue, but at that point I understood the meaning of his visit. He was persistent and asked if I had come across anything in the house during my visit that Luca might have wanted to give to the Order. He even went so far as to imply the gift was something belonging to the Order all these years! I thought that was nervy and had no answer for him then, but my silence made me seem guilty. Then Costa looked at me, his eyes squinting, and boldly asked if a sum of money – or even Katrina's house – had been left to the Order in Luca's or Katrina's wills.

"I was shocked at his suggestion, but my mind turned to the boxes hidden behind the locked short door in the rear of the wine cellar. I immediately thought the contents must be related to Luca's 'promise.' I said nothing and began to think. I recalled reading Luca's will at the Fellini law firm outside Ciampino, but nothing suggested a gift. I concluded those boxes in the basement held something Costa wanted.

"He was sharp and could see my mind's wheels turning. My five seconds of silence must have seemed like a minute to both of us, and his face grew stern when I said I had no answers. He squinted again and looked into my eyes. I could tell he didn't believe me. Then he turned and walked away without saying goodbye. He believed I knew something about Luca's so-called 'promise.' His intimidating behavior was more like a future *capo di tutti capi* than the role of a friendly and wise Grand Master.

"I watched as he got into his bright-red sports car, but I was so nervous that my insides turned, and I ran to the john. As I pulled down my pants, I noticed the damn hammer and screwdriver from the basement sticking out of my pocket, and my shoes were all covered with dust. So, I sat on the toilet, knowing Costa was wondering what I'd been up to.

"An hour later, I let Carlo leave early. Then, knowing I was completely alone, I returned to the cellar, wondering about the contents of the other crates. Did Luca purchase the items? Were they something Luca was holding for some reason? Or were they stolen and hidden there by Paolo? Rather than open them, I moved more pieces of wood to completely hide the door and returned upstairs—the truth about what was inside needed to wait."

"Who were all these knights? What do you know about them?" Massimo asked.

Brian gave a halfhearted shrug. "I know a little about the Knights of Malta, the Knights Hospitaller, and the Templar Knights. Did you know the Templars grew immensely rich and powerful during the Crusades? They loaned a huge sum of money to King Philip IV of France to help finance France's role in the Crusade. It turned out to be a disaster for them because when the king realized he couldn't repay them, he told the pope lies about the Templars, and their grand master, Jacques de Molay, was arrested on charges of heresy, blasphemy, and Satanism, and burned at the stake."

"My God, that's barbaric! And all these fellows... aren't they all Catholics?"

Brian nodded gravely. "The pope permitted the king of France to massacre all the remaining Templars. Most of the killings took place on Friday the thirteenth in 1307. It's why Friday the thirteenth is still considered unlucky." Brian paused and let out a deep sigh. "You know, I do kind of feel better now."

Massimo nodded. "I figured you would. Well, my friend, the king's and pope's horrific behaviors are disgusting, and I can't imagine they made it into your Catholic-branded heaven. You know, Brian, I was raised Catholic, but I've avoided Church after coming out with my lifestyle. Some understand, and some just don't get it. But back to the boxes, you're right to ask Nina to help you figure out what's in the rest of those crates and determine where they all came from. And now you have something else to worry about because everything could be valuable. And speaking of value, I rolled up the two Argyle paintings you wanted to purchase and put them upstairs in your room before I left for lunch."

"Thanks. I'll transfer the money to your account when I reach Amsterdam tomorrow or the next day."

Massimo looked at his watch and stood. "Sorry, Brian, but I must leave you again. I need to get to the club for tonight's meeting. Besides the two dicks vying for my role as commodore, we have some legitimate new business to consider. Hearing what happened in Malta, one of my wealthy neighbors has expressed interest in buying Paolo Luzzi's yacht before it's sent back to Naples. I'll shower and change when I return and see you downstairs at seven. I've made reservations at my favorite restaurant, Ristorante La Darsena, overlooking the water. I've invited Isabella and another couple to join us. I'll have my housekeeper pick up a special dessert for when we return here later to continue our evening."

"Sounds good. With everything that's happened, I haven't been sleeping well. I'll head upstairs now and close my eyes for an hour. See you down here when you return from your meeting."

CHAPTER TWO

Nina and Solie

After moving into her new house, Nina began a daily routine of walking through Vondelpark, going over to the Van Gogh and Rijks museums, and returning home. Long walks in Amsterdam's fresh air were helping Nina recover from her recent injury, when glass from a broken window sliced her thigh. Solie Van de Berg, her next-door neighbor, occasionally accompanied Nina on the walk.

One day, as they returned home, Solie asked how Brian was feeling.

Nina sighed. "The past six weeks have been so upsetting for him! First, as he was leaving to go back to his home in New Jersey, he emailed me to say he still loved her and he wanted to recommit to their marriage, maybe get Grace to see a new doctor and get on a different medication. Brian wrote, 'Despite our problems, I've loved her for many years. I wished things between us were more loving and friendly – life with Grace has been difficult for so many years.'

"But, my God, what happened after returning to New Jersey was unthinkable. He emailed me the night he arrived at an empty house. All of his belongings were either moved out to his adoptive mother's house in Staten Island or boxed and sitting in the garage. Upon arriving he also discovered Grace's plan to divorce him. He wrote saying that he was seeing her the next morning. They had breakfast at a diner – she walked out on him. Minutes later, Grace's car was broadsided by a tractor-trailer. Her death crushed Brian. Then, just a few weeks later, his birth mother, Katrina, died from a heart attack. Unfortunately, it happened so soon after he found her living in Malta. It hit him hard and

11

broke his heart, but at least he spent some time with her."

"That's tough," Solie agreed. "What he's gone through is enough to break anyone's spirit."

"You got that right. And all this happened on the heels of his losing his adoptive mother – Mrs. O'Sullivan, in a car crash. Not to mention Erick's death! They'd worked together for years before I joined their team. They were so close."

Solie gave a grim nod. "I know. I've lived here two years, and I'd see them laughing as they came and went from the apartment. I knew Erick was gay, so I wondered about Brian for a while. Erick was such a sweetheart. A real good guy."

Nina considered this. Then she spoke again. "Here's another thing that makes all this even worse and has gnawed at Brian. His sisters helped him go through the house after Grace passed. Among Grace's collection of books was her diary. One of his sisters began reading it and discovered a letter addressed to Brian tucked in the back of Grace's journal. She'd written it five months before Brian's adoptive mother died, but never gave it to him."

Solie's interest heightened, her raised eyebrows in an invitation for Nina to continue.

"She wrote about a botched abortion – before she met Brian. The scarring in her uterus made it impossible to get pregnant. That was the cause of her depression. She felt guilty for being unable to give him a child through their entire marriage and, even worse, for never telling him the truth about her condition. Brian told me she wrote, 'I regret what I've done. I feel my emotional instability as I've aged is all my fault and the cause of our marriage falling apart.' In the letter, she also admitted she could have been more engaged in and supportive of his career if not for the constant sorrow for not having children. Brian said, 'Grace filled her letter with apology after apology.' He called it 'her litany of sorrows.'"

Solie swiped a rush of tears from her eyes. "Oh, my God, Nina, that's so sad! Brian must be an emotional mess. Why didn't Grace ever share the letter with him?"

"I don't know. I know it's bothered Brian a lot since finding out. One of his sisters speculated the group of women urging Grace to divorce might have tilted her feelings from being remorseful and sorrowful to blaming Brian for her depression and her state of mind."

"That's terrible! I feel so sorry for Brian. I wish there were something we could do to help ease his pain."

Nina hesitated before responding. She gave a pensive nod. "It takes time, but a change in setting or a huge distraction can help. That said, I have two pieces of news for Brian when he gets here. I'm hoping they'll be just what he needs."

Curiosity piqued Solie's interest. "What's that?"

"First, the woman in Leipzig, whose mother worked in Berlin and gave her the German SS soldier's diary, has contacted me via email. At my suggestion, she's taken one of these new genetic tests. It turns out that the woman who turned in the diary is a half-sister to Brian. Her birth date is nine months to the day after the Russian army crushed the Germans in the Battle of Berlin. Karl von Richter must have gotten her mother, Hilda, pregnant in the Bendlerblock building – that's where he lost his journal as the war was ending."

"Wow… that's amazing!"

"That's not all."

"Oh?"

"When Brian visits, I have special – *personal* – news for him."

Solie's eyebrows shot up; her eyes widened. "Can you tell me?"

"Remember you asked me about all my color choices for the rooms in the house?"

She nodded.

"I had the small room next to the main bedroom painted bright yellow because it'll be a nursery. Brian's going to be a father."

"Oh, my God! Are you pregnant?" Nina nodded and smiled. "How wonderful!"

"I know," Nina bubbled excitedly. "I can't wait to tell him! He went to Malta and stayed for ten days after his birth mother passed. He took care of Katrina's burial and then handled legal things with the Fellini law firm that managed her estate. And he arranged for the care of her villa. It's in such a beautiful location overlooking the ocean. He's due to stop in Sicily to see his friend Massimo… something about buying a painting he liked when we were there.

"He'll be here tomorrow and is planning to stay in Amsterdam for a few days, but I'm hoping he stays longer – once I tell him about the baby. Despite his recent hardships, Brian finds time to email me every day with his plans for the day. Sometimes, it's just a brief note. And sometimes his words… uh, well, he's charming… and it seems he misses me. I think he, uh, you know, I think he loves me."

"How do you plan to tell him about the baby?"

"When he shows up, we'll take a casual walk around Vondelpark, then come back and relax. I'll show him how a woman's touch transformed Erick's former place. Then I'll suggest we have a late lunch or early dinner at Restaurant Bellavista. We'll sit in the back. He'll ask me what type of wine I'd like, and I'll say, 'I won't be having any.' He'll ask why, and I'll look him in the eyes and smile. Then he'll know."

"Oh, Nina. You're making me tear up again."

They returned from their walk and stood next to Nina's front steps. Solie checked her watch as they were finishing the conversation. "Nina, I'd love to stay and talk some more, but I need to prepare for a call in fifteen minutes. I'll see you tomorrow. I'll stop by to say hello to Brian."

Neither woman noticed the tall man in a dark coat who had been following them. He slowed down so as not to get too close as they paused to say goodbye. As Solie entered her apartment, Nina turned and walked a few more steps to her front door.

Still twenty feet away, the man called out to her. "Miss von Scholz. Excuse me. Miss von Scholz."

Startled by the voice over her shoulder, Nina turned. Seeing the man advancing quickly toward her, her pulse raced, and she reached for the side-holstered handgun she'd worn since the dreadful events in Malta. As the tall man drew closer, she released the tense breath she didn't realize she'd been holding.

"Ah, Senior Director Van Deusen! Good afternoon! You surprised – and scared – me for a moment. What brings you here?"

"Good afternoon, Miss von Scholz, and please, call me Pieter."

"Of course. Please call me Nina. How can I help you? Would you like to come inside for a cup of coffee?"

"No, thank you. I'm glad to see you're walking without a limp."

"Thank you. The long walks around Vondelpark are good, and my leg's healing nicely."

"Miss von Scholz – uh, Nina – I tried calling Brian earlier this morning. I knew he planned to stop in Siracusa to see his friend Massimo Marini after leaving Malta."

"Yes, he's been staying a few days to unwind after all that's happened. He's also buying two paintings from his friend's collection. Brian's flight from Catania to Schiphol arrives tomorrow morning around eleven-thirty, and I was planning to pick him up."

"Perfect. Nina, I have two pieces of news for you."

"Oh?"

"First, we learned only four days ago that Erick Schmidt is alive."

"What?" Nina gasped. Her eyes widened in amazement.

Van Deusen went on. "He was shot in the lower back and left on the side of a road to die. An elderly couple found him in a ditch. The bullet barely missed his spine and vital organs, but he suffered extensive bleeding and almost died. Besides the gunshot, he had a severe concussion and suffered memory loss for several weeks while he was healing. He was nursed back to health in a small veterinary clinic in a remote area southeast of Seville. His papers were missing, so his identity wasn't immediately known, not even to himself. Those caring for him didn't see our all-points bulletin. He regained his health over the past eight weeks, but with the head injury, his memory was slow to return. Once he remembered who he was, he initially feared contacting the Agency. As his memory improved, he remembered his old friend, Kristofer Bronn, in Leipzig and reached out to him. That was four days ago. Bronn told him about the Muellers, Luzzi, Gozzo, and the fixer who lived in Malaga. Bronn wired him money, and

Erick returned to his sister Monica's house in Zaanse Schans last night. He called me this morning saying he's well and eager to return to work."

"Oh, Pieter, that's wonderful news! I'm going to cry! I met Monica two weeks ago when she picked up his things. I'll call him at his sister's when I go inside."

"Next, you already know the Agency sent Brian a letter a few months ago. It was a demand notice saying he must retire from the agency within ninety days. Well, I rescinded that notice yesterday, and I'm extending his commitment to the Agency by two years."

"Really? You can do that?"

"Yes. Interpol can extend an agent's obligation to serve under Section Fourteen-point-four.

"Why?"

"I'll explain why in a moment. Now, Nina, I've come here today to see how you are doing. I watched as you and your neighbor walked back from the open market, and I'm delighted you're doing so well! So, let me get to why I'm here: Something unusual came up several days ago. The situation and circumstances are unique, and no team is better suited to deal with this challenge than you, Brian, and Erick. So, I'm assigning your team to the case and promoting you to team leader.

"Getting to the bottom of this case won't be easy, but with Brian's extension with the Agency and Erick's miraculous recovery and interest in returning to work, your team's critical-thinking skills, intelligence, perseverance, and extensive art knowledge will allow us to unravel the facts and discover what's been hidden."

"What is it?"

"I'll share the details with you tomorrow. When Brian arrives at Schiphol, bring him straight to my office in The Hague. I've set up a 3 p.m. meeting. Erick will be at the meeting as well. Good day, Miss von Scholz."

"Wow! Yes! Good day, Director Van Deusen. We'll see you tomorrow!"

As she watched Pieter walk away, Nina sat on the porch steps and began thinking.

Gosh, Erick's alive? Working together again with the team would be great... but I wonder what the case might be. Why does he want Brian back so badly... and will Brian even want to stay on with all that's happened – and with his new fortune? Still, he may have no choice. And if he is interested, will he still want me on the team once he learns I'm pregnant?

CHAPTER THREE

In Siracusa

Eight minutes after Massimo left the house, Rosa, the house-keeper, heard a car rumbling on the gravel driveway. Thinking Massimo was returning, she opened the door and saw three young men in dark jumpsuit uniforms exit a black Mercedes van.

"*Signora*, we're here to fix the air conditioning."

Surprised Massimo had said nothing, she backed up to let them in, but when two rushed past her without tools, she sensed something was wrong. Immediately panicked by the intrusion, she took a deep breath to yell, but the third man put an ether-soaked rag to her nose and mouth. She passed out in his arms a moment later. The intruder lowered her slowly onto the floor, rolled her onto her side, and placed a hood over her head. He then tied her hands behind her back and, bending her knees, pulled her feet up behind her and tied her feet to her hands.

Looking up as he tied her hands and feet together, he saw the other two watching him. "Luigi! Franco! Don't just stand there, watching me. Follow the plan. Quickly!"

The three began in the living room, then moved to the den. One by one, they removed Massimo's entire collection of paintings from the walls of his seaside villa – including several pieces he'd bought in Greenwich Village over several years at the annual art show along 6th Avenue. They also removed six paintings worth millions by up-and-coming Greenwich Village artist Argyle. In all, fifteen paintings were loaded into the van.

In the upstairs bedroom, Brian lay awake, thinking about seeing Nina tomorrow, initially unaware of the intruders. Hearing voices downstairs, he thought it was the housekeeper and her son. A moment later, he headed to the bathroom. From the hallway, he looked through the banister down to the first floor and saw two men in dark uniforms carrying paintings into the foyer. When he saw a third uniformed man hovering over the hogtied Rosa, he realized he was witnessing a robbery.

"*Filipo*, we've only got fifteen. There should be another two."

Brian's heart pounded as he quickly ducked into the bathroom, barely squeezing into the shallow linen closet. *Oh, Jesus, can I fit in here? Thank goodness these shelves are set back. Who are these guys? Massimo's art! It's worth millions!*

Downstairs, the thieves were finishing up, but the number of paintings they had gathered didn't add up.

"Franco, help me get these into the van. Luigi, go upstairs. Look for two more paintings, but be quick about it."

Luigi nodded and headed up the stairs while Filipo and Franco continued moving the framed artwork outside and into the van.

The youngest of the three intruders looked in two upstairs bedrooms and, seeing nothing, entered the bedroom where Brian was staying. He scanned the walls and then noticed a white tube on the desk. He pulled off the end cap, peeked inside, and saw rolled-up canvases. "Aha!" he murmured.

With his brief trip upstairs a success, Luigi returned downstairs with the last two prizes in hand. "Filipo, look what I found. It's the other two paintings. They're rolled up together."

"Okay! We have everything we came for. We're done here."

"What do we do with her?"

"She'll regain consciousness in a few minutes and be okay when he returns from his meeting. *Andiamo!*"

Brian's heart was still pounding against his chest when he heard the front door slam. He exited the linen closet and opened the bathroom door. He stepped into the hall and, as he peeked through the banister, heard the van drive down the gravel driveway. He headed downstairs and found Rosa on the floor. He took the hood off her head, removed a rag from her mouth, and untied her.

Rosa slowly regained consciousness as he finished untying her hands and feet. It took a minute for her to gather herself. Looking around, she started crying. *"Signore!* The paintings, the paintings! Look at the empty walls! Massimo's paintings!"

Scanning the room, Brian saw the bare walls. *God, they're all gone!* He helped Rosa to her feet and sat her in a chair.

She continued crying, *"Jesu Christo, Dio mio!"*

Brian suddenly remembered that the paintings he was buying from Massimo were rolled up and sitting on the desk in the guest bedroom. He ran back upstairs. The tube with the two Argyles was gone. It felt like a gut punch. But worse, Brian knew Massimo's collection of valuable paintings – his prized possessions worth many millions – were gone.

Brian returned downstairs and attempted to comfort the distressed Rosa. *My God, how could this happen? Massimo needs to know – right away!* He grabbed his cell phone.

Massimo saw Brian's call come in but let it ring. The meeting at the club wasn't yet thirty minutes old, but, as expected, the argument between the two combatants had escalated quickly. It started with mutual accusations of falsehoods and marital infidelities… and came to a head with face-to-face shouting, pointed fingers landing on each other's chest, and threats of whose family would get even with the other's family.

Massimo's pocket buzzed a second time. He felt he had no choice but to ignore Brian's call again.

Just then, another vehicle pulled up on the gravel driveway. Brian and Rosa looked at each other and panicked. He helped her up from the chair, and together, they ran into the pantry, closing the door behind them.

The front door opened. *"Momma, dove sei?"*

The housekeeper, recognizing her son's voice, opened the pantry door and ran to him. *"Filio mio! Signore Massimo …"*

Just then, Rosa fainted but Brian caught her as she began falling to the floor.

"Massimo has been robbed of his paintings!" Brian exclaimed. "He is at the yacht club. You must go to him and tell him to return! Go now! Hurry! I'll take care of your mother."

The son left the house and pulled away. Only a moment later, Rosa took a sudden deep breath and woke. Still shaking from her ordeal, Brian helped her sit up.

Brian called Massimo a third time, but it went to voicemail again. He turned to the housekeeper, who was still crying and mumbling to herself. He held her hands as she spoke in broken English.

"*Madre di Dio! Signore* Brian, I could have stopped them! He will be so upset!"

Brian opened and closed the kitchen closets, and finally finding a French press, he started boiling water for a pot of coffee.

Just as the coffee was ready, Massimo called. "Sorry, my friend. What's up with all the calls? Is something wrong?"

"You need to come home. Right now. Something terrible has happened."

"What could be so terrible?"

"Massimo, leave your meeting and come back immediately."

"Okay. Okay! But first, please tell me what's so important you had to call me three times. What's going on?"

"Three men came to the house shortly after you left for the club, posing as service people to fix something in the house. After Rosa let them in, they knocked her out with ether and tied her up. Massimo…" – Brian hesitated – "they went through your house and stole all your paintings. One guy even came upstairs and grabbed the tube with the two Argyles you wrapped for me."

There was silence at the other end of the call.

"Massimo! Do you understand what I'm saying? They robbed your house, and your entire art collection has been stolen. It's all gone!"

"Have you called the police?"

"No. Not yet."

"Don't. I'll be there in ten minutes." *Oh my God. My paintings! My paintings are my life. I'm nothing without them. I'm broke. I'm broke.*

Massimo excused himself from the meeting, saying he was urgently needed at home. He was about to get into his car when Rosa's son pulled up, telling him to return home. Massimo sped away from the meeting, Rosa's son close behind.

CHAPTER FOUR

The Bookcase

Four thousand miles away in Amsterdam, Nina's unexpected face-to-face conversation with Interpol's Senior Director Pieter Van Deusen echoed in her mind. Troubled by his comments and suddenly nervous, she hurried inside to the kitchen to make a cup of tea.

After a few sips, she thought to unpack her boxes of old books and place them into her home's new built-in bookcase… anything to take her mind off tomorrow's impending meeting. A few minutes into unpacking, she spotted a favorite old book – Leo Tolstoy's 1867 classic, *War and Peace*. Knowing it once belonged to her grandfather, whom she had never met, she paused momentarily and caressed it, running her hand over its smooth-worn leather cover. She opened the cover and found the letter her grandfather had written long ago. She moved to her couch, sat, and carefully unfolded the yellowing and age-brittled paper.

Nina's grandfather, Heinrich, was the chief administrator of a hospital in Friedrichshafen, Germany. He was a brilliant and insightful man during a career that spanned the 1920s to a few years past the end of WWII. In the letter written to his daughter, Nina's mother, he expressed his horror at what had just happened to Jewish shopkeepers and synagogues on Kristallnacht, and the rumors he was hearing about Jews and Romani being placed in detention camps in northern Germany and Poland. He also expressed concern about the recent transition in local factories, where tanks were being built instead of farm equipment. His words were enough to put him in jail or be sent away if the Gestapo knew his views and contempt for Hitler's extreme Nazi propaganda and right-wing nationalistic beliefs concerning the promotion of a pure Aryan race. He knew it was genetically impossible.

She was still reading his lengthy epistle when there was a knock at the front door.

It was the delivery of a framed painting she'd bought in downtown Amsterdam. The colorful artwork, by a famed local artist, depicted an iconic view of a small canal, a church steeple, and several houseboats. She had the delivery people place the painting beside the wall where it would be hung in the morning – before Brian arrived.

Nina finished reading her grandfather's letter, closed the book, and found a special location for it on an easy-to-reach shelf. As she placed the book, she noticed the sunlight from the front window had grown dim. She looked at her watch and then emailed Brian to confirm she'd pick him up at Schiphol just before noon the next day.

There was another knock on the front door.

Not expecting another delivery, she cautiously opened the door. Upon seeing her surprise visitor, she began crying. She unhooked the door's safety chain, and there stood Erick, alive and well, grinning. His sister Monica stood behind him. On tiptoes, Nina reached up around his neck, gave him a big hug and kiss, and welcomed them both inside.

"Oh my God, Erick, Pieter only told me an hour ago you were alive. I don't understand what happened to you. We have so much to talk about."

"We sure do! I just had to come to see you tonight! My sister has filled me in on some of what's happened in the last month. Hey, the place – I should say '*your* place' – looks great and comfy! Look at all the art on the walls! You're awesome, Nina. You certainly have a woman's touch."

"Hey, it's almost five-thirty. How about dinner? I'll fill you in on a few things that happened your sister doesn't know about."

"Sounds great."

"There's a great Italian place near here called Ristorante Sardegna. It's cozy, and we can catch up. I have so much to tell you."

"Let's do it!"

Unaware of the dilemma in Siracusa at that very moment, the three left for dinner.

* * *

Massimo looked at his watch. It was 5:30. His heart raced as he drove back home. *How can this be? I've paid the local capo for my protection. It's good Brian didn't call the police.*

Brian heard the car sliding hard over the small gravel as it came to a stop. As he went to open the front door, Massimo stormed in like a bull, knocking Brian backward against the wall.

"What the hell happened here? Please, tell me all my paintings aren't gone!"

Before Brian could answer, Massimo rushed into the living room and spun around, looking at all the walls. Three were completely bare. The fourth was a dozen floor-to-ceiling windows and sliding doors overlooking the Mediterranean.

Massimo fell to his knees and started crying, putting his hands to his face. "My God! They've ripped my heart out! My precious paintings. They're my children." He cast about frantically, looking from wall to wall, then implored, "Tell me what happened. This ... this is devastating."

Brian took Massimo through the events of the past hour.

Rosa, who had been inside, came and sat at the island. Her eyes were filled with tears. *"Oh, signore!* So sorry, so sorry."

"Are you okay, Rosa?"

"Si, uh, yes. *Ma guarda!* Uh, look! *Tutti!* They took all your things. *Tutti!"*

"Rosa, please, my medicine. Please hurry and bring my blood-pressure medicine to me. Brian, coffee. I need coffee. I need to sit."

"Settle down. Just sit. Here's a glass of water. A fresh pot of coffee will be ready in five minutes," Brian calmed his friend.

"A few weeks after I moved in, I was visited by one of the locals. A short guy. He was dressed in all black. He wore a funny old Italian hat, had a pencil moustache, and thick glasses. He acted like a little capo and said, 'I take care of the South Side. For a small price, I provide you with extra protection – what you Americans call insurance – but this is *special* protection. You're a big man. I think you know what I mean. It's the kind of protection to keep you safe from the corrupt police in this town.'

"Then he rubbed the side of his nose with his thumb and straightened his tie. He was talking about selling me protection against local police corruption! I didn't care much for his gangster looks. That Mafia dress code of wearing all black and the 'service' he was offering didn't suit me, but I had no choice. Since then, I've paid my annual dues for special insurance protection to little 'Tony Four-Eyes.' The guys at the yacht club call him *'Piccoli Quattrocchi.'* They say he's the wise guy in charge of our neighborhood. How's that for you?"

Brian shrugged and gave a helpless headshake. "This heist is out of my league, Massimo. But I'll do what I can to help if you find any information."

Massimo shook his head. "BJ, I can't do dinner tonight. I'm too upset. This horrible act" – he put a beefy hand to his heart – "it crushes me."

Brian suggested bringing in Chinese.

"Let's do that, but just the two of us. I need to talk something through with you."

"What do you mean?"

"I've got to get Four-Eyes over here. He needs to find the bastards who did this. I'll discuss it with him before going to the police. Hopefully, the local capo can help."

"But you'll need a legit police report for the real insurance company, right?"

Massimo looked down at the floor, then ran his hand through his thinning grey hair.

"Hey… everything's insured, right?" Brian prompted.

"I wish."

"Damn it, Massimo! I hope to God you're kidding!"

The big man shrugged. "I'm not."

"You're telling me you have *no* insurance?"

"That's right."

"How about cameras? You've got cameras outside, right?"

"Nope. Nothing. Nada."

"Christ, Massimo! How in heaven's name can you not have insurance?" He raised a hand in dismissal. "Never mind. What's done is done. Jesus! And here I thought you had your act together."

The next morning, Brian was up early and, feeling uncomfortable, recalled last night's Chinese dinner. The wonton soup and moo goo gai pan arrived cold. The boneless spareribs had bones, and there were no wraps for the moo shu chicken. He had watched as Massimo opened a fortune cookie. The little paper said, 'Today will be a day you will never forget.' Then he watched Massimo tear up as he found the second, third, and fourth fortune cookies he opened missing their paper fortunes. It was sad but amazingly fitting.

Then Brian remembered the somber discussion that followed dinner. Massimo had failed to live within his means or properly manage his income to cover payments on his huge mortgage, fancy car and extravagant yacht. Those expenses created the necessity of a grim choice, so he chose not to buy insurance on his treasured paintings. Brian shook his head, recalling Massimo's confession of having made a colossal mistake.

Brian shaved, showered, and dressed, then headed downstairs with two bags in hand at 7 a.m. Massimo sat motionless at the kitchen island, holding a coffee mug and staring into the blue sea beyond the living room's glass wall. Brian coughed lightly to announce his presence.

"I still can't believe what happened yesterday," he said, his lips barely moving. "I have a call into the little capo already. He's coming by around noon. I'll learn more about what's going on then. It's got to be a local heist —someone who knows someone, who knows someone, and told the thieves about my paintings."

"I need to get going – you're taking me, right?" Outside, a car horn sounded.

"I've arranged for Rosa's son to bring you to the airport. That's him.

Coffee to go?"

"No thanks. I'll call to stay in touch. After seeing Nina, I plan to return to Malta to investigate those boxes in the basement of Katrina's house. Let me know if anything happens or if you need money. Good luck, my friend."

The horn sounded again. As Brian walked to the front door, Massimo stood.

"Hey, I might be reaching out to you soon. My cash flow sucks, and the truth is I was counting on the money from those two Argyles you were buying to get my finances back into the plus column."

Brian nodded. "Call me in a couple of days. I'll do what I can to help."

The flight to Schiphol in Amsterdam from Catania, Sicily, would take just over three hours. The weather was perfect, and the flight was expected to be smooth. As the plane rose above the morning mist, seeing Mount Etna in the sunlight reminded Brian of a visit to Sicily twenty years earlier. It was his first opportunity to work with Erick. The case required two months of research and a trip across North Africa to places he'd not previously visited as an art-history professor. For six months of intermittent visits to the desert, he and Erick traced Rommel's path and eventually recovered a small statue taken from Egypt by the Germans during WWII. But the adventure seemed more important for Brian than the artifact's recovery. It excited him and completely hooked him into his new position with Interpol.

The flight leveled off at 30,000 feet, and as the pilot announced their estimated arrival time, Brian recalled the events of the last few months, each one flickering in his mind like a surreal highlight reel. *Mom's death in that car accident... finding that German family Bible with Katrina's letter tucked inside... the discovery of Karl von Richter's diary and the chase into Andalusia...being followed at the Mezquita... getting involved romantically with Nina... finding Luca's safe-deposit box in Rome...the carnage at Paolo's birthday party...seeing Nina tied up, and her life threatened... shooting Paolo... that awful gash in Nina's thigh... going home to New Jersey… our home void of all my things… that contentious last breakfast with Grace… and the accident. My God – Grace's accident!*

The film reel came to an abrupt halt as a chill ran down his spine. In his mind, Brian suddenly envisioned the horror that must have encompassed Grace's final moments: *running the light and getting broadsided by that tractor trailer… Grace's SUV flipping and rolling so many times from the impact. The first responders had to cut her bloodied body from the vehicle's crushed wreckage.* Brian cringed at that mental image.

And then when that police car pulled up to the house…I immediately knew something was wrong.

Brian shuddered and choked back a swell of emotion as he recalled going to identify Grace's body.

Still feeling guilty, his thoughts flashed back to when he first met Grace at McSorley's in downtown Manhattan. *The accidental bump, the spilled beer, her glare, that red hair, those striking green eyes. She was so beautiful!* He continued reminiscing about their good times, dating, marrying, and moving into their tiny cape-style house in Tottenville on Staten Island. *The flower garden… the tulips and irises, and the fresh smell of spring air after a light rain.*

The jet engine hum soon lulled Brian to sleep, and he awakened when the flight touched down smoothly on the runway in Schiphol.

<u>CHAPTER FIVE</u>

Amara Chikere

Early that same morning, as Brian was flying to Amsterdam, Pieter Van Deusen – in charge of several investigation units besides the Art Research and Recovery team – was sitting in his Interpol office in The Hague when his colleague arrived.

Amara Chikere was a West African native, educated at Kings College in London and McGill in Montreal. Chick, as most of his co-workers called him, had joined Interpol ten years earlier and was recently promoted to manage West African operations, which focused on international drug trade and sex trafficking.

"Thanks for meeting me this morning. Let me explain what's come up and why I've asked you here. Ursula and I attended a cocktail party in the Brussels Royal Palace, across from Brussels Park, two weeks ago. It was a fabulous evening. We stayed overnight; Leuven is a nice little town. I should probably mention that Ursula and I started seeing each other before Wilhelm Mueller took charge of the Art unit. Our relationship cooled a bit while he was still here, but she's been living with me since he passed."

"Don't worry, Pieter, more people know about the two of you than you realize. And yes, I remember the event. Sasha and I were invited but were out of the country that evening."

"It was a much larger event than I expected. Bigwigs from several European law-enforcement agencies, and the American CIA were there. I was also surprised to see NATO represented. Before the small award ceremony, I spoke with Bill Pattison, CIA's section chief of operations for Europe and North Africa, about what went down in the recent KvR Diary investigation. I explained how a Nazi soldier's diary ended up with our Art Research and Investigation team, who, interpreting information in it, scouted several towns and sites in Andalusia, and eventually recovered two missing paintings stolen from Paris by Nazis. Agents Brian O'Sullivan and Nina von Scholz worked to break up a ring of crooked Interpol agents run by Klaus Mueller, his son Wilhelm – who worked here – and Paolo Luzzi. Their decades-long art-theft escapade was unconscionable. I finished telling Pattison the story just as the award ceremony began. He said, 'Great story. Congrats,' and headed over to his wife, sitting on the far side of the room. That's the last I saw of him that night.

"On Friday, I got a call from Pattison. He wanted to come in and sit down with me to go over something. When I said, 'Sure,' and asked, 'When?' He stunned me when he responded, 'How's tomorrow at 8 a.m.?' I was surprised by his tone and heard urgency in his voice. It made me wonder what he needed to discuss."

Chick nodded. "How well do you know him?"

"Bill and I go back to college. My father grew up in Utrecht – our family home for over two hundred years. A distant relative to the royals, Dad was a Dutch diplomat and worked in The Hague after World War II. We moved to Bethesda, Maryland, just outside the Beltway in the seventies. I was a year ahead of Pattison at Georgetown. I spent a year at Columbia and met him again at Yale Law School in New Haven, Connecticut. After law school, I returned to the Netherlands and started my career at Interpol. Bill returned to D.C., joined the FBI, and then moved into the CIA at Langley. The breakup of the Soviet Union caused a lot of activity in the CIA. We worked together and saw each other at a few events but didn't send Christmas cards."

Chick nodded his understanding. "So what did he want?"

"He arrived in my office on Saturday with a briefcase and a flat box tucked under his arm. By the way, Ursula brought in pastries this morning and made a pot of coffee for us. Would you like a cup? It's fresh."

"No, thanks. I'm good."

"I asked Ursula to join me in the meeting to take notes. As the meeting began, he started pulling papers from the box, unfolding them, and spreading them on the conference table. The papers were eight-by-ten-inch color photos, Scotch-taped together. Though unclear at first, the images revealed an island. He then laid out more photos, covering the entire conference table. I chuckled to myself because, at one point, Bill was momentarily confused trying to assemble all the papers. It turned out that they were satellite photos of the Canary Islands and the Azores.

"He told me how, during the war, the Germans were interested in taking control of the Canary Islands, the Azores, and the Channel Islands. They sent troops to occupy and control a few islands for several years. German U-boats would refuel in the islands' small harbors and then go out to the North Atlantic in small groups called 'wolfpacks' to destroy American and British cargo ships. I knew the story but let him continue. Bill said the SS and Gestapo eventually sent most folks living on Grand Canary Island to concentration camps in Germany. Frankly, I wasn't sure why he was telling me all this. It seemed like a repeat of an old high school world history lesson.

"He then began saying how the newest American satellites use new radar technologies called LiDAR and Ground Penetrating Radar – GPR – with multispectral imaging. LiDAR can see very small land features, even through vegetation, right down to ground features. GPR sensors can penetrate the ground to a depth of two meters. Interpretation of the combination of signals can be complicated. For example, he showed me how, in one location, a GPR imaging photo revealed the foundation of a house previously not visible in another satellite photo only a year earlier. When he laid another group of photos on the table, I saw what he meant by comparing different photos of the same location."

Amara nodded. "Yes, Pieter. I've heard about these new capabilities in briefing meetings. The newer Lockheed-Martin KH-11 spy satellites are remarkable, and the NROL-49 launched into space last year has some unique capabilities. But what made Pattison's visit so urgent he had to see you on a Saturday morning?"

"These images are feeding a resurgence of interest in several post-WWII conspiracy theories. When these LiDAR and GPR images are combined with old rumors, they create reasonable scenarios that need to be debunked. A new investigation began shortly after these new images were seen nine months ago as people hoped to get to the bottom of a particular fifty-year-old rumor."

"Interesting. And what rumor is that?"

"Years ago, a British reconnaissance plane reported finding a previously undisclosed airfield with a very long landing strip along the eastern edge of Grand Canary Island. It was forgotten after the war ended, and in the late 1950s, a new airport was built nearby.

"These new infrared thermal image photos show remnants of the previous concrete runway, which was much longer than average for the time. As these facts resurface, they've generated questions about the kind of airplanes the very long runway may have served.

"Next, in 1943, Germany's largest plane, manufactured by the Junker company, was the JU-290. Using four radial aircraft engines manufactured by Bavarian Motor Works, the plane could carry enough fuel to fly nonstop across the Atlantic. Germany considered using the JU-290s to bomb New York City, but those flights never took place. In late 1944, a larger plane with six engines, the JU-390, was built. It could easily fly from Berlin to New York and back. Depending on the cargo weight, some say it could have reached Brazil nonstop and other countries in South America, even as far as Argentina."

"Okay. Go on."

"In 1940, Johannes Siegfried Becker, a German agent using the code name 'Sargo,' handled most of the Nazis' intelligence gathering in Latin America. He and his Nazi partner, Heinz Lange, built a network of spies focused on stirring up attitudes against U.S. imperialism in South America. Their goal was to have the South American people favor Germany's push against Jews and communists. As a result, by 1944, German influence in South America was strong and thriving. Brazil and Argentina became places where Nazi officers planned to flee if they lost the war in Europe."

"So, what's up with the re-emergence of the 'long runway' theory? And what's with all the photos?"

"The rumor is Hitler not only hid stolen paintings in Germany – later found by American soldiers called the Monuments Men – but he moved some paintings and gold to underground caves on the Canary Islands. The theory is based on events in the late summer of 1944. As the Allies carpet-bombed German industrial cities, Hitler realized the war was going badly and changed his mind about where to hide the stolen treasures. Some believe he decided to ship the artifacts to caves on Grand Canary Island. Another theory says the move of those assets was to be temporary. The final plan was to move the gold and art to a friendly country, like Argentina, aboard JU-390s."

Amara nodded. "Makes sense."

"Pattison said the new satellite images from the satellites launched last year now reveal ground-based images that were not apparent in the last fifty to sixty years because of the growth of dense vegetation. GPR images confirm an airfield with a long runway embedded beneath the soil alongside the beach on Grand Canary Island. Today, the area is used for agriculture. The location isn't far from the current Aeropuerto De Gran Canaria. While regular photos don't show a runway, the GPR images show concrete elements integral to an airport runway – like shallow concrete boxes that hold runway lights.

"Furthermore, these new LiDAR images also reveal hundreds of cave openings from the natural gaseous lava flows when the islands were formed. So, the idea that Hitler had items hidden in caves is gaining traction. A think-tank in D.C. believes one or more of these caves may still hold lost paintings and artifacts. It's also believed gold bullion may still be hidden there."

"Why doesn't the CIA work with the Spanish government to look for the caves?"

"Good question, Chick. I asked him the same question, and it was like he didn't hear me or just ignored me. Bill then presented photos revealing similar caves in the Azores and Cape Verde."

"The Canaries are a more direct flight path between Berlin to South America."

"Exactly. But now here's the next level of this little mystery, where it gets sticky – and why I've asked you here this morning. The folks in D.C. know the Russians who first entered Hitler's underground bunker had several days to access and remove all the secret papers left there. Many of the documents and reports were burned in the pit where Hitler's body was burned with his new wife, Eva. But we know some papers survived. These were taken by the Russians, who arrived at the bunker later that day. So, the current thinking is the Russians might have come across information at the time about Hitler's decision to use an alternate location to hide art and gold.

"In the Nüremberg trials after the war, it was noted that Albert Speer, Hitler's architect and minister of armaments and war production, and Martin Borman not only had frequent personal access to Hitler, but both were with Hitler in those last few hours in the bunker. And while most believe Hitler committed suicide, others still believe he survived. Some D.C. think-tank folks theorize those two poisoned Eva, then shot a Hitler body double to fake a suicide. They believe Speer and Borman moved Hitler through a tunnel located behind a toilet in the Führer Bunker built by Fritz Todt. Soldiers left behind were ordered to burn the double's body immediately so it couldn't be confirmed as a double. After intense questioning at the Nüremberg trials, Speer said he knew nothing about such a plot.

"But now, here's what's making Bill anxious. The CIA has recently learned that a team of students from a college in southern Belarus recently arrived on the Canaries to do archeological research. They're spreading out to a few locations in the hills. We believe they're using imaging technology similar to our newest satellites – or there's a leak in Langley. And somehow Moscow is in the same mindset as our D.C. think-tank folks, believing art and gold are hidden in those caves."

"Wow! Interesting story. So Pieter, why am I here?"

"Bill was given the task a few weeks ago to develop a response to the Russian activity on the islands. It's up to him to assemble a task force of

CIA operatives to investigate. He told me that before we met at the Brussels Royal Palace, he'd been going through internal CIA personnel records to find young agents who've had hobbies of being in the wilderness, doing mountain climbing and spelunking – you know, cave exploring. He's also looking for anyone with an art-history degree. He said that from our conversation about what happened in Malta, he got the idea to include Interpol and our team of Schmidt, von Scholz, and O'Sullivan in the effort."

"Really? This sounds like a tall order for your group, Pieter. Isn't Schmidt the guy recovering from a gunshot? And wasn't the von Scholz woman badly injured in Malta? And O'Sullivan—he's the art-history professor, right? I heard through the grapevine he's retiring. Correct?"

"On the surface, our team sounds like a bunch of walking wounded. But they're all fine now, and I'm proud of their accomplishments. O'Sullivan's back for another two-year stint. I never intended to put them into a situation like this."

Amara winced, then scratched his head. "Pieter! You haven't already agreed to involve them, have you?"

"Chick, Pattison was smart and went right to the top. The deal for our participation was made a few levels up from me, and the order for the art team's involvement came downstream.'

Amara shook his head and cleared his throat. "I don't think I need to tell you this assignment sounds difficult and dangerous!"

"The bottom line is, I have no choice. The three of them will be here later today. Now, let me share why I've asked you to meet me here this morning."

Chick paled. "You sound serious, and I'm already feeling uneasy!"

Pieter grabbed several small maps from his desk, brought them to the conference table and spread them out. "If you look here, the distance from Grand Canary Island to the west coast of Morocco is sixty-two miles. The D.C. folks and top CIA brass say a Junker could easily fly across the Mediterranean and Morocco to reach Grand Canary Island. But there are alternative flight paths to consider. For example, a flight travel-ing inland would cross over Algiers and Marrakesh. Or, if it traveled along the coast, it would have passed over Algiers and Casablanca before getting to Grand Canary Island."

"Your point being? Where are you going with all of this?"

"These alternative flight patterns cover a huge swatch of western Africa. I'm sharing this with you because it's your area of expertise. Chick, you not only grew up in Western Sahara, but it's where you currently oversee things for Interpol."

"Pieter, you're in deep with this. Are you trying to pull me in, too?"

"Actually, I did that yesterday morning when I laid out the plan with my boss. I expressed the need for a few extra bodies to help my team. Your name came up, and he agreed."

Amara stood and put his hands on his hips. His gaze grew intense, and his brow furrowed. The edge in his voice mirrored the irritation on his face. "Just like that, Pieter? You couldn't even ask me if I was interested in participating in this new case? You just assumed?"

"Chick, whatever we discover in your area will be a feather in your cap."

Shaking his head, he asked, "And when does all of this start?"

"At four. My team will be here this afternoon at three. I'll review the information with them and trust them to tell me what they think and need regarding resources.

"I know this is sudden, Chick, and I haven't given you time to digest it. You might want to consider who from your team you'd want to have involved. Some folks from Pattison's team will also join us in today's meeting."

Amara smirked. "Good God. This already looks messy." He gave another headshake, accompanied by a resigned sigh. "Nevertheless, I'll see you then."

CHAPTER SIX

Arriving at Schiphol

N ina woke early the next morning, excited about Brian's arrival. She read for an hour, then showered and dressed. The doorbell rang as she was descending the long staircase. Her cleaning lady, Julia, was there to do last-minute cleaning and dusting and to help her hang the new painting in the dining room. After a few pleasantries, Nina brought the step stool and a hammer up from the basement. She took measurements and carefully hammered two six-penny nails into the solid plaster wall.

"Yikes! That was harder than expected! Julia, please help me with the painting."

They each grabbed an end and lifted together, carefully hooking the braided wire over the two nails.

"Ah! There. Is it even?"

"You have a good eye, Miss von Scholz. It looks perfect!"

A few minutes later, the doorbell rang again. It was her next-door neighbor, Solie.

"Good morning. I just wanted to let you know I'll be leaving in a few minutes, and I'll be out the rest of today. Brian's due around noon, right?"

"Yes."

"Can you please put Bashful on a leash and let her explore outside for ten or fifteen minutes before you get Brian? I'll be back after six tonight."

"Of course."

"Thanks." As Solie turned to leave, she looked past Nina into the living room. "Nina. I love the new painting. It's beautiful and looks great where you've hung it."

"I hope Brian will like it."

"I'm sure he'll like everything you've done to Erick's place. I mean, *your* place." Solie looked at her watch. "I must run. Thanks for the help with Bashful."

When Solie left, Nina returned to her room. She continued her research and wrote a few notes on an index card to review with Brian.

An hour later, Julia called up to her in her hard-to-understand English accent. "All finished. See you in two weeks."

"Thank you."

The cleaning lady let herself out, and a minute later, Nina headed to the store for English muffins and orange juice for Brian. She returned to the house, put things away, then grabbed her carry-on bag stuffed with index cards, jumped into her new-to-her used car, and headed to the airport.

On the way, she thought more about Director Van Deusen's visit yesterday and this afternoon's meeting at The Hague. She wondered about Brian's response to having his work commitment extended.

The drive to Schiphol seemed quick. She parked and took the long walk from the parking lot to where he'd exit customs. As she was walking, she found herself biting her lip, becoming more anxious. *It's already nine weeks since I left him in Malta to return to Amsterdam. He's gone through so much. I wonder how he's feeling. Hopefully, the few days he spent with Massimo helped him to rest. The tragedies he's endured in the past three months are unbearable. Maybe seeing Erick this afternoon and the house renovated tonight will brighten his outlook. Perhaps he'll also notice I've put on a few pounds. Oh, dear God! I hope I see a big smile when I tell him about the baby.*

Brian's plane arrived an hour later than planned. When she finally saw him exiting the customs doorway, she was relieved, and her heart fluttered excitedly. She watched him stop for a moment to adjust his tie and coat. *He's so handsome. His face is thinner. He's been through so much since our time together in Malta.*

Brian looked up and saw Nina just ahead. His heart jumped. *Wow. She looks great.* He flashed a big smile. He continued to her and then dropped his bags. They wrapped their arms around each other and kissed.

"Oh, Brian! It's so good to see you," Nina gushed between kisses. "And you look so wonderful. It looks like you've got some sun on your trip."

"Thanks, Nina. You look terrific, too! It's like there's a sparkle in your eyes! Hey, sorry about the delay. I changed planes in Ciampino, but it had last-minute equipment trouble. The pilot said a light on the instrument panel needed to be replaced. It took longer than expected, and we lost a travel slot – whatever that means – so we left an hour late."

As they headed to the parking garage, he paid particular attention to Nina's gait. "You're walking well. That leg of yours healed fast."

"Yes, thank God," she said. "Here we are."

"That's your car? It looks small."

Nina shrugged. "Fits my needs for now."

As they left the airport complex, Nina told him about the house and her ongoing remodeling efforts. She regaled him with details of her challenges with some of the contractors. But she didn't mention that the house needed a new roof, nor that the foundation and footers needed new concrete work – something commonly required in Amsterdam to stabilize buildings on the soft, wet ground to prevent tilting.

About twenty minutes into their drive, Brian asked, "Shouldn't you be driving in the other direction?"

"We're headed to The Hague."

"Really? Why is that?"

"Director Van Deusen came by my house late yesterday. We spoke briefly, and he asked us to meet him in his office this afternoon."

"Do you know why?"

"So you haven't read last night's email I sent you?"

"No. For some reason, my battery never recharged last night at Massimo's. And there's more to tell you about what happened at Massimo's."

"Well, there's a few things you need to know, too. Pieter's extending your time with the Agency."

Brian looked perplexed. "Really? I thought they wanted me out. I was happy to be a short-timer."

"When he came by, he said something unusual had come up and wants to see us today to discuss it."

"Hmm. Wonder what it could be?"

"Whatever it is, he said he wants to extend your service another twenty-four months."

"Twenty-four months? You're kidding me, right?"

"I wish. He was serious. He cited a line in small print in our employment contracts. It says they have the right to extend our service."

"Why do they want me at this point in my career? I'm spent emotionally. Besides, I'm no spring chicken."

"I don't know. I guess we'll find out. But I know there's be a surprise waiting for you when we get there."

"Please don't tell me this is all a joke, and it's a retirement party."

"No. It's nothing like that."

"Can you tell me?"

"I shouldn't."

"Never mind. I'll wait."

After a brief silence, Nina changed the subject. "How was your visit with Massimo?"

Brian shook his head. "You won't believe what happened."

On the forty-five-minute drive, Brian shared details about his visit with Massimo. He told her about the art robbery and how distressed Massimo had been the previous night and this morning when he left.

"My God, Brian, that's awful! Poor Massimo!"

"The paintings I was buying from him were stolen as well. Massimo was counting on my purchasing them. He needs the cash, and he asked for help as I was leaving. I'll need to stop at a bank tomorrow to wire him money.

"You're such a good friend. Have you eaten anything yet?"

"No."

"We're only a few minutes from the office. We can grab a bite in the cafeteria."

CHAPTER SEVEN

At The Hague

That same morning, while Brian landed in Schiphol, Erick Schmidt arrived at their team's offices. He went upstairs to HR to fill out paperwork and file a report on what had befallen him. In his report, he attached a note from the Spanish doctor who found him. When he finished, he went to Pieter's office, where they discussed details of his harrowing experience.

"I felt the sharp burning sting after being shot. I remember hitting my head falling into the trunk, but I went blank after that. I was dumped in a ditch. About fourteen hours later, a local vet found me and brought me to his animal clinic. My lower back, where I was shot, was pushed up against a plant, which helped stop the bleeding. I was in and out of consciousness for three days. Once I could stay awake, I had no idea who I was – that went on for three weeks as my memory slowly returned. He said I was lucky to recover at all."

"Why didn't he call the local authorities?"

"He said they had a lot of trouble in the area, but seeing I was Dutch, he and his wife decided to care for me."

"Well, Erick, we're all happy to have you return to work. Nina just texted me; they'll arrive in another ten or fifteen minutes. Here, take this. It's a summary of the new case. Make yourself comfortable and take a few minutes to read through it."

Erick was half finished reading when Ursula called into the office on the intercom. "Nina and Brian are downstairs. Shall I bring them to your office?"

"No. Nina texted me before she left the airport … 'Brian hasn't eaten anything today.' Have them go to the cafeteria and get started on lunch. I'll bring Erick down there in ten minutes. He and Brian can catch up. Then, when Brian's finished a sandwich, we'll go to the large conference room. Call Amara. He's bringing two of his people to the meeting. Let him know we'll be starting in thirty minutes. Is Bill Pattison here with his CIA team yet?"

"Yes, Pieter. They're in the small conference room."

"Okay. Keep them there for now, then bring them into the large conference room in ten minutes to set up his PowerPoint presentation. Is the laptop and projector all set? And did you put out the placards?"

"Yes, to both. Refreshments are set up as well."

"Thanks, Ursula. You're welcome to stay in the room while we have our discussion."

"Thank you. I'll have a tape recorder running for you as well."

"Good idea. See you in a few minutes. I want to see the look on O'Sullivan's face when he sees Erick."

At Ursula's direction, Nina and Brian went to the cafeteria to eat. Brian was happy to be with Nina, but his thoughts became preoccupied with why the Agency would want him back. He put down his sandwich. "Nina, do you know what's going on?"

She shrugged. "I don't, but something's up."

In his office, Pieter asked Erick for his first impressions of the case.

"I do have a few questions."

"Hold them for now. Let's head to the cafeteria. I asked Nina to keep it a surprise that you've returned. I hope your presence will make the extension of Brian's term with the Agency more palatable. You two can catch up, and then we'll meet in the conference room."

As Nina and Brian were chatting about his return, she saw Pieter and

Erick enter. Brian's back was to them as they approached the lunch table. Nina tried to appear as if nothing was happening. Then Erick grabbed Brian from behind.

Startled, Brian turned. "God almighty! You're back from the dead! Where have you been? Nina, did you know Erick would be here?" He wiped away the tears that sprang to his eyes and gave Erick a bear hug. "Damn it! Erick, we were heartsick, thinking you were dead. What the hell happened?"

"It's a long story, BJ. I was shot and this close to death. We can talk later. I asked Nina to make dinner reservations for this evening. We'll catch up then. But now it looks like we have an interesting challenge ahead of us. Hopefully, you'll step up to the plate and, as you Americans say, 'make a good swing.'"

"I'm not sure what this is about, but it sounds like you've already been briefed."

Pieter spoke up. "Erick came into my office earlier. I gave him a brief overview of what you and Nina have been through in Malta, including the murders of Paolo and the others. You'll probably want to spend more time with him reviewing the details later."

"BJ, my sister, and I visited Nina last night. We stayed for an hour. She shared what you've been through. I'm so sorry, my friend, for what's happened at home in New Jersey with Grace and in Malta with Katrina's passing."

Brian shrugged. "Katrina was old, and she'd lived a long life, so it's easier to understand. But everything with Grace was so unexpected" – he shook his head – "It's devastating – like having a millstone around my neck that keeps dragging me down into dark places."

Brian's companions spontaneously observed a moment of silence out of respect for the losses Brian had endured.

Pieter abruptly – and thoughtlessly – broke the silence. "Okay. Brian and Nina, here, take this report. Take a few minutes to speed-read it so you'll understand what the meeting's about. Erick already has a copy. In ten minutes, I'll meet you all upstairs in the large conference room."

CHAPTER EIGHT

The Meeting

Brian and Nina finished reading, spoke briefly, and then headed upstairs while Erick made a pit stop. Ursula was serving coffee when Brian and Nina entered the conference room. The two scanned the visitors' faces and were surprised to see Nina's neighbor, Solie, sitting across the room. They walked around the conference table to greet her.

"Wow! We sure didn't expect to see you here!"

"When I was told about the meeting's topic at dawn this morning, I figured I might see you."

As Erick entered the room, he walked up to and tapped Solie on the shoulder.

She turned and was shocked!

"My God, Erick! I thought… I thought you were—"

"Stop. Don't say it! I'm here, and I'm okay. But more importantly, how's my Leo, or should I ask, 'How's your Bashful?'"

"She's fine but missing you. Like all of us were missing you."

"Well, I'm back. I feel good, and I'm excited to be here with all of you. I love you all." Erick dissolved into tears, releasing the tension of his past two brutal months.

Nina and Solie teared seeing Erick get emotional.

Again the spoiler, Pieter spoke up. "Okay, everyone. We have work to do. Please find your seats so we can begin." He first introduced Interpol's 'Art Research and Investigation Unit' now led by Nina Scholz and supported by twenty-year Interpol veterans Erick Schmidt and Brian

O'Sullivan. Pieter mentioned how Erick survived a recent attempt on his life and that Brian O'Sullivan had graciously agreed to extend his service with Interpol for another two years. The comment drew a small applause and an unhappy sneer from Brian, which he tried to hide by rubbing a hand across his mouth.

Next, Amara Chikere stood to introduce his team. "Felix Freeman, sitting next to me, was born and raised in Liberia. He's a descendant of enslaved people who were freed in America. Ladasha Daddah, to my left, was born and raised in Mauritania and is the granddaughter of Ould Daddah, the country's first president, after it gained its independence from France. Both agents held a 4.0 index in their undergraduate studies. Felix attended King's College in London, and Ladasha attended the IE Business School in Madrid. Both took a semester of courses abroad at UCLA in California and traveled extensively through Europe before joining the crime-fighting arm of Interpol." After the introduction, he continued with a brief explanation of their accomplishments and current duties.

Then CIA Section Chief Bill Pattison stood. "Thank you all for coming today. Some of you already know Solmaz Van de Berg as 'Solie.' For those who don't, Solie resides in Amsterdam and has been assigned to this case for several reasons. First, she earned her undergraduate degree in European history at Dartmouth, where she was a member of Dartmouth's Mountaineering Club. She completed her MBA at NYU and graduated from Harvard Law before joining the CIA. Solie has been with the Agency for eight years, six of those years right here in the Netherlands. She's an excellent investigator and has been instrumental in solving several cold cases. Her expertise is in mathematics, and she dives deep into data and numbers to assess, recognize, and highlight criminal patterns.

"The next member of our team is Jay Stemmler. Jay grew up in Connecticut and graduated *magna cum laude* from West Point. After twelve years as an Army Ranger, he joined the operations side of the CIA. His experience as a Ranger and hobby as a recreational mountain climber has led Jay to climb some of the highest North American peaks, including Denali, Mount Logan, Mount Saint Elias, Mount Foraker, and Mount Lucania. His climbing experience is perfect for this case.

"Our third team member is David Smith. Unfortunately, Smith's been delayed in New Orleans, but he'll arrive shortly. Smith grew up in Llano Esticado outside of Lubbock, Texas. His doctorate in geology and his unlikely hobby as a spelunker give our CIA team a member familiar with cave exploration. David fits well, based on what we believe might be a huge challenge in this case. We recognize we may need to add one or two more spelunkers to the team once we begin our exploration."

"Okay. Thanks, Bill and Chick. Ursula, please lower the lights. Bill, your presentation is loaded. Here's the clicker to advance your slides."

"Thanks, Pieter."

Pattison began his presentation, repeating the assumptions and speculations he'd told Pieter a few days earlier. But, unlike his review with Pieter using Scotch-taped photos, his PowerPoint presentation integrated translucent photos layered over topographical maps and included more satellite radar imagery. The evidence, given point by point, slowly and meticulously developed the argument supporting a search of Grand Canary Island. Thirty minutes later, every up-to-date photo was displayed, and each attendee was awestruck by the well-developed hypothesis of gold and art being hidden in the caves of Grand Canary Island.

As Pattison ended his presentation, he said, "The project will initially involve eight people – three from the CIA and five from Interpol. Today's meeting was not to decide whether to go forward, but rather to introduce all of you to the challenge this case presents, and allow each of you to get acquainted."

Pieter stood. "Our agencies have worked together in the past, but this case is different. To many folks, dealing with what people call 'historical fiction' is a thing of fantasy. It happens, however, that on multiple occasions, Erick, Nina, and Brian have researched what seems implausible or farfetched situations and have come up with the goods. With their efforts, their investigations have uncovered art treasures worth millions. In this case, as Bill's presentation has pointed out, we're focused on tangible evidence of possible hiding places. In other words, the satellite photos speak for themselves.

"We don't know what was in the minds of the men closest to Hitler. Nor do we know what Hitler demanded of them at the time. The speculation of Hitler leaving his Führer Bunker alive hours before his apparent suicide remains a strong possibility. And the idea of Hitler redirecting art and gold from being hidden in Germany's mountains to another location was, for years, just rumor and speculation. But now, with these satellite photos, the old rumors and speculation of his moving his assets, leaving the bunker, and flying from Berlin to a remote location in the Canaries, the Azores, or South America take on real legitimacy. Our goal in supporting this project is clear: Look for hidden art and anything else stowed in caves on Grand Canary Island.

"We discussed the idea of having four teams for the project. Bill suggested having a CIA member and an Interpol member on each team. I'm not necessarily an advocate of that approach, but we should consider the idea. I suggest our new team leader, Nina, work with Solie to discuss how best to set up the teams and approach the search. Bill and I believe we all should meet again here, the day after tomorrow, at 1. This will give you time to digest what you've seen and heard today. Get with your teams tomorrow to work out your respective plans. Use presentation software. Report back with recommendations on how you will search the island. Save your files on either 3½ inch disks, CDs, or small flash drives to Ursula, and she'll load the files for the meeting. She'll have them ready for the meeting. Any questions? Yes, Erick?"

"Is there a bonus for the team who finds the treasure?"

Nina and Brian looked at each other and cringed.

Pieter understood the bad joke. "Ah! So, you'd like a prize. How's this? You'll have an office in this building – the vacant office next to mine. Is that okay with you?"

"Uh, no thanks. How about a nice dinner in Amsterdam?"

"You got it. Chick, any questions?"

"I'm good. We might have a few more tomorrow."

"Get with me if you need to. Okay. Everyone, be back here in two days. Same time, same room."

As the meeting ended, members of each team stood and chatted with their supervisors. Grimaces and head-scratching prevailed.

Solie walked over to Nina. "Wow, neighbor! This was a surprise! It'll be interesting working together."

"I guess."

"You seem worried. Are you concerned?"

Nina nodded. "A little."

"How do you feel? Have you said anything to Brian yet?"

"I'm okay – a little queasy in the mornings. I thought I'd tell him tonight, but now it looks like we'll be eating dinner with Erick."

"At least you'll have the ride back together afterward."

A few feet away, Erick turned to Brian. "Interesting project. But I can't stop thinking of what you've been through."

"It's been an emotional rollercoaster for eight straight weeks. It'll take time before I put everything behind me. I'm thinking of staying here in town tonight. I need to catch up with Pieter and HR about my employment extension and get a good night's sleep. I'll pass on dinner. I'm sure Nina can make her way home and get back in the morning. How about you?"

Erick nodded. "Sure. We'll have dinner another night. I enjoy my sister's cooking, so I'm not missing anything. I'm using her car so I'll be able to return early tomorrow morning."

Nina finished with Solie and headed to the foyer with Brian and Erick. Brian shared his thoughts with Nina about staying at a hotel in The Hague for a good night's sleep. Solie heard Brian's comment and noticed the disappointed look on Nina's face.

"How about we meet here at ten," Brian suggested. "Are you okay with that, Nina? I mean, are you okay with heading home tonight by yourself?"

"Sure. Uh, so we won't have dinner tonight. Right?"

"Right. I'll grab my luggage from your car."

Brian didn't notice her obvious disappointment. "Okay," she said with a shrug. "I've got a few things I need to do anyway. I'm good."

An awkward silence descended among the four as they waited for the elevator, which was taking forever to arrive. The silence lingered during the entire ride down to the lobby. Nina felt acutely aware of the stifling tension. Even Brian seemed to notice the prevailing awkwardness in the elevator car.

What the heck is going on? Erick wondered. *What's different? Something's wrong.*

Solie knew the answer but said nothing.

When the doors slid open at last, Erick and Solie exchanged hugs before heading to their respective cars. Brian and Nina silently walked to her car, where he retrieved his bag.

"Is everything alright?" Brian asked.

"Yes. Uh, well, to be honest, no. I'm disappointed you're staying here tonight. I made dinner reservations at Bella Vista."

"I'm sorry. How's tomorrow night? We'll have lunch with Erick and then have dinner together—just you and me. I promise. We can go to Ristorante Sardegna."

A smile lit her face. "I'd like that."

Standing on her toes, she kissed him on the cheek.

He smiled. "Thanks, Nina. I'll see you in the morning."

With a travel bag in each hand, he returned inside, intending to ask Ursula to book him a hotel room. While waiting for the elevator to Pieter's office, Brian thought about Nina.

CHAPTER NINE

Kristofer Bronn Calls

Just then, before stepping into the open elevator, his phone rang.

"Hello. *Das* Agent Brian?"

"Yes."

"*Yah*, Brian, *das ist* your friend Kristofer – Kristofer Bronn – you know me – *der* one who owns *der* antique store in Leipzig."

"Hello, my old friend. I hope you are well."

"*Yah.* Very well, Agent Brian. I have something. It's something for you."

"And what is that, my friend?"

"My cleaning lady. *Yah.* Once a year, she comes to my store. She is very *gute! Yah.* She does *der* cleaning all over *der* place. Today, she got on her knees to clean under my desk. She find something. *Yah, der* thing. A piece of paper. She put *der* paper on my desk."

"Nice! So, Kristofer, you are calling me about a piece of paper?"

"*Yah!* She found *der* old paper. *Yah! Der* old paper is from *der* diary. You know, *der Nazi. Der von Richter* diary. I think it is *der* middle of *der von Richter* diary. *Der* paper is ripped where *der* little staples are sup-posed to hold it in *der* book."

"Really! Interesting."

"*Yah.* Agent Brian, I read *der* words. *Der German* words. *Karl von Richter* had other business during *der* SS service. I think you find *der* words interesting."

"Can you tell me more?"

"*Yah,* but I have an idea. I will take a picture with my phone, and I will send you *der* picture. *Dis* okay? I will send *der* page tomorrow."

"Yes. Kristofer, send me the photo now, but please send the page tonight."

"Okay. But where are you, Agent Brian?"

"At the Interpol offices in The Hague. Send it to Pieter … uh, no. Kristofer, send the paper you found to Nina von Scholz in Amsterdam. Please send it to her using overnight delivery tonight. I'll text you her address when we hang up. And I'll reimburse you for the shipping."

"Okay, my agent friend. When will you visit me? We can have schnitzel and beer."

"Soon. I promise."

"*Danke,* Agent Brian. *Gute nacht.*"

Brian rode the elevator to the third floor and went to Pieter's office.

Ursula looked up as he walked in. "He'll see you now."

"Thanks. Can you get me a room for tonight? Just one night."

"Sure. Non-smoking, queen bed, extra pillow, low floor, away from the elevator. Right?"

"Is that in my profile?"

"Of course. Do you want to know what *else* is in your profile?"

"Uh, I'm not sure. Maybe we can discuss that another time."

Just then, a voice bellowed from inside. "O'Sullivan, are you coming in here or not?"

Their conversation about his employment extension started in a friendly enough way. But when Brian pushed back on signing on for another two years, Pieter got straight to the point.

"Listen, O'Sullivan, I'll be frank. The Agency needs you back for this one. You can see for yourself these other agents are youngsters. This case needs a mature agent like you. Not to do the heavy lifting but as a leader. Your presence alone will lend legitimate guidance – especially for those two CIA fellows and the woman. Those young Americans are often more like reckless cowboys than sleuths in their approach."

"I get it, Pieter, but listen: This case needs to be the end of my work with Interpol. I don't care if I have another two years of service. I'm only doing this to help Nina get her feet under her as a team leader. Once this is done, I have a few personal things to address with the inheritance, including residential and commercial building properties I recently learned I own in Italy."

"Of course. Is there anything else you want to share with me?"

Brian looked surprised by Pieter's question. "No, why?"

"We have eyes and ears all over this place. Ursula told me the four of you were dead silent in the elevator. We would've expected some chatter among you."

Brian's mouth formed a grim line. "No. We're good. There's been a lot on everyone's minds. I'm staying in town tonight, and I'll be with my team first thing in the morning. We have a lot of catching up to do with each other tomorrow."

Half believing Brian's response, Pieter replied, "Okay. Good evening, O'Sullivan."

Summarily dismissed, Brian left the office feeling spied upon. *Is he any different than Wilhelm Mueller?*

Showing no shame in having spied for Pieter, Ursula handed Brian a slip of paper with the hotel address. "You are all set. It's the company suite. I decided you deserve a nice room tonight. I've called a car for you. It's waiting downstairs."

"Thanks, Ursula. See you tomorrow. Oh, one more thing. Can you please get me a new laptop? The battery in the one I have isn't taking a charge."

"Actually, a new laptop has already been ordered; you'll get it first thing tomorrow. I've also ordered you – and the team – new, updated phones."

"Great. Good night, Moneypenny."

"What?"

"It's a joke."

"Who's Moneypenny?"

Brian gave a dismissive headshake. "Never mind."

That was interesting. Everyone who's ever watched at least one

James Bond movie knows Bond's secretary at MI-6. Where has Ursula been not to know that?

It was a six-minute ride to the hotel. After checking in, Brian changed into sweats and returned downstairs to the hotel's small business center. He printed four photos, one for each side of the paper Bronn's cleaning lady found. It was all in German. He folded the pages and returned to his room. He'd review them with Nina tomorrow if the overnight delivery didn't arrive at her place. He called for room service, ate, and read a bit.

But as he was falling asleep, Ursula's comment came to mind yet again: "Who's Moneypenny?" *It's strange she didn't know.* He was asleep by 8 – earlier than usual.

It was late when Nina arrived back in Amsterdam. Still curious about Pattison's earlier presentation, she went to her PC and spent the next two hours online, looking for historical information about Grand Canary Island. She first read how Hitler's early attempt to align with Generalissimo Francisco Franco enabled the Germans to set themselves up with an outpost with over fifty airplanes stationed at Gran Canaria Airport.

She also read about a huge villa built by Gustav Winter on another Canary Island in an area called Fuerteventura. An article written by Island locals said Winter arrived in 1939 with suitcases full of cash to buy the entire peninsula as a strategic location for the Nazis. Nearby residents believed his newly built villa was vital to Germany's plan to control all the Canary Islands. Island natives claimed they often saw high-level Germans visiting the villa. In later years, natives speculated the villa was used by high-ranking German SS officers receiving plastic surgery before flying on to South America to hide.

Nina read another later article from 1947 written by the Madrid bureau chief of the U.S. Office of Strategic Services, the precursor to the CIA. It described Winter as a German agent overseeing several observation posts, using wireless telegraphy to reach German U-boats at sea.

Nina's last read was how the British considered a plan to invade the Canary Islands in late 1940 or early 1941 and take it back under British control under a maneuver dubbed 'Operation Pilgrim.' However, British intelligence abandoned the plan after learning Germany's new focus was to invade Russia in the summer of 1941 rather than launch military activity against the neutral Franco in Spain.

Finally satisfied with a better understanding of the islands, Nina turned in for the night. As she lay in bed, she thought about her time with Brian earlier in the day. She grabbed her long body pillow and held it tightly. With her anxiety somewhat relieved, her mind wandered back to Pattison's earlier presentation, the rumors, the assumptions, and satellite photos. Something didn't fit.

At the hotel, Brian began dreaming. It was a spring day years earlier. It was near Easter. He was walking with Grace toward their just-purchased house, a small cape. He carried her over the threshold. It smelled so fresh. Early purple irises and giant yellow and red tulips stood proudly in a tall, etched-glass vase on the delicate hand-woven lace runner he'd purchased in Burano during an art research trip to Venice. The home's newly painted interior was bright white, and the recently refinished and varnished plank flooring sparkled in the sunlight. They entered the bedroom, where the bedspread's floral print matched the vase's flowers. Suddenly, they were in bed. The sheets were new and cold. Grace's pale Irish skin was such a contrast to her dark red hair and green eyes. He reached to caress her breasts.

I love you, Grace. I'll always love you.

Just then, the bedside hotel phone rang.

"Good morning, Mr. O'Sullivan. It's 6 a.m. This is your requested wake-up call. Have a nice day."

He lay back down for a moment. Unlike most of his others, this dream remained fresh in his mind. He thought about Grace. *She's gone. Grace left me a long time ago. I need to move on.*

Then he thought about Nina and fell back to sleep.

CHAPTER TEN

Day Two at The Hague

It was 7 a.m. when Brian's trusted wind-up travel alarm sounded. Always used as a backup, he jumped up and called Nina. "Good morning, team leader! Were you awake?"

"About thirty minutes – resting here in bed – thinking."

"Of?"

"Things. Lots of things – and about you."

Brian sighed. "Our time together in Spain and Rome this spring was special, and I don't believe I've thanked you properly. I want to spend more time alone with you. But, honestly, right now, I'm still a wreck inside... and feeling guilty. I'd call it Irish guilt, but apparently, I don't have a shred of Irish in me. But these last three months have been hell."

"I get it. You're a good man, and it's your nature to hurt deeply. Solie and I have become friendly since my return to Amsterdam, and we've talked a lot on our walks through Vondelpark, Museumplein, and the open markets. Our discussions have helped me understand what you're dealing with. I want you to know I'm here for you."

"Thank you, Nina. Sometimes, Grace still shows up in my dreams. But I'll get past this. As Massimo told me, I need to turn the page and start my next chapter."

Nina glanced at her watch. "I'm about to shower, and I'll be leaving in thirty minutes. I want to be in the office when Erick arrives. We can have breakfast together, and I want to go over some ideas I had after reviewing Pattison's presentation and doing research last night."

"Great. I'm going in early, too. According to Ursula, we're all getting new phones, and I'm getting a new laptop this morning. I'll see you there. Gee, I forgot to mention why I called. Do you have an overnight delivery on your front steps?"

"I'll look. Just give me a moment." She put her robe on and walked to the front door.

"Uh, no. Nothing's here, Brian. Did you send something?"

"Something came up late yesterday with the old gent, Kristofer Bronn, in Leipzig. I had him send an envelope to your address using an overnight courier. It should be there within the hour. I'd like you to wait for it before you leave. Okay?"

"Sure. I'll give you a call when I'm leaving."

In Zaanse Schans, just outside Amsterdam, Erick was finishing a cup of coffee and once again thanked Monica for letting him use her car.

"Thanks, sis. Your dinner last night was awesome! See you tonight."

"Erick, please be careful," Monica cautioned. "Whatever you do for work – it scares me."

He offered her a quirky grin. "I'm just going to the office today. And, you know, I'm only into researching art."

"I hear what you're saying, but you seem to be putting yourself in danger lately."

"Yes, 'Mother.' I'll be careful," Erick replied, only half teasing. He turned away quickly so she wouldn't see the tears welling in his eyes. After all these years, he still missed his mother.

Monica watched him go, heartbroken by the hurt tone beneath her kid brother's words. *Life was so difficult after Mother passed. And when Father couldn't accept Erick's being gay, our home life became toxic. Thank God I found my love and moved out. But I should never have left Erick alone there with Father! I should have known he'd throw Erick out of the house. I hope he finds someone who loves him.*

Brian finished a brief but intense workout on the treadmill and showered. His A-fib was under control with a new med prescribed by his doctor in New Jersey. He took a taxi back to the office and headed to the fourth-floor IT department to pick up his new laptop from Dirk. Equipped with several new applications, it was configured with a small device slid in the side, enabling a connection to the building's local area network. A few of the latest laptops could also access the building's network through a new feature Dirk was testing. He casually called it 'Wi-Fi.'

"Wow! I feel like James Bond getting a new, fully equipped Aston Martin for whatever happens next!"

"You're also getting a smartphone to replace your flip phone."

"Interesting. A Blackberry, right? I've read about the 'Torch' model."

Dirk shook his head. "Not here. Those Blackberry phones have peaked. This is an Apple."

"Looks kind of flat for an apple." When Dirk rolled his eyes at his kidding, Brian added, "Okay. So we're staying with fruit but going from berries to apples. Interesting."

"Not just interesting. This thing's incredible! This phone with the cute logo of a little apple and bite mark will be the next big thing. It'll leave those berry phones in the dust. Give me a minute to transfer your contacts. Brian, what's your Agent call sign? Is it a number?"

"I go by ten point five. It's my U.S. shoe size – so it's easy to remember."

"You're funny. Here. You should be all set now – the new phone has all your old contacts. Let me know how both work for you before you leave the building today."

"Thanks. Hey, Dirk, any chance an Aston Martin will be waiting downstairs for me?"

The IT whiz grinned. "In your dreams, Agent. And here. Your new password is 'EUR44.'"

"How am I supposed to remember a password like that?"

"Don't worry. It's written inside your shoe in case you forget."

"Dirk, you're a comedian – NOT!"

Brian left carrying a new laptop under his arm and a new phone in his pocket and headed to the third floor to meet Pieter.

Ursula told him Pieter wasn't in yet, but she'd already prepared the papers for him to sign to extend his time with Interpol. She spread the paperwork on the edge of her desk.

"So, Moneypenny, is this all legit? They can enforce my stay?"

"If you mean, can the Agency enforce extending your time? The answer is 'Yes.' And who on earth is this Moneypenny?"

"Just an old friend."

He reluctantly signed where the small yellow stickies indicated, then left the office before Pieter showed up.

It's interesting that she still doesn't know who Moneypenny is.

In the cafeteria, Erick and Nina were huddled at a table, deep in conversation while waiting for Brian. She filled Erick in on all that had happened since he went missing, all the way up to the deaths of Paolo, Wilhelm, and the Luciano cousins. She began by explaining how they found the paintings hidden in an arch inside the Mesquita, and then they disappeared overnight. Her return to Rome with Brian, the use of the code left by Katrina, and the incredible treasure they found in a safe deposit box.

"Then we were asked by Wilhelm to follow Paolo. So we flew to Siracusa, then sailed to Malta with Brian's friend Massimo for Paolo's birthday party."

She explained how Paolo went on a killing spree, killing three agents, Wilhelm, two of his cousins who owned a bank, as well as a nurse and a doctor.

"We went down to the house where Brian's mother was resting. It was a warm night. The wind outside waved the palm trees back and forth. Clouds were racing across the night sky, sometimes blocking the bright full moon. It was frightening.

"We spotted Paolo inside. Brian told me to wait, but I made the mistake of going alone, thinking I could sneak in without being seen. But Paolo spotted me and was waiting behind a door. I approached ever so slowly. Suddenly, I felt him put the muzzle of his handgun to my head. He moved me to the kitchen, sat me down, and taped my hands behind my back. Then, straddling over my legs, he reached behind me, unhooked my bra, and started touching my breasts.

"Suddenly, a palm tree's frond came crashing through a tall kitchen window, sending slivers of glass over Paolo and me. The moonlight reflected on the piece of glass stuck in Paolo's neck's artery. It looked terrible as the blood began spurting. He was in trouble. Another piece slashed through my pants, slicing deep into my upper thigh near my artery. I was bleeding badly. I don't remember much after that – other than waking up in the hospital. Brian told me he shot Paolo through the broken window, and he used his mother's wheelchair to take me to an ambulance a few houses away from where the party had been, and where the others were killed.

"But Erick, that wasn't the end. A day later, I left the hospital, returned to Katrina's house, and was resting with Brian. Wilhelm's father, Klaus, and the fixer from Malaga showed up. We heard them sneak into the house. Brian helped me limp into the atrium. As we got down onto the floor to hide among the plants, Brian's A-fib was raging, and he passed out next to me. I was on my stomach with my gun drawn.

"This huge, mean-looking guy approached and spotted us. He grinned, then lifted his gun and took aim. As he did, I raised my gun under a giant philodendron leaf and pointed it at him. I shut my eyes and was about to pull the trigger when a thunderous shot rang out. I thought I was dead."

Erick let out a sharp gasp, and his eyes widened.

"Unknown to Brian and me, Interpol got wind of a revenge plot against Brian, and Pieter made plans for the Agency's special squad to hide outside and keep an eye on us. It was an Interpol sniper who took the shot through the Atrium's glass window, killing the intruder just in the nick of time. The guy landed on the floor right next to me – and facing me with his eyes wide open. I'll never forget the expression on his face. He was dead, but I shot him again anyway."

"Oh, Nina. I had no idea of these details. It had to be absolutely horrible for you."

"After all that tension from the shootings, killings, and the house invasion, Brian decided to take a break. He said goodbye to Katrina and flew back to New Jersey to deal with his A-fib and to be home with Grace. But when he arrived, he learned Grace had filed for divorce and moved everything that belonged to him out of the house. He slept on a couch that night. The next morning, he and Grace went to breakfast to talk. A terse discussion ensued. She walked out, leaving him alone in the diner, and drove away."

"Is that when it happened?"

"Yes. She was, no doubt, distraught and distracted because she drove through a red light, got broadsided by a huge tractor-trailer truck, and was killed instantly. Since then, Brian's taken her death extremely hard."

Hearing the entire story for the first time, Erick teared up. Pieter had only partially told Erick how Paolo, Antonio, Wilhelm, and Klaus were in cahoots and were killed. "Oh my God," he moaned, "What a terrible series of events you and Brian endured. I'm sure there's more, but it must be hard to recall everything. It's making me cry just listening to you."

Nina hugged him. "There is something else. Brian and I became… close to each other in Spain when you didn't return. I have strong feelings for him, and he has expressed strong feelings for me. I hope you understand."

"I get it. And I'm sure you two feel even closer after sharing all that—Brian's such a great guy. I feel terrible for what he's been through. I must say, his wife could be a real bitch at times. Instead of supporting his career and frequent trips, she was like an anchor chained to his neck. I don't know how he put up with her all those years and carried on in his career as a professor and on the Interpol team. Brian's historical art knowledge is brilliant. We're damn lucky to have the professor on our team."

Nina considered mentioning her pregnancy, but she pushed off the urge and, looking over Erick's shoulder, saw Brian entering the cafeteria. Her face lit up with a smile. *He's here. He's so attractive.*

"Well, good morning, my favorite people. It's a beautiful day."

Brian leaned over, gave Nina a peck, and then shook Erick's hand.

"Good to see you so chipper this morning, BJ. You must have had a good night's sleep."

"I did! Thanks. I didn't expect you here yet, Nina. Did you get the envelope?"

"It arrived moments after we spoke."

"Great."

"What's in it that's so important?"

Brian deflected Erick's question. "Let's get our breakfast first. Then I'll share what's been going on in my life… and the contents of the envelope."

As they ate, Brian shared about being back at Katrina's house after her passing, handling the real estate going into his name, and stumbling upon the secret door behind the bookcase and the stairs leading to the wine cellar. He described the dark basement space filled with empty wine barrels. He told them about finding a small door behind the last barrel and how he got on his hands and knees and crawled and found six wooden crates. They were amazed to hear him describe the old statues in the first crate. Nina asked if he thought they were local art or from elsewhere. Brian suggested they could be Egyptian but said it was too dark to see any markings. When he shared the contents of the second crate, both were stunned.

"Do you think Katrina's husband purchased the contents of those crates?" Erick interrupted. "Or could they have been stolen and hidden there by Paolo?"

"I've asked myself that several times. Regardless, I could use you both in Malta at some point to go through what's down there."

"I thought I'd had enough of Malta after Paolo's party," Nina quipped. "But it seems like I need to return."

He went on to say how the new grand master of the Knights of Malta visited to introduce himself and how he became uncomfortable with questions the man asked about promises made by Luca.

Erick nodded. "The Order of the Knights of Malta is a well-known and reputable organization. They may have a legitimate claim based on Luca's promise. Or – and I'd hate to think this – the local chapter had issues back then, and someone was reaching into the purse before anyone else knew if a monetary gift had arrived."

"Well, there's more than meets the eye in those crates. I need to determine who put them there. How were they acquired? What's inside? Is it worth anything? And to whom does it rightfully belong?"

Brian explained about the break-in at Massimo's house, how he barely fit in the shallow towel closet, and how all his friend's paintings were stolen, including the two Argyles he'd agreed to purchase for a million dollars each. He said Massimo had a modest pension but had been financially ruined by the robbery, as all his savings – including his 401k, which he pulled out years ago – had been invested in his art collection.

Nina and Erick were stunned to hear of his misfortune, especially since Massimo had no insurance.

"He seemed like a smart man," Nina observed. "Erick, you'd like him. You need to meet him."

Brian took a bite of his bagel with veggie cream cheese and sipped his black coffee. He opened the special delivery envelope, looked inside, and smiled.

"Good. It's exactly what Bronn said."

"What is it?"

CHAPTER ELEVEN

The Center Page

Brian pulled the paper from the envelope, looked it over, and showed it to Nina and Erick.

"Our old friend Kristofer Bronn called me late yesterday from his antique shop in Leipzig. His cleaning lady found this page while cleaning the floor under his desk. Look closely."

"My God, Brian! Is that…"

"Yes. It's the center page of Karl von Richter's diary. It must have fallen out when Bronn was given the diary by the daughter of the woman we know as Sweet Hilda – the woman who worked in the Bendlerblock building in Berlin and was referred to in KvR's last entry. If you look closely, you can see the paper's ripped where the staples would have held it in place. The sheet has four pages of information. Bronn sent me photos of each page last night. I picked up a few German words but haven't had time to do any translation. Nina, since you're fluent in German, can you take a few moments to read it and tell us what it says?"

"Sure. Hmm. Wow. Well, this is interesting," she mused after glancing at the pages. "I seem to recall we'd wondered if there was a time gap of a few weeks in the diary."

"Yeah, it did look like something was missing," Brian agreed.

"Our last case, when we found the art hidden in the Mezquita, didn't require this information. But now, having these four missing pages of the diary is intriguing. Let me read it again."

Brian and Erick looked at each other with raised eyebrows. Brian took another bite of his bagel, patiently waiting for Nina's translation and assessment.

"Okay. Here goes. First, I can tell you what's written covers several weeks of von Richter's activity. A quick guess is that the pages could comprise six to eight weeks of his time."

Nina read the pages a third time while Brian sipped his coffee, then reached for his briefcase.

"Erick, I printed these upstairs when I arrived this morning," he said, handing sheets of paper to Erick. "They're photocopies of what Bronn sent. You know some German. Have a look while Nina goes through it again."

"The information on the pages of the diary is interesting. And what's amazing is the information comes at a perfect time for what we are being asked to work on as our next case. It's *spürsinn!*"

"In English, please," Brian prompted, a half-smile lighting his face.

Nina smiled back at him. "In English, it's called serendipity! What Bronn sent us may fit perfectly into the challenge we're faced with, and it seems to tie directly into Pattison's presentation yesterday. I'll take a few minutes to write out the translation. I may be able to catch more of what he intended to say or implied in these notes."

"Good work, Nina. Erick, I'm going to have another cup of coffee. Can I get you a refill?"

"Sure. I'll stay and watch our Sherlock Holmes at work."

Nina began writing a translation of Karl von Richter's words; she erased a few of her own words and wrote more. Erick watched her full-motion body language, delighted as she wiggled with excitement as she sat. At one point, she paused, stood, and walked around the table. She sat again and wiggled some more. The information unraveling at her fingertips seemed incredible.

Brian returned with a tray carrying his and Erick's coffee, a cup of Chamomile tea for Nina, and three apple Danishes.

She looked up as he sat. "Are you guys ready to hear what I think KvR was thinking when he wrote this?"

"You're kidding. We're on pins and needles waiting for your

assessment!"

"Look here, on the first page. KvR writes about Neuschwanstein Castle and the paintings hidden there. We know Hitler directed stolen art confiscated by the Gestapo to be stored there and how the American soldiers called the Monument Men beat the Russians there and began a huge recovery effort. Next, Karl writes, 'Why does the Führer keep changing his mind?' Then, in the next line, he writes, 'Can it be? New orders for a new location? Something interesting is happening. I question the source of these orders.' "

"Does he say what the new orders are?"

"Hold on, Erick. The next words on the second page say, 'Transferring the art will be manageable. But the rest of the prize? It will take a mighty effort. And why there?"

"Does he give a location? Where is 'there'?"

"Erick, please. I'm going slowly, trying to get in his mind and make sure I have this right. 'We will need a large transport plane – a Junker can carry the weight, and the heavy load will require a long runway.'

"The next sentences go from pages two to three and are the most revealing. KvR writes, 'One stop or two?' He worries again and writes, 'But how heavy?' His next sentence is telling: 'Island or inland? Is not inland better?' His comment about stopping on an island or inland is pure luck for us."

"Wow! Nina. You're truly a sleuth. Is there more?"

"Yes, on page three. He rambles and alludes to the mystery: 'Failed landing. Busted bodies and cargo. Any Nazi friends nearby?' There's more bad news in his next words: 'Hans is upset. Bad engine. This bird is on its belly, dead in the sand, and can't fly away. Heads must roll. Devilish heat.' I believe he means the plane can't take off unless the engine, landing gear, or both are repaired – or perhaps he means it can't take off at all.

"Then he detaches himself and concludes his role on the fourth page: 'I was right – extra fuel and the Au – too heavy for a 290. A Ju-390 would have reached the target. Bad engine. Unexpected dead. Unbearable heat in a sea of sand. The little birds have found us. Hans Pancherz returns to Berlin. I will go finish building Ravensbrück.'""

"Well done, Nina. I got a copy of his diary from Ursula this morning. Where the newly found page four ends, KvR begins with a reference to arriving in Ravensbrück. We know from historical records that the Organization Todt construction team arrived there in September of 1944 – that's when Karl supervised the completion of the gas chambers and crematorium he proposed two years earlier. In mid-December, when construction was completed, Karl managed the use of the new equipment and instructed others. We know from notations in his diary Field Marshal General Kristofer von Schultz reassigned Karl in mid-April 1945 to the Bendlerblock building in Berlin. He's there a few days before being given orders to extract Hitler from the Führer bunker. He has a quickie with Hilda, makes an entry about it, and then loses his diary. That must be when Hilda found it."

Brian praised Nina. "Sounds like your translation is completed. Terrific job! Now our real work begins. The paper Bronn sent is in sync with the diary, and its timely arrival is perfect given the upcoming mission. But Karl's notations leave me with new questions: Where did the plane land? Was it ever able to leave? What happened to the plane's cargo? Karl's use of the letters 'Au' implies gold was on board. And what happened to the plane itself? It's got to be out there someplace."

"I have an idea about the landing," Erick said. "The landing runway was too short or too narrow for the large plane, and its tires rolled into the sand. Maybe a tire blew? Or did the landing gear's hydraulics break, hit the sand, and collapse? Are any of those things possible… or likely?"

"Those are all reasonable conclusions, Erick. What do you think, Nina?"

"We heard Pattison say those new satellites saw an old landing strip on Grand Canary Island, but we can conclude, with this latest information, that Grand Canary Island is the wrong place to investigate. The diary says they landed inland, and it didn't end well. Lots of sand and unbearable heat – not exactly the coast of an island with cool breezes."

"I agree. It was late August 1944 when the failed flight occurred. And

I agree it must have carried gold bullion from Germany to a new hiding place."

"So, von Richter's missing diary pages validate the rumors the think-tank guys in D.C. believe about gold being transferred," Erick pointed out. "They indicate the plane landed where it was hot and sandy, and the landing gear failed. So what's next? What do we bring to the next meeting? As good as it is, I feel the information from these diary pages puts us in a more difficult situation."

Nina spoke up to answer Erick's concern. "My immediate thought is to learn more about the capacity of the Junkers the Luftwaffe used at the time and do some math. I need to consider where such a plane might have taken off. Then, given a hypothetical load, I can design vectors or flight paths taking the plane a certain distance. From those numbers, I can figure out how far it could go nonstop, see which path they might have taken, and determine where they might have landed. The diary notes made it sound like something unforeseen happened, or something went wrong, and they stopped unexpectedly. And if the landing gear failed, as Karl wrote, they might not have been able to taxi down a runway to take off again."

Erick turned to Brian, "My guess is the plane never took off again, based on his notation, 'impossible repair without spare parts.' Your conclusions are spot on. It also leaves a big plane sitting somewhere… somewhere those newfangled satellites should see."

"And Nina, as you pointed out, it has a serendipitous account of events in sync with our new case."

Nina smiled. "It has. Now, let me recap for you both. We now believe a large Junker transport plane, with its load of heavy gold bullion and art, landed in a hot, sandy place – not on an island – and couldn't take off again. Right?"

Erick nodded, and Brian spoke up.

"Nina, our team, or perhaps you as the new team leader, need to approach Pieter gently to say that we've suddenly acquired the missing innermost four pages of von Richter's diary. He's up to his neck in this case, having the three of us, plus Amara and his team, committed to supporting the CIA's investigation. It'd be a huge embarrassment if this new information came up in tomorrow's meeting with the CIA. It might even cause an unfriendly rift between the agencies if we come out and say the CIA is wrong and Interpol wants to back away from exploring Grand Canary Island. How we reveal what we've found in these new pages, and what we believe and will do about it must be clear and concise. Your thoughts, Erick?"

"I think we just tell Pieter, Amara, and Pattison what we've found."

"Maybe, but it could be more complicated. If there's a lot of gold, the recovery could become contentious and make access to the resources we need for the search more difficult. Perhaps we should reflect more on how we want to present this to Pieter."

Brian looked around at his teammates. "Okay. Break time. Let's each of us take a walk, get some fresh air, and do some more thinking. Let's meet back in the library in thirty minutes."

"Brian, before you go, something's already puzzling me. With all these satellite images, wouldn't a large plane stuck somewhere in or near the desert have been seen and investigated by now?"

Brian's brow wrinkled. "Yes and no. During the war, thousands of planes crashed, and I'm sure dozens went down in North Africa. So, it might have been seen but overlooked. Okay? See you both in the library in thirty."

Brian took the elevator and headed outside for some fresh air. Erick took a different elevator car and went to the roof to walk around the outdoor track. He took a deep breath and appreciated the cool air, happy to be alive. Nina headed to Dirk's office to retrieve her new laptop and phone. After instructions on connecting to the building's LAN, she went to the third-floor library to research the specs of Junker planes built in the 1940s, identifying fuel and weight capacity, and started doing "What-if" calculations. As she worked, something distracted her for a moment. She wasn't sure what it was.

CHAPTER TWELVE

The Art Collection

Brian was ten minutes into his walk when his new cell phone rang – its ringtone surprised him.

"My friend. It's Massimo. Do you have a moment for me?"

"Of course. How are things there? Do you have any news?"

"I met the local capo and Tony 'Four-Eyes' for lunch yesterday at my club. The capo said he knew nothing, but after a few glasses of grappa, he began complaining about some teenagers trying to get into the game and prove themselves to a few in the organization. He speculated they could be tied to an offshore organization. He finally suggested I wait another few weeks and allow something to reveal itself. He said, 'Perhaps the ambitious hoods will try to move the stolen art."

"Well, that sounds positive."

"It is, but Brian, I need your help.

"Of course."

"I mean, your *financial* help. I have a payment due, and I was counting on your money from the sale to help me."

"Sure. You already mentioned that, and I don't have a problem sending you money. I'm sorry, but I've been busy here since I arrived. I'll stop at a bank this afternoon and send a wire."

"Thanks. How is your girl, Nina? Are you two… uh, you know."

"I stayed here last night; she went home. I should have told her to stay." Brian paused and shook his head. "I don't know, Massimo. Our time together and conversations didn't help. I'm still feeling bad about

Grace dying. The Irish Catholic guilt my parents laid on me has my insides tied up in knots. Grace is even haunting my dreams."

"I told you, Brian. It would be best if you let go of that guilt. Get back in bed with Nina. It'll make you feel better. Relax with her. Remember, it's time to turn the page in your life and open a new chapter."

"Easier said than done. Hey, I need to get back to a meeting. Anything else?"

"How much can you send me?"

"How much do you need?"

"One million U.S."

"You'll see it by tomorrow afternoon."

"I owe you, my friend."

"Find those two Argyles, and I'll send another million; then you won't owe me anything. But now I need to go. Take care."

Brian slid his phone back into his pocket and resumed his walk, thinking about what Massimo had said. *He's probably right about being with Nina... but going to bed with her? She was so good, but sex seems so out of place right now. It seems like our lovemaking was a dream. I'm so confused. Maybe I'm too old for her – maybe I'm just too old, period.*

He returned inside and headed to the library, intending to look at some maps of North Africa and West Africa. He saw Nina at a desk, focused intently on a new style, large computer monitor. He approached her slowly and quietly and stood behind her. Seeing the information on the screen, Brian realized she had the same idea. In fact, she was several steps ahead of him. *Her sleuth-like thinking is what makes her so good.*

While standing over her shoulder, he smelled her perfume. Its sweet fragrance flashed his thoughts back to Spain. *It wasn't a dream.* As he remembered looking up at her as she mounted him, he felt aroused. *She is such a terrific lover. Where do we go from here? I'm right next to a beautiful young woman and tormented by Grace's death.*

He laid a hand on Nina's shoulder.

"What you have up on the screen looks impressive."

She turned and looked up at him with a smile. "Thank you. I've drawn several lines; let me explain my reasoning. Each line has a starting point for a plane leaving from Berlin and heading to several locations. Look. This first line goes to Marrakesh. The next one takes a slightly different course and crosses Casablanca.

"But as I'm doing this, my thoughts have become complicated. Let me explain why I used Berlin as a starting point."

Brian nodded in interest, signaling for her to continue.

"My focus, when we three aren't together in the field, is to work from a compilation of lists made by the Nazis during WWII of what they gathered – such as paintings, statuary, and other valuable artifacts. Many of those items and other stolen items were headed for the town of Linz, where the Führer's new Reich Museum, designed by Albert Speer, was to be built. We also have old lists compiled by over a dozen European art collectors after the war. In some cases, they match the Nazis' lists of missing paintings. Other lists gathered by the European Art Collector Association in the 1980s identify more art that's still missing. Very recently, a new list has been put together based on family requests. In some cases, these people believe their parents or grandparents owned art pieces before the war based on paintings or statues appearing in old family photos that survived the war. There's been more of this happening with the growth of the Internet."

Just then, Erick returned from his walk and, thinking similarly, joined them in the library and began listening to Nina's new idea.

"Hi Erick. I was about to share an idea about Hermann Göring with Brian. We know he started an art collection for himself. Some paintings and art pieces Göring collected were gifts. But other paintings, statues, and art pieces confiscated by the Gestapo, the Nazi unit which Göring started, and were shipped to his estate, Carinhall, Göring's estate."

"Interesting premise," Erick said. "Go on."

"Göring kept a meticulous journal that listed each piece of art at his house, with details explaining the piece's name, its creator, description, quality, and origin, along with special notes on where it would be placed inside his home. His list of art stolen from Jewish collectors consisted of fourteen hundred paintings and more than four hundred sculptures and tapestries – including works by Botticelli, Velazquez, Renoir, Monet, and Van Gogh. Since the end of the war, Göring's collection has been the subject of many publications. Art dealers have tried to assemble a complete list of the works he gathered based on his wartime archives and his letters to a group of art dealers with whom he dealt in the sale and purchases of art.

"So, as I think more about those lists and this situation and study the new pages of KvR's diary, I focused on his comment when he questions the source of his order to transport art to a new location not previously used by Hitler. It's making me think the load of art and gold on the Junker airplane wasn't Hitler's cache, but part of Göring's personal collection, sent by plane from Berlin."

Brian looked like he was about to talk, so Nina held up a hand to forestall any interruption. "Stay with me on this. Here are my reasons: First, Hitler admired Hermann Göring for his success as a World War One flying ace who flew in the same fighter group as Baron von Richthofen. Göring was a committed Nazi who was wounded in the same failed Beer Hall Putsch as Hitler. He was appointed to create the Gestapo, and later, besides being named to head the Luftwaffe in 1939, Hitler declared Göring would be his successor and gave him the special rank of 'Reichsmarschall.'

"Göring became the most popular Nazi leader with the German people, as well as foreign ambassadors and diplomats. During the war, Hitler gave Göring the freedom to create his own art and gold collection to enrich himself.

"But Göring's downfall began when Germany's Luftwaffe failed to win the Battle of Britain in 1940. Then, in the summer of 1944, the Luftwaffe couldn't prevent the Allies from bombing cities in Germany, and Hitler openly spoke of replacing him with another World War One flying ace, General Field Marshal Robert Ritter von Greim. When this plan was leaked, Göring lost most of his authority.

"Knowing the Führer's war could no longer be won, and that he'd lost favor with Hitler, Göring claimed poor health and retired to

Carinhall – the residence he built after the death of his first wife, Carin von Kantzow. But even in the final twelve months of the war, he kept records at Carinhall showing he continued to add spoils from occupied countries to his art collection. Brian, it's long been speculated among European art collectors that he'd begun relocating his loot away from Carinhall."

"Relocating where?" Erick asked.

"Good question. During my post-grad studies, I read that in the final weeks of March 1945, his art collection was loaded onto a private train and sent south toward Berchtesgaden in Bavaria. Göring blew up Carinhall after the train left to prevent the Soviets from ransacking the house. American soldiers in the US 101st Airborne Division later stopped the same train from reaching its destination. Only art and statues were found inside the train's box cars."

"How about the gold he amassed?"

Nina shook her head. "The soldiers didn't find any gold on the train. I think it might have been shipped away earlier by Göring."

Erick spoke up. "You're right, Nina. I'm a bit older than you and know that European art dealers assembled many lists of stolen art after the war. Art collectors found a list of Göring's diverse collection. It was later determined his collection was much larger than the statues and paintings recovered in the train cars. Many of the listed items in his collection were never found."

"Exactly, Erick. So, here are my conclusions: Von Richter initially thought he was following orders to move the Führer's stolen goods from Neuschwanstein Castle. Next, the flight was to move Göring's cache of gold along with only the best paintings. Third, the event occurred in August 1944, long before the end of the war. Despite his emerging conflict with Hitler, many Luftwaffe pilots remained faithful to their former commander, and if he needed a plane, he'd have no trouble getting one – of any size and to any destination. Fourth, Göring initiated the order, and that's why it seemed different to KvR. Last, I suspect the art pieces in the plane may have included a few late arrivals in Göring's collection, and he didn't catalog all of them. Thus, they were not listed, nor were they on the captured train because he had previously sent them away. Those would be the set of paintings on art lists that were never found. Last, I believe much, or all the gold he acquired was moved. The amount of gold bullion made KvR question whether it was too heavy for the airplane."

Brian nodded. "You're probably right on all your points, Nina. Here's what we also know to be true. When Göring gave himself up to American soldiers and was tried at the International Military Tribunal at Nüremberg, he believed he'd be treated lightly because he wasn't involved in the horrific activities at the death camps. He saw himself getting out after a few years in prison, and figured he'd have his treasures, taken from Carinhall, waiting in a secure location."

"BJ, I'm surprised Göring didn't fly away himself that summer. Or he should have left Berlin in February or early March of 1945 while he still had the chance."

"You're right, Erick. It's been documented that many SS and Luft-waffe commanders flew to South America. He could have commanded a flight at any time to get away. For some reason, he remained in Berlin until the end. I'm not sure why." Brian paused and shook his head.

"And instead of reclaiming his stolen art after the war, Göring ended up taking a cyanide pill two hours before he was scheduled to hang."

"Another crazy and inauspicious ending for a bad guy with a huge ego," Erick scoffed.

Brian beamed at Nina. "Well done! You've identified the events leading up to the Junker's departure with Göring's goods. I'd also say you've successfully identified what was on the plane. Now, we need to figure out how far the plane traveled, where it landed, and what became of its treasure. It'll be like finding a needle in a haystack."

"Brian, look closer at the image on the screen. That's why I drew the different vectors. Dozens of scenarios could have caused the plane to land short of its initial destination. Here's one scenario I've imagined: A gauge on the plane's instrument panel indicated something was wrong. Needing to land the plane, the pilot looked for an airfield short of their destination. He likely found a roadway and landed. The landing gear was damaged when the overloaded 290 traveled off the old road as it landed. Or the landing gear was damaged when the heavy plane landed too hard. Either way, according to von Richter's words, the plane landed in a hot and sandy remote place."

"I like your iteration of what might have happened. All plausible. Based on your data, how far do you think the plane traveled? Or, the better question to ask: 'Where do you think the plane landed?'"

"Depending on the pilot's preference to avoid the US and British allied air traffic, the math says it could have landed in Libya, Tunisia, Algeria or Morocco. The map on my computer screen and KvR's words tell me they landed someplace in Morocco."

"Why there?"

"I looked again at the entire diary. Let me read and translate an excerpt from the next to last page. Karl writes, 'It's been a harsh, frigid winter. The situation was bad, but the heat in *Parikesh* was comforting.'"

"So what do you have in mind? Where do you think he landed?"

"He writes about the cold in Ravensbruck and anticipates the warmth where he landed. I think it's his misspelling or his misunderstanding. I believe he means to say he's somewhere near Marrakesh. It must be where the pilot tells him they landed. It would explain the heat, the sand, and the short runway. I think we solve the 'where' of this puzzle if we put a seventy-five-mile circle around Marrakesh."

Suddenly, it was quiet. Brian and Erick looked at each other in astonishment at Nina's revelation. Both thought she was right and took moments to absorb the information she laid out.

Brian cleared his throat. "Well, once again, the old Karl von Richter diary seems to reveal or at least get us closer to the answer our team was seeking. And, Nina, we have you to thank. Your intense focus had led the way. Erick, thoughts?"

"Agreed! So what's the next step?"

"Ha! Good question. It's your call, Nina."

"How do you figure?"

"With your recent promotion, you're now officially our group leader. So, the question remains: How do you want to handle this?"

Nina paused for a moment. "We go see Pieter. Just Pieter, initially."

"And say what?"

"I'll tell him what's been discovered and what we've concluded with that new info."

"And just back out of the Canary Island escapade entirely?"

"Yes."

"And we fly to Morocco instead?"

"Of course."

Erick held up his hands. "Whoa! Slow you two down. BJ, take a moment to step back on this. What do *you* think?"

"I like Nina's conclusions about the plane's track over Morocco and Marrakesh, but it changes everything. Frankly, my head is spinning. I've got so much going on in the back of my mind with Massimo's art theft, the discovery of God knows what in that wine cellar, the Knights of Malta questioning my honesty, learning I now own a dozen rental properties in Capri and on the Amalfi coast, Grace's death, and all the murders in the last two months. And I'm not sure another two years with this damn agency suits me."

Then Brian's frustration with technology bubbled to the surface.

"Plus, I've been forced to swap out my flip phone for this fancy smartphone and deal with this Wi-Fi stuff. And what in God's name is a virtual private network? I need a fucking break."

Brian shook his head as the others stared at him, realizing he'd un-loaded horribly on his teammates – and it had nothing to do with the case.

"Excuse me for that. I'm going back to the hotel. I was up early. Now I'm grouchy and need some shuteye. I'll be back around four. I'm sorry, Nina. It's not a reflection on your work."

Brian's comments were very unexpected as his voice elevated in frustration. He seemed angry as he stood and walked away.

Nina stared at Brian as he left—his temper more than his words upset her, and she wanted to cry. *I've not seen this side of him before. He's not prone to cursing. He's exhausted. I hope that's all it is.*

Brian walked out and headed to the elevator.

"Don't worry, Nina. He needs some space right now," Erick assured her. "I've known him for years – he always bounces back after a nap. Trust me."

"I sure hope so. There's a lot more to discuss. We need to decide about telling Pieter, and we need a plan."

CHAPTER THIRTEEN

The DiBotticino Family Legacy

One morning in early March 1945, Giovanni Cardinal DiBotticino, then living at the Vatican, woke from a dream in which he vividly recalled a family legend he'd learned about as a child. Later that morning, during the Celebration of the Eucharist, he became distracted thinking about the dream.

After Mass, Giovanni left the altar, removed his vestments, returned to the rectory, then sat and penned a letter to Katrina Amorino. He began by citing his connection to young Katrina. Twenty years earlier, the cardinal's sister, Valentina DiBotticino, had married Otto von Richter and had a son they named Karl.

Valentina's and Otto's son, Karl von Richter, worked in the factory with Otto. He frequently skied in the Alps. On one trip, he met and fell in love with Katrina while skiing. He enticed her to go and live with him in Germany, but after his initial training at the Nazi Officer school at Bad Tölz, he was transformed into a treacherous SS Nazi officer. His reputation became legendary among German commanders for his design to oxygenate furnaces in Nazi death camps to speed the complete incineration of bodies put in the ovens.

Giovanni and Katrina had met twice in Brescia's Old Cathedral soon after he became a bishop. She wished to give her and Karl's baby boy – the product of rape – up for adoption, and she also sought his approval to enter the convent. A week later, Katrina left the child with Giovanni and, after a brief visit to her parents' home in Lecco, traveled to a convent in southern Italy to hide from Karl. Upon entry to the convent as a postulant, Katrina prayed for God's forgiveness for her impetuous and reckless decisions allowing Karl into her life, having had passionate sex with him before marriage, and for her painful and crushing decision to give their infant boy, born out of wedlock, up for adoption. Her mistakes led to her litany of sorrows.

Weeks later, the cardinal's letter, addressed to Katrina and bearing a Vatican postmark, arrived at the convent in Bernalda. The convent's Mother Superior, a cousin of Katrina's mother, opened the letter and read it. Like the cardinal's intuition, Mother Superior knew Katrina's time in the convent would be limited.

His letter began, "My Dearest Katrina – An interesting dream this morning has caused me to write to you today. I have no idea why it came to me now. Perhaps it is because the Allies have freed Rome and are pushing toward Berlin. This horrible war has brought such pain, hardship, and misery to Italy and its faithful."

The body of the Cardinal's letter revealed the tale of an Italian knight, the centerpiece of the DiBotticino family legend.

"The knight was a fearless Italian prince who sailed with other Crusaders from the coastal city of Naples, considered part of the Kingdom of Sicily at the time. The knight was a fierce fighter who became a Templar. He eventually fought bravely in the Siege of Acre in 1291. After losing thousands of men in the fight against the Mamluk Muslim army led by Sultan al-Ashraf Khalil, a remaining group of Crusaders and Templars escaped through underground tunnels and sailed to safety on the island of Cyprus, where the Templar order established its new headquarters.

"After a brief time in Cyprus, the brave Italian knight sailed to Ephesus, where he met and stayed with an old family who claimed to be descendants of the apostle John, who fled there with Mary, the mother of Jesus of Nazareth, after His crucifixion. A year later, the knight sailed to Crete, where he stayed for two more years, learning the stone-cutting trade.

"Although defeated in the Holy Land, the Templars remained a powerful Christian organization during the knight's time in Cyprus, Ephesus, and Crete. Eventually, Templars were seen as threatening the pope's authority in Rome as they gained more power. Some years later, King Philip IV of France, who owed money to the Templar Order for financing France's participation in the Crusades, took advantage of the emerging conflict between the Templars and the Roman Catholic Church. The king approached Pope Clement with a devious and horrific plan.

"In 1307, Pope Clement gave King Philip permission to pursue and kill members of the Templar Order in France and elsewhere. It was on the thirteenth of the month, and it was a Friday when Templars were arrested and killed. Many were first tortured into giving false confessions of heresy and sexual misconduct and then burned at the stake. Groups of Templar knights, after hearing of King Philip's actions, immediately scattered and hid their identities. In 1312, two hundred years after the Templar Order was founded in 1119, it was disbanded by Pope Clement V."

The cardinal wrote how the princely knight from the Kingdom of Sicily returned to Italy from Crete sometime in 1308 or 1309 and, using his stone-cutting skills, began the stone quarry just north of Brescia. The family legend says it wasn't long after arriving that he married, and the DiBotticino family was established.

The cardinal further explained what he learned as a youngster – that items had been hidden in wooden boxes at the stone works.

"On more than one occasion, when my sister Valentina and other children in the family were together for family holidays, we would hike up to a secret spot with Uncle Vincenzo, the eldest brother of the DiBotticino generation at the time. He would show us the contents of two wooden boxes brought back by the knight. One box included odd-looking statues of people with heads and faces like dogs. Another box included the Crusader's sword, chainmail, a tunic, and a banner emblazoned with a red cross."

Giovanni continued, 'There were four other boxes, but Uncle Vincenzo said they were special, and we couldn't open them. And so we never saw what was inside.'

In closing his letter, he wrote, "I would go back and look for those boxes myself if I had the time. But I am busy here in the Vatican, trying to rebuild our Catholic Church and recruit new young priests to restore attendance and rebuild damaged churches in southern Italy now that the Nazi invaders have been eliminated from southern Italy and pushed north of Rome by the Allies."

He finished, "Now I say this with all due respect, dear woman. If you were to leave the convent, you and your child would be the rightful heirs to the DiBotticino family legend and the contents of the boxes hidden in the family quarry. I'm enclosing a small map to help you find them. If you ever find those boxes, please write and tell me what Uncle Vincenzo never allowed us to see.

God bless you, dear woman."

Katrina was uninterested in Karl's mother's family and DiBotticino's Templar Knight legend. She folded the letter and tucked it away in her drawer under her clothing. Only weeks later, after the Russians captured Berlin, Karl, the despicable Nazi, and Katrina's nemesis, discovered her hiding location in Bernalda, Italy, and arrived at the convent. A heated confrontation between Karl and Katrina ensued. An unexpected shooting by one of the convent's sisters resulted in Karl's death. As anticipated, Katrina left the convent soon afterward and married Luca Luciano, the former parish priest, six months later. She never thought about the cardinal's letter or its contents, but it remained among her things, including letters from her parents.

Years later, when she and Luca had settled into their home in Malta, Katrina found the cardinal's letter among a stash of memories in her hope chest – her first-anniversary gift from Luca. After rereading it, Katrina gave the letter to Luca, who was primarily focused on building his wine distribution business at the time. Nevertheless, he agreed to investigate the DiBotticino family legend, and the boxes hidden at the quarry if the opportunity presented itself on a business trip to northern Italy.

As Luca's business grew, he eventually made good on his promise to Katrina. She joined him on a trip to Lecco, where they took a side trip to look for the DiBotticino family stone works and quarry. Upon arriving in Brescia, they followed a local map to the general area of the quarry. They climbed the barely visible trail, where they found the remnants of the DiBotticino family's stone works building on a hillside. The area was filled with boulders and rubble from bombing by the Allies in WWII. They walked carefully and made their way among the giant stones strewn about like pebbles. Luca followed the directions in the cardinal's letter where Uncle Vincenzo said the boxes were hidden. A few unmistakable markers on the path soon revealed themselves, making them feel they were on the right track.

As they looked closer for more clues, they both noticed something that may have once been hidden. There, ahead of them, under a wide rock ledge sat six wooden boxes protected from rain and snow. Katrina turned to Luca with a surprised look. She kissed him and thanked him for the effort, but there was no way they could carry the six crates. Luca marked each one as 'Property of Luciano Wine Export Company' and they returned to town and hired some locals to carry the boxes down from the hillside. They were excited by their find but, due to limited time, didn't open any. Luca marked each box 'Property of Luciano Wine Export Company.' The next day, the boxes were on a train to Milan; a day later, they would be flown to Malta.

A week later, Luca finished his business in Milan and Genoa, and returned with Katrina to their seaside villa in Malta. Over breakfast the following morning, they discussed the DiBotticino legend and the prince, wondering more about his original home in the Kingdom of Sicily. After finishing, they went to the garage, where the boxes had been placed upon delivery.

Katrina watched as Luca struggled to open the first crate. Inside, under layers of straw, they saw the knight's sword and his chainmail. Next to the chainmail was his washed-out white tunic, a large banner, and a triangular flag, all bearing faded red crosses. Luca and Katrina looked at each other in awe.

"Wow! Luca! It looks like the DiBotticino family legend is true!" Katrina exclaimed.

When Luca opened the second box, Katrina gasped! Inside were two odd-looking statues, each with a dog's face atop a man's body.

Luca said he saw similar statues in a museum near the Ghetto in Rome while studying to be a priest. "These are Egyptian statues."

He carefully picked one up and looked it over.

"This represents Anubis, the Egyptian Lord of the Necropolis," Luca explained.

"I wonder how the family crusader came across these pieces."

"Perhaps the statues were taken by Roman Legionnaires from Egypt to Jerusalem during the time of Christ, then found and taken as a memento as the knight fled Jerusalem."

While Luca's imagination turned to the treasures in the other boxes,

Katrina remained focused on the statue's role of helping Egyptians into the underworld. She saw their presence as a bad omen.

"Please, Luca, put that back," she urged her husband. "It's making me nervous."

He agreed. Then, looking at his watch, he saw their time was too limited to open another box because a special visitor was due to arrive. The meeting was important. A vast international company had recently approached Luca about buying his business, and the visitor was the CEO and deal maker.

Katrina returned inside to prepare for the guest while Luca, now believing the boxes contained valuables, called the groundskeeper to have all six boxes, marked 'wine,' moved into the cellar.

Carlo Vernieri was a friendly local man who, along with his father, had built Luca and Katrina's house twenty years earlier. Once given the task, Carlo knew the easiest way to the wine cellar was through the root cellar, and he proceeded to trim the twenty-year-old overgrown hedges, then carried the crates down the cleared path with assistance from a helper. Unfortunately, the small door leading from the root cellar into the wine cellar was locked, so Carlo left the six wooden crates in the cool root cellar.

It was Carlo who had urged Luca to join the Order of the Knights of Malta shortly after moving in. But despite joining, try as he might, Luca could only attend two meetings that year. Luca's business of acquiring exclusive distribution rights of small vineyards and promoting and exporting Italian wines kept him busy, and he was often out of town on business.

Another week passed, and negotiations for Luca to sell his wine-distribution company reached a frenzy. Closing the deal was down to four points in the acquisition agreement, which the international distribution company needed to modify to Luca's benefit. After some phone calls, the worldwide giant finally met Luca's demands and agreed to purchase his holdings.

Excited by the upcoming sale of his company, Luca shared the news that afternoon with Carlo, who mentioned there'd be a meeting that night. Feeling blessed, Luca planned to attend the meeting to donate cash and the knight's equipment to the Order after closing the sale of his business, provided Katrina approved. That night at the meeting, he promised something special would be forthcoming, and the next day, he wrote to his attorney outlining his plan to make the cash and material donations.

Two days later, with the guidance of the Fellini law firm, the giant international distributor's purchase agreement for the Luciano Wine Export Company was in place. The documents would be signed four days later at the Fellini offices in Rome. Luca insisted on being there in person to thank his old lawyer friend. Knowing the deal was about to close was a massive relief for Luca and Katrina. All his hard work since leaving the priesthood and starting the wine-export company was coming to fruition. But more important to Luca than all the money from the sale was the idea of settling down, traveling by choice, and enjoying life with his love, Katrina.

But sadly, only two days later, Luca unexpectedly fell ill and died. It was determined days later, after tests, that Luca had been poisoned. No one knew at the time his murderous stepson, Paolo Luzzi, was attempting to take control of the company before the deal closed and plotted Luca's death.

Luca's business was sold days later, despite his death, and his promise to the Order of the Knights of Malta was never fulfilled, disappointing many. Additionally, several provisions in Luca's will were triggered. Those provisions put money from the closing into trust accounts for Paolo Luzzi and Katrina's natural son, who had been adopted by an Irish couple in New York and renamed Brian O'Sullivan.

CHAPTER FOURTEEN

Tomorrow's Afternoon Meeting

Just past 4 p.m., having enjoyed a restful nap, Brian returned to the office building. As he entered the lobby, Van Deusen was on his way out.

"Finished for the day?" Brian hailed him.

"Unfortunately, no. I have a function to attend this evening. I'll be seeing Bill Pattison once again."

"Uh, Pieter, about tomorrow afternoon's meeting…"

"You're scowling, O'Sullivan. Why the concerned look?"

"Expect a text requesting an early-morning meeting from our team."

"About?"

"Let's just wait until the morning."

"This doesn't sound good."

"Have a good evening, Pieter."

"Ha. Doubtful. You just spoiled it."

Brian headed inside and took the elevator to Pieter's office. Ursula, wrapping up for the day, ended a cell phone call when she saw Brian enter.

"Hi, Ursula. I don't remember you saying anything about extending my life insurance and health benefits. They will be continued, won't they?"

"Uh, sorry, Brian. No time for you right now. I need to catch Pieter. We can discuss your questions tomorrow." Suddenly in a hurry, she ran from the office and, passing the elevator, opted for the stairway. But, unknown to anyone, she stopped on the landing one flight down the stairwell and made a call.

Annoyed at having been shoved aside, Brian headed upstairs to the cafeteria, where he found Erick and Nina chatting. Despite being dissed by Ursula, he felt better than he had and was happy to see them both.

Erick saw him enter. "See, Nina. I told you he'd return with a smile on his face."

"Brian, I've decided we need to tell Pieter about our discovery. I wanted you to know before I text him. I want to meet with him tomorrow morning – around 8. How's that sound to you?"

"Sounds good. I'm not surprised. In fact, I gave him a heads-up a few minutes ago as he was leaving, saying we'd want to meet with him first thing tomorrow. And I want to apologize for being abrupt with you earlier. Too many unresolved issues… it makes me tired and grumpy."

"No shit, Sherlock," quipped Erick.

Nina rubbed her hands together. "Okay, then. So now we discuss how we approach Pieter with the facts we've uncovered, how we will set up our next search, and lay out the steps we want to take. My goal is to leave our meeting with him tomorrow with our action plan approved."

"And our plan is?"

"Well, that's what we need to iron out. Let me text him now to tell him the time. Meanwhile, you can write a few next steps individually and see how we can align our thinking."

"I like your style, boss."

"Erick, I'm not your boss. I'm the team leader. And to function as a team, we need to communicate and coordinate with each other."

"Haven't we done that for the last few years since you joined us, boss?"

"Well, to be honest, Erick, I've felt left out a few times in the past. Sometimes the two of you made me feel like I wasn't even there."

"Well, you were young and just learning the ropes back then. Now that's in the past. I promise you'll know exactly what I'm thinking from now on. How about you, BJ?"

"Of course! Having Nina running the show is a breath of fresh air."

She smiled. *I need to remember this moment and remind them the next time they go off and do something without me.*

For the next hour, they shared notes and ideas, agreed, disagreed, wrote a plan, made changes, laughed, and reached a conclusion the three could live with. The meeting with Pieter would be direct, positive, and eye-opening. When Erick left to use the john, Brian turned to Nina.

"Good job, Nina. Dinner tonight, right?"

She hedged. "Gee, I was thinking about that, and I feel torn. It's my first chance to show Pieter his decision to make me team leader wasn't a mistake."

"So?"

"So I'm feeling the need to skip dinner with you and return home to begin working on this. I want tomorrow's presentation to be perfect in every detail. And I want to ask myself tough questions as if he was asking me. Being fully prepared and anticipating questions the three of us didn't discuss in the past hour will make me more relaxed."

"I get it. Okay. I checked out of the hotel earlier today, thinking I'd be staying at your place tonight, but you're making a smart choice since we've never put a plan in front of Pieter. For the past few years, we worked under Wilhelm, and whatever we decided to do was often done on a wing and a prayer. So, young lady, let me give you a hug and a kiss, and I'll see you here bright and early tomorrow morning."

"Thanks for understanding. We do need to have dinner. I have something I need to catch up with you about. And, Brian, you need to know I want to be with you."

Brian smiled. "Thanks. I've been thinking it's time to let go of all the pain that's happened in the past six months – and the struggles some years before that." He paused. "Nina, you need to know I want to be with you, too."

He gave her another hug, tighter this time, then kissed her lips.

She felt a tingle and whispered, "It feels good to be in your arms, Brian."

"Likewise. Tomorrow night."

They were reluctantly parting as Erick returned. He'd missed the tender kiss but saw the handholding after their hug.

"Hey, I'll see you two tomorrow morning. Gotta run."

"Good night, Erick."

"Hey Erick, not so fast. Can you take me back to the hotel where I stayed last night? Nina's heading home to prep for the morning's meeting with Pieter."

"Sure. But let's go now. I promised my sister I'd be home to watch her kids. She's sitting with some ladies tonight sewing quilts or something like that."

Nina stayed behind as the two left the room. Earlier, she had asked Ursula to put the Pattison presentation back up on the conference room's overhead projector so she could see it again before heading home. Something curious in it had caught her attention.

<u>**CHAPTER FIFTEEN**</u>

Meeting Pattison

Pieter was waiting outside in the car. "Jesus, Ursula, what took you so long?"

"O'Sullivan came in and started asking me questions. I didn't finish with him, so he'll be back in the morning. Don't worry, I'll deal with it."

"Well, I just got a text from von Scholz. She's asked for a meeting with their team at 8 a.m. tomorrow. And I didn't tell you, but I got a call from Pattison this afternoon. He wants to see me tonight. He texted me an hour ago where to meet him."

"About?"

"Something new is showing up on the satellite photos on the island. He wants to clue me in on what's going on."

"About?"

"I'll find out tonight."

"Am I going with you?"

"No. We're meeting at the Irish pub near the apartment. He was already in town for tomorrow afternoon's meeting. And, by the way, where were you this afternoon?"

"With Dirk. There was something wrong with my phone, and I had to get it fixed."

Erick looked at his watch as he and Brian headed to the lobby. He realized he'd be getting to his sister's too late if he had to take Brian to the hotel. Brian understood and offered to take a taxi. A guard at the front desk overheard them and suggested Brian use a new type of car service, new to the Netherlands, called Uber. The guard made the call for Brian, and the car arrived quickly. Brian was amazed at the efficiency and, upon arriving at the hotel, was surprised he could pay using a credit card.

Inside the hotel, Brian explained to the hotel's front desk clerk he needed to stay another night.

"Not a problem, sir. The room is open; besides, that room is perpetually reserved by Interpol for its employees and guests coming into town. Your wake-up call? Will it be 6 a.m. again, like this morning? And shall we send breakfast in the morning?"

"Yes, for the call, and no, thank you for breakfast. Have a nice evening, Miss."

He went upstairs, unfolded his clothes, and returned to the dining room. He had a salad and, while he ate, recalled the day's events. He dwelled on the idea of a huge German Junker plane landing in the Moroccan desert. *It should be easy to find with those new satellite photos.* He finished supper and went up to his room to read. He set the portable alarm for 6:30 a.m. and fell asleep.

Erick arrived at his sister's house in Zaanse Schans on time. He fumbled about while trying to manage his two young, rambunctious nieces as they finished dinner. They prepared for bed and returned to watch a television show but continued to tease and challenge their uncle. Erick shook his head a few times, and wondered how these two young, mischievous girls would someday become functional adults. A short time later, he fell sound asleep on the couch.

As Erick began to snore, his naughty nieces painted his fingernails bright red-orange. One added sparkles to the wet polish on one hand, saying to her sister, "Uncle Erick will like mine better than yours." The other replied, "Well, I'm painting tiny Xes on these five fingers. It will look like the flag of Amsterdam."

Having used her thinking time wisely in the car, Nina arrived home in Amsterdam and immediately opened her laptop. She began laying out the framework of her presentation. She wanted to make several critical points to Pieter. First, she'd present the recent find by Kristofer Bronn and show how it physically fits into the KvR diary. Next, she'd show how the written comments on the four pages fit perfectly into the timeline of his activities. Then she'd point out how KvR's comments implied a plane he was in was flying from Berlin with a heavy load, landed inland where it was very hot and sandy, and not on the cool shores of an island enjoying tropical breezes. She wanted to point out how rumors escalated by the D.C. think-tank folks driving this case might be moot with this new information. Her last point was to justify the logic behind her team's preference to research the plane's route as if it traveled over the Sahara Desert. And that suggested the large German Ju-290 plane unexpectedly landed somewhere near Marrakesh as described and misspelled in KvR's diary.

Her last point would be the most challenging. She wanted to extricate the team from going to Grand Canary Island and travel instead to Morocco and search in Marrakesh and an area farther north, toward Casablanca. She summarized her findings with math, showing vectors drawn on maps retrieved from the Internet.

Pieter returned to his apartment just past 11. Ursula, dressed in a sheer negligée, sat in bed reading. His breath smelled of alcohol, but she was more curious about what Pattison had to say.

"You're later than I expected. What'd you talk about?"

"It took a while – and a bunch of drinks – for Pattison to get to the point, but he thinks there's a mole in his organization. He's unsure if it's one of the folks in Langley or one of the young ones he's assigned to this case. He said there's been more activity this past week by the Russian students on the island. He says there may even be another smaller group there. He also said the agency began investigating the origins of airline flights landing on Grand Canary Island in the last few weeks. The initial report says the first group was from Belarus. Now, another group has arrived."

"What else did he say?"

"Not much. He sent you his regards and said, 'The cinnamon donuts at the last meeting were tasty.' Okay, I need to close my eyes."

"Did you see I dressed for you?"

"I did. You look great, but we have an early morning. Good night."

Pieter was asleep in a minute. Ursula got up, changed into a flannel nightgown, and then headed into the kitchen to send a text.

Nina sat back and smiled. She checked the time and was surprised to find it was already 1 a.m. After five hours of work, she was finally satisfied with her presentation. *I feel good! I think I can answer any question Pieter asks, and I think if Pattison drills me, I can do the same.*

She closed the laptop, washed her face, and headed to bed. As she lay in bed, her thoughts turned to Brian and his words earlier. *He's been through a lot. We'll have dinner tomorrow night. I'll turn down having wine. I'll smile. He'll know I'm pregnant. I sure hope he'll be happy. We'll skip dessert, and we'll return here. I'll take him to bed, and we'll make love like we did in Cordoba. He liked that, and it'll put him right to sleep.*

<u>CHAPTER SIXTEEN</u>

The Presentation

Nina was the first member of the team to arrive at the offices in The Hague. She headed upstairs and was loading her presentation on the conference room's laptop when Ursula walked in with a pot of coffee.

"Good morning! Pieter tells me you'll review something new this morning related to the Grand Canary Island case."

"Yes. We've obtained new information Pieter needs to know about."

"Oh? What's that?"

"It's about finding a— Oh, good morning, Erick."

"Hi, Nina. Hi, Ursula."

"Good morning, Agent Schmidt."

"Ursula, instead of my explaining what's come up, Pieter authorized you as our secretary to sit in and listen."

"Thanks. I'll get some cinnamon buns and return in a few minutes."

Nina gathered some papers, showed them to Erick, and, after a brief discussion, inserted a 3½" floppy disk through the laptop's thin side door. She then downloaded the presentation file onto the laptop's hard drive. She had hoped Brian would be there by now for her initial run-through but started her presentation by flipping through the PowerPoint slides with Erick present.

Ursula returned to the conference room with the buns, taking great interest in what Nina was proposing. Standing unnoticed at the back of the room, she put the plate on the credenza and jotted notes on a paper napkin. As the presentation ended, she quickly stuffed the napkin into her pants pocket and casually approached Nina while Erick wrote notes about what he'd just seen.

"Well, Nina, I'm impressed! It looks so interesting. So, do I understand you want to change the CIA's request and not go to Grand Canary Island?"

Nina beamed at the other woman's praise. "Thank you! That's right. Two days ago, a sheet of paper was found on the floor in Kristofer Bronn's antique shop in Leipzig. I'm sure you remember him. The paper came from the von Richter diary and represents the four middle pages. Unexpectedly, those pages have clues about the Grand Canary Island case. We've thoroughly reviewed the information, including the specific German-to-English translation. In this meeting, I'll try to convince Pieter that we must explore an area in Morocco instead of spelunking through caves on GCI."

"Is this just your idea? Or are agents O'Sullivan and Schmidt on board with this change of plans?"

"The three of us agree on the findings."

"Well, good luck trying to convince Pieter of such a change. You know he can be a real stickler."

"I'm prepared – and feel confident."

"As a heads up, he met with Pattison last night. Something was going on, and he returned to the apartment grumpy and tired. Expect the worst. You know he's an old chauvinist like the other department heads at the Agency. You don't see women running teams in any other department, right?"

"What apartment last night?"

"Oh! You don't know?"

"Know what?"

"Pieter and I have been together for over a year. We've shared our bed for the last five months."

Nina shook her head. "I didn't know."

"It's getting more serious. But, Nina, I can help you now that you're a team leader. If you keep me in the loop on what's happening, I can persuade him to adjust his thinking in your favor by whispering in his ear. I just need to know what's going on. Are you okay with that?"

"Got it loud and clear. Thank you, Ursula! I appreciate your support. I have a feeling I'll occasionally need it with Pieter."

As they were chatting, Brian arrived. He grabbed a cup of coffee and a fresh cinnamon bun and saw Ursula and Nina talking.

Then Pieter walked in. "Good morning, everyone. Nina, you asked for this meeting, so let's get started. It's your show."

Nina tensed. She'd hoped to go through her presentation with Brian quickly, but Pieter's early arrival prevented that.

Everyone sat. Taking a deep breath, Nina picked up the small clicker and moved to the front of the room. Slide by slide, she addressed the recent discovery of the missing diary pages and translated several of von Richter's notations. She watched Pieter's body language while translating several of KvR's notations, point by point. Nina's impeccable logic contributed to her self-confidence while she spoke.

Brian and Erick likewise eyed Pieter's body language. His crossed arms and stern look gradually relaxed as Nina spoke. He rubbed his nose and chin and nodded, revealing a growing receptiveness of her ideas.

Meanwhile, Ursula sat in the back, taking more notes.

Nina wrapped up her presentation by making the team's recommendation on the last slide. Brian and Erick looked at each other and smiled. Having Nina in the lead felt good.

Pieter asked Nina several questions. She responded to each one confidently, without hesitation. Then he paused and looked up at the ceiling.

The intervening silence seemed like an hour to everyone in attendance.

Then Pieter turned to Erick and Brian. "Are you two confident in this development, and the idea of going to Morocco?"

Brian nodded. "We are and wouldn't have requested this meeting if we weren't on board as a team. The diary played a key role in finding those paintings at the Mezquita, and if it weren't for this newly found page, we'd all be planning a spelunking excursion to the Canaries. But now there's no doubt the Agency needs to redirect our efforts."

"Nina, you did an excellent job in putting that together. We must get Amara Chikere in here to see what you've just presented. Ursula, is Amara in today?"

"I believe so."

"See how soon he can come up and sit with us, and please see if his people are already here. Our meeting with Pattison is still set for 1 o'clock. Amara, Felix, and Ladasha need to see what Nina put together before we meet Pattison. Then we need to decide what to do regarding the CIA's take on the project and how best to deploy our resources."

Ursula rose from her chair, and Nina expressed her appreciation to Pieter.

"No thanks are necessary, Nina. Your presentation is compelling. The facts are clear, and your logic supports repositioning our resources. You've shown that looking in Morocco for a failed flight makes more sense than hiking in the Canary Islands looking through caves. Besides, your hypothesis about Göring's art collection being removed from his home before the end of the war is spot on. Elements of his art collection have eluded European art experts and collectors and are among the top items on Interpol's priority list. It's one reason I argued to establish the Art Research and Recovery Unit twenty-seven years ago. You three are professional art experts and, as investigators, you're the best I've ever seen."

Hearing the accolade, Nina felt even more satisfied that Pieter found her presentation convincing. Erick smiled at Brian and proudly rubbed his loosely curled fingers on his chest. Then he noticed glitter all over his shirt and realized he'd missed cleaning his mischievous nieces' sparkly handiwork from one fingernail.

When Ursula returned, she told Pieter and the others that Amara and his team would be ready in about twenty minutes. Then she went outside for her morning walk and to make a call on her new smartphone, the same type she had Dirk ordered for Nina and her team.

Pieter headed toward the door. "O'Sullivan, I'm headed back to my office. Did you want to see me about your extension?"

"I had a question, but it can wait for another time."

"Ursula told me you were hammering her with questions yesterday. Is that not so?"

"No. I just asked whether my insurance and health benefits were being extended."

"Of course."

Pieter left the room. He'd intended to call Pattison to give him a heads-up about the new information but decided to wait. He walked back to his office, wondering. *Why would she say O'Sullivan had asked a bunch of questions?*

CHAPTER SEVENTEEN

Brian's Call to Shawn

Brian left the conference room and called his sister Shawn while standing at the far end of the hall. It was almost 3 a.m. in New Jersey, and he purposely called then, knowing it would go right to voicemail. He left a message apologizing for not calling lately, sent his love to Stephen and the children, and asked if she could please let Tricia and Kathy know he was busy with a case that would keep him overseas.

"I'll be here at least another two to four weeks, and I'll be back to New Jersey after that."

As he spoke those words, he recalled previous calls to Grace in which he'd promised the same thing. A sting of guilt came over him.

He then called Massimo and left a message asking whether there'd been any news about his stolen art.

Then, concerned about the crates stashed under the house, Brian called Carlo, his groundskeeper in Malta, to ensure everything was okay there.

Carlo's phone went straight to voicemail, so he left him a message as well.

Brian's last call was to the Fellini law firm in Rome.

"Pronto, pronto. Come posso aiutaria?"

"Senora, questo e' Brian O'Sullivan."

"Ah, Signore O'Sullivan. How can I help you today?

"Is Signore Fellini in the office? I'd like to speak to him briefly."

"Uno momento."

"Pronto, ah! Signore O'Sullivan. *Come stai?"*

"Bene. Good. I'm good."

"Cosi dispiaciuto... uh... So sorry to hear about Katrina. I so adored her. I envied Luca for so many years. Did you give her a rose from me when you saw her?"

"I did. She smiled, and tears filled her eyes."

"Grazie, molto grazie. Signore O'Sullivan. Do you need something?"

"Yes. I wanted to know whether Luca committed to making any donations when you prepared his will as he was selling his business."

"Ah. What you're asking – it's many years ago. Give me a moment. I remember now. Luca was talking about the Knights of Malta. He was going to join them. No. He had already joined them. He wanted to donate money from the proceeds of the sale of his business, but we never talked about specifics, and then his death was so sudden."

"Did he mention anything else to you?"

"Such as?"

"Did he say anything about Katrina's family and their ownership of the DiBotticino stone works at a quarry north of Brescia?"

"Yes. He mentioned Katrina's family and talked about a legend of an Italian prince who became a Crusader."

"Did he mention finding some boxes in a quarry north of Brescia?"

"He did."

"And?"

"He said he found equipment worn by a knight and some statues."

"Anything else?"

"Yes."

 "What else did he tell you?"

"Luca was nervous about the contents of the other boxes. He said he'd tell me more when we spoke in person, but he never came to Rome."

"Grazie, signore Fellini. I hope to be in Rome soon and will come to say hello."

"Buona giornata, signore O'Sullivan."

Inside, Erick, still elated from Nina's presentation, was munching on a cinnamon bun. He poured himself another coffee and turned to Nina.

"Great job, boss. I'm proud of you. What you put together was impressive."

Nina scowled. "I'm not your boss. Don't call me that."

"Okay, boss. Hey, Nina, when Chick and his team get here, focus on Chick like you focused on Pieter. And remember, you're talking about a case in his territory."

"What do you know about Morocco, Erick?"

"Very little. When Brian first started with Interpol, he was assigned to me. Our work took us to a few cities across North Africa. We spent only a little time in Morocco."

"Where in Morocco?"

"We started in Casablanca and headed east. Why do you ask?"

"I'm getting nervous about this."

"Why would you be nervous?"

"I feel like I've opened Pandora's box, and I'm just feeling… I don't know. Different."

"Nina, you'll solidify your reputation with this case. Just relax. Besides, you've got two great teammates." Erick grinned at her.

Brian returned to the room from his calls. "What are you two talking about?"

"The case. Nina's nervous."

"About what? It's our job to go and investigate places where the art might be hidden."

"But, Brian, it's *Morocco*. Just the thought of it makes me tremble. And besides, I'm…"

"You're what?"

Nina shook her head. This wasn't the time. "Never mind."

Less than twenty minutes later, Amara, Felix, and Ladasha arrived. After everyone had greeted each other, they sat for a repeat of Nina's presentation. This time, Nina included more details while spinning the information. Her comments about Hermann Göring struck a chord with

Pieter, who was again impressed by her facts and suggestions, and felt even more convinced now than earlier. The information excited him and made him want to return to the field to participate in this search. It was the first time he'd felt this urge in many years. But he held off letting anyone know his feelings.

When Nina finished, Pieter turned toward Chick and his team. "What do you think?"

"Damn interesting – and convincing. Well done, Agent von Scholz," Amara commended her.

Nina beamed at the West African team leader's praise.

"We've never come across anything in the field to suggest a plane went down in or near Marrakesh," he continued. "Nor have we heard of any art or gold being stashed away any place. And I say 'field' broadly. The physical territory under my direction is huge, and my team is limited to just two staffers. Then again, we're not art sleuths like you. We focus on crimes of a different kind. But I like your idea about the direct path a plane would take to the Canaries going over Morocco and Marrakesh. Your point about that German fellow you call KvR – his misspelling of Marrakesh is convincing. I'd say you're spot on to something. Well done."

"Based on what you've seen, do you believe it's plausible that art and gold might be stashed in Marrakesh or nearby?"

Amara rubbed his chin. "Well, anything's possible, Pieter. Like I said, it's a big area. It seems like you're about to go all in with your resources and begin searching Marrakesh and the nearby desert, not Grand Canary Island. Is that correct?"

"Exactly."

"Where does that leave you with Pattison and the CIA?"

"Good question. It's why I asked your team to come in early."

Pieter spun his chair. "Nina, I'd like to discuss this further with you and Chick in my office. Let's do that now. The rest of you can get back to your outstanding to-do lists. Uh, did any of you see Ursula?"

The meeting ended.

Brian and Erick went to the cafeteria to chat while Nina and Amara returned with Pieter to his office. As he approached his desk, he saw the large writing on Ursula's note.

"Hair appointment! Back in two hours."

That confounded woman! It's always her hair or nails or taking breaks to smoke. And it's so blasted inconvenient when she runs out. I swear, sometimes it feels like she's out more often than here.

CHAPTER EIGHTEEN

Pattison's Call

Twenty minutes into Pieter, Nina, and Amara's conversation about the case and staffing commitment, Pieter's office phone rang. Expecting Ursula to pick it up, he remembered she was getting her hair done. He reached for the receiver.

"Van Deusen here."

"Hey Pieter, it's Pattison. Listen, I'm sorry to call you at the last moment before this afternoon's meeting. I just got a call. Something's come up with the boys back at headquarters in Langley, and I'm being asked to focus on another case instead of this Grand Canary Island case. But listen, I have an idea. Solie Van de Berg lives there in Amsterdam. Two others on my team – Jay Stemmler and David Smith – are already in The Hague. You can take those three. Well, uh, let me rephrase that. Let's say they can all be yours for the next three months. The guys have been chewing at the bit after I told them about this case. The three will stay on my payroll. The case can be all yours – all under your agency's direction. You'll get all the glory at no cost!"

Pieter hesitated. "Well, you've caught me a bit flat-footed, Bill. Give me an hour to review the logistics, and I'll get back to you with my decision."

"Great. Thanks. I'll expect to hear from you in an hour."

After hanging up, Pieter turned to Nina and Amara, sitting across from his desk. Both looked curious, having only heard Pieter's side of the conversation.

"That was Pattison."

"We gathered. What's going on?"

"This afternoon's meeting is off. The CIA's redirecting him to another case, but we can have his three people: Van de Berg, Smith, and Stemmler. They'd work directly for us for the next three months. I think he's making the offer assuming we're going to Grand Canary Island to follow the case he presented."

The two looked at each other.

"What do we do now, Pieter? Must we investigate Grand Canary Island?" Amara asked.

"No. It's our case now, and I say we follow Nina's idea to search Marrakesh and the nearby desert."

"Pieter, this comes at a convenient juncture as it allows us to change our direction without confronting the CIA about the new information. Now we can look for Hermann Göring's stash in Morocco. Amara, wouldn't you agree?"

"Absolutely, Nina, based on what we just heard, and having three more people under your wing could help our efforts. But, Pieter, are you sure that's what *you* want?"

"I'm not sure. That's why I said I'd call him back in an hour. It's really up to you two."

"Pieter, if we all feel convinced about changing our focus to Marrakesh, Casablanca, or somewhere in between," Amara mused, "we could really benefit from integrating the others into our plans. Morocco is a large area. We could use them."

"What's the status of those three anyway?" Nina asked. "Did Pattison say he briefed them about being assigned to our unit?"

"Not yet. He's waiting for me to call him back with a decision." Pieter looked at the time. "It's eleven now."

"I'll get with Erick and Brian and discuss what Pattison suggested. I'll be back in thirty minutes. Amara, please have the same chat with your team."

Chick nodded. "Will do. Pieter, are we all done here?"

"Yes. I'll see you both back here at 11:30, and then I'll call Pattison with our decision."

CHAPTER NINETEEN

The Works

Nina and Amara left Pieter's office to huddle with their teams. Pieter reread Ursula's note. The small writing said she was 'getting the works.' He smirked. That meant she was getting her usual haircut and dye job at the private hair salon near the office. Her note assured him she'd return in time for the meeting with Pattison. He shrugged and chucked. *I know she's not a natural blonde.*

Ursula visited the exclusive one-seat salon to have her hair cut and dyed, like clockwork, on the last Thursday of the month. But Pieter failed to notice that today was Wednesday. In this case, a week and a day early. And Ursula's sudden visit to the high-end beauty parlor had nothing to do with the state of her roots.

Instead, in the confines of the private salon, Ursula was about to brief Olga – the parlor's owner-operator and her Russian Federal Security Service handler – about the Interpol case focused on Grand Canary Island.

* * *

Born Tamara Ehrlich in East Germany, Ursula Bloom was the daughter of Kuhrt Ehrlich, a senior officer in the East German army, and Sofia Muratova, a Soviet gymnast who won a combined eight medals in the 1956 and 1960 Olympics. Kuhrt and Sofia met a few years after the '60 Olympics and lived together in East Berlin. Tamara, their only child, was born in 1965.

As a young teenager during WWII, Kuhrt Ehrlich was in the Hitlerjugend – the German youth movement that taught Nazi ideological

108

messages of hatred and prejudice against Jews and other minorities. When the Soviets took control of East Germany after the war, eighteen-year-old Kuhrt joined the military. In early 1950, he was offered a position in East Germany's newly formed Stasi. The Stasi was the intelligence agency under the direction of the Soviet Socialist Party that successfully collected large quantities of intelligence on the East German population. Like the Soviet's KGB, the Stasi created an atmosphere of fear and enabled the Soviet-controlled East German government to squash any plots against it.

Tamara learned about her father's activities in her teens while listening to his anti-West rhetoric. She loved her dad and supported the idea of the Stasi's control. After Tamara spent a few years as an elementary school English language teacher, her father's long-time supervisor suggested she consider a role in Stasi. Recommendations of entry into the East German intelligence agency were rare, customarily done as favors among old comrades.

The Stasi quickly vetted Tamara, whose role as a spy was immediately approved. Careful background planning and impeccable credentials showed her resumé as a trustworthy former educator seeking a career in journalism. Her fluency in English gave her instant credibility, and it wasn't long before she took a position working for an East German newspaper suspected of having staff journalists leaning toward Western democratic ideals.

In June 1987, a speech by American President Ronald Reagan and subsequent speeches by Mikhail Gorbachev destabilized the East German government and its post-WWII political position. On November 9, 1989, crowds of Germans gathered and began dismantling the Berlin Wall, a barrier symbolizing the Cold War division of Europe over the previous thirty years. Its dismantling created a massive shift in the East German spy community. As a result, Tamara and her comrades were again vetted and initiated into units of the KGB.

In October 1990, West and East Germany were reunified. The monumental event triggered the collapse of Soviet control over other

Eastern European nations. After the reunification, Tamara moved to West Germany with her parents, and her life as a spy was thrust forward to play her role in the free, united Germany. Meanwhile, the collapse of the USSR heralded the end of the KGB, which then became known as the FSB.

After working in three different German newspapers, Tamara, now known as Ursula Bloom, eventually made her way to the Netherlands under the direction of a new FSB handler. She eventually made her way to the Netherlands under the direction of a new handler. In Amsterdam, she gained employment as a writer for *De Volkskrant*. Three years later, she applied for an open position as a secretary with Interpol's offices in The Hague. With bullet-proof credentials dating back to her birth and baptism, she was thoroughly vetted by Interpol and hired. Her first assignment was as a secretary and administrative assistant to Director of European Operations Klaus Mueller, who oversaw several units, including the Art Research and Reconnaissance Group. She enjoyed the work and was proud to silently contribute to the FSB's efforts. Besides her regular job, the FSB generously compensated Ursula with monthly stipends in an offshore account.

Her position gave the FSB the deep access they desired to keep an eye on many of Interpol's activities. After Klaus retired, she became secretary to his successor, George Hobson, a Brit with the United Kingdom's foreign intelligence service – MI6. When Hobson retired after a brief stint, Interpol named Wilhelm Mueller, Klaus' son, the new director.

When Wilhelm was killed in Malta, Senior Director of European Operations Pieter Van Deusen decided not to fill the position of director, instead taking on the responsibility of the Art Research and Recovery unit himself, along with his other responsibilities. Pieter had known Ursula Bloom to be an excellent administrative assistant. When his secretary retired, he promoted Ursula to work in his office. But having her work for him didn't come as a complete surprise.

For the previous few years, Pieter occasionally joined Ursula for lunch, initially to keep track of the younger Mueller's activities and erratic behaviors. During those casual lunch meetings, he found her attractive and wanted to become better acquainted. Unbeknownst to others in the office, they began dating and, before long, found themselves in a sexual relationship. Wilhelm's death in Malta created a convenient path for their mutual sexual interest, and within a week, Ursula moved into his apartment. In doing so, she could satisfy her intense sexual desire to be with Pieter while reaching a new level of success in her commitment to her FSB comrades.

In the last several months, her visits to the salon and chats with her FSB handler focused on her emerging relationship with Pieter, his performance in bed, and comparisons between her former on-again-off-again relationship with young Wilhelm. Wilhelm's forceful approach to sex and Pieter's slower, more mature, and tantalizing techniques.

In these conversations, Olga's interest in Ursula was often aroused as Ursula detailed her sexual exploits with both lovers. Olga longed for the day she would find herself in bed with Ursula. But not today. Ursula's call for an impromptu visit prompted Olga to take an uncommon step. In turn, she summoned her FSB handler, Dmitri, to the tiny salon, anticipating unusual news.

<u>CHAPTER TWENTY</u>

Taken from Carinhall

At 11:29, a knock at his open office door caused Pieter to look up.

"Come in, come in." Pieter looked at his watch as Nina and Amara entered. *She is precise! Now, what have they come up with?* "Please sit."

Amara moved to the couch while Nina remained standing and began to pace as she began to outline the plan for the mission.

"The European Art Dealers Association's most current *'Master List of Art Stolen During WWII'* has many pieces of art identified on Göring's personal list of art assets unaccounted for. Thus, our unit's primary goal is to retrieve what KvR referred to in his diary notation, which we believe to be elements of Göring's art and gold."

Pieter nodded.

"Göring planned to use Luftwaffe pilots loyal to him to secure a Ju-290 to move a portion of his collection. We know he didn't move it all because the American soldiers stopped a train with two boxcars filled with his stolen art assets.

"I strongly suspect Göring knew of von Richter's reputation, background, and outstanding service and tapped him for the assignment. However, when the U.S. Army Air Force and British allies gained air superiority and clamped down hard on German Luftwaffe air traffic, few planes could successfully support the contents of the flight.

"Our aim is to determine where the 290 might have landed based on von Richter's notes and develop a perimeter around an area where the bounty may be. The downside risk is that locals might have found and carted away the goods. However, we can assume the art or even the gold might be in and around our target cities, and some or all may remain hidden – or some of the art could be in plain sight and not recognized for what they are.”

“Well done, Nina. I fully support your theory and your plan. And the CIA Agents?”

“Thank you, Pieter. I recommend we agree to accept the CIA agents' help. I'm suggesting we pair them with our agents. Amara and I agree on this.”

“Is that right, Amara?”

Chick nodded. “Absolutely. Nina has a good strategy. She's a brilliant young woman. And based on the diary pages, we've concluded that while the satellite photos show remnants of a long runway, this case will not proceed to look for stolen art or gold hidden in caves on Grand Canary Island. Are you okay with that, Pieter?”

“Yes.”

“Great. My lead agent, Felix Freeman, will team up with Jay Stemmler; Ladasha Daddah will partner with David Smith. Both teams will go to Marrakesh.”

Nina nodded. “Erick will team up with CIA Agent Solie Van de Berg and go to Casablanca. They know each other and will work well together. Brian and I will cover southern Casablanca and move south to a small town called Settat. It became an essential agricultural trading center in the 1800s and grew quickly under French colonial control at the turn of the last century. The countryside south of there is mostly fertile but has sandy and desert-like areas with dunes. I've drawn a long single vector and the most likely flight path we believe the 290 might have taken.

“I'll be the single point of contact for everyone in the field, and I'll relay their findings to Amara. Pieter, you'll be his backup.”

“Sounds good.”

“Next is timing. If we make the decision today to move on this, we can be in the field as early as tomorrow or the next day. The plan would be for team members to meet and speak with locals, native Moroccans who grew up in those towns, to see if we could produce any leads. Hopefully, we can get this done quickly. How's that sound?"

Pieter nodded. "I like everything you've said. I'll call Pattison and let him know we plan to use his people. Remember, you have his people for ninety days. I have nothing budgeted for this expedition. I can transfer some funding, but if your search takes longer than three months, I'll have an issue with my upline manager at headquarters.

"Okay, it's 11:40 now. Let's meet in the conference room at 1:30. You can reveal your plans to the CIA folks then. You and Amara should meet with your teams now and put something together to present to everyone at 1:30."

Nina nodded. "Thanks, Pieter. See you then. Will Ursula be available to take notes?"

"She should be. She just went to the beauty parlor for her regular Thursday appointment."

Nina looked at him strangely. "It's Wednesday."

"So it is." Pieter shrugged. "Well, her note said she'd be back in time for the Pattison meeting."

CHAPTER TWENTY-ONE

Years Earlier – Late August 1944

At 7 a.m., twins Ahmad and Chadu mounted their camels, waved goodbye to their grandfather, and headed south. The early morning sun cast long shadows as the boys rode along the empty desert road leading away from Settat, located on the outskirts of Casablanca. Keeping a good pace, they would camp overnight, then arrive home in Marrakesh around noon the next day.

The teens descended from the Rahamna tribe, which had occupied the extensive plains north of Marrakesh in Western Sahara since the 1500s. Local custom dictated a boy would visit his paternal grandfather upon turning thirteen to obtain his blessing. However, the German Afrika Korps occupation of the region had delayed their visit two years.

Like the twins' father, their grandfather was a trader who dabbled in raising piebald camels. The grandfather was pleased with the young men during their two weeks together. He enjoyed his teenage grandsons' company and shared many family stories. But now it was time for them to return to the small settlement where they were raised.

Four hours into their trip, the teens heard a strange noise in the distance. They looked around, scanning the bright, cloudless blue sky, but saw nothing. Within a minute, the unfamiliar sound grew louder. Ahmad pulled up on his camel and stopped. The noise came from behind, so he turned to look again. Coming directly toward them was a giant airplane. It was nothing like anything they had ever seen. The plane was so massive, and the roar of its four engines became louder and louder as it approached.

Terrified, Chadu turned to his brother. "Oh God! Ahmad, it's coming right at us! It's going to hit us!"

"Something's wrong. It wants to land right here on the road."

"There's smoke coming from the plane's wing. Look! I see flames!"

"It's the engine. Quick! Let's get over there behind that tall sand dune. Hurry, Chadu."

Each kicked his camel's sides and immediately were on a fast trot toward the rear of the dune. As the camels ran, Ahmad and Chadu looked back again and saw the plane's landing gear and huge wheels were down as if ready to land. Filled with fright, they arrived behind the dune in seconds, jumped off their dromedaries, and pulled them down to lie flat on the sand.

The plane's long, wide wing suddenly passed overhead by only ten feet. The engine's roar deafened the boys, and the air pressure from the enormous propellers pushed the air down on them, scattering sand and dust in all directions as the plane passed. The frightened camels grunted loudly and bucked, but the boys managed to keep control, hiding safely behind the tall dune, perfectly positioned to peek over the top.

They watched in awe as the plane's left tires landed on the old road's hard stone surface. But the road wasn't wide enough for the right wheels; they missed the road surface entirely, and the plane's weight and motion began driving the entire landing-gear assembly, including the wheels, deeply into the sand. Suddenly, the right-side tires exploded on impact, and the right-side landing gear collapsed. The plane's nose was jerked down abruptly, crashing hard on the road, sending sparks flying everywhere.

As the landing gear embedded deeper in the sand, the craft pivoted and spun hard to the right. The screech of metal as the plane turned was deafening and sent shudders down both boys' spines. More crashing sounds came from within the plane. The plane's motion stopped with a huge jerk and a thump as the fuselage hit the ground while sand and dust thrown into the air rained back onto the ground.

As the airplane lay mainly on its belly, its nose was tilted downward, partially buried in the sandy ditch off the side of the slightly elevated road, leaving the plane's tail jutting ten feet in the air. The massive radial engines sat on the ground, and the long, broad wings rested lengthwise atop the road. The propellers – those that didn't snap off the engines altogether – were bent and twisted. Luckily, the sparks had subsided because aviation fuel poured from the broken wing into the sand. Fine dust particles hung in the air for another five minutes.

Watching in awe from about two hundred yards away, the brothers couldn't believe what they had seen! Not only were they astonished at the plane's size, but now both were even more amazed at the crash and all the destruction they'd just witnessed.

Chadu looked at his twin.

"Oh God! What do we do?"

"Nothing. We need to stay here, be patient, and watch what happens."

"But we must continue our journey home. Momma and Papa are expecting us tomorrow."

"I know. But for right now, we need to be careful. There are bad men inside that plane."

"How do you know?"

"Look at the plane."

"What about it?"

"It has no markings."

"So?"

"If the people inside were honest, the plane would have some marking or flag painted on the side. So they must be bad."

"I think you're right, Ahmad."

"Of course I'm right. I'm older and smarter than you."

"You're only six minutes older than me. I would have had the same answer in four more minutes."

"No."

"Yes."

The brothers shoved at each other momentarily, as quarreling brothers do, forgetting their difficult situation. Then Chadu's camel, Blue, named for his unusual eye color, grunted, and both were reminded of their terrifying circumstances. They slid back down the dune to consider what to do next.

Chadu again suggested they leave for home. "We can travel on a path that keeps us hidden behind this dune before turning toward home."

Ahmad remained resolute. "No. We can't leave now. Whoever's inside might see us. We need to stay hidden here. The full moon will rise tonight, an hour after sunset. By 4 a.m., it'll be in the western sky. We'll leave for home then and be home by dinner time. Let's get back up the dune and see if people come out."

"I'm scared."

"Of course you are. Just keep Blue quiet. Whisper in his ear, 'No grunting!'"

Ahmad and Chadu inched their way back up the side of the dune and peeked over the top again. Just then, a wide ramp descended from under the rear of the plane's fuselage, down to the road. Moments later, after it fully opened and rested on the road, three Nazi SS officers in stark-looking uniforms walked down the ramp and stepped onto the road. They circled the plane and began a discussion, arms waving and fingers pointing south and north. Two men in gray overalls emerged, carrying a slumped body by its arms and legs down the ramp. They placed it at the road's edge.

"Ahmad, the man they're carrying – he has blood all over him. Do you think he's dead?"

"I think so," Ahmad whispered in reply.

Another minute passed. A third man in a pilot's uniform descended the ramp carrying a tarp. After placing it over the bloodied body, he and the flight engineers, the men in overalls, walked to the front of the airplane. They looked at the chunks and scraps of rubber from the blown tires, and the broken wheel hubs snapped off the landing gear assembly. They surveyed the right-side landing gear buried at least two feet into the soft sand. The pilot inspected the broken wing, then walked over to the two flight engineers looking at the engine that had caught fire. The pilot started yelling at the other two.

The brothers heard the yelling but couldn't determine what was being said.

"Ahmad, it looks like they're not happy, and that's scaring me. I'm sliding back down the dune and will say my prayers."

"I'll keep watching."

Two minutes passed.

"Ahmad, I can't concentrate on my prayers."

"Ah, you don't know how to pray properly anyway."

"I do."

"No, you don't. You couldn't even say your prayers in front of Grandfather."

"As if you're perfect."

"Shh! Chadu, you're getting loud."

"You're a pain. I hate you sometimes."

"Quiet. We have a bad situation going on here."

Chadu scrambled back up the dune.

They watched as the flight engineers finished arguing with the pilot and headed back up the ramp into the plane. The Nazi officers followed. The teens continued to watch but saw no movement outside by any of the plane's occupants.

The brothers remained vigilant, taking turns to see if anything was happening, while the other kept Baba and Blue calm. As the hours dragged, both boys moved back down the dune and hid in the shadow of the camels as the hot sun beat down.

As the sun began to set in the west, the moon began its rise in the east. It wasn't long before the desert sand began cooling. Feeling the chill in the air, the twins took the blankets from under the camels' saddles, then wrapped themselves and nestled against the warmth of the camels. Exhausted from the anxiety of the day, they fell into a deep sleep.

The next morning, as the sky brightened, the brothers woke to the hum of a small plane's engine as it circled overhead before the sun had risen over the horizon.

"Ahmed, do you hear that?"

"Yes. Look at the markings on the side and wing of the plane."

"Is it German?"

"Yes. Grandpa said German planes have a black cross and not a swastika."

"Really?"

"Chadu, you weren't paying attention when he told us that," Ahmad scolded.

"Stop picking on me."

"I wouldn't pick on you if you weren't so stupid."

The brothers kept an eye on the plane as it circled. A minute later, the small plane easily landed on the narrow road. They watched it taxi and spin around behind the crashed 290. The engine stopped, and they heard another plane in the sky. It landed less than a minute later and, similarly, rolled up to the first small plane and spun around. The pilots of both planes climbed out and walked over to the flight engineers. The three Nazi SS officers descended the ramp to the road. The small planes' pilots saluted the officers, who clicked their heels and returned the Nazi salute.

After a brief, animated conversation, two of the SS officers, a flight engineer, and the pilot of the crashed plane climbed into the second plane. With a few puffs and sputters, its engine reached full speed, rolled north along the narrow road, and flew away.

"Wow. Did you see that, Ahmad?"

"Of course I did. I'm right here next to you."

"Those Nazi guys sure look scary."

"They sure do."

A minute later, the third Nazi, an SS officer, the tallest of the three, spoke briefly with the pilot of the first plane, who climbed back into the small plane and started it. The officer turned to the remaining flight engineers. They had a brief discussion marked by smiles and small laughter. He shook their hands and saluted them. They proudly returned the salute. Then, without warning, the officer pulled his Luger from its holster and shot both men. The flight engineers' bodies slumped to the ground at the base of the plane's rampway.

Shocked at witnessing the murders, Chadu began crying.

"Be quiet!" Ahmad hissed. "Do you want him to come here and shoot us, too?"

The Nazi officer stepped over the bodies and climbed into the idling plane. It sped down the road and took off.

The teen's sobs continued.

"Oh, stop your crying, Chadu. The bad men are gone."

He sniffed and asked, "What are we going to do now?"

"I don't know about you, crybaby, but I'm going to look inside that airplane."

"No way."

Ahmad eyed his brother and gave an impatient sigh. "Are you always gonna act like a little kid?"

"Please, Ahmad. I don't want to go down there. I'm scared."

"You're always scared of doing stuff because you're the baby. Here, hold Baba's reins and keep Blue quiet. I'm heading down there, and I'm going inside."

Ahmad stood from his crouching position and clambered over the top of the dune. Then, step-sliding down the sand, he reached the road and walked toward the ramp. About two hundred feet from the plane, his young heart throbbed with excitement. He grew nervous as he approached the plane. Then, within fifty feet, his heart began to race.

The plane's sheer size overwhelmed Ahmad. It was so much larger than anything he'd ever seen. Looking down, he saw the bodies of the two men murdered by the Nazi officer. Both had been shot in the heart. The bloody broken arm and mashed bones of the compound-fractured leg of the third body weren't covered by the small tarp. Flies from nowhere in the middle of the desert that had already arrived for the first body were now inspecting and enjoying all three. Ahmad wanted a closer look at the dead men but kept his distance.

Neither seeing any movement nor hearing any noise, Ahmad took a step onto the ramp. It felt solid. He took a second step. A massive rush of adrenalin surged through him. He looked back to see if Chadu was watching. He was. Ahmad gave him a thumbs up, turned, and, continuing up the steps, disappeared into the wide fuselage.

As his eyes adjusted to the dark, he saw large wooden crates scattered about. Some were broken, others smashed against the inside of the plane. Stepping in a little further, the teen saw two more dead bodies. Both were wearing grey overalls; they were covered in blood, crushed between huge crates and the airplane's shell.

Then he saw something baffling. A crate shoved up against one dead body had broken open; its contents, a stack of shiny yellow bricks, had scattered outside the crate. Intrigued, he reached to lift one and found it surprisingly heavy. Unaware of what he held, he reached for a second. Then he noticed a swastika embossed into the gold bullion's surface.

Ahmad innately sensed the shiny, yellow bricks' value and carried two back to the ramp. As he slowly made his way, stepping over scattered debris and then stepping carefully down the ramp, he noticed Chadu waiting for him at the bottom. Blue and Baba stood nearby, sniffing the dead bodies.

"I think these must be important. Feel how heavy they are. They even have a swastika thing on them."

"I bet they're valuable."

"I'll bring one back to Grandfather and see what he thinks. We should take the other one home to Papa."

"No," Chadu insisted, shaking his head. "We can't do that. It's stealing."

"Chadu, they're not going to miss one or two. There must be hundreds of these things all over the place inside the plane. I also saw a crate of paintings inside. They must be important."

"If it's so important or so valuable, won't the men in the black boots be coming back?"

"Probably. That's why we must hurry. Let's go now. I'll try to get Grandpa to come back. You do the same with Papa."

"Okay."

CHAPTER TWENTY-TWO

Olga Briefs Dimitri

Happy with her stylish trim and dye job, Ursula felt even better about sharing the latest intel about the Interpol case with Olga. It was almost one o'clock when she left and hurried back to the office, unaware the meeting with Pattison had been canceled.

Olga walked to the salon's back room where Dimitri, her next-level FSB handler, and his assistant, Katya, were waiting.

"Comrade, we arrived late and listened to your conversation up front with Ursula. What do you take from her last visit and today's sudden visit?"

"Before today, she had said a senior member of the CIA visited her boss, Pieter Van Deusen. A new American satellite launched last year has revealed there might have been a long runway on Grand Canary Island. Parts of it are hidden below the ground's surface. The finding is a link to a decades-old rumor of a plane that flew art and gold from Germany to the island during World War Two."

Dmitri nodded. "Our people already know about this, and we have a small group there right now, searching the caves."

"She said the CIA agreed to have several agents team up with Interpol's Art Research and Recovery unit to search on Grand Canary Island. However, her urgent visit this morning is because the new Art Research team leader has new evidence that suggests the art and gold are elsewhere."

"Did she say where?"

"Ursula said it's somewhere in North Africa. She mentioned Morocco."

"What else did she say?"

"The art and gold belonged to Hermann Göring."

"Interesting! Göring was a close friend of the Red Baron. Both were World War One flying aces whom Hitler greatly admired."

"Ursula also said she heard of an art robbery in a Siracusa home owned by a Massimo Marini. I'm not sure what that's about."

"My superior purchased art from an Interpol Agent, Paolo Luzzi, for many years. He's still upset Luzzi was killed, and he blames O'Sullivan. After Luzzi's death, my boss arranged for several comrades to track O'Sullivan's activities, including his visits to New Jersey, Malta, and Siracusa. That theft from O'Sullivan's friend was arranged by my boss, an art lover who serves in a very high-level role in the FSB with access to the Kremlin's inner circle.

"The three locals who hit Marini's house believed the robbery was ordered by a *capo di capo* in Reggio, Calabria, who would reward them by bringing them into the organization at a prominent level. They had no idea who really ordered the theft. They were just instructed to bring the art onto a yacht owned by one of our oligarchs. Now, do you have anything else for us?"

"Ursula also overheard a tense conversation Van Deusen had with O'Sullivan. It seems O'Sullivan's employment contract with Interpol was extended. O'Sullivan told Van Deusen he didn't need to work anymore because of – get this – the fifty-three million U.S. dollars sitting in his Swiss account."

Dmitri's eyebrows rose. "I see. Is that it?"

"One more thing. With O'Sullivan's time being renewed, Ursula arranged for him and the two others to get new cell phones and laptops. She also convinced an IT technician in their office that O'Sullivan was under internal investigation and suspected of thievery as part of the old group under Wilhelm Mueller. Ursula used Van Deusen's digital signature to sign off on purchasing the equipment and is tracking his movements using a new feature in his phone. The IT department also continues to tap the antique dealer's line in Leipzig."

"Ursula also said O'Sullivan promised to withdraw one million U.S. dollars from his Swiss account and wire it to his financially strapped friend, Marini."

"Anything else?"

Olga shook her head. "That was it."

"Excellent. Did you do her nails today?"

"No. She needed to get back."

"Good. Text her. Bring her in again in a day or two. We want to stay close to any new developments in their plans in the next 24 to 48 hours. Olga, you've done well to have Ursula arrange the phone tap and plant listening devices with Ursula in the hotel room assigned to the Interpol division guests. I'm surprised you didn't take advantage of being in the hotel room with her."

"When Ursula visits, she often looks deeply into my eyes. I take her stare to believe she might be interested. I'm so tempted to go down on her."

"Of course you are! But you're smart to be patient. Your chance to fuck with her will come soon. Continue staying close as Ursula transitions herself deeper into Van Deusen's life. Encourage her. Send her flowers with a 'Thank You' note from the beauty parlor. It'll confirm you support her work, and Pieter may appreciate her visits here if fresh flowers occasionally arrive on her desk. She'll be happy – and he won't have to spend the money."

"Good idea, Dmitri. As a reminder, everything said at the hotel where O'Sullivan is staying and in Pieter Van Deusen's apartment is transmitted and recorded here. The equipment is in that closet. Since Ursula has been living with Pieter, I've enjoyed replaying and listening to her in bed with Pieter. I think she's forgotten the listening device is there. She's so vocal, and she gets loud when she lets go in bed. She thoroughly enjoys her role as a spy. And he is, no doubt, enjoying fucking a younger, well-endowed woman. I'm amazed at his stamina – and, frankly, jealous!"

"Ha! You make me laugh. You'd prefer being with Ursula, no?"

"Yes. But it doesn't matter. I could take both on."

Olga had just finished her debriefing with Dmitri and Katya when a late-model black Mercedes SUV pulled up outside the tiny shop. A moment later, Dimitri's cell phone rang.

"We just pulled up outside. He's waiting to hear the latest."

Dmitri ended the conversation with Olga, went outside, and climbed into the SUV with Katya.

"Good afternoon, comrades. Latest information, please?"

CHAPTER TWENTY-THREE

Ivan Sokolov

Sitting in the SUV and listening intently was a high-level FSB mastermind, Ivan Sokolov, a Russian official with extraordinary access to the Kremlin, who had full responsibility and control for art stolen by the Gestapo during World War Two and then carried back to Moscow by Russian soldiers.

Sokolov's story began years earlier when, after studying at Leningrad State University, he had the chance to attend Columbia, on the upper west side of Manhattan, for graduate studies in Political Science. During his time there, in the mid-1970s, he met a group of students called lefties who leaned toward communism. Sokolov was initially surprised at their anti-American beliefs. He eventually joined the group and shared ideas and perspectives on socialism and communism versus capitalism.

He returned to Moscow after graduation, planning to continue his education. Unexpectedly, Sokolov was approached by the FSB, who had watched him carefully during his meetings with other college students and his visits and presentations at coffee shops in Greenwich Village. Recognizing his strong interests in art and art history at New York City's art museums, the FSB made him a tempting offer he couldn't refuse. The opportunity would allow him to continue to focus on the art world in a way he never expected. Thus began his spy career, which promised additional studies in art.

Within weeks, Sokolov was introduced to Andrei Konstantinov, a WWII Russian war veteran and curator of art initially stolen by the Germans during the war and moved to Moscow and St. Petersburg by the

Russian Trophy Brigades – comparable to the U.S. Army's Monuments Men. As Konstantinov's protégé, Sokolov was immediately elevated to a position on the Soviet Art Committee and began working alongside him. It wasn't long before the two became like father and son, but three years later, Konstantinov died of old age. After his mentor's death, Sokolov was given full responsibility for overseeing all the art stolen by the Soviet Trophy Brigades and took the senior position on the Soviet Arts Committee.

According to records that came under Sokolov's control, the Trophy Brigade had looted, captured, and controlled an estimated half million works of art, including statues and paintings, along with millions of books and manuscripts. In his new role, Sokolov desired to continue growing the stolen private collection hidden in St. Petersburg and deep underground in the Kremlin's basement in Moscow. Under his oversight, the Russian collection of art and ancient manuscripts grew as additional art pieces from museums and private collections in East Germany and the Soviet Occupied Zone of Berlin were transferred to Moscow and St. Petersburg in the years leading up to 1989.

But unlike the old war vet Konstantinov, Sokolov had a view of the emerging world and knew what it would take. To achieve his goal, he contacted the KGB agent who had kept track of him in New York. Sokolov established a strong rapport, giving him access to a unique art world. Next, he sent a note to a Leningrad State College classmate who'd made his way up the chain inside the FSB.

With the demise of the Central Party of the Soviet Union in 1990, Sokolov was given the okay to pursue his ideas further, allowing him to act autonomously but still in accordance with the FSB. A few years later, another FSB agent friend continued further up the ranks, and Ivan's ability to make decisions independent of FSB higher-ups went even more smoothly. Sokolov, now in his senior role and with the most authority to date, traveled widely to art shows and conferences.

Sokolov's love of art and efforts to protect antique paintings and other artifacts in the 1990s had moved him to the highest level of Soviet politics in Moscow. He continued to manage and guide the distribution of the assets the Russians had secured decades earlier. But Sokolov was no ordinary comrade.

In 1994, at a huge art show in Vienna attended by art collectors from across the globe, Sokolov was making the rounds and collecting business cards when he spotted two well-dressed gentlemen examining a painting with a magnifying glass. One gentleman was the well-known Rutgers University art-history professor Brian O'Sullivan. The other was Erick Schmidt, whose background and expertise in European art were known throughout Europe, the Middle East, and Africa.

Both seemed intrigued by the Italian artist's brushstrokes on the painting, which seemed ever so slightly different from other works by the same artist. As they whispered and gestured with pointed fingers, they quietly discussed the notion of Professor O'Sullivan's joining Interpol's Art Research and Recovery unit. Intrigued, O'Sullivan nodded while their concern over the artist's brushstrokes diminished since both art experts concluded the painting was an excellent copy.

Nearby, Sokolov watched the two. Curious, and looking to expand his reach into the art world, he approached the Dutch art expert and his friend and introduced himself, portraying himself as an art-history professor at the University of St Petersburg. During their pleasant encounter, Sokolov boasted of his extensive knowledge of European art. As he spoke, Sokolov focused on the two men's facial expressions, style, and characters. He studied the quality of the fabric of their suits and ties, and took note of whose Florsheim shoes were highly polished (Brian's) or dull and badly scuffed (Erick's), utterly unaware he had just introduced himself to a current and a future Interpol agent.

When Brian returned home to New Jersey days after the art show, in addition to thinking more about becoming an agent focused on finding lost art, he ran Ivan Sokolov's name through a database of college professors. The name didn't come up on the first query. It made Brian wonder at the time because, in support of his Ph.D. research, he'd worked on a program to establish a database listing American and European colleges with art programs and college professors teaching art and art history. Brian ran another query against a different database; Ivan Sokolov was identified as a Columbia University student. After that incident, the name stuck with him.

* * *

Seeing such wealthy people from around the world in the art business enticed Sokolov to find a way to make the Russian-controlled art a profitable venture. After the 1994 show, he returned to Moscow with an idea and pushed for a meeting with his friend in the FSB. He said, "A day may come when we could covertly manipulate the sale of state-owned assets to the wealthy oligarchs. If I'm given full control, transactions could be profitable for both of us." Ivan's friend liked the idea and suggested that he develop the plan.

Over the next few years, Sokolov's social activities with oligarchs occurred more frequently, and his connections with the FSB intensified. And even better, his Leningrad State College friend, Vladimir, became the president of Russia in 1999 after Boris Yeltsin's sudden departure. Soon, Sokolov watched how Vlad catered to the new class of wealthy Russians.

Then, one day in 2007, his classmate unexpectedly called Ivan into his office. Vlad was about to make Ivan's idea to sell the stolen paintings sitting in the Kremlin's basement a reality.

"Comrade! Come in. Come in. Sit and have a vodka with me. It's good to see you. You have done an excellent job with the Moscow and St Petersburg art collections. I asked you here today because I remember your idea of growing the repository of art and paintings. Your concept was like a mustard seed. It has remained with me for many years, and the idea has grown significantly. Ivan, I brought you here today to tell you your idea is officially approved."

Ivan could scarcely believe the news.

"Under my more relaxed system of government, many Russian businessmen are accumulating great wealth. I hear these oligarchs are looking for art to dress the walls of their newly built homes and their huge yachts worth millions of rubles. So listen closely, comrade. Here is my plan. You will begin to release and sell the art stored for decades in the basements. At the same time, you will also acquire more art with the money you are paid. The sale of each art item will carry a twenty percent tax. You will call the tax 'overhead.' Fifty percent of the overhead tax will go in my pocket, and ten percent will go in your pocket. The remaining forty percent will go to my friend to fund his military group enabling him to cause mayhem in Africa. Comrade, all your activities of buying and selling art to the oligarchs will be fully supported. Here, I give you this embossed paper with my signature as my commitment to you in writing."

"Thank you, Vlad. I've been waiting for this day for many years. You've made a wise and profitable decision!"

From that day on, Ivan Sokolov had an official license to sell, as he pleased, all the art pieces and paintings collected during WWII by the Russian soldiers in Germany to the wealthy Russian oligarchs. Sokolov's prestige and power rose quickly, and his reputation grew in wealthy Russian social circles as 'the man to know if you want classic art.'

* * *

Just over a year after he met with Vlad and received permission to do as he pleased, Sokolov came across a scheme for acquiring and selling art – with a slight twist. A Maltese FSB spy revealed information about a small team of agents inside Interpol who searched for and recovered lost WWII-era art. According to the spy, a team member who lived in Malta was corrupt because he did not always return 'found' art to its rightful owners. Intrigued by the scheme, Sokolov ordered the Maltese spy to pay closer attention. Soon, the team's members were identified as Paolo Luzzi, Antonio Gozzo, and their supervisor, Klaus Mueller. Not long afterward, Sokolov reached out and, at arm's length through the Maltese spy, made his first deal to purchase a piece from Luzzi.

Sokolov took another step shortly after that. Interpol's Art Research and Recovery unit was seeking a new secretary, and the timing was perfect. Then, like a puppeteer, he set in motion several steps that placed a young woman – a rising star within the FSB and living in Amsterdam – to a job at Interpol's art unit.

With the former Tamara Ehrlich in place, Ivan Sokolov soon began receiving information about how Klaus Mueller ran his operation through the regular FSB channel. Antonio Gozzo was attracted to the shapely Ursula and foolishly boasted that one or two 'discovered' paintings were occasionally sold for profit. Intrigued at hearing of the ring's activities, Sokolov nevertheless kept his distance.

A few years later, Klaus Mueller retired and was eventually replaced by his son Wilhelm. Sokolov watched to see if the son would behave like his father. He guessed right when Ursula revealed a developing situation to her hairdresser, Olga. A Nazi diary had become the focus of a new investigation into lost WWII paintings hidden by a Nazi soldier. Ursula watched closely as Wilhelm, revealing himself to be crooked like his father, negotiated a deal with Luzzi and Gozzo the day before the Andalusia investigation began.

Greedy Wilhelm contacted his father's fixer in Malaga. It resulted in Erick's being shot, thrown into a trunk, and left for dead in a roadside ditch south of Cordoba. The fixer also murdered Antonio Gozzo by blowing up his car.

Ursula had a front-row seat and continued to share information with Olga. After finding art hidden at the Mezquita, Paolo Luzzi hid the paintings in his cousins' bank in Rome instead of returning them to Wilhelm. Seeking revenge, Wilhelm followed Luzzi to Malta. Luzzi murdered him, both of his cousins, and several others. Then O'Sullivan shot and killed Luzzi.

Getting all the details from Ursula through Olga and Dmitri gave Sokolov a huge edge in understanding the group's illegal activities, including activities by the bankers who'd gifted forged paintings to the Vatican for years.

Sokolov was annoyed when he heard Paolo Luzzi was killed. His death had shut down his most lucrative source for new high-end paintings. But now, two months later, Sokolov was hearing new information about the art group's involvement in another case. He listened carefully to the reports and began arranging pieces and thinking of moves in his devious mind – as a Grandmaster would in a championship chess game. He had a new idea to enrich himself aside from selling art. Moreover, he had a new target: Brian O'Sullivan.

CHAPTER TWENTY-FOUR

His Plot

S okolov was a chess expert and devious planner from whom Vlad often sought answers to questions. His arrival outside the private beauty salon minutes after Ursula's departure had more than one purpose. He was greeted like a king but went right to work.

"Comrades, let's review where we stand. Besides reviewing the latest information about the search of Grand Canary Island caves for lost art and gold, my goal now includes capturing Brian O'Sullivan's newfound fortune. According to what Ursula and Olga said and what you shared, our art-history professor turned Interpol agent has had a difficult time recently. I'm about to make his life far more miserable. I'll tell you why.

As Sokolov revealed his devious plan to avenge Paolo Luzzi's death, Olga and Dmitri listened intently.

"Marini's art is being held in a secure FST-controlled mausoleum east of Tropea," he said. "O'Sullivan wants to keep his friend afloat financially, so he'll call the antique dealer's nephew, who set up his Swiss bank account, to arrange the transfer. Fortunately, we've got all those lines tapped. Ursula told the Interpol IT manager O'Sullivan was siphoning Interpol funds into a Swiss account. When O'Sullivan calls Leipzig, the IT manager will intercept the account number and password and send both to Ursula, who will pass them along to Olga. We'll allow the transfer into Marini's account. Then, a few days later, when he least expects it, we'll withdraw the balance of the money from O'Sullivan's account. We should be looking at $51 million."

"Ivan, shouldn't there be more remaining?"

Not used to being challenged, Sokolov scowled. "O'Sullivan said he had the expense of legal transactions to transfer land, and we know from Ursula he sent money to a woman in their group to purchase a building on Johannes Verhulstraat two blocks south of Vondelpark."

"Will we take the money from Marini's account?"

"No. It's too small a prize and not worth the effort. Our spy in Malta has been a member of the local chapter of the Order of the Knights of Malta for over a decade. He messaged me this morning, saying last night's meeting focused on a promise made by Luca Luciano years ago. It's unclear what that promise was, but the chapter leader was heated in the meeting and said there's no question O'Sullivan is hiding something. I told our man there to offer to assist the new leader with any of his needs and to get closer and investigate this further.

"By the way, the sale of Luca Luciano's international wine distribution company is the basis of O'Sullivan's millions. Paolo Luzzi was Luciano's adopted son and had expected to inherit everything. But O'Sullivan showed up at the last minute, causing havoc and mayhem for Luzzi. O'Sullivan is Luca's wife's natural son."

Dmitri looked confused. "Ivan, I'm new to handling Olga and reporting to you, so I'm confused by the relationships."

Sokolov explained. " I met Paolo Luzzi at an art show in Brussels years ago. He was looking to sell two expensive paintings. One is by Antonio Allegri, who is known as Correggio. The other was by Giacomo Adolfi. I never saw the paintings and sensed Luzzi was not to be trusted. After all, many of these high-end paintings are expert copies."

"Were they?"

"Of course. Nevertheless, with Vlad's directive to acquire and sell paintings, Luzzi and I stayed in touch. Eventually, I bought two paintings from him for half a million each. When I put Ursula in place and she began her tenure as Klaus Mueller's secretary in Interpol's Art Research group, the information she provided connected all the dots.

"Mueller and Luzzi were thieves and skimming millions. They'd find two paintings, return one to the rightful owner, and sell the other. Ursula pretended to be naive to their illegal transactions, but she caught on quickly and passed along what they were doing to the comrade who ran this beauty shop before Olga. Once I knew about their act, I bought a rare, expensive painting from Luzzi for Vlad. He still keeps the Renoir in his palace home near Gelendzhik, on the Black Sea. I was never told how Luzzi came to possess a piece of art worth sixteen million – and I didn't ask. I just knew it'd make Vlad happy.

"During those years, the oligarchs began making more demands for me to release and sell them the art stolen by the Germans during the war and recovered by our Trophy Brigades. Of course, Vlad wanted them to remain content as their wealth grew.

"I paid little attention to Klaus Mueller's British replacement at first. Ursula made us aware of Wilhelm's stepping into his old man's shoes while Luzzi and Gozzo continued their criminal sideline. Then, recently, Ursula told me about the activities of O'Sullivan and Schmidt and a woman called Nina. They found two pieces of art hidden in Spain by a Nazi officer during the war. All those murders and Luzzi's death at the party in Malta followed.

"This old Grand Canary Island caves rumor had life years ago and was all but forgotten, but it sprang to life four weeks ago, rekindled by technology. Our spy inside the CIA at Langley sent us the information the new radar satellites saw. We responded by sending cadets from a Belarus military school to explore the caves and hills. Our comrade in Langley believes we're in an excellent position to quietly capture and extract anything of value we find hidden there.

"Then, ironically, the CIA asks Interpol for the Art and Recovery unit to get involved in the search. So, unexpectedly, Agent O'Sullivan is again in my sight. As I see it, if this was a game of chess, you can say I've already captured the 'queen' – that's O'Sullivan's gay friend's art worth almost twenty million U.S. dollars. And, once I make the right moves with the remaining pieces on the board, I'll capture O'Sullivan's huge inheritance. Checkmate."

"So, what's next?"

"What's next is we'll learn from Ursula about plans being made by the CIA's Pattison and Van Deusen in this afternoon's one o'clock meeting. I'd like to hear from her tomorrow morning after she gives her boss a workout in bed tonight. She delights in her craft of seduction and spying! She'll get him to share what's really going on once she's had her way with him."

Olga and Dmitri nodded and grinned, familiar with Ursula's sexual escapades.

"I'll leave the two of you now. I'm busy this afternoon here in town. I have a dinner date tonight back in Amsterdam, and I'll return to our embassy in the morning. We will talk again in the morning, or text me if you hear from Ursula before then."

<u>CHAPTER TWENTY-FIVE</u>

Spring 1944 – The Twins' Grandfather Abraham

On the porch of his small house in Settat, Abraham reflected on his extensive trading career. His family were renowned traders dating back to the 1600s. They originally ventured east on the Silk Road for spices and exceptional hand-crafted products. At the turn of the last century, as the family focused its trading efforts and interests in northern Africa and the northwestern Sahara, Casablanca became a hub with its ready access to the sea. However, they still traded with Cairo and ventured farther east to Bagdad and Tehran every two years.

The 1920s' growth of air transportation prompted Abraham to explore new opportunities. He aggressively built trading relationships with new contacts in Europe and as far away as America. Life as a trader was good! But in 1929, the stock market crash in the United States triggered an economic depression that sent the world into a spin.

In the mid and late 1930s, trading with Europe grew difficult. Germany's military activities supporting General Franco in the Spanish Civil War caused many traders to pull back and pause. A few years later, Nazi U-boat wolfpacks roaming the Atlantic disrupted commercial shipping, and overseas trading for small North African entrepreneurs became impossible.

Tired from the struggles of the past couple of years due to Germany's occupation of North Africa, Abraham decided it was time to retire. He transferred half of his trading business to his son, Youssef, in Marrakesh, the twins' father, and the other half to his daughter, Manasa, and son-in-law, Benjamin, who lived near him in Settat.

Now retired and more relaxed, the active Abraham took on his son's hobby of raising piebald camels, still the primary form of transportation in the region. In less than a year, the ever-astute businessman had created a new business for himself, raising and trading camels.

On a hot, sun-drenched day in late August 1944, Abraham sat with his daughter and her husband, who were visiting for dinner. Sipping khoudenjal tea prepared by his wife as a dinner aperitif, Abraham smiled and spoke of one of the activities he'd enjoyed with the twins during their recent visit. He then began sharing the details of negotiations and a sale of two camels earlier that day. As he spoke, Abraham heard a disturbance outside. His small flock of camels in their pen was grunting and growing restless. Curious, he rose and, looking through the window, Abraham saw his grandson Ahmad jumping from his camel, Baba, and running to the front door.

Breathless, young Ahmad struggled to speak as he entered the house. All were surprised by his presence but, more so, worried about Chadu's absence.

Abraham greeted him with open arms, but Ahmad quickly removed himself from his grandfather's hug and lunged for the table, grabbing a glass of water. After downing it in one long gulp, he took a few seconds to catch his breath. Then, after respectfully hugging his family, he began his story, rattling through the words so quickly they were almost incomprehensible. Catching some of what the twin had experienced, the elders looked at each other with curious expressions, suspicious and doubtful of what they had just heard. Abraham took the boy to his chest and told him to relax and speak slowly.

"My dear grandson, please tell us again. Your story sounds so incredible! This time, speak slowly and take your time recalling and explaining every detail once again. I must remind you my ears are old and tired, and of course, I want to believe what I am hearing."

Ahmad smiled, but before saying another word, he reached into his pocket. "Here, grandfather, let me show you what I'm talking about."

He pulled the small gold bar from his cloak and placed it on the table. Then he flipped it over, revealing the embossed Nazi logo. Suddenly, Abraham's old ears and eyes opened wide, as did the eyes of the others sitting at the table. They all sat up at attention, in awe of what they saw.

Abraham picked up the small gold bar weighing about three pounds. "Good God, Ahmad, where did you get that?"

"I just told you, Grandfather."

"Well, tell me again!"

They listened to Ahmad's story, and then, still in disbelief, they asked him to repeat it. Abraham asked question after question. At first, Ahmad felt like he was in trouble because of all the questions, but slowly, he felt more confident – and more important.

Meanwhile, 150 miles south, in Marrakesh, Chadu arrived home late that same day. His camel, Blue, had developed an issue with its leg, so the trip took longer than expected. The twins' father, Youssef, immediately launched into a rage, yelling at his son for arriving a full day and a half late and not being with his brother. After he calmed down, Youssef became concerned about Ahmad's absence.

Chadu stopped crying and began telling his father the story of the enormous plane and Nazi soldiers and the murders he'd witnessed.

Still upset, Youssef lunged for Chadu with the intent to spank the boy for inventing his wild tale. But just as his father raised his hand to take a swing, Chadu pulled the gold bar from his cloak and waved it in his father's face.

"Wait! Here's proof, Father. Look at the symbol."

"Where'd you get that?"

"Inside the crashed plane. Ahmad took a bar like this and returned to Grandfather. He said he'd ride as fast as he could. He should be there by now."

"Chadu, tell me again. Where is this plane that you are talking about?"

"Off the desert road near Settat, north of the village of Ben Guerir. Besides hundreds of gold bars, there are paintings in wooden crates. Ahmad says everything inside is valuable. Father, what are we to do?"

Perplexed, the father walked away, rubbing his beard.

On the farm near Settat, Abraham leaned back in his chair, sitting silently for a moment, and then spoke. "Ahmad, by no choice of your own, fate has bestowed upon you the title of 'young trader.' You have brought gold to your family. In return, we must respond to the venture before us. Tonight we will pause and take time to pray about this. Our minds will be clear in the morning, and we will know the steps we must take. Right now, you look exhausted. Have some more water and something to eat, then go to sleep. I'll wake you in the morning."

"Thank you, Grandfather. I feel safe here with you."

That night, after Abraham finished evening prayers, he thought more about the impending task. It weighed heavily on his mind. He knew it wouldn't be easy, and he recalled stories of his ancestors who had bravely protected their community in times of distress. Determined to follow in their footsteps, Abraham knew he had to act swiftly and wisely because the men described by Ahmad as Nazis could return soon with more planes. It worried him as he laid his head on his pillow and fell into a deep sleep.

CHAPTER TWENTY-SIX

The 1:30 Meeting

Ursula returned at 1:20. Surprised Pieter wasn't in his office with Bill Pattison, she quickly walked around. Not finding him, she headed to the conference room to set up for the 1:30 meeting. She was proud of her debriefing with Olga and curious to hear more about the upcoming operation. Nina sat at her laptop in the conference room, running through a slide presentation.

"Where is everyone? I expected Pieter to be in his office, but he's nowhere to be found."

"The meeting with Pattison's been canceled."

Ursula looked startled. "Really? Then what are you doing?"

"We're still having a meeting, but the plans have changed."

Now Ursula reached for the high back of one of the conference room chairs to steady herself. She tried not to appear desperate for details. "Oh? What's going on?"

"Don't have the time to go into it now. I need to finish this before the group comes in."

"What group?

"Everyone except Pattison."

"Where's Pieter now?"

"Don't know. Maybe the men's room?"

Quietly fuming, Ursula clenched her fists and stormed out. She wondered how things could have changed so quickly in two hours. She returned to her office and was about to sit as Pieter entered.

"Hair looks good. Well, actually, it looks the same."

"What's going on, Pieter? Why isn't Pattison here? And what's happened to the plans since I left?"

"Easy there, Ursula! Remember, I'm the senior director, and you're my admin."

"My apologies, dear senior director! My appointment took longer than expected. But I returned when I said I would, and now everything's changed." She realized she was sounding like a cranky child. "I need to breathe and center myself."

Ursula straightened up, pulled her shoulders back, and took a few deep breaths. Pieter smiled, admiring her shapely body, then went over everything that had taken place in her absence, including the temporary transfer of CIA personnel to his department's budget.

"You'll need to set them up in our personnel system to keep track of things, but zero out the individuals' income."

"Of course. Uh, Pieter, I'm feeling compelled to tell you I'm shocked at the change in plans. Is it a smart decision? And, frankly, is Nina even capable of being a team leader?"

"Ha! My dear admin! You sound jealous!"

"I'm not. But I'm concerned about your interest in this, and I hope it doesn't end in an embarrassing debacle for you, my dear senior director," she parroted mockingly. "For example, you don't even have a budget for this project. In fact, the O'Sullivan-Schmidt-von Scholz team's existence has been questioned since Wilhelm took over the department because of their cost."

"You're right. But considering they recovered assets worth millions on their last search, maybe now you can understand why I didn't put anyone in the position after Wilhelm died. I decided to save the cost of his salary."

Ursula nodded. Then, backing down and recognizing her role as his administrative assistant, she asked if there was anything she could do.

He suggested she go and offer Nina assistance and make sure refreshments and snacks were in the conference room for the meeting.

She looked him in the eyes, then lifting her chin defiantly, turned and left.

Pieter watched her leave, admiring her backside in the tight-fitting pants. *Something's going on. Ursula's defiance is bubbling up... and I don't like it.*

Ursula headed downstairs to the lobby and outside to smoke and send a text. It was 1:28 p.m.

The meeting started promptly at 1:30. Nina and Amara stood together at the front of the room as Nina began making her presentation focused on the case and how the teams would work, and was only minutes into the presentation when Ursula walked in with cookies. Pieter lifted his wrist to check his watch. 1:44. He glared at Ursula, noting her tardiness. She returned a stare that could kill and turned her head, her nose raised in defiance again.

The CIA members and Amara's agents were amazed at Nina's story about the Interpol team's recent success finding art in Cordoba's Mezquita using clues in KvR's diary. She introduced the recently found center page of the diary, explaining how keywords and phrases by its author helped her arrive at the conclusion that due to a mechanical problem, a large plane carrying art and gold in the late summer of 1944 likely landed somewhere in Morocco, short of its destination. She then announced team assignments.

Amara spoke next, citing where and how each team would concentrate its efforts and how they'd go about the daily work of looking for clues. Although surprised at the differing intel, the CIA members welcomed the challenge of the new plan and the team assignments.

By the time Amara and Nina finished reviewing all the details and answering questions, two hours had passed.

Pieter stood to address everyone. "You all know we have an unusual situation here. Two agencies coming together like this is something not often done. But Pattison liked what he heard about the success of our Art Investigation team, and he thought, by working together, we could resolve a persistent post-World War Two rumor about art, and maybe even gold, hidden on Grand Canary Island. The location we'll focus on has changed, but the general idea behind the investigation is the same. Now, you all are experts in your fields, and I want to see this project completed within ninety days. Good luck, everyone."

Pieter then announced all the team members were invited to an early dinner together – on him. He took a count, and getting a thumbs-up from everyone, he asked Erick to call and make reservations for nine.

In a brief chat with Solie, Nina said she'd hoped to return to Amsterdam with Brian for the night, and she was disappointed because he was planning to stay there this evening.

Brian watched Nina from across the room; her usually cheerful face wore a frown. Anticipating her thoughts, he walked over to her and whispered in her ear that he still had the hotel room and suggested she stay with him tonight. While she didn't immediately agree, her smile returned, and her eyes sparkled through her tears.

The conference room had not emptied when Pieter turned to address Nina and Amara.

"Ursula's been taking copious notes about your plans. I'd like you both to be in my office in thirty minutes. She needs your definitive input to set up flights, and she'll help you get started on your journeys. She's wonderful with travel arrangements."

Erick walked back in. "Dinner is set for 5:30. Why don't you and Ursula join us?"

"Thanks, but I'll pass for both of us. Ursula and I have more work with the budget for this case, and it's best you all coalesce into your individual teams. We'll take a raincheck and celebrate when your team unravels the mystery."

As Pieter headed for the door, Ursula said she needed a cigarette and would be right back. Seeing her looking anxious, Pieter watched as she walked to the front stairwell. Curious, he raced to the rear staircase and rushed down to the lobby. He slowly opened the stairwell door, he saw her holding her cell phone to her ear. She strode past the guards and outside. Pieter watched from the front window in the lobby. Seeing her unusual hand gestures to the person on the other end of the call made him wonder. *Something's up. That's not like her. And who could she be talking to?* Then she put the phone in her pocket and finally lit up.

Pieter legged it back up the rear stairs to his office and hid his being out of breath when Ursula arrived back at her desk. He saw her sit and then watched as she lit yet another cigarette.

"Missy, you know smoking inside is against regulations."

"I need another cigarette," she snapped.

"What's going on? You seem upset."

"Things."

"Like?"

"Just things. Nothing you should be concerned about."

"You've seemed on edge since you got back from your hair appointment."

"It's nothing, Pieter. Now, please, leave me alone and go do your stupid budget."

He looked at her strangely. "Did you forget? Nina and Amara are coming to finalize the flights in a few minutes. I saw you taking plenty of notes so you should be all set with where everyone's going, right?"

"Yes, senior director. I'm all over it, senior director. Please pardon me for lighting up my cigarette. Oh, and don't call me Missy, mister senior director."

He backed off. *Whatever it is with her, it's serious.*

* * *

Dimitri and Katya were at the rear of the beauty parlor, packing and preparing to leave. Olga was sweeping the floor, cleaning up from her visit with Ursula, when her terse text arrived at 1:27. She was brief.

"Art Investigation team plans changing. More info when available."

She sent a second text requesting another visit to the beauty parlor tomorrow morning under the guise of having her nails done.

Olga texted back.

"OK for 9 a.m. visit for nails."

Olga discussed the situation with Dmitri.

He, in turn, called Sokolov. "Ivan, we're still with Olga. Interpol and the CIA have changed plans. We're expecting to hear more from Ursula in the morning."

"I'm at the embassy. My luncheon appointment has just finished. The young oligarch told me how well he was doing. So, I tripled the price, and he still agreed to make the purchase. What an idiot. We have planned special entertainment for him – the type of entertainment your new partner, Katya, provides. Stay there for now. I'll be over to you a bit later."

At 3:45, Sokolov's driver stopped at the beauty parlor to pick up Dmitri and Katya. They were driven to a nearby parking lot, where the three of them sat in the back of the SUV, first discussing what seemed like a panic text from Ursula at 1:27 and again at 1:28,

"She texted again just minutes ago at 3:40. She was in a hurry, saying she would set up flights for three or four teams to Casablanca and Marrakesh. Something to do with the lost gold. She said she'd have the details in the morning."

"Is that right? 'Casablanca and Marrakesh' and not 'Grand Canary Island'? Interesting. But she did mention the lost gold, right?"

"Yes, exactly. Then she said something about the agents finishing up and heading to a dinner sponsored by Van Deusen."

"Okay. I'll drop you both back at Olga's place. Then I have something to do."

* * *

In the office, after kowtowing to and being pissed at Pieter, Ursula began making the arrangements from her notes. Amara and Nina arrived fifteen minutes later, confirming the target cities. With the cities and flights identified and schedules outlined, Ursula would print the tickets in -house and access the department's cash box to dole out funds to each Interpol team member.

Nearby, her steno pad sat in plain view on the desk's return. Although most of her notes were written in Gregg, Pieter was surprised to see a few details printed in English. Coupled with seeing her make the earlier phone call, he began to wonder even more.

It was now 4:20. Most of the meeting's attendees had finished milling around the conference room with introductions and sharing old stories and began to leave. Nina found Brian and, after gathering their things, they left the building, feeling like two kids about to play outside at recess.

They headed across the street where Nina had parked her car that morning. She reached for his hand as they stepped off the curb. Feeling the touch, he lovingly accepted it and clasped her hand tightly – the sensation of her hand in his drenched his brain in endorphins in nanoseconds.

She began speaking as they waited for a slow-moving SUV to pass. "Brian, you didn't say much about my car when we came here today. Brian? Are you listening to me?"

As she spoke, a large black Mercedes SUV drove past. The rear passenger-side window lowered as the vehicle rolled along. Inside, a white-haired man sporting a trimmed van dyke-style beard stared hard, making eye contact with Brian. Having met hundreds of people in the field over the years, Brian nevertheless needed only seconds to recognize the man's face, but it took another few moments for the name to arrive. *Jesus! Why him? And why now?*

CHAPTER TWENTY-SEVEN

Before Dinner

Nina continued speaking while Brian remained fixated on the face. The encounter sparked his memory, returning him to Milan twenty years earlier. *My God! That day, Erick took me aside and asked me to consider joining Interpol. He's the guy who came up to us claiming he was a professor but wasn't. He'd been a student at Columbia. What the heck was his name? What's he doing here in The Hague? And why the drive-by? He was watching me. It's as if he knew I'd be here. And his stare! It sure as hell was meant to be intimidating. I need to let Erick know.*

"Hello? Hello? Earth to Brian! Are you here with me? Or are you suddenly back in New Jersey?"

"Huh? Oh. Sorry."

"What just happened? I was talking to you, and suddenly, you zoned out!"

"I'm sorry."

"Listen, Brian, I've been hoping you could relax while you're here in Amsterdam and forget all that's happened these last few months. We need time alone."

Brian nodded mechanically. "Of course. That would be nice, Nina. I'm getting past Katrina's death, and shaking Grace is taking longer. But that wasn't it just now. Something else popped into my head and threw me for a loop."

"So, I asked you – do you like the car?"

"Which one?" he asked distractedly.

"*My* car. The one we're standing next to. The one I drove you in yesterday."

"Oh. Well, yes. It's nice, and yesterday I said it's small."

She rolled her eyes, opened the trunk, and placed her laptop next to her carry-on bag.

Brian opened the passenger-side door and threw his travel bag and laptop into the back seat. "I'd like you to stay with me tonight and avoid the drive back to Amsterdam."

Nina looked downcast. "I wanted to show you my new house."

"Don't you remember? I used to stay in the guest room when Erick lived there."

"But you haven't seen it since I fixed it up. I made a few changes to the floor plan and added a woman's touch with colorful paint instead of Erick's drab white walls. And I've acquired a couple of nice art pieces. I'm certain you'll like it."

"I'll stay there for sure tomorrow night. I need to call Erick and review what distracted me right now."

She pulled up to the front of the hotel and, as Brian grabbed the door handle to exit the car, she grabbed the collar on his shirt.

"Brian, I have an idea. If I stay here tonight, maybe we can just relax and be with each other like in Spain. And you can speak to Erick at dinner about what distracted you."

He smiled – and she smiled back.

She looked at her watch. "Dinner is in an hour. Maybe we can have some time together right now – before everyone gets together."

"An hour isn't long."

"No, but it's time enough," she countered. "Then I'll stay tonight." She leaned into him and gave him a special kiss.

They grabbed clothing bags, left the car with the valet, checked in, and went straight to the Agency's reserved room. The two stripped each other naked and were rolling in bed within a minute. He caressed her warm body and told her how beautiful she looked as he admired her large breasts.

"Nina, you have a sparkle in your eye. And you are so... well, uh..."

She laughed as he reached for her breasts. Nina pushed him onto his back, climbed over his legs, mounted him, and draped her hair over his face. She began doing all the right things to make him forget his nagging Catholic guilt. He was feeling alive and twenty-five years younger.

Massimo was right. My next adventure has just begun, and this new chapter feels incredibly good. Gosh! She is so gorgeous.

Within moments, feeling each other's warmth, both climaxed and closed their eyes.

* * *

Inside the beauty parlor, Olga was about to say goodbye to Dmitri and Katya when she got another short text from Ursula.

"A group of nine agents have reservations for dinner at Dekxels."

Olga shared the news with Dmitri, who called Sokolov.

After hearing Dmitri's update, Ivan set a plan in motion. "Dmitri, I want you and Katya to go to the restaurant where those agents will be. Go inside and have a nice dinner. Pretend it's your anniversary. You won't be recognized. Even if Ursula shows up, she won't know who you are. Pay attention to the nine agents. Let me know what you think about the older man. His name is Brian O'Sullivan. Meanwhile, I'll have Olga text Ursula to reserve a room where O'Sullivan is staying tonight. You'll be booked under the names on your Dutch EU passports, 'Kristofer and Bobette von Gostout.' Enjoy the food. I hear it's good."

When Dimitri told Katya where they were headed to dinner, she rolled her eyes.

"When do I get to decide anything? How do I know the food there is any good?"

"Katya, you're becoming difficult." Then he turned to Olga. "We need to leave now. Good night, Olga."

"Yes. Good night."

As Olga stowed her broom in the back closet, she noticed the automatic voice recording machine had turned on, and the tape was rolling. She reached for the headphones. At first, she could barely make out noises and whispers. But within minutes, Nina's whimpers grew louder and more urgent. Olga's imagination took over. *Whoever's in bed, they're enjoying each other.* Then she sat and, reaching down, Olga began her own satisfying episode in the windowless back room.

Minutes later, the black Mercedes SUV sat motionless in the end space of the restaurant's parking lot, obscured by several other SUVs. Ivan watched for the agents' arrival. He hoped to see O'Sullivan again and catch a better look at the woman with him. *So, Grand Canary Island is no longer the target? Why is a young woman now running Interpol's Art team? Their team has been good at finding lost art, but Morocco? I don't understand.* He recalled his past visits to Casablanca and Marrakesh. Then he returned to his plot to steal O'Sullivan's millions. Calabria shimmered into his mind, so he called to confirm the paintings by the artist Argyle were secure. They were.

* * *

Almost sixty minutes had passed when the call to Brian's cell phone woke him and Nina.

"Hey, BJ! You and Nina are coming to dinner, right?"

"Of course! We, uh, we were going over the plans again. We'll be right over."

"Well, hurry up. The clams Casino, fried calamari and hot antipasto are awesome. And it's all on Van Deusen! And we just had the waiter open a few bottles of a super Tuscan."

"Save some for us. We'll be right here!"

Both looked at each other and laughed. They kissed again, then quickly dressed, brushed their hair, and headed downstairs, holding hands. Both of them glowed. She was ecstatic. He was relieved. Once outside, Brian thanked the valet and tipped him for keeping the car out front for them.

"Brian, I have something to share with you," Nina said as they waited for the valet to return with the car keys.

"What's that?"

As they got into the little car, Nina's phone rang. She started it anyway.

"Nina, it's Solie. You and Brian are coming to dinner, right?"

"We're on our way now."

"Good. This Stemmler guy is hanging on me. I've already pushed his hand away twice. He's very inappropriate. I'm going to break his finger if he tries to touch me again."

"Good for you! We'll be there in five."

"Have you told Brian yet?"

"I was about to, but then you just called! Bye."

Nina hung up, made the next turn, and stopped at a red light.

Brian asked, "What were you about to say?"

"I won't be drinking any wine tonight."

"Okay. So?"

"Brian, I'm pregnant."

It was an exceedingly long four seconds. The traffic light turned green, and Nina pressed her foot on the gas pedal.

"Oh my God, Nina. Uh, congratulations. That's wonderful. Who's the lucky—"

"You, Brian. It's you. I'm having your baby."

Stunned by the news, he didn't know what to say.

His prolonged silence made her nervous.

"Brian, we're going to have a baby. Are you okay with that? You've always wanted to be a father, right?"

"Uh, yes. I'm just… uh, I'm shocked by the news."

"It's good news, right?"

"God, Nina, it's great news. It's absolutely terrific news!"

Brian's smile suddenly became a mile wide as Nina turned into the restaurant's parking lot. She parked the car, and they held hands as they entered the restaurant. *Wow, a new chapter in my life. Just like Massimo said, and so far, this first page is perfect. What a wonderful feeling it is to be loved so passionately. I do love her. She makes me feel like a kid.*

She needs a bigger car.

<u>CHAPTER TWENTY-EIGHT</u>

The Caravan – August 1944

The following morning, Grandfather Abraham rose before dawn's light and stepped outside to pray. He asked for blessings and guidance because he'd decided the gold bars and the paintings must be moved, and it must happen quickly. Moments later, his son-in-law, who had stayed overnight, emerged. They estimated the trip south from Settat to an area just north of Ben Guerir called Loara would be about 56 miles. They knew a camel's average pace of 3 miles per hour would take too long. Therefore, the animals would need to travel 4 miles per hour to reach the site in 14 hours. It also meant they'd need to leave by 6:30 a.m. to arrive by 8:30 p.m. without stopping. If they took two thirty-minute breaks along the way, it would be 9:30 when they arrived, just after the sun had set.

After formulating the story they would share, Abraham and Benjamin left the house and immediately went to friends and nearby neighbors to assemble a caravan. In an hour, as the sun's rays peeked over the eastern horizon, eighteen volunteers, thirty-six camels, and four pull-carts moved forward on Abraham's command. The men of his community understood the challenging task and were ready to support the venture.

Abraham knew Youssef would be doing the same, and he was right. At that exact moment, twelve men with twenty-four camels and six pull-carts stood ready to leave from Marrakesh in a caravan. As father and son commenced their journeys from different cities, the fifteen-year-old twins anxiously sat in positions of honor on the first camels, leading the way.

It had been years since many of the men in the community had been on such a camel train, and some younger men had never had the chance. Abraham considered each rider's experience level but set a swift pace with the expectation of arriving near the crash site by nightfall. But being a wise and gentle man and considering the volunteers, Abraham slowly moved alongside each rider as the trip progressed, speaking words of encouragement. He told stories about their fathers, with whom he had taken similar adventures years earlier, bringing agricultural products grown in Settat north to Casablanca and south to Marrakesh. Abraham felt proud on the ride and, at times, melancholy. More importantly, Abraham felt blessed to watch his grandson participate in this critical and potentially dangerous expedition.

As the day wore on, the caravan made its way without issue. Two stops were completed as planned, and everyone remained in good spirits. As the daylight faded, Ahmad sensed the crashed plane was not much farther ahead. Then, with his eyes straining, a tiny dot appeared on the horizon. He turned to his grandfather and pointed ahead to the plane. Abraham smiled.

"Purpose, patience, and persistence, my grandson. In life, we are happiest and most successful when we keep a steady pace – and so are our ships of the desert."

Within ten minutes, the members leading the lengthy caravan arrived near the crash site. They were only a hundred feet away when Abraham waved his hand, and the first camels came to a halt. The men were astonished at the size of the plane sitting on the ground before them. The scene was exactly as had been described. Nothing was exaggerated.

"We stop here. The men and the animals will rest," Abraham directed. "Ahmad, come with me. We will inspect the plane. Ali, bring along your shotgun. Have your friend Farid and the others keep watch and have their rifles ready."

Daylight was disappearing as the three walked past the dead bodies and stopped at the ramp at the rear of the plane. Anticipating the darkness inside and smelling no gasoline fumes, Abraham lit a small torch and handed it to Ahmad. "Lead us inside and show us what you found."

Outside, the second caravan, led by Chadu and his father, Youssef, was just arriving. The twins' father gave similar directions to his men, then he and Chadu went to the rear of the plane and walked up the ramp into the fuselage's interior, where they saw Abraham and Ahmad inspecting the scattered contents.

"My son!" Abraham exclaimed. "Bless you for coming. Look at this incredible bounty."

"Father, I'm so glad to see you. This is amazing! But we must act quickly if what Chadu has told me is correct. The men in Nazi uniforms may return in tomorrow's light."

Abraham and Youssef returned outside and together, briefly estimating the number of gold pieces and their weight. Then, fully agreeing, they gathered the men assembled in both caravans and explained what needed to be done. Without concern or complaint, the men immediately positioned the camels in two rows, set up in an assembly line, and began moving the gold bars from inside the plane. As the gold moved down the ramp, it was placed into large saddlebags on each camel. When those were filled, the remaining gold was placed onto eight carts. Four men moved paintings from the broken crates onto three carts while the gold was being loaded. The last of the gold was placed on the remaining carts as they neared completion. The operation to load everything was facilitated by a full moon and finished by 2 a.m.

Fifteen minutes later, after a short break to refresh themselves, each of the thirty volunteers walked to his camel. Abraham spoke and, holding up a bar of gold with the embossed Nazi emblem, reminded everyone that although they were removed from the war by a significant distance, the international community deemed Hitler and the Nazis as evil. He shared in a heartfelt manner how the Jews in Germany, brothers to those living in Casablanca's small Jewish quarter, were being persecuted for their religious beliefs. Then he promised everyone a fair bounty for their work on the caravan and swore them to secrecy for their own safety.

Youssef led the men in a brief prayer and gave the command to mount their camels. He then told them where they were headed with the camels and carts laden with 1,800 three-pound bars of gold bullion worth millions of dollars and the carts filled with paintings by some of Europe's finest artists. As they departed, not even Abraham knew the value of these twenty-three paintings would someday surpass the total value of all the gold.

CHAPTER TWENTY-NINE

The Cadets Are Moving

After skipping last night's supper with the teams, Ursula and Pieter arrived at work early. She reviewed all the flight arrangements she'd completed late yesterday, making sure there were no mistakes. Then she secured hotel reservations in each city for the various team members.

Meanwhile, Pieter reviewed his budget and was moving money around to ensure he had adequate funds in case the project took more than ninety days. It was still early when his cell phone rang.

An angry voice at the other end launched into a tirade. "God damn it! What the hell is going on over there, Pieter?"

"Well, good morning, Bill. What's your problem?"

"Morning? It's the middle of the night, and I'm someplace over the Atlantic on a red-eye right now. I just got a satellite call from my guy embedded with the Russian cadets on Grand Canary Island. He says they received word moments ago to stop their work on the island. They're packing up and moving."

"Moving! Moving where?"

"To Morocco. They're heading to the Grand Canary Island airport now. Word is they're splitting into two groups and heading to different cities. Damn it, Pieter! Is that true?"

"Perhaps. Where are you now?"

"My assistant told me we'll land in Brussels in two hours."

"It's best we talk privately, Bill. Let's meet at the Royal Museum of Fine Arts in Antwerp. It's about halfway for both of us. How's noon?"

158

"See you then. I'm interested to hear what you know."

Pieter stepped from his office to tell Ursula to cancel his 1 p.m. meeting.

"I overheard you say you're meeting Pattison in Antwerp. Shall I put that on your calendar?"

"No."

What's so important that you have to meet with him suddenly?"

"It's those Russian students on Grand Canary Island. Something's going on. They're leaving the island this morning. He said they're flying to Morocco and splitting up, going to Casablanca and Marrakesh. It means they're a step ahead of us. Something is going on."

Ursula did her best to look shocked. "How can that be? And how does Pattison know the cadets are leaving the island?"

"He's got an undercover guy at school embedded with the rest of the students doing the cave hunting."

"Interesting. Can you sign this? It's to approve the tickets I purchased last night before we left. In a few minutes, I'll have another document for you to sign for the hotel reservations in Casablanca and Marrakesh."

Pieter paused. Something in his mind fell into place. *How did she know they were cadets? I can't recall it being mentioned in any meetings she attended that the youngsters hunting through the caves were from a Belarusian military academy. This is not good.*

He went to the cafeteria for another coffee and returned.

"Besides finishing these tickets, what are your plans for today, Ursula?"

"I ran out of time yesterday when I had my hair done because I was supposed to be back on time, so I'm headed back for my nails. And Pieter, I meant to tell you earlier that you were terrific in bed last night. That is until you fell sound asleep on top of me and started snoring. I couldn't breathe. I had to push you off. You still look tired. Have you had enough coffee? And you've been quiet. Where's your head this morning?"

"My mind's been spinning – even before Pattison's call. Bill said after we meet later, he has another meeting, and then he's flying back to

Langley for a meeting of the Joint Chiefs in D.C. tonight. I don't know how he does it."

"Nina texted me. They should be here by 9. Here. I'm ready for you to sign the authorization for the airplane tickets. But why don't you close your office door and take a quick morning nap on your couch? You look like you'll need some more sleep before your drive to Antwerp later. I'll finish the hotel reservations, and you can sign for those and the plane tickets when you wake up."

Pieter shut his door, slipped off his shoes, and lay down. He thought about Pattison's call, his schedule, and Ursula's comment. *There's no way she should've known those students were cadets.*

* * *

A mile away, Olga had made a fresh pot of coffee and was waiting for Dimitri and Katya's arrival. They entered through the rear door. It was nine a.m.

"Any word from Ursula?"

"She sent a lengthy text last night and another twenty minutes ago. Oh, and she texted again as you walked in – oh my! This one begins with an SOS! She says she'll be here at eleven to have her nails done."

Olga then read Ursula's first text to them.

"Wow! Interesting. She had a lot to say." He turned to Katya. "Call Ivan right now. Let him know Ursula will be here at eleven with the latest intel. He should be awake by now, and there's enough time for him to return from Amsterdam."

"Do you know why he went back there last night?"

"He had dinner with an old college flame from eons ago when he attended Columbia in New York City."

Olga quipped, "Maybe he'll be too exhausted from last night's sex to make the trip."

"Not Ivan. He's in good shape for his age. He, Vlad, and another former KGB comrade have access to a private, well-appointed place on the coast where they throw parties and entice the oligarchs to buy art. They have those tall, skinny, pale-faced fashion models come and drape themselves over the men. It typically turns into a huge orgy."

"And how do you know this, Katya?"

She gave a disinterested shrug. "Been there. I took on Vlad myself in '09. It was the evening of the day they took that photo of him riding shirtless on a horse. Vlad was pumped up and feeling good about himself that night. He tried to prove his endurance with me, but I wore him out. Then, as I finished him, he asked, 'What can I do for you?' I climbed on him again and said, "Let me be a spy." He just smiled. When we left the room, he grabbed my hand, dragged me to Ivan, and said, 'This is a good one. Make it happen for her.' Well, you can imagine how pleasurable – and difficult – the next year was."

Olga was practically drooling. "Great story. I'm jealous!"

Dimitri chimed in. "That's enough, ladies. Let's focus on the challenge at hand."

* * *

At the Interpol offices, everyone working on the case arrived in the conference room by nine. Ursula handed Amara the plane tickets and hotel arrangements; he distributed them to each team.

Then Nina went to the end of the conference table and addressed the teams.

"Please listen, everyone. We leave tomorrow morning from Schiphol. Here's a list of things you should bring. Look it over. If you have any questions, I'll be here for another hour, and Amara will be here the rest of the day. Instead of calling me, Amara will be our single point of contact. If you come across any information about the search, share it with him immediately.

"And here's a second list. Hermann Göring was fastidious in keeping a detailed record of his art. This list identifies the paintings and other art pieces, such as statues known to have been under his control in his house, 'Carinhall,' in Berchtesgaden, Germany. At least two dozen of those paintings were not among the items found on the train captured by the U.S. Army Airborne unit as the war ended. The items on the list in bold font are still missing. As for the gold, he kept no record of that.

"Next, although we're searching for art and gold, it will help most if we discover or learn from someone that a large German plane crashed nearby. If we find that, we need to determine who found the wreckage, what happened to the contents, and where they were hidden. Was the gold melted? Was any of the art sold? Or was everything hidden with plans to disperse the bounty decades later? In other words: Were the plane's contents considered too hot to be sold right away, and they knew it all should sit for the benefit of the next generation?"

The agents murmured among themselves.

Nina raised her voice a bit. "Your task is to meet and speak with locals who might know something about a significant plane crash in the summer of '44. That event was sixty-eight years ago. So, for example, someone who was a youngster then would be in their seventies or eighties now. It means you'll be looking for an older man or woman who knows the story of the plane crash. A younger person might have heard about the story and still might be a lead to follow. But your best bet would be talking with the older residents who've lived there all their lives."

"Thanks for a good summary and good marching words, Nina. I need to speak with Erick for a few minutes. We can return to Amsterdam. Solie, you're welcome to join us on the ride back."

The meeting broke up, and the agents began discussing the lists with their partners. Solie told Nina if it didn't upset her privacy with Brian, she'd accept his offer of a ride back.

Off to the side, Brian steered Erick to the cafeteria, where they sat with coffee. He told Erick about yesterday's drive-by and, after a good sleep, his having recalled the name.

"It was Ivan Sokolov, whom we met twenty years ago in Milan."

Erick immediately remembered Sokolov, whom he recalled had winked at him at the end of their conversation. "What do you think it means, BJ?"

"Can't say yet. But something's going on for him to be here. The drive-by seemed very deliberate. I wonder how long he's been following me?"

Just then, Pieter found the two speaking.

"I was looking for both of you. I have interesting information you'll want to hear."

He shared the information from Pattison's early-morning call about the students' departure and their move to the mainland.

After running through a set of possibilities, all concluded there had to be a leak, but they imagined it to be in the CIA's house.

Then Brian told Pieter about Ivan Sokolov, his drive-by, and the long stare.

"I thought we were in front of this expedition and had the edge based on Nina's evaluation," Erick said. "But now, with the Russian students moving to Casablanca and Marrakesh, matters will become complicated. Walking around the Moroccan markets and asking questions with Russians floating around will be more dangerous. And this Sokolov fellow adds another layer of complexity to this. Someone should write about this case. It'd make a great story."

"Let me make a few calls to get a handle on Sokolov," Pieter offered. "I'll see what I can come up with. For now, we need to keep this latest development among the three of us and Nina."

They thanked Pieter for his willingness to follow up with other Interpol agency offices for the latest on Sokolov. Brian said goodbye to Erick and agreed to meet at the airport in the morning.

Brian then found Nina and told her about Sokolov. He told her he wanted to keep Solie out of this latest Sokolov situation on the ride back to Amsterdam because there could be a leak inside the CIA.

Nina found the Sokolov information startling and worried for the first time since being flat on the floor in Katrina's atrium and staring at a shooter. She'd hoped finding a plane in the desert would be a fun-filled challenge. Now, the search had a huge twist – and a new antagonist.

Why must it always be this way in our line of work? Who is this Sokolov? And will he try to affect my relationship with Brian… and our baby?

<u>CHAPTER THIRTY</u>

Back to Amsterdam

The ride back to Amsterdam for the three was unusually quiet as each focused on their priorities. With the tiny trunk filled with Brian's carry-on bags, Solie found herself crunched in the back seat of the tiny car, shoved up against pocketbooks and computer bags. Despite her uncomfortable position, she reflected on those not-so-unwelcome passes made by that cute CIA agent, Jay. *It's a good thing he's not my partner in this. But then again, maybe I should have been more receptive.*

Nina's thoughts bounced from Morocco's oppressive heat and sandy terrain to the baby, her due date… and having a life with Brian with their child. Her mind drifted to imagined walks through Vondelpark, pushing an old-style baby carriage along a path exploding with a colorful array of springtime tulips.

Meanwhile, Brian pondered Sokolov's drive-by. *Why was he there? How did he know I'd be there? And that black SUV he was in! Jesus, it made him look like a spy. A spy? Good Lord, maybe he is a spy. God, I'm so tired. I'm making no sense.*

He yawned, closed his eyes, and fell asleep. Ten minutes later, he awoke with a loud snort. When the women laughed, he felt momentarily embarrassed, but it broke the tension.

Solie, giggling about the CIA guy who wore a cowboy hat to the meeting, told them about being in Billy Bob's in Fort Worth, Texas, and riding the mechanical bull. She shared her dilemma of barely hanging on to the contraption that jerked and revolved like a bull trying to throw its rider. When she got to the part about falling off and splitting the crotch of her brand-new $200 jeans, she had them roaring with laughter.

When the laughter subsided, the others urged Nina to share an embarrassing moment story, but she declined.

Ten minutes later, they arrived and parked in front of her new house on Johannes Verhulststraat.

Solie thanked them for the ride and headed to her apartment next door. Nina unlocked the two deadbolts, went inside, and turned on the foyer light. Brian followed her through the short foyer and stepped into the new open space she had made by her design improvements to the interior. The transformation from Erick's former home to this new, welcoming environment astonished him. The interior colors, the tasteful art on the walls, and the accent lighting highlighting them were stunning. Nina's touch was well beyond what he had expected.

"Brava, young lady. What you've accomplished here is amazing! I'd never know I was in Erick's former place. It's hard to believe Erick was so unimaginative for an art lover."

Nina took his arm. "Come upstairs with me. I want to show you something."

They climbed the fifteen steep steps to the second floor and rounded the corner.

"Look at this room! Do you like the bright yellow?"

"Yes."

"It'll be the baby's room. I'll add some more decorations as the time gets closer."

"Beautiful!"

He turned and put his arm around Nina's waist. He gave her a big hug and kissed her lips. Then, slowly, he maneuvered her backward, past the nursery door, and across the hall into the next room. Then, with his arms still wrapped around her, he slowly pushed her toward the king-size bed. It was beautifully decorated and loaded with extra-large pillows. He lifted her onto it, and within minutes, both forgot about everything else.

An hour later, it was dark outside when Brian woke. He looked over at Nina, smiled, and kissed her forehead. She felt his kiss, opened her eyes, and smiled. The cozy warmth under the covers was hard to leave. Since they had not eaten dinner, they dressed and walked around the corner to Sardegna.

The restaurant's best new customer was greeted warmly.

"Good evening, Miss Nina. Your usual seat?"

The maître d' ushered them to the last booth in the rear of the restaurant, where they were handed menus. He lit the candle and returned with sparkling water, slices of lemon, a basket of thinly sliced focaccia, and a dish of crushed kalamata olives. A red pepper flake dispenser and a black pepper mill stood adjacent as sentries.

Brian's smile melted away, and he asked the question. "Why are we doing this?"

Nina squeezed some lemon into her water glass. "Dinner?"

"No. Why are we running off to Morocco? I have all this money – more than I could spend in a dozen lifetimes. I should ignore Interpol and retire and let someone else search for Göring's gold and art." He paused and took a sip of water. "Maybe I'll just go AWOL and let the Agency sue me."

Her eyes widened in alarm. "Wow! This isn't the art professor turned Interpol detective I know. What's wrong? Is it because I'm pregnant?"

"No, of course not. I'm thrilled you're pregnant, Nina. You're the best thing that's happened to me in years! And the baby… well, that's a wonderful surprise. But I'm worried."

"About?"

He sighed. "Something going wrong. I don't want anything to happen to you or the baby."

"Brian, you've been through a lot. But you, or should I say *we*, can't live our lives in fear, waiting for the proverbial 'other shoe to drop.' You and I make a great team, and we've got a tiger by the tail with this project. Be positive. Everything will be fine."

They ordered salads with protein. Then she poured olive oil over the crushed kalamata olives and added more grated Pecorino Romano cheese, freshly milled black pepper, and a few red pepper flakes. Then she put a spoonful of the mixture on a piece of the thinly sliced, warm, crusty bread and raised it to his mouth.

"Eat this. It will magically cure all your worries and make you feel better."

He smiled and laughed. "You already made me feel better this evening. But I sure could use a cure for all my worries." He took a bite. "Hmm. You sure do know how to make a man happy." He smiled again and reached for the slim, leather-bound wine list. "Wine with dinner?"

"Not for me."

Brian nodded. "Right. What was I thinking?"

Still excited about showing Brian through her new place, Nina chattered about the challenges she faced with contractors during the renovation process.

Brian half listened, tuning out the details. He couldn't shake his pessimism and slipped back into his concerns and fears. His mind returned to Luzzi, pointing his gun at Nina. Then it jumped to Sokolov staring at him and again to Tony Costa's eyes squinting in disgust.

I need to find out what's in those unopened boxes in Katrina's basement.

"Brian! Nina to Brian… You're zoning out on me again, just like yesterday."

"Sorry, Nina. I have an idea."

"Did you hear anything of what I've said these past few minutes?"

"Some of it. Listen. I need to take a quick trip to Malta. Uh, let me rephrase that. Would you visit Malta with me tomorrow for a few days? We can still fly to Casablanca from Malta. It'll delay our start by three days. I'll tell Pieter that I need to finish up some family business. He shouldn't bark too loudly since he's got me tied up for another two years – and the rest of the team shouldn't mind."

Nina looked askance at him. "Do you *really* have things to finish?"

Brian hedged. "Well, not exactly, but let me explain. Something suspicious is going on, and it's gotten into my head. I've got to figure it out. But I need you to be with me."

Over dinner, Brian outlined what he had been thinking, especially questioning how the young Russian students were now heading to the mainland only one day after she'd convinced Van Deusen to skip searching the island.

"Maybe the Russians didn't find anything, and the move could just be a coincidence."

Brian shook his head. "No, Nina. Trust my instincts on this."

They finished dinner and skipped dessert, then left. They held hands on the walk home and went right to bed. Brian fell asleep quickly while Nina lay awake, wondering about tomorrow.

CHAPTER THIRTY-ONE

The Flight to Malta

The next morning, they arrived at the airport early. Brian changed the destination of their tickets while Nina emailed the other teams. She said an unexpected need required Brian to go to his mother's house in Malta, which would delay their commencing work by a few days in south Casablanca and then Settat by two or three days.

They received acknowledgments from each team, also headed to the airport, and from Amara Chikere, who was hanging maps of the target cities at the office.

Nina was concerned about the lack of response from Pieter, but as she and Brian had the rest of the teams' support, Pieter's opinion was insignificant.

The flight to Malta was smooth. They arrived on time, and the car Brian rented online was ready. They left the parking lot and had driven for ten minutes when Brian made four righthand turns around a block, putting him on the straight again.

"Brian, why did you make those turns? We're right back where we were a minute ago."

"We're being followed."

"Oh my God. Not again!"

"Relax. It's only a little Fiat, even smaller than yours."

"You were right about worrying."

"Well, for now, don't worry. It's probably just a scout following anyone who enters town to see where they're going. They'll pass the information along to a local capo. If they recognized me, even the

Knights of Malta guy will hear I'm in town. I wouldn't be surprised if one or two guests were waiting when we arrived at the house. While I'm thinking of it, let me call Carlo to let him know we're coming. He and his father built the house many years ago. When Luca bought the place, he offered to make a few upgrades the original owners wanted but never had done. He constructed a wrap-around veranda for Luca and began caring for the house and grounds after Luca died. I got to know him last time I was here. Good guy."

They noticed a red sportscar in the driveway as they reached the house. Tony Costa sat in the shade on the side veranda. As they parked, Brian reminded Nina of his accusation of an unfulfilled promise made years earlier to the Order of the Knights of Malta's local chapter.

"*Bon giorno*, Tony. This is my associate, Miss von Scholz."

"*Ciao, signore* Brian and Miss von Scholz. What brings you back to Malta so soon?"

"A brief stay at my mother's house."

"I see. Have you any news about Luca Luciano's promise?"

"Not yet. I've been busy working in the Netherlands and needed a break. You have my word. I'll continue investigating your claim in our family records and with Luca's law firm in Rome. I'll be sure to let you know when I learn more."

"Working? I heard you were retiring. Is that not true?"

"It's a long story, but I'm still working."

Tony rose. "I see. Well, enjoy your stay with your beautiful associate. *Buon pomeriggio*."

As he drove away in his Ferrari, Nina turned to Brian. "I don't like him."

Brian disregarded her comment. "Why didn't you buy a car like that?"

"I got a red car."

"Not like that." A teasing grin lit his face.

"Brian, please be serious."

"Okay. I'm not sure about him yet. He's just trying to do his job running the Chapter – and since this is Malta, his position as head of the Order of the Knights of Malta is incredibly prestigious."

"I'm a bit anxious about going inside. I'm not sure I want to see the atrium where we both were on the floor and almost died."

"Fair enough. Then, instead of seeing the atrium, let me bring you into the living room. I'll show you the moving bookshelves and the hidden stairway leading down into the spooky dark cellar filled with lots and lots of spider webs."

"Brian! Please! Don't scare me."

Another car pulled up as they were about to head inside.

"*Ciao signore* O'Sullivan."

"*Ciao, Carlo!* It's nice to see you."

"Ah, it's nice to see the beautiful young lady who was with you last time."

"Nina, you remember Carlo Veneri."

"*Certo! E' cosi bello rivederti!*"

"*Ah, bellissima! La bella signorina!*"

Brian smiled, appreciating their exchange, and then led the way inside.

Slightly stooped, Carlo was still remarkably mobile for a 78-year-old man.

He led them through the house. "*Signore* Brian, the bullets fired by the Interpol sniper saved your lives – but shattered the tall glass window in the atrium. The broken glass was replaced this week. And I've trimmed the bushes on the side of the house, just as you asked before leaving ten days ago."

"Excellent, Carlo. Thank you. Do you know anything about the hidden stairway behind the bookshelves that go down to the basement?"

"*Si.* The original owner asked me to incorporate the stairway into the house when we built it."

"Do you remember being in the basement when Luca lived here?"

"Yes, a few times. The last time was when Luca asked me to bring several boxes of wine down into the wine cellar. He got them in northern Italy near Brescia. We carried them down the path and left them in the root cellar by the tiny door. That's the outside entrance into the wine cellar where he made and kept his wine. Luca made me laugh. He could afford the best wines in Italy, but he loved his homemade wine – a rare but delicious blend of Grenache, Alicante, and Muscat grapes. He never added yeast. He'd just crushed it and let it sit outside in the sunshine, where it would ferment. Then he'd ask me to help him bring the juice through the root cellar door and pour it into his barrels. Luca was particular about flavor, and his barrels were made from oak found in the Basque region of Spain."

"Can you show me the outside entry?"

"*Certo.* Follow me."

As they walked around the side of the house, Carlo pointed beneath the west side's veranda. "There. Just walk down this stone path and bend over to get under the porch. The root cellar is there, and entry into the wine cellar is at the end through a small door."

"I didn't see this on my last visit."

"It's because these sun-loving bushes grow like weeds, and this was all overgrown. I cleaned it up after you left."

Brian made his way down, ducked under the wood beam, sitting on a column of stones carrying the weight of the porch, and disappeared. Nina looked at Carlo's sun-drenched face and smiled. He smiled back.

"Nina! Come down here," Brian called. "You need to see this."

She carefully made her way so as not to trip on the vines firmly rooted in the path.

"Now, wait here."

Brian left and went upstairs. He moved the tall bookcase and quickly went down the dark stairs. He walked the length of the wine cellar, quickly knocked out the pins to the small door's hinges, and crawled into the root cellar.

He called out, "Nina, can you hear me? Come closer."

As she moved toward his voice, and while bending over, she saw the six boxes on pallets in the open root cellar next to the tiny door.

"Now I can see exactly what you were talking about."

"Okay. I need to speak to Carlo." They both crawled out from the root cellar.

"I need to move those six boxes from the root cellar into the garage. Can you arrange for someone to do that?"

"Of course. I remember carrying the crates down there at Luca's request. There was an old lock on the door going into the wine cellar. Luca couldn't find the key and said to leave them there. I think he forgot the root cellar was open to the outside, and then he died, and the bushes and shrubs overgrew the entrance. Let me get someone to help and a hand truck. I'll get that done this afternoon. I hope the old wine is still good!"

Carlo departed, and Nina followed Brian into the house.

"Let me show you the other way down to the root cellar."

She watched him pull a concealed lever inside a shelf in the living room. She gasped as the bookcase swung open, revealing the hidden door.

"Follow me. Careful. These steps are rickety."

They made their way through the musty wine cellar draped in cobwebs to the end of the long, dark room. He pointed to the small door and the unpinned hinges.

"Since we're here now, let's crawl through and try to get those boxes outside ourselves if they're not too heavy for you."

Lifting together, the two found them to be lighter than expected. Taking their time, they moved all six crates into the garage in less than twenty minutes. Brian brought the hammer and screwdriver to the garage atop the last box.

"I figured the crates I hadn't opened on my last trip would be heavier – assuming they were filled with bottles of wine."

Using the hammer, Brian pried up the top of the first crate.

"Here, I've got this end. Lift the top off your end."

"Wow! Brian!"

"I told you about the contents of this first box, which I opened when I found them."

A ray of daylight coming through the open garage door illuminated the colors of two statues. This is 'Anubis,' the Egyptian deity of death and mummification. He accompanied kings like Tutankhamun into the afterlife."

"I'm just blown away at the pristine condition of these pieces!" Nina exclaimed.

"The next box has similar markings. Let's see if the old DiBotticino legend about the knight is true."

"Remind me."

"When I started going through the house, looking for old messages Katrina might have stuffed away and forgotten, I found an old letter from Giovanni Cardinal DiBotticino to Katrina when she was in the convent. According to the letter, his uncle Vincenzo would let the children in the family see the 'dog-faced' statues and the knight's equipment, but he wouldn't open the other boxes."

Brian pried open the second box and removed the straw used as packing material. He exposed the Crusader's sword, his chainmail, and a tunic and banner, both emblazoned with the uniquely styled red cross, emblematic of a Templar.

"I had this open when I was here the first time. The evidence certainly supports the DiBotticino family legend about a Templar hiding in the hills above Brescia and starting their quarry."

"Amazing!" Nina remarked. "To think this was worn – and used – by a real Crusader."

"Let's open the third box. In his letter to Katrina, the cardinal remembered his uncle said the other boxes were special or sacred and not to be opened."

Brian struggled to get the lid loosened. "Here goes… Jesus, this isn't easy. This box and the remaining three look like they're constructed differently than the first two. Let's try again. Pull up on the edge here while I use the hammer claw."

As the two struggled, Brian noticed the rusty old nails looked different and were not coming out quickly because they had been hammered in and bent over. He put the claw under the nail and gave another pull.

"Ah! Finally. Let's have a look after I remove the straw."

"Brian, my God! That's the Crusader's helmet! It's in perfect condition, except for that awful dent."

"He must have been hit in the head pretty hard with a sword to cause a crease like that in the metal."

"Let's see what's in the next one."

They struggled again with the fourth box, then pulled the top off and removed the straw.

"What is it?"

"Goodness! It's an old Persian helmet from the time of the Crusades. It's in excellent condition."

"Wow! It's so different. It's such a unique style."

"Let's see what's in the fifth box."

Like the previous two, the fifth crate was difficult to open. They finally succeeded. It contained a clay vase about three feet long and maybe eighteen inches in diameter. The cover fit snugly into the top and was tied to the neck with a cloth band – cotton or linen. While it still lay in the box, Nina tried to unravel the fabric, but it merely disintegrated into dust in her hands. A substance, much like beeswax, sealed the top.

Nina looked at Brian. When he nodded, she gently grasped the top, slowly twisted it off, and set it down on the packing straw.

"Brian, look! There's something inside."

"It's a scroll."

"Wait. It looks like two scrolls. They're rolled up together."

"Careful, Nina! Don't pull them out. Those could break apart easily."

"What's the material?"

"One looks like a papyrus scroll; the other looks like it's made from leather, maybe a sheep's skin. The Dead Sea Scrolls and the fragments were made from tanned or lightly tanned parchment, and some were on leather. I wonder if what's written on the papyrus scroll was also written, or perhaps rewritten on the leather scroll."

"Brian, I'm speechless just looking at these."

"Nina, this find is priceless – and likely sacred! In Cardinal DiBotticino's letter, I recall he wrote, 'The knight stopped in Ephesus where he met and stayed with an old family who claimed to be in the direct line of the apostle John, who fled to that city with the mother of

Jesus of Nazareth after His crucifixion.' This is just wild speculation on my part, but I'll step out on a limb and say this scroll could date back to the time of Christ."

"You could be right, Brian. Now, what can be in the last box?"

Just then, as they were about to open it, they could hear a car pulling up in front of the house on the long gravel driveway.

"We need to put this on hold and see who that is," Brian said. "Quick, let's pull that tarp over the boxes. Run to the house, go in the back door, and act like you've been there all along. I'll walk around and see who it is."

After they covered the boxes, Nina took off running toward the house. Brian went to the front of the house as the car pulled to a stop. It was Carlo, returning with a friend from the Knights of Malta chapter to move the boxes.

"*Signore* O'Sullivan. We're here to move the boxes of old wine."

"Oh, Carlo. I should have called you. Nina and I moved the boxes out of the root cellar already, and we're all set. I won't need your help after all. But thank you."

Not understanding Brian's indirect message suggesting he leave, Carlo noticed the blue tarp at the edge of the open garage door.

"Ah, I see you put the boxes into the garage."

Brian didn't bother to look back. Had he looked, he would have seen that, in their haste, he and Nina had only partially covered the boxes.

"Yes. They were lighter than we expected. Thanks again for returning."

Brian did his best to get rid of the friendly Carlo, mostly because he didn't know who the other person was.

"Did you open the boxes to try the wine?"

"We opened one, but the corks in the bottles were spoiled, and I'm sure the wine wasn't good, so we are going to throw it all away."

"You can leave it all there, *Signore* Brian. I'll return tomorrow morning with a larger pick-up truck and dispose of everything. *Ciao!*"

As they left, Carlo's friend Sebi was all eyes, stretching his neck to catch a glimpse of the partially exposed boxes from under the tarp in the garage. "Carlo, what's in those boxes?"

"Many years ago, I thought it was wine. I thought it was something Luca wanted to give to the chapter."

Sebi understood and offered to help Carlo in the morning. But when they got back, Sebi went to see his chapter leader, Tony Costa, and told him a tarp was covering some interesting boxes in O'Sullivan's garage.

Sebi would also make a second call to an associate, his comrade and upline spy chief, Ivan Sokolov.

CHAPTER THIRTY-TWO

What To Do

As Carlo drove away, Brian went inside. He wasn't sure whether his stomach ached from hunger or nerves. He went to the refrigerator and, realizing there was no food in the house, got a glass of water.

Nina returned to the kitchen. She saw Brian's face, which was grim and pale. "Are you okay?"

"Houston, we have a problem."

"What? Who's Houston?"

"Sorry. It's a misquote from a movie. But it means we have a serious problem. I told Carlo the wine in one of the boxes wasn't good, so he's coming back in the morning to take them away."

"Well, that complicates matters. Who was that with him?"

"Don't know."

"Let's see what's in the last box. Then we can decide what to do. Maybe we can consolidate the boxes. Maybe the two helmets will fit into one box."

They returned to the garage and, after struggling with rusted bent nails for several minutes, Brian opened the final box. Inside was another piece of pottery, twelve inches round and just as deep. This pottery had its top wrapped in silk cloth and sealed with beeswax. Nina unraveled the silk, pulled off the top, and found more straw stuffed inside. She carefully pulled out the straw and found another piece of pottery, a glazed ceramic cup the size of a small water glass. As she picked it up, she got an incredible chill through her body, and for the first time, she felt her baby move. She handed the cup to Brian. Inside was a piece of leather. Brian unrolled the light-colored leather. On it, some writing. The ink was faded, but he could barely make out what it said.

"This writing. It's Latin. Look. It says, *'Hoc pocumum est Paulus apostolus nocte ultimae cena usus est.'*"

"Oh my God, Brian, I think that means—"

"Yes. It says, 'This is the cup the Apostle Paul used the night of the Last Supper.'"

"Is that real?"

"Well, two things. Most early Christians believed Paul was an apostle, but he wasn't among the original twelve selected by Jesus. That would mean he wasn't at the Last Supper. The Gospel story says Paul was a Jewish tax collector whom God called by knocking him off a horse and making him temporarily speechless. He converted, regained his voice, began following Christ, and wrote many letters to Christian communities. One of the communities where he spent more time was Ephesus, located in present-day Turkey. And as for the cup, only God knows if Paul used it. As for the authenticity of what's written, Latin wasn't all that common among those people at the time. But it's possible. As for the dating of what's written on the scrolls, carbon dating should reveal whether they're from that time, in which case, the cup may indeed be Paul's. The scrolls will need to be translated by scholars at the Vatican to reveal what they say and determine if they're originally from the period."

Nina bit her lower lip. "I know I've been telling you not to worry, but I'm worried. What do we do now?"

Brian smiled. "First, stop worrying. I have a plan. I'll call Tony Costa and get him over here. He can have those first four boxes – the statues, the Templar's tunic and banner, the sword, chainmail, and helmet. I'll even throw in the Persian helmet and say it's from the Siege of Acre, which, unfortunately, the Templars lost. Luckily for him, the DiBotticino prince returned home to Italy in one piece. Costa will be thrilled with all that. I'll tell him it's what Luca promised to give the local chapter. Those items are exceptional, but ordinary in many European museums.

"We'll keep the contents of the last two boxes. The scrolls and the cup must go to Monsignor Borrelli at the Vatican. He's the guy who helped us unravel the art thefts, and exposed the forgeries being made by that old guy living in the Luciano bankers' attic and being given to the Vatican. The scrolls will have to be prepared before they can be unfurled."

"How do we do that? How do we get the two boxes to the monsignor?"

"You ask too many questions," Brian teased, giving her a kiss on the nose. "I don't have that part figured out yet. I need life's author to write a few more pages in the next chapter of my new life with you to figure that out."

"I knew it when I first started working with you years ago. You can be silly at times and romantic at times!" She leaned over and kissed him.

Nina carefully fit the cup inside a small wooden box Brian found in the garage. She then nestled that into the long box with the tall pottery vessel holding the two scrolls. Then, they meticulously stuffed straw into all the nooks and crannies to make the contents snug and reattached the top of the box by inserting and re-bending all the nails.

Brian then called Costa, who seemed surprised at the call and even more so by Brian's hint of what the boxes contained. Costa said he'd call Carlo and Sebi, and have them bring the truck in the morning to pick up the four boxes and bring them to the chapter's hall. Costa hung up without so much as a thank you.

"Okay. We're all set. Now we need to eat and figure out how to get this box to Rome."

"And did you forget? You and I need to get to Casablanca to start our search."

"Yes, I know. Casablanca and Settat are next, but there's one more thing we need to do right now. You and I are bringing this box inside and putting it at the foot of our bed. I'm not letting it out of my sight tonight."

After the two carried the box inside, they left the house and dined at a local restaurant known for its assortment of fish dishes in white wine, garlic, tomato, and caper-based sauces. They considered ways to get the box with the scrolls and the precious cup to Rome. Nina suggested having Massimo's boat captain friend come and get them and the box back to Siracusa. Brian agreed because the crate wouldn't be put on a plane leaving Malta. Then he would fly to Rome and go directly to the Vatican.

* * *

Earlier that same afternoon, the other Interpol teams arrived in Marrakesh and Casablanca after air-traffic issues delayed their respective late morning flights from Schiphol. Following Nina's "Steps to Take" list, they settled into their hotels, and then, using local maps provided by the car-rental companies, headed out and drove around, familiarizing themselves with the layout of the cities. They began identifying all the houses of worship and major roads in and out of the cities. One team chuckled at Nina's suggestion: "Find and locate the closest large dunes the KvR diary pages implied were nearby."

The teams were then instructed to take walks and get used to the communities. Nina's last recommendation was to get a good night's sleep and avoid too much alcohol. That advice didn't go over well with Jay, the Texan CIA agent, who'd also been told to leave his cowboy hat in Amara's office.

<u>CHAPTER THIRTY-THREE</u>

The Following Morning

The following morning, Carlo beeped his truck's horn as he came through the front gate precisely at 7 a.m. His surprise helper was Tony Costa, uncharacteristically dressed in overalls and without his red sports car. Brian came outside to greet them, and he took five minutes to explain more about the contents of the boxes as well as the story behind it all – the DiBotticino family legend. He said there was no doubt that Luca had these items in mind when he offered to make a gift to the chapter. His busy international schedule and sudden death kept him from fulfilling his promise and making the gift to the chapter. Brian concluded Luca may have wanted it to be a surprise, which could explain why nothing specific was ever said about the contents of the gift.

Tony thanked Brian with a shallow smile for following through in the search for Luca's promise. After loading the boxes, he opened the door of the old green farm truck and then turned back to Brian.

"*Signore* O'Sullivan, you will be remembered at a High Mass this Sunday as we celebrate another anniversary of our chapter's history. Good day."

Brian gave a Hollywood wave as they drove away, immensely relieved to have Tony Costa out of his life. He and Nina returned to the bedroom and carried the box containing the precious scrolls and cup to the car. Only after a mighty struggle and with a final umph did they barely manage to wedge the box into the Fiat's back seat.

Their drive to the dock was quick. They found the captain, who left

Siracuse long before dawn, standing on the pier waiting for them, having already delivered wine and other goods to his customers – the two restaurants.

Brian and the captain lifted the box from the car onto the boat's rear deck. Once it was secured, Nina joined them on board for the ride back to Siracusa.

Brian pulled Nina to himself and breathed another sigh of relief as the boat pulled away from the dock into the harbor and slowly motored by picturesque Saint Elmo's Breakwater into the open Mediterranean. The small village of Valletta and its city gate looked beautiful in the morning's orange-tinged sunlight. They held each other, watching the skyline slowly fade in the distance. Nina kissed Brian. She was so happy Brian felt more relaxed, keeping Luca's promise and putting the task behind him.

Two minutes later, as they were about a mile from the shore, Brian's cell phone rang.

"*Signore* Brian. This is Tony Costa. You are a cruel and heartless man. The boxes you gave us this morning – they are empty. Do you hear me? Empty! Was this your idea of a joke to tease me by giving me straw-filled boxes? Shame on you. You have embarrassed me and disgraced our Order of the Knights of Malta chapter. By the power of almighty God, I curse you and your family! You will forever remember this moment and my words, and you will shudder in fear at the thought of revenge for the rest of your life." Costa ended the call.

Numb, Brian fumbled to put the phone back in his pocket, his face ashen.

"You said nothing while you were on that call. Who was it?" Nina asked.

He shook his head. "You don't want to know."

"Brian?"

He remained silent, released her hand, walked away, and began to simmer.

A mile inland from the port of Valletta, Sebi relaxed on the roof of his two-story house adjacent to Malta's airport. Being the local scout in support of the needs of the Maltese capo, the head of the Order of the Knights of Malta, and several other small bosses on the island wasn't easy – or so he thought. He leaned back and watched as a Ryanair flight from Barcelona was about to land. In a few minutes, once it was on the ground, he'd drive two blocks to the airport, park in a favorite spot, and watch for well-dressed strangers hailing taxis while keeping an eye on the car rental lot.

But today, he decided to pick up his cell phone and make a call. As the call was connecting, he took a drink from a glass of freshly squeezed orange juice. Proud and smiling, he recalled his one-man overnight caper.

"*Ciao!* It's done," he greeted the person who answered.

"*Bravo*, my friend. How is your family? Your wife and your children – they are okay?"

"*Buono, multo buono.* My wife tells me we will soon have another grandchild, a boy. My daughter says his name will be Matteo Pietro – after my two brothers recently lost in a storm fishing off the coast of Africa."

"Yes. I remember. Very sad. But my old friend, you are blessed with beautiful daughters who make beautiful babies."

"Ivan, what shall I do with these relics I picked up? Toss them in the ocean?"

"Hold on to them for now, comrade. I will let you know what to do soon. They may have some value. Have a good day. Your payment will be in the mail."

"*Grazie*, Ivan. *Multo grazie!*"

Brian continued to seethe about Costa's call. Finally reaching its limit, his temper flared with an outburst of cursing. His sudden frenzy surprised Nina. Realizing Brian could become so angry scared her. Despite his Mediterranean complexion, his face flushed with anger and turned beet red as his heart raced wildly.

Minutes passed before he finally calmed down. When he did, he shared Tony Costa's words – the root of his anger. Costa's allegation and his curse astonished and shocked Nina. But Costa's curse to instill fear of revenge and punishment in another person's heart was extreme.

She gripped Brian's hand, and her touch further calmed him. His appeared to cool down more as they watched Malta begin to disappear on the horizon. Before he lost cell service, Brian phoned Massimo, but it went directly to voicemail. He left a message noting their ETA and then pocketed his phone.

Nina suddenly felt something. She quickly grabbed his hand and placed it gently onto her belly. "Do you feel that?"

"No," he replied distractedly.

"Our baby. It's moving."

He managed a smile but said nothing because his thoughts had returned to Costa's call. *How could the boxes be empty? Who could have done this? And how? My gift of the DiBotticino family's legend has become a complete bust, and those missing artifacts have resulted in another new mystery... which I don't need on my plate now.*

His hand still lay against Nina's belly. He looked at her again, noting her smile had diminished, and she now looked worried. Seeing her like that saddened him.

Nina's brow wrinkled in worry and concern. In addition to their search for the missing art and gold – and now the missing DiBotticino relics – she had a new concern. The handsome and wonderful art professor she loved – and the father of her unborn baby – had an explosive temper.

Both were filled with anxiety as the boat headed back to Siracusa.

CHAPTER THIRTY-FOUR

The Boat to Siracusa

The journey to Siracusa continued as the western sky grew overcast and dark. The sea became choppy as a long line of thunderstorms headed southeast between Tunisia and Sardinia stirred the water. The boat's captain skillfully navigated the large, unexpected swells as the storm approached their position between Malta and Sicily.

Nevertheless, within minutes, the ride became daunting. Nina grew nauseated and rushed to the rail. Holding on tightly, she threw up overboard. Although he tried to help her, the smell of her vomit made Brian sick moments later.

Nina hurried below to clean up as the boat got tossed about, and remained there, bucket in hand.

Brian reached for a hose on deck to wash his face when a sudden flash of lightning and a clap of thunder brought drenching rain as the storm clouds let loose. Soaking wet, Brian needed to hold on dearly while being careful not to slip and fall on the wet deck as he made his way across the back of the boat and inside, near the captain.

As quickly as the storm came upon them, it passed. The remaining storm clouds in the western sky, left by the fast-moving front, became a dazzling display, reflecting all shades of the rainbow. The sea calmed, and the ride was smooth again, as if nothing had happened.

Brian looked down the stairs to the deck below and saw Nina asleep on a couch. Seeing her there made him pause and think. He smiled. *She's going to have my baby. How lucky I am to have her in my life! I need to hold onto her now. Suddenly, she's become everything to me.*

Just then, the captain spoke. *"Signore* Brian, we'll arrive in Siracusa in one hour. If you need a nap, go below and do it now."

"I'll do that, but first, let me ask you something."

After their conversation, Brian headed down the steps five minutes later, sat, and rested his head against a pillow on the couch across from Nina. He looked at her lying there and fell asleep.

Brian and Nina both woke to the sound of the boat's horn as it neared the entrance of Siracusa's harbor. It seemed like no time had passed, let alone a whole hour. Brian called Massimo again and, this time reached him. He explained they'd be docking in ten minutes. Massimo assured him he'd be there in time since he lived eight minutes away.

Nina sat up. "How are you feeling, Nina?" Brian asked when he had ended the call.

"Better, I think. Still a bit queasy. How about you?"

"I napped. It helped. That was quite a storm! We'll get some ginger ale for you once we're off the boat. Uh, Nina, I'm sorry for getting so upset earlier. I know my outburst… uh, well, I know it upset you. I'm thrilled you're pregnant, and you need to know how much I love you. I've had a lot on my mind, but I can't lose sight of what's most important to me: you and the baby."

He wrapped her in a strong, comforting hug.

"Massimo said he'll meet us at the dock in a few minutes. He'll help us unload the box, and we'll bring it to his house. Before I fell asleep, I spoke to the captain. I've arranged for the captain to take me to Naples using this boat tomorrow morning instead of flying. I'll rent a car in Naples and drive the box to the Vatican. After it's secure with the monsignor, I'll fly to Casablanca and meet up with you the next night. I suggest you get a good night's sleep tonight. You'll fly out from Catania for Casablanca. Massimo will bring us to the airport before we return to his house to make those arrangements."

Shaking her head, she balked at his idea and took a moment to respond. "You should fly to Rome. Forget the boat. It'll take too long. Next, being apart from you makes me nervous. Can't we stay together?

It's only one more day I'd be away from the case."

"I thought you'd want to get there to get started."

"I do, but not without you," Nina insisted. "We'll still have eighty-eight days. That's plenty of time to come up with something."

"I'm glad you think so," he replied with a hint of sarcasm. "The answer to the mystery initiated by the loose middle page of KvR's diary is like finding a needle in a haystack. I think you should get started."

"Who made you team leader?" she retorted, ending the matter… for now.

As the two finished speaking, the boat pulled along the dock. It was tied up, and its engines were shut off. They came up on deck and saw Massimo standing beside his SUV to greet them. A deckhand and a dockhand carefully used a small hoist to move the gangway in place. Brian and the captain carried the precious cargo down the ramp and into the back of Massimo's SUV. Nina followed behind, dragging their clothing bags and computers down the expanded metal ramp.

"Good to see you again, my friend," Massimo greeted Brian, "and it's good to see you with the little lady. It looks like you two are a happy couple!"

Nina smiled and, getting up on her tiptoes, kissed Massimo. "Life is good, Massimo. It's nice to see you again."

"Massimo, the captain, and I talked earlier, and he agreed to take the box and me to Naples in the morning. He'll make good use of the trip to pick up some high-end Tuscan wines for his return trip to sell to his Maltese customers. I'll drive to Rome and drop this at the Vatican. It's a straight three-hour drive."

"You'd be wiser to fly to Rome," Massimo advised. Nina gave Brian a pointed look. "What's in the box anyway?"

"I had mentioned I opened a couple of boxes when I visited you. But your mind was elsewhere during my stay. I'll tell you again at the house tonight. Something else has been going on that we need to discuss."

"I have some interesting news for you, too."

At the house, Massimo opened a bottle of dry rosé, opened some ginger ale for Nina, and shared what he'd spoken about with Tony Four Eyes the previous night. Tony came to explain that the local capo, to whom he had reported, had discovered the names of the thieves who'd robbed his house.

"The three young men claimed they were contacted by a stranger claiming to be from Reggio, Calabria. A handwritten note was given to the oldest promising to catapult them into assistant roles to the *capo di tutti capi* in Calabria if they stole paintings from a specific house in Siracusa. They were given a hefty sum for the initial theft and were promised a much larger reward when they brought the paintings to Calabria. They were instructed to use some of the initial money to rent a vehicle, take the stolen art to a ship, and then journey with the art to Reggio to meet the *capo* in person.

"After delivering the stolen art onto a two-hundred-foot yacht sailing under a Venezuelan flag, the three 23-year-olds were told to wait on deck for the hefty reward balance before being assigned accommodations in guest rooms below deck. As the boat left the dock, they were walked to the rear of the ship and told to wait. Two minutes passed when four men came on deck wielding modern Kalashnikov assault rifles and ordered them off the boat. The young men were stunned and frozen in a panic as the men with guns slowly advanced towards them. One of the boys, the leader, a real wise-ass kid who's been in trouble since he was twelve, balked. He was thinking it was a test of their courage. When one of the gunmen fired a burst of rounds over his head, all three jumped overboard and swam at least a mile back to the harbor.

"The three heard the gunmen and their contact on the boat speaking Russian. Feeling lucky to have their lives spared and regretting their mistake, the trio confessed their sin to the local parish priest – who happens to be Tony Four Eyes' brother, Father Emilio Quattrochi."

Brian almost laughed out loud but struggled to hold it in, knowing the robbery was still a sensitive and heartbreaking loss for his friend's delicate emotions. Despite the early time, Nina found herself falling asleep and excused herself to take a nap upstairs.

That evening, Brian and Massimo met over dinner to discuss 'things' while Nina was absent and still sleeping. Brian shared information about the newly discovered diary pages and the project in Morocco. But, beginning to recognize the Russian connection amid the string of recent events, he held off telling Massimo about seeing Ivan Sokolov – especially after hearing that the three thieves heard the men on the boat speaking Russian.

The art history professor, turned Interpol Agent, was beginning to recognize a Russian connection in the recent events, and those previously loose pieces were starting to fall into place, forming a pattern. He figured a connection existed among the art theft from Massimo, Sokolov's drive-by, the Russian students' leaving Grand Canary Island for Morocco. But he was unsure about last night's theft, leaving empty boxes at Katrina's home in Malta.

He didn't know what would happen next but hoped to connect more dots for a clearer picture.

CHAPTER THIRTY-FIVE

Leaving Siracusa

Brian wished his friend a good night and headed upstairs. He found Nina reading and sipping her remaining ginger ale.

"You're looking better. The color in your face has returned."

"Thank you. I feel much better. Brian, please make sure you're careful on your journey to the Vatican. What you have is incredible and priceless. When you land in Naples, call Pieter and see if you can use your position as an Interpol agent to get an audience with the pope. He needs to know about your discovery. And don't forget to use your new phone to take photos of the box while it's closed, then take one with you and Monsignor Borrelli showing it open, with the contents. I'll call Chick in the morning to tell him what we're doing."

"Of course. But I'm sure the pope has better things to do than to stop to see me."

She kissed Brian goodnight, turned off the bedside lamp, and whispered, "The baby and I be waiting for you."

Then, spooning together, they fell sound asleep.

Brian was up at 3:45 a.m., long before sunrise the next morning. He left a note for Massimo, apologizing for the delay in sending him the money he requested, but he'd get to it soon. The housekeeper's son picked Brian up at 4 a.m. for the ride to the boat. After putting the box in the rear of the van, Brian climbed in and thought about the day ahead. During the ride to the dock, he recalled leaving Massimo's less than a week earlier after the art theft. He'd heard the thieves going through

Massimo's house methodically, as if they knew where each painting hung in the house. It made him wonder how they knew. And he wondered about his driver, the housekeeper's son, whom Massimo casually mentioned recently turned twenty-three. At 4:20 a.m., the box with the scrolls and cup was safely onboard, and Brian and the captain were heading to Naples.

Nina slept in a few extra hours. At 8 a.m., she was similarly being chauffeured to Catania by the housekeeper's son. Nina called Amara from the airport to check in. She explained what had been found, Brian's change in plans, and that she'd be heading to Casablanca alone.

Amara listened, then broke the news. "Nina, two CIA people are being pulled off the job."

"I don't understand. What do you mean?"

"Smith and Stemmler are being pulled off the case. Fortunately, Solie Van de Berg will continue working with Erick. Pieter got the call ninety minutes ago from Pattison just after seven this morning. He said the order that came from Langley was unexpected. Bill said he was embarrassed by the sudden decision. He said he called two levels up but was told to stand down. Then Pieter called me to share the news.

"In your absence, I called Ladasha and Felix and told them to wrap things up in Marrakesh and head to Casablanca tonight or tomorrow morning to work the area alongside Erick and Solie. So later, when you arrive, rent a car and drive south to Settat. With these changes in play, you should start your search there. Is that okay?"

"Well, yes. But this is a huge surprise. Does Pieter have any idea what's really happened?"

"He says no. But I've known him for a while. Pieter's pissed and knows something's up. Call me tonight. I might know more then. I'll also let Brian know you'll be in Settat tonight, and I'll tell him he should catch up with you there."

CHAPTER THIRTY-SIX

The Path Back

Grandfather Abraham stepped away from the group and silently prayed, 'Protect us on our journey home.' A moment later, he rose and mounted his camel. A confident smile came across his weathered face as he looked at the length of the camel train. He straightened up, and with a slight snap of his whip and a piercing whistle, the camels stirred, and the caravan took its first steps north toward Settat. The twins waved goodbye and turned their camels, Blue and Baba, south toward home in Marrakesh while their father headed north with the group.

The ride back to Settat would be slower than the hurried pace on the way to the plane, given the heavy load. Youssef and Benjamin rode at Abraham's side. The plan was to continue straight through, stopping only four times. The idea of camping overnight on the return had been discussed briefly on their way there but was dismissed.

The ride was good, and the men's spirits were high. They liked the idea of using one of Abraham's old tricks. Before they left Settat, he had them bring four dozen palm tree fronds in the carts. As they readied to leave for home, he instructed the riders to tie the branches to the last two carts, which would ride side by side. The dragging branches would erase most of the camels' hoof prints if anyone tried to follow them from the crash site. The men liked the idea. It convinced them Abraham had led caravans in the past.

Less than two hours into the journey back, Abraham's age betrayed him. He was exhausted and needed to sleep. He should have rested in a cart for a few hours and closed his eyes. Instead, he alternately gritted his teeth and bit his lip to remain awake and upright in the saddle, holding tight to the reins and hoping the morning's light would stir him. While he struggled, the challenges he'd spoken of with Youssef entered his mind and ran like a repeating loop through his brain. *Where should we bring this bounty initially? Where will it be held? How can we protect it? Should some be used and the rest be hidden away for tomorrow?* His concerns were endless and exhausting. Then, after struggling to remain awake, Abraham finally gave in. He closed his eyes as his camel's gentle gait slowly rocked him into a deep sleep.

It seemed like an eternity, but within a minute, he fell from his camel, crashing down onto the road's hard surface, badly twisting his leg and hitting his head. Although the train was long and spaces between the camels were further than usual, the caravan immediately came to a halt. Youssef and Benjamin, riding in the rear and encouraging others to remain awake, sensed something had happened to stop the caravan. Moonlight allowed them to see the silhouette of a small group gathering in front. They quickly came forward and found Abraham on the ground. One man said Abraham's leg was broken, and he was losing blood. It worsened when a camel carrying extra saddlebags laden with heavy gold cargo accidentally stepped on him. Unbeknown to the men, the camel's misstep caused the simple break to become a compound fracture, and a sliver of bone pierced the femoral artery in his thigh.

One rider with medical experience came forward and attempted to stop the bleeding using a tourniquet. Youssef and another man laid Abraham in a cart and cushioned his body and head with blankets. One of the oldest men in the caravan volunteered to ride with Abraham. Benjamin agreed, and the camel train once again moved forward.

An hour later, at the first planned stop, Youssef discovered the old volunteer sleeping soundly, and his beloved father, Abraham, was dead. It was so unexpected and came as a shock to all the men, especially Youssef, who cried in disbelief his beloved father was gone. He loved him deeply. Even Benjamin, who'd lost his father when he was seven years old, felt deeply distraught at the loss, as Abraham's loving ways had filled the paternal void in his life.

After openly expressing their grief, as did many of the men, Benjamin and Youssef spoke and decided Benjamin should take on the responsibility of the caravan. He called the youngest rider forward and instructed several men to unload his camel's gold onto a cart. Then he told him to ride toward Marrakesh and return to Settat with Ahmad and Chadu. The young man left with his camel in a trot, heading south as the moon was setting in the west.

The weight of their emotions gradually outweighed the men's concern for the gold they were hauling, and the rest of the ride back became unbearable for everyone. While the caravan moved north, Benjamin pondered what Abraham would have done when they arrived. He recommended to Youssef that they use Abraham's beautifully constructed riad to conceal the carts temporarily and put the camels into the large corral and a smaller covered pen Abraham recently built for his growing herd. But it would be Youssef who had the final say.

The rider never told the twins why they were asked to return. Both were excited by the invitation but fell into deep despair when they caught up with the rest of the caravan and were given the sad news of their beloved grandfather's death.

Eventually, after a week of mourning, Youssef had an idea.

CHAPTER THIRTY-SEVEN

Nina Arrives in Settat

Nina's flight from Catania, Sicily, to Casablanca was delayed over three hours. A faulty light on the instrument panel of a connecting flight in Malaga was the cause of the lengthy delay. Adding to her woes, when she finally arrived, her rental car had been released, and she had to wait half an hour for one to become available.

While she was waiting for the rental, she called Erick. Not getting an answer, she left a voicemail. "Hi, Erick! It's Nina. I've just arrived in Casablanca. Amara called me, so I'm headed south to Settat. Call me when you have a few minutes to let me know what you two are up to. Bye!"

Twenty minutes later, her phone rang. It was Erick.

"Sorry, I missed your call. Where are you?"

"Leaving the rental car lot. I'm driving to Settat, and I'll be there tonight and for the next few days."

"Amara called with the news about the CIA guys being withdrawn. He told me you're heading to Settat. Solie and I are good here. We began our canvassing after we arrived. We have a good part of this area covered, and Ladasha and Felix are coming north to help us. But, Nina, I have to say that our chances of finding anything here are slim because there's very little sand around here."

"Remember, Erick, we're looking for people, not the plane. We want to find someone who might have seen what happened in 1944. So, continue to execute your search pattern like I asked."

"Sure, boss."

"Erick!"

"Okay. Have a good evening, team leader. And Solie says, 'Hi.'"

After a salad for dinner, Nina returned to her room and prepared for the next day. She planned to follow her own guidelines: Visit mosques, churches, and synagogues, look for excessive use of gold in those houses of worship, and look for paintings on her list worth millions that, by chance, might be hanging in plain sight.

Her list of paintings, similar to what she distributed to the others, included unrecovered paintings by European artists known to have been in Hermann Göring's possession, according to a small group of modern-day European art experts. When she finished sketching the path to visit as many locations as possible, she held the city map up and laughed. It looked like a Pac-Man game. Satisfied with her plan, she turned the lights off, got into bed, and fell asleep.

Nina woke early and showered, thoroughly enjoying the warm water and ample water pressure. She dressed and called Brian. He said the boat trip to Naples and the drive to Rome went as planned. The wooden box with the scrolls and cup sat safely on the floor beside him.

"Where are you staying?

"In a hotel across from the Trevi fountain."

She winced at hearing where he'd stayed, remembering it was where Wilhelm's nephew was murdered.

"I have an appointment to meet with Monsignor Borrelli tomorrow after lunch. I'll fly out and meet you later."

She told him Amara's news about the two CIA agents being pulled from the case and the reassignment of his two people to Casablanca. Then she asked Brian to fly directly to Settat, where she was now.

Brian told her he already had his tickets to Casablanca in hand, so he'd get a car and drive down to Settat the next day. They agreed to speak again when he arrived in Casablanca.

CHAPTER THIRTY-EIGHT

Settat

Nina's second day in Settat was long, hot, and dry. She faithfully followed her Pac-Man map, even laughing at her habits. As the day wore on, her feet ached from all the walking, and worse, her thigh muscle stabbed by the broken glass was throbbing. She realized it wasn't fully healed and was now paying the price.

She checked her watch. It was later than she realized, and she decided she'd done enough for the day. A new app on her new smartphone showed she'd walked 19,800 steps. That was impressive, and it was well beyond anything she'd ever walked with Solie in the Amsterdam city parks since her injury.

On her way back to the hotel, she stopped occasionally to rub her cramping thigh. Then, during her last stop, from the corner of her eye, she thought she noticed movement a fair distance behind her. She turned and, seeing nothing, figured it must have been a dog or a cat that had run behind her.

Nina resumed walking. Hearing footsteps, she turned quickly and caught a glimpse of a hooded man dashing into an alcove of a storefront. *Oh my God, I'm being followed. I need to get to the hotel.* Estimating the distance, she judged it to be about the length of a soccer field.

Nina picked up her pace. Fifty yards from the hotel, she was still being followed as she limped in pain. *I need to reach the front desk in the lobby. My leg is killing me. I need to get through this. Oh God. Please, my baby.*

Suddenly, her throbbing thigh muscle cramped badly, and her entire leg became as stiff as a baseball bat. Exhausted and in severe pain, Nina hopped along for the remaining fifteen yards to the hotel's front door. Once inside, she hobbled to the center of the lobby, hoping whoever was following her would stay outside. She found a chair, and overwhelmed with pain, she began rubbing her leg's quadriceps, hoping to release the cramped muscles. When she looked up, the hooded figure was gone. She felt some emotional relief, but her leg still hurt badly.

Nina regained her composure over the next minute and realized she was severely dehydrated. After sitting a few more minutes, the cramping eased. She carefully stood and, slowly regaining her footing, scanned the lobby. Seeing no one in a hood, she took small steps, slowly moving across the lobby toward the corridor and to Room 122, the last room at the end of the long hallway.

As Nina turned to enter the hallway, she looked back and caught sight of the hooded figure emerging from behind a sprawling potted plant in the lobby. She picked up her pace and resumed hopping because her thigh cramped and stiffened again. When she peeked back again, the hooded man was following her. He'd be in the hallway, and she'd have no escape. About to panic, she noticed ice and soda machines set into an alcove less than eight feet ahead.

Reaching the alcove, she slipped sideways into the narrow space between the machines. Then she reached for her gun and held it tightly. As the hooded figure approached, she saw it was a teenage boy.

I'm doing this! So, with a burst of energy, Nina lunged from the space, straight across the hallway, and shoved him up against the corridor's wall with one hand, and with her other hand, she pushed her handgun into his ribs.

"Who are you? And why are you following me?" she demanded.

The boy's eyes widened in terror. "Madame! Madame! Please! I don't want to hurt you, and please don't hurt me."

"Why are you following me?" Nina repeated.

"Madame, I have a message for you."

"From whom?"

"Please, madame. Please. I don't intend to harm you. The message is from my grandfather. The community elders called him and told him about your visits to the mosques and churches today, and they told him about the questions you asked. He sent me to find you. I tried to find you this afternoon and only found you twenty minutes ago when I saw you struggling as you walked."

"What does your grandfather want?"

"It's about the message, Madame. He told me to tell you."

"Tell me what?" she barked impatiently, wincing as her leg cramped again.

"He said, 'Tell the woman I saw the plane. I saw it crash.'"

She paused. Her breath caught in her throat. *Is this the needle in the haystack? Could this be the lead I'm looking for?*

"Madame, please. My grandfather wants to talk to you. He said, "Tell the woman I've been waiting all my life for someone to come and ask about the plane."

"Your grandfather – how old is he?"

"He's very old. He was just a boy during World War Two."

Where is he?"

"At his house. He said to come right away. I can take you now. This is how to get there." The teen held out a small piece of paper with a sketched map.

In silence, Nina replaced her gun in its holster, then took the note with the tiny map. She shoved the teen away and looked at the note.

He held his hands together as if in prayer, bowed slightly, and looked at her. "Madame, please. Grandfather lives on the edge of town, south of here. Please, will you go with me?"

"Young man, you scared me half to death – and you almost got yourself shot," she scolded.

"My apologies, madame. My sincere apologies. I was tasked with finding a beautiful woman with hair flowing freely from under her shawl. And, madame, I must tell you that you are the most beautiful woman I have ever seen. Your face is pure, and your eyes are clear and bright! I can only imagine how you must look…"

"Stop. That's enough. What is your grandfather's name?"

"Ahmad. He's a sincere and honest man."

"Tell your grandfather I will visit him tomorrow at 10 a.m."

"I will." The teen nodded and backed away. "Thank you, madame, and good evening."

The young man walked back to the lobby and left the building. Nina checked her watch as he left. It was 4:45 p.m. She hobbled in pain to her room, waited two minutes for her cramp to subside, and then slowly limped back to the ice machine with a bucket. Again, she returned to her room, placed the ice in a small towel, and placed it on her thigh. Then, she made her first call.

"Hi, Nina. I was just about to call you."

"Erick! Listen carefully. I need you and Solie to pack all your things and check out of your hotel as soon as we hang up. Next, I need you to pick up Brian at the airport in Casablanca tonight; his plane arrives at 8:20. Bring him to this hotel where I'm staying in Settat. It's an hour south. I'll reserve two rooms here for you and Solie. "

"Will do. No problem getting Brian, but what's happening that you want us down there this evening? It sounds urgent."

"I have a strong lead here. It happened just a few minutes ago. Some young kid approached me. Said his grandfather saw the plane crash. I'll tell you, Brian, and Solie the details when you arrive. There's a restaurant here in the hotel. We all can eat when you get here."

"It's amazing you were approached. Tell me again. How do Germans say "Serendipity?""

"I have to go. Call me with anything. Cellular service was spotty on the way down here."

Her 5 p.m. check-in call to Amara Chikere went straight to voicemail. In the message, she said she had been given a message that an old man in town saw the plane crash, but she'd confirm that tomorrow after the meeting.

Next, she called Pieter to share the exciting news about the lead.

The call rang his office phone a few times. Ursula picked up as Nina's call was about to time out and transfer to voicemail.

"Good afternoon, Pieter Van Deusen's line."

"Hi, Ursula. It's Nina. Has Pieter left for the day?"

"He's been out of the office, hosting two foreign law-enforcement officers. He said he'd return here to the office around six."

"Please tell him we have a lead here in Settat. Also, tell him that if tomorrow's lead is good, additional support from Felix and Ladasha might not be necessary, and Pieter can take them off the budget for this case."

"Of course, and congratulations! That was fast work! Have a good evening."

Nina felt relieved and excited about tomorrow morning's visit. She undressed, filled the old-style clawfoot bathtub, and climbed in, hoping the warm water would relax her leg muscles. She also wanted to be fresh for Brian's arrival later.

After hearing Nina's news, Ursula called Olga and told her about the lead in Settat. Olga then called Dimitri with the update. He, in turn, called Ivan Sokolov.

"Dimitri, you and Katya must go to Schiphol immediately. Get a plane to Casablanca, or better yet, get a direct flight to Settat if possible. Go to the hotel where that woman, Nina, is staying and follow her where she goes tomorrow morning."

"Yes, comrade. We'll go immediately. What is the hotel's name?"

"Call Olga. She'll get it from Ursula."

* * *

Nina finished her bath and blew her hair dry. She put on her robe, sat in a comfortable, high-back chair, and flipped through her notes. Before long, her mind drifted to being with Brian and making love to him tonight.

But a moment later, her mind flashed back to the confrontation with the young man at the soda and ice machine. *He was a cute kid, but he could have gotten himself shot! I'm so lucky to have found someone who saw the plane crash. It's almost unbelievable that within one day here, they came to find me! But I knocked on a lot of doors today – my canvassing plan worked. But is it the plane with the gold and art? Gosh!*

I bet other planes might have crashed near here during the war. Gee, this lead sounds so good, but it could turn out to be a dead end. I guess we'll find out more tomorrow.

She returned to the bathroom and disrobed. She looked at herself sideways in the full-length mirror. *I think I'm beginning to show.*

CHAPTER THIRTY-NINE

Brian Arrives in Settat

Erick pulled into the hotel's parking lot at 9:35 p.m. Brian, asleep in the back seat, awoke when the car jerked as the front tires hit the concrete bumper in the parking space.

"Wake up, BJ, we're here."

"Uh, I'm awake. Thanks for picking me up."

"Let's get our bags and check in."

As they headed inside with Solie, Nina greeted them with hugs – and a kiss for Brian. Since she had already registered them at the front desk, she handed Erick and Solie their respective room keys and asked the young man assisting at the front desk to take their bags to their rooms.

"And please take Mr. O'Sullivan's bag to Room 122."

She turned to Erick. "The dining room is open for another hour, and I bet you're hungry. Let's head inside."

Erick began discussing the day's events in Casablanca and Brian's flight from Rome when Solie excused herself and headed upstairs for a few minutes to make a call. When she returned, the waiter took their orders. Nina started with a request for a salad with hummus and grilled goat as the protein. Solie followed.

"Salad with hummus for me, but no meat, please."

Erick asked for a hummus burger, and Brian said he would pass on dinner.

After a few comments about the day's traveling, Nina told the team how her lead developed. During her story about being followed, Erick grew uncomfortable, recalling the moments before he was shot. As Nina reached the part about hiding in the alcove next to the soda machine, Brian held up his hand like a stop sign.

He leaned forward and whispered, "Keep your heads down and speak quietly. The couple who just walked past our table… I recognize them."

"Gosh, BJ, old friends here in Settat?"

"No. Remember the other night when we gathered for dinner after our meeting in The Hague on Pieter's tab? The same couple that just entered are sitting over there came into the restaurant that night. I remember them distinctly."

"Really? Why's that?"

"His ears are deformed like he was a wrestler in school."

"And her?"

"Well… her long blonde hair and that figure! But there's one more thing about him."

"What's that?"

"I walked to the men's room that night, and as I passed their table, I got a whiff of his cologne. It was a popular brand back in the '60s and '70s called Jade East."

"BJ, I didn't know you had a nose for our investigative work."

"Please, Erick, hush," Nina hissed.

"But my concern about his wearing Jade East gets worse. That's the same cologne Ivan Sokolov wears; he's the guy Erick and I met years ago at an art show. And I distinctly remember the fragrance because I bought a bottle after that show when I returned home to New Jersey. And now I'm even more certain it was Sokolov who drove by me the other day. He's back in my life; only God knows why he's following me. I'm convinced he's sent those people here to Settat to find or track us – or both."

"BJ, if what you're saying is true, they probably weren't expecting that we'd all be sitting here as they walked in. They must be careless, inexperienced, or both."

"So, now what, Brian? How'd they know to come *here*, of all places?"

"Let's think about this for a moment. Nina, besides me and Erick, who did you call after your run-in with the young man who gave you his grandfather's address?"

"I left a voicemail message for Amara, then I called Pieter."

"What did Pieter say?"

"He wasn't in, so I started to leave a message."

"On his office voicemail or on his cell phone's voicemail?"

"Well, actually, neither. It was right at five o'clock. Ursula was still in the office and picked up my call. She said Pieter was due back at six, so I gave her the message."

"What did you say?"

"All I did was tell her the good news."

"Can you be more specific?"

"I told Ursula I'm in Settat and was approached late this afternoon by a young man who said his grandfather saw a plane crash when he was young, and we have what seems to be a good lead that we'll be following in the morning."

"I also said if tomorrow morning's news is positive, we might be able to release Amara's people from the case. I thought she'd pass this along to Pieter, and it'd reduce his stressing over his budget."

The table's hushed conversation went silent as everyone absorbed what Nina had said. It was a pivotal moment as they each reached the same conclusion, recognizing the source of the security breach.

Nina cringed, a cold, empty feeling in the pit of her stomach. Erick felt emotional. Solie appeared stoic but cringed inside.

"Oh my God, Brian. Does this mean…"

"Yes, Nina, it probably does."

"Ursula… a spy? My God, that's ridiculous. Why would she be a spy?"

"Who knows why? It's certainly hard to imagine."

"She's been with the Agency long before you arrived, Nina, and even before Brian became my partner."

Solie spoke up. "Spies are placed as sleepers for years to gain the trust of a neighbor or employer. Sometimes, they're with several different employers before they become active. They look for positions where critical information is available, then slowly creep their way in. During their hibernation period, as we call it, they are compensated well."

The others nodded in numb acknowledgment.

Solie continued. "It's evident your team has a problem, so let's talk about how to isolate the problem immediately, but not here. I swept my room just before we ate to detect any devices, and it was clean. I suggest we only speak about this in my room. I'll leave now and see you all in a few minutes. I'm in 224."

While the two FSB spies began eating dinner in the rear of the restaurant, the team members slipped away one at a time to Solie's room. Once there, they brainstormed several alternatives to deal with the Russian agents.

Solie spoke first. "Brian, consider this: Your art research department has had a spy in a critical position where the most delicate communication about every case has passed through her hands for at least a decade. I'm guessing this case is seen as worth much more than others in the past, and she's been activated because of the value. And Brian, your comment about Sokolov – I know about him from my work in the CIA. Years ago, probably when you first met him, he was head of the Soviet Arts Committee. He still controls all the art stolen from Germany after World War II by the Russians, and his role has broadened. He has earned a very high position inside the FSB, which affords him direct contact with Vlad Putin and Putin's social entourage.

"For now, I suggest we discuss one or more ways to misdirect the two FSB agents sent here to follow you. For example, Erick and I can run interference tomorrow by causing them some mayhem."

They continued the discussion. After a few minutes, concern grew among them about whom they could trust. Solie gingerly suggested their boss, Pieter Van Deusen, might also be an FSB spy, and Ursula was only accidentally exposed.

Solie continued by sharing her experience in the CIA undercover game and finished by expressing concern about the next steps the team would need to take if they found the gold and art from this lead.

Erick speculated the four of them could be seriously outnumbered if all the Russian students moved off Grand Canary Island and were directed to Settat.

"Whatever action we take, we'd have to do it quickly," Brian advised.

Nina agreed.

As the impromptu meeting in Room 224 neared its end, Solie suggested she'd call Pattison to inform him about the lead, the two spies, the Sokolov drive-by, and that Ursula was likely a spy. Solie commented, "It'd also be wise to share that Van Deusen may be on the wrong side in this."

Nina nodded, giving the okay. Solie stepped onto the balcony and made the call. Meanwhile, the team continued chatting, considering alternative ways to misdirect the Soviet agents the next morning.

"I have an idea," Erick said. "I'll go out to the parking lot and feel the hoods of the cars to determine which car they just drove here. I'll give them a couple of flat tires to disable their vehicle."

Brian smirked. "Erick, I bet you'll find the hood of every car outside is still warm from today's heat."

"Well, BJ, this is getting complicated. We haven't met the person Nina's telling us about. We have a Russian spy in our office, two Russian spies are downstairs, and a super-stud Russian spy that smells good is stalking you. The situation's become a bit like our search in southern Spain. I'm nervous, my stomach hurts, and I may need to throw up that hummus burger."

Unlike the jovial exchanges the trio often shared, the atmosphere in the room had become quiet as they wondered why Solie's phone call was taking so long.

CHAPTER FORTY

The Misdirection

Although it seemed longer, only seven minutes passed before Solie returned from the balcony.

"Okay. I spoke with Bill. I outlined the situation and your concerns regarding Ursula, Sokolov's presence, and Pieter's possible involvement on the wrong side of this case. Let me explain what he's suggesting. Do any of you know about the Ksar Tamentit or Ksar Draa?"

Erick and Nina exchanged a look and shrugged. Neither had an idea what she was talking about, but Brian nodded. "I've heard of both in my studies of North Africa."

"The Ksar Tamentit is in a historical village dating back to the tenth or eleventh century AD," Solie explained. "The village is in the heart of the desert and was a stopping place for caravans because of the availability of water."

"An oasis?" Nina asked.

"Exactly. The Ksar Draa is another ancient building located in Algeria. Today, centuries later, it sits like a boat stranded amid the Saraha's thousands of sand dunes. Legend says great treasures remain hidden in both Ksar locations because of the old caravan routes."

"Talk about looking for a needle in a haystack!" Erick added, "Or a treasure in a sand dune."

Brian nodded, understanding where Solie was headed.

"Pattison suggests we throw misinformation and mislead the two

FSB agents here in Settat and the Russian students currently headed this way. He's suggesting Nina email Pieter, then call his office and leave a message saying, 'I just received additional information confirming the gold and paintings found in the 1944 plane crash were moved and hidden near the Ksar in Tamentit.' Pattison believes this will give us the time to do our local research tomorrow, here in Settat."

Erick asked, "But what happens if our intended misinformation turns out to be true? What if the gold and paintings were there? We'd unintentionally be giving them a head start."

"It's not likely, Erick. Bill did a quick check on the distance. It's over five hundred miles as the crow flies, and not likely that an individual – or even a large caravan in the 1940s – would have moved the gold and paintings that distance."

"Won't they realize that?"

"Maybe. But if Nina sounds excited and sells the idea of having learned the exact location where the bounty is hidden, we can hope they swallow the bait."

While they were still together, Nina called Pieter and emailed him the same information from her phone. She tried to write in a way that sounded as excited as possible in the email, indicating the additional information was unexpected.

"So, now that Nina took that step, what do we do about the two FSB agents here in the hotel?"

"If our trick works, we might see some movement from those two in the next few hours – or certainly by the first thing in the morning. Erick, you drove here and must be tired, so I'm willing to take the first watch from now until 2 a.m. to see what happens. Hopefully, they will leave here and drive away to get a flight. Brian, Nina, and Erick get some sleep."

"I'll take the two-to-five shift."

"Thanks, Erick. Brian and I will relieve you at five. Thanks, everyone. Let's hope Ursula somehow sees Pieter's message, and it prompts those two to leave tonight."

* * *

Pieter's afternoon meeting at the local bar extended well into the evening, and he and his old law-enforcement friends hailed Uber drivers to get home after leaving the bar. Pieter was still inebriated when he arrived home and collapsed on the bed.

Ursula had prepared herself for sex when he arrived and was hugely disappointed seeing her boy-toy boss incapable of pleasing her. She undressed him and rolled him under the sheets. As she was doing that, she heard Pieter's cell phone buzzing in his pants pocket, and, out of curiosity, she read the incoming email from Nina. The baited hook was swallowed.

Ursula rushed to the kitchen, where her cell phone was charging. She grabbed it and stepped outside for a smoke and to call Olga.

 Hearing the update, Olga passed the news along to Dmitri, who immediately called Sokolov. Within eight minutes, the FSB spy network had shown its effectiveness and efficiency.

Sokolov texted Dmitri.

"Return immediately with Katya to the Russian embassy here in The Hague."

Then Sokolov called the agent in charge of the Russian cadets, saying arrangements would be made in the morning to secure two buses – one to bring half the group from Casablanca to Timimoun, the town near the Ksar Draa, and the others to leave Marrakesh for Ksar Tamentit. His orders were accepted without question.

As Sokolov lay awake, he realized Ursula's activities had reached the point where her undercover role was now exposed. He texted Dmitri with these instructions:

1) Have Olga text Ursula with instructions to come to the beauty parlor at 10 for a facial in appreciation for her work late last night.

2) Arrive with Katya at 9:50 a.m. Use the back door. Stay in the rear.

3) Instruct Olga to garrote Ursula during the facial by 10:10.

4) Shoot Olga in front of Katya. A behavior lesson for the sex brat.

5) The fixing team will arrive at 10:20 to remove both bodies, the voice recording equipment, Olga's financial books, and the paper records of customer visits.

6) Exit with Katya. Take nothing. Leave everything behind. Return here.

7) The fixers will set an intense fire to destroy the parlor's interior.

* * *

Given their displeasure for one another, Dmitri and Katya were sleeping in separate rooms. At 2:05 a.m. in Settat, Sokolov's step-by-step text arrived on Dmitri's phone. He realized they needed to leave immediately. He crossed the hall and knocked on her door.

Seeing who it was, Katya opened the door wide – completely naked. "Ah! So you couldn't resist the urge to come to bed with me?" she greeted him in an enticing purr.

"Get dressed. We're leaving," he told her, taking arrogant pleasure in her look of disappointment.

"Dimitri, this spy stuff sucks," she told him huffily. "This isn't what I signed on for."

"Tell it to someone who cares," he snarled, adding. "tell it to your boy *Vlad.*"

Sans showers, they dressed quickly, left the hotel, and hurried to their rental in the hotel's parking lot. They pulled onto the road heading to Casablanca at 2:30 a.m.

Erick was sitting at the edge of his bed, peering through the window. His elbows were firmly against the sill, propping up his chin as he tried to remain awake. Despite napping during Solie's watch, he remained tired from the drive to the hotel earlier that evening.

Despite his drooping eyelids, he spotted the two FSB agents heading to their car. He sat up attentively as they put their bags in the trunk and drove away. He went to Room 122 and knocked.

A shirtless, sleepy Brian answered. "It's not time for my turn."

"Someone swallowed the bait. The two spies just drove away. My

God, it means Pieter's in this with them."

"Hold on, Erick. There's a chance Pieter's not in on it if Ursula intercepted the message."

"Well, Brian, either way, I'm exhausted and going back to sleep."

"Good idea. We've got a big day ahead of us in a few hours. See you at eight."

Erick returned to his room, wrote a note about the two agents' departure, and slipped it under Solie's door.

Ninety minutes later, Dimitri and Katya sat in the Casablanca airport, awaiting the 5:30 a.m. flight to Schiphol.

"We'll get in about nine, then it's a thirty-five-minute drive to The Hague. We'll have to hustle to get over to Olga's by 9:45.

"Dmitri, why didn't we just go to their rooms in the hotel last night and kill all of them? Why were we sent there anyway?"

"We were sent to *track* them, not *kill* them. And now we must follow Ivan's next set of orders. Have you learned nothing about your role in assisting me? Your problem is that you're undisciplined. You only have your position because you've been a pleasure machine for Ivan and his friends at Vlad's villa in Sochi."

"You're right!" she hissed in contempt. "I've had sex with Ivan and Vlad, and I've fucked Vlad's friend Yevgeny. He used to be Vlad's chef. Now he's a big shot causing mayhem in Africa with a rough bunch called the Wagner group. They all love me in Sochi because of what I do to get them off."

"Yeah, you're so talented," Dmitri scoffed.

She paused a moment. "Ha! I finally got it! You're not angry; you're jealous!" She paused again, then looked directly into his eyes. "You want me, don't you, Dmitri? Let me take care of you. Look, there's a family bathroom over there. I can be quick. I'll make you happy like the others. Then maybe you'll be nicer to me."

"Enough talk. Just shut up and do as I say. If you fail this assignment to work for me, there'll be no more vacations for you and no more 'happy endings' for Vlad and his entourage. We must do as we're told.

We've been directed to fly to Amsterdam and return to our embassy. Now, can you be quiet?"

She fell silent. A minute later, she told Dmitri she needed to pee. He nodded. But before standing, she reached over and rubbed his crotch. "Oh, Dmitri! See... you *are* thinking of me!"

She stood and, grabbing his belt, pulled him from the seat into the family bathroom.

Wanting to find out how good she was, he offered no resistance.

CHAPTER FORTY-ONE

Meeting Ahmad

The team members were up early and met for breakfast at 8 a.m. The conversation focused on Pieter's background, his tenure at Interpol, and whether he could be a deep FSB agent. Afterward, they returned to their rooms, but in Room 122, Nina's emotions ran uncharacteristically all over the place. Nina swung from excited and nervous to fearful, weepy and anxious.

It was the first time Brian had seen Nina like this. He thought of giving her some encouraging words but wisely knew words wouldn't suffice. So he wrapped her in a huge, reassuring hug. Then he kissed her cheek and, looking into her eyes … gave her a long kiss on her lips. It worked. He felt her settle into his arms and could feel her relax as she regained her composure.

"Brian, when Erick came and knocked on the door to tell you the spies left the hotel, I felt the baby move. It startled me. At that very moment, I became more alert – more conscious of having our child inside me. Then, at that moment, there was a little kick. It was amazing. Feeling the baby move – Brian, it was like a tipping point. It was as if the baby was saying to me, 'Hey, don't forget I'm here with you.'"

Nina teared up again and paused to gather her thoughts. Brian saw her swallow hard as she was about to speak.

"This case, searching for Göring's gold and art here in Africa – and, well, being team leader just doesn't matter as much to me this morning as it did just two days ago. At that very moment last night, all of this took a back seat to what's most important to me. I can't get over how my thinking feels so different this morning. I'm carrying your baby, our baby. It's right here between us."

She reached up and, standing on her tiptoes, kissed Brian. She put her arms around him and held him close. The moment was tender for both of them. For the first time, he was truly emotionally in sync with her and understood it. And it seemed as if it was the first time the three of them were together as a family.

But only seconds later, he blew it with words she didn't need to hear.

"Well, Nina, you have a big day ahead. Meeting someone claiming to have seen the crash will be so exciting!"

Nina agreed but felt he had just missed an opportunity to show her more love.

In her room, Solie made another call to update Pattison before leaving for the meeting. It was the middle of the night in Langley. After teasing her about the time on the US East Coast, he said he'd support the project if they found the bounty.

"The Moroccan Royal Air Force has a base south of Settat in a town called Ben Guerir. It was once a U.S. Strategic Air Command base with a two-mile-long runway for a group of nuclear-armed B-47s. We have friendly relations with the Moroccan base commander there, and I've met him in person. Keep me informed. I can get a C-5 transport currently stationed in Malaga into the Ben Guerir base if you need it.

"Those Interpol folks with you are intelligent, efficient, and great researchers, but remember, they're art hunters, not trained CIA agents like you. Keep them under your wing. I'm surprised those FSB agents took off like that. I'll do some more checking to see where Van Deusen lands in this debacle. Do you have your satellite phone with you?"

"I do."

"Continue to stay in touch."

At 9:30, the four got into their cars for the trip to the meeting place. Brian led, driving Nina's rental. She co-piloted while reading the small map the young man gave to her. The drive would be about twenty minutes on a paved road. The road eventually became hard dirt and gravel, with the tires kicking up gravel and small stones. As both cars neared their destination, they slowed down because the road narrowed. Brian feared driving off the edge and getting stuck in the sand.

"I'm getting nervous," Nina fretted, toying with the map.

"Relax. If the guy we meet saw the plane go down, I'm sure the bounty isn't in his house. We have questions to ask, and we'll need help to retrieve the plane's contents. Your estimate is accurate – maybe a small truck or a short tractor-trailer."

Not far ahead, a farmhouse stood on a rise of land silhouetted by the morning sun.

"Brian, I think that's the house."

"Could be."

"I wonder if that young man will be here?"

"You said he was flirtatious. I'd guess he'll be there to see your long hair and shapely curves again."

"Can you please be serious? This is important, and I'm nervous."

Following the map, they turned off the dirt road onto an even narrower road leading up to the house. They came to an open gate. Brian stopped and told Erick and Solie to wait there. Brian continued and stopped twenty feet from the house. He parked and shut the ignition. They looked at each other and took deep breaths.

"Brian, my stomach feels nervous."

"Mine, too."

They exited the car and walked toward the house.

The front door opened as they approached, and a handsome older man draped in a flowing, white robe emerged. His whiskers were pure white, and strands of his long white hair flew freely from beneath his turban, in sharp contrast to his tanned, leathery skin. He once might have been five foot nine or taller. His grandson, standing beside him, easily stood a head taller. He stepped onto the porch to greet them.

Nina spoke first. "As-salam aleikum."

The man smiled and replied in English.

"Good morning, madame, and peace be upon you, as well. Welcome to my humble abode. My name is Ahmad. I am the person you have been seeking. Please, come with me."

Ahmad led them through the front door into a living room. His teenage grandson stood in the background, ogling the beautiful lady, just as Brian had teasingly told her.

"Yesterday, you met my grandson, Abraham. He is named after my grandfather."

"Yes. We met at the hotel. My name is Nina von Scholz. And this is my associate, Brian O'Sullivan. We work for an agency called Interpol. Here are our identification badges."

"Ah! Yes. I know your agency."

It didn't take long for Nina to pitch why they were in Morocco, searching for something believed to have been lost sixty-seven years earlier in a plane crash. She explained how art and gold were taken primarily from Jewish families throughout Europe during WWII in Gestapo and Nazi raids on their homes. She shared the sad fate of most of those same Jewish families.

Ahmad listened intently, nodding. At times, he appeared uncomfortable hearing what became of the Jews brought to camps. Her story refreshed his memories.

"Yes, Madame Nina, I am well aware of the horrors of the war."

Nina continued by identifying the name of the senior German military officer heading the German Luftwaffe. "While reporting to Hitler, Hermann Göring personally collected a huge cache of stolen art and gold at his German home called Carinhall. It's believed he wanted to move it to South America before the end of the war. We have reason to believe the plane crashed nearby."

Ahmad's eyes opened wide upon hearing her detailed explanations. He shifted in his seat, realizing he'd just received answers to his life-long questions.

"Yes, madame, I trust you. I believe your story, and I'm glad you've finally come. All my life, I've been waiting for this moment to learn the truth of what I witnessed as a boy. My body is old now, but in my mind, the plane crash – yes, the plane crash, and what I saw afterward – seems like it happened just yesterday."

Ahmad let out a huge breath – a sigh of relief. He thought for a moment and, leaning forward, took a sip of tea. He smiled a Cheshire-cat grin and sat back against his couch's colorful cushions. He reached for a small carved wooden box on the table beside him and pulled out a white Turkish Meerschaum pipe. Then he reached into his colorfully stitched vest for a package of aromatic tobacco and packed the pipe's bowl. He lit a match and waved it about the surface while drawing in the flame. The sweet aroma filled the small room.

Ahmad, who had witnessed the crash with his twin brother Chadu, sat cross-legged like a sultan in a regal position and, puffing away, began his incredible story, revealing – and reveling in – his family history. "Madame Nina, thank you for coming today. Your quest will be satisfied, but first, let me tell you my story."

He puffed on his pipe again, creating a ring of smoke that swirled above them.

"My ancestors originated in Judea and belonged to a tribe of Israel. Ha! I see your reaction, and I know what you're thinking! Yes. We are Jews. And I know you're surprised to find a Jew dressed like an Arab living here in Morocco. Madame Nina, the Jewish diaspora began long before Jesus of Nazareth walked the earth. The dispersion of our twelve Tribes grew when fighting the Roman occupiers intensified. It prompted my ancestors' great migration across the Sahara. They made many friends and eventually settled in Casablanca and the valley to the south, where you and I sit today.

"My family began conducting trade between northwestern Africa and the East, where the brilliant Persian people lived. We traded even in the Far East, where Marco Polo once ventured."

Ahmad's family history and pipe puffing stopped when he got to his trip with Chadu to Grandfather Abraham's home, originally scheduled for the boys' thirteenth birthday. Ahmad slowly shared the scene: the sound of the plane's engines, the plane's one-wheel landing and sudden crash and spinning into the sand, the ramp's opening, the German soldiers in tall black shiny boots, the dead man, and the tall Nazi shooting the two men. He mentioned the caravan and the sadness he felt at being told how his grandfather had fallen and died.

But the old man stopped short of revealing what Nina and Brian were waiting to hear.

And so, with dozens of questions tumbling through Nina's head, she blurted out the most important one when Ahmad paused to relight his pipe.

"Kind sir, after the caravan, what became of the contents of the airplane?"

He struck another match and placed it above the pipe's bowl. After several puffs, he was prepared to answer her when his grandson leaned over and whispered into his ear.

"Grandfather, there's a reflection of the morning's sunlight near the front gate. Where are your binoculars?"

"In the kitchen." Ahmad turned to Nina. "Did you come alone, or do you have associates with you?"

Brian spoke. "Another team of agents is at the gate to protect our being here with you. Unfortunately, others seek to enrich themselves, and sometimes we find ourselves being followed." Ahmad nodded. "I understand."

Nina leaned forward and inched her bottom closer on the seat. Then, with her hands open and palms up, she asked the important question. "Ahmad, our purpose this morning is to find and return the stolen goods to whom they belong. Will you help us?"

He looked at her. "Agent Nina, my family has long waited and prayed to return the goods to their rightful owners someday. It was my grandfather's wish and my father Youssef's wish to do so. And now it is my wish to see good prevail. But agent Brian, we also have feared this situation all these years."

Ahmad methodically emptied the tobacco from the pipe's bowl. "Madame Nina, you will ride with me into the desert, and I will reveal where the art and gold are hidden. We will go only a short way by camel."

Nina froze at the suggestion and looked anxiously at Brian. "Ahmad, may Brian and I speak privately a moment?"

When he nodded, they stepped to the side.

"Brian, I don't want to go. I'm not sure if I can ride on a camel while I'm pregnant. Please, you go with him."

"He seems trustworthy, and pregnant women have ridden camels for thousands of years. They're easy to ride. Just rock back and forth – like you did with me last night in bed."

"Are you kidding me? Here I am, a nervous wreck, and you're making a joke out of it?"

"Nina, what you identified in the diary's pages and your theory about a plane carrying art and gold is proven. It's a great accomplishment. Focus on celebrating! You've found the needle in the haystack. And now, the person who saw it happen has invited you to go with him. He said it's just a short ride. You can do this."

The grandson, standing nearby, saw the worry on Nina's face and approached them. "Do not be afraid, madame. Our camels are gentle and walk slowly. When we reach our destination, there will be a car, and I will take you back to the hotel."

"Nina, I'll go with you if you want," Brian offered.

She reconsidered and shook her head. "Never mind. That won't be necessary. I'll be alright."

"Okay, go with them. Find the answer. I'll see you back at the hotel when Abraham drops you off. I'll head back out front and let Erick and Solie know what's happening."

Still nervous and half-convinced of her decision, Nina turned to Ahmad and accepted his offer to ride with him. They all stood. Brian said goodbye and walked to the gate.

Nina reluctantly followed Ahmad and Abraham to a large corral, where a small herd of forty camels was held. The grandson continued walking to a small pen holding six camels. He swiftly saddled three mature piebald camels. Then, pulling one camel down to the ground, he knelt on one knee and offered his other knee as a step for Nina to mount the camel. She anxiously stepped on his knee and, reaching up, grabbed the front of the saddle, then swung her leg up and over and landed perfectly.

"Are you okay, madame?"

She nodded but wasn't. The smell of all the animals and manure was nauseating her.

"Hold the front bar as he rises. Then, hold the reins and pull back tightly. Let the camel know you're boss."

Oh God! Erick would love to have heard that!

Nina adjusted her bottom in the saddle and smiled at Abraham. Seeing she was set, Abraham gave a command, and the camel stood.

Nina let out a loud "Whoa!" as the camel took a step to steady itself. She thought of Brian. *I'll remember he made me do this.*

"Oh my God! Abraham, how long will this take?"

"Only ten minutes. Just rock with the camel. You'll be fine, madame."

Ahmad and Abraham mounted their camels in a flash, and their trek began. Brian and the others watched the three camels plod away from the pen at the rear of the house across the sandy ground. He saw Nina was uncomfortable, leaning from side to side.

I know she knows how to use her hips to rock back and forth. Doing it with the camel's gait should be easy. Geesh! I may never hear the end of this!

CHAPTER FORTY-TWO

Calling Pieter

After watching the trio ride slowly into the distance, Erick asked, "What's going on, Brian?"

"It's an interesting story. The lead seems legit so far. The old fellow at the house says he saw the plane crash and described it in detail. He says he was just a young teenager when it happened. He cited the date of the crash as being in late August of 1944. It fits with Nina's assumptions. I can tell he's trustworthy and has a good soul. Nina rode off with the old guy to get information about the plane's contents. The grandson who followed her to the hotel yesterday went along, and he'll drive her back to the hotel when they are done."

He looked at his watch. It was 11:30.

"We're done here. Let's head back to the hotel and keep our fingers crossed. Erick, try calling Pieter at the office on Solie's satellite phone."

Erick and Solie turned their car around and headed back. Brian followed.

While Solie drove, Erick made the call. After a few rings, Pieter answered.

"Van Deusen."

Erick knew from the slight echo he was on the speakerphone.

"Good morning, Pieter. It's Erick."

"Yes, I know your voice after all these years. How are things going there?"

"Good. Is Ursula there in the office with you?"

"Uh, no. She had an early appointment at the beauty parlor… but come to think of it, she should have been back by now. What do you need?"

"Hey, uh, sorry, Pieter, something's just come up. I'll call you back in twenty minutes."

Erick hung up and turned to Solie. "He said Ursula's out right now. I'll text him when we get closer to town and have him call back from outside the building."

The ride got quiet as Solie and Erick mulled all the possible permutations of what might be happening. As they approached the town, Erick saw the cell tower in the distance and hit <Send>.

Expecting a phone call, Pieter was surprised to receive Erick's text. He texted back, 'Need five minutes to finish updating the budget for Nina's case.' After printing it, Pieter put the finished spreadsheet on Ursula's desk, then left the office and headed down to the lobby. As he walked through the lobby doors, he wondered. *Where the heck is Ursula? No woman needs <u>that</u> much time at the beauty parlor!*

Outside, he called Erick. "Okay. I'm outside, as you requested. What's going on? And why the text when you said you'd call?"

"Pieter, what did you think of Nina's message?"

"What message?"

"The message she sent you."

"Sent me when?"

"Late yesterday. Ursula took Nina's phone call, which was intended for you. Ursula said you were out with some guests. Did she not give the message to you?"

Pieter ran a hand through his hair. "Uh, that visit… ended much later than expected. We were at a bar, and I took an Uber straight home. I was feeling under the weather, but Ursula never said anything about a message from Nina – not last night *or* when we got up this morning. And why are you drilling me?"

"You should ask her about the message. Or, better yet, confront her."

"What do you mean, 'confront'?"

Erick explained that Nina had called him to report the news of a new lead. "Her message, intended for you, said she was told by a man who saw the crash that the gold and art had been moved and hidden in Ksar Tamentit."

"Are you getting this?"

"Yes."

"But let me tell you what happened last night."

Erick revealed the arrival of two people at the hotel who Brian recognized and believed were spies and then mentioned their middle-of-the-night departure.

"Pieter, there's no way those two Russians could have known we were here in Settat last night – unless Ursula fed the information to someone on the outside. We've concluded Ursula is an FSB spy."

Pieter was quiet for a moment. *Ursula's been gone all morning, and I don't know why. He's right. It feels like something's up. But spy? Is it possible? I had my suspicions long ago when she worked for Klaus, but those concerns diminished when she began working for Wilhelm. What time is it anyway?* He looked at his watch. 11:36. *Where is she?* He didn't share the thoughts flashing through his brain, so he tried to sound surprised in his response.

"My God! I hope you're wrong, Erick, but I'll bring your concern to the attention of our security division immediately, and I'll check with IT. What's the team's next move? And why isn't Nina reporting this to me?"

Then, in his exuberance, Erick spilled the beans despite agreeing not to divulge details of their morning's activities. "Nina's with the person who says he witnessed the plane crash. They left for a short ride where he'll tell her the location of the art and gold."

"Erick, I thought you just said Nina left a message saying the gold and art are stashed in some Ksar. Yes, you said Ksar Tamentit."

Erick gulped, realizing his mistake. Then, feeling there was no reason to hold back from Pieter, he shared the concerns he'd discussed earlier with Solie. "Pieter, let me explain. Our team is concerned about the group of Russians Pattison said is flying to Casablanca and Marrakesh, which could be redirected here to Settat. It's where we are right now. If that happens, and if they learn where we are, we'll be outnumbered. We need more people here, and we need them here fast."

"Say again? How do you know the Russians are headed to those two cities?"

"Solie shared that a young American CIA agent is embedded in the group. It's a huge part of the reason Pattison approached you in the first place. Remember those satellite photos, all that radar stuff revealing the long airstrip and all the caves on the island? All that is what renewed the old post-World War Two rumor about hidden gold. The embedded agent gave the Agency insight into the Canary Islands case, but Bill chose not to tell you about the guy when he first brought the project to you. They've got their own issues because someone there in Langley has been passing our new satellite info to the FSB, and they've narrowed it down to inside a small think-tank group. That's why Pattison bailed on you and is back there now, keeping a close eye on how this develops."

"That's a lot of stuff, Erick. Is Solie sharing all that with you?"

"Yes, she's just like one of us."

"Regarding your position – and the possibility that Nina's lead yields information about the location of the art and gold – how many people do you need to support your efforts there?

"There's only the four of us right now. We thought we didn't need Amara's people, but now we may need another six to ten people and a truck if what we find is hard to move. Maybe more if this spy thing blows up in our face, and we need to secure our position to defend what we find."

"Let me see what I can do here, then I'll speak with Bill. It's almost noon. Let's talk again at two – sooner if something comes up."

As Erick hung up, Solie turned to him with a surprised look.

"Gosh! Erick! We agreed only ten minutes ago you wouldn't tell Pieter the details of what Nina was doing this morning or about the embedded CIA agent! And now, if Pieter is an FSB spy handling Ursula, we may have a much bigger problem."

"Sorry. I got carried away by the news and only realized my mistake as I was saying it."

"Well, one thing's certain from your mistake. Whatever happens next will determine if Pieter's involved with the FSB. I'll ask Pattison if the Russian group directed to Ksar Tamentit last night was redirected again. If that happens, then Pieter is the source of the leak."

CHAPTER FORTY-THREE

The Visit

Twenty miles southeast of Settat, after a twenty-minute camel ride, Nina, Ahmad, and Abraham arrived at a beige adobe house set on a small rise. An older woman sitting on her shady porch saw them coming. Recognizing Ahmad, she stood to greet them. As they approached, Abraham jumped from his camel and commanded Nina's camel to kneel. He helped her off, then took the camels to the pen in the rear of the house.

Nina and Ahmad followed the woman inside.

Samira, a few years younger than Ahmad, greeted her late husband's best friend with a customary kiss on each side of his face. Tears rolled down her cheeks. Seeing Ahmad always reminded her of her husband since they had grown up together.

In her local dialect, she asked Ahmad, "And who is this beautiful young woman?"

He replied in her dialect. She listened, smiled, and nodded. Then she led them into the kitchen. Ahmad took a chair and moved it against the long cupboard. Carefully, with one arm on the counter, he climbed onto the chair, and, standing erect, reached up to the top of the cabinet. Without seeing what he wanted, Ahmad reached, touched, and retrieved a scroll sitting in the open behind a dozen decorative teapots of all shapes and sizes. He slowly stepped down from the chair and unfurled the scroll on the table.

"Agent Nina, you have a good mind. Look carefully at what I'm about to show you on this map. The gold and art removed from the crashed plane were brought to my grandfather's house – the house where I now live. When my grandfather died, my uncle decided to keep the bounty covered in the camel pen for the next two years. During that time, my father, Youssef, commenced and completed the construction of a mosque."

Nina eyed him in surprise. "A mosque? Didn't you tell me your family is Jewish?"

"Yes, my grandfather, father, and I are Jewish. However, my mother – whom they called Sanam – was Muslim. My father was a wise man and, to make my mother happy, he built a mosque. But most importantly, the building became the hiding place for the plane's treasures.

"Now let me show you where it is on this map. Look. There is a town south of here called Ben Guerir. Do you see it? It's grown quite a bit since the war. West of Ben Guerir is a small village called Labrikiyéne. Construction began in December 1945 and was completed two years later. My father financed the project by melting a few gold bars, and local artisans – some of whom helped retrieve the bounty – created and sold jewelry. My father paid the artists for their work and used the profits for the materials and labor for the construction. The building has a regular first floor, a basement, and a secret lower level. My father's friends who constructed the building were all sworn to secrecy to never reveal anything about the lower level.

"In January 1948, several caravans moved the gold and art into the secret lower level down a long ramp. It begins at ground level and leads downward through a large set of double doors. The start of the ramp is hidden at ground level, buried under a pile of heavy rocks about twenty feet away from the building.

"There's a secret door on the first floor behind a wall panel. The panel opens to a door, which opens to an enclosed circular stairway. The stairway leads from the main floor down past the first basement level, ending in the secret lower level. The secret circular stairway is uniquely designed. Its diameter is small, and the diameter of the stairway gets smaller the further down you go. Only a tiny woman, less than one hundred twenty pounds, can fit into the circular stairwell and go all the way down to the bottom and exit into the secret lower level. For example, your agent friend, Brian, could get into the circular stairway, but after taking eight to ten steps down, the circular stairway's diameter gets smaller. At fourteen steps, his weight would trigger a trap with swords jutting out above his head. He would not be able to return up the steps to escape, and he would not be able to go down. He would die there in the stairwell.

"My goodness! That sounds dangerous!"

"Yes, my father wanted the treasure to be protected with virtually no access, with one exception. A small woman could descend the staircase and look at the treasure once a year. So, the only path to retrieve all the art and gold is to drive down the hidden ramp that begins outside. And its opening begins under several tons of rocks. A large machine must first lift the stones from the top of the ramp's opening before the treasure can be retrieved. Three statues of Moroccans sit atop the rock display. They will also need to be moved.

"Three years after the mosque's construction was completed in 1951, as the art and gold were finally moved into the secret basement, my father was shocked to learn the United States Strategic Air Command began constructing an air base and a very long runway several miles away in Ben Guerir. The base was for big American planes to carry nuclear bombs to Russia if another war broke out. The presence of the U.S. military made my father nervous when the flights began, but the basement and upper walls of our mosque never developed cracks. In 2005, the U.S. Air Force left the Ben Guerir base with the long runway, and today it's home to the Royal Moroccan Air Force, where three squadrons of Morocco's American-made jet fighters reside."

"That's a fascinating and impressive story. But you're saying the gold and art are still in the mosque's secret basement. Is that correct?"

"Yes. All the paintings are covered in canvases and sit atop wooden pallets in the dry basement beside the gold bars embossed with the Nazi emblem. As I said earlier, our family knew the gold and the art weren't ours to keep. My father said, 'Using some gold to construct the mosque will serve God, and we will protect what someday must be returned to its rightful owners.' Agent Nina, do you understand everything so far?"

"Absolutely. You've been very clear, Ahmad."

"Wait here a moment, and I'll bring you two keys. One gets you into the mosque; the second opens the steel door behind the wooden wall panel and provides access to the circular stairway. Remember, only a woman your size or even smaller should attempt to access the stairway of death."

Nina's eyes widened in alarm. "Is that what you call it?"

"Yes. It's what we call the circular stairway after my father and I found a decayed body trapped inside decades ago."

Oh my God! Riding a camel is one thing, but I will not be talked into going down that stairway!

"Now, Agent Nina, do you have the location committed to memory?"

"I do."

"And the warning? Is that committed to memory, too?"

She gave a solemn nod. "Yes."

"Good. Then I will be right back with the keys."

CHAPTER FORTY-FOUR

Dirk in IT

It was 11:48 a.m., and Pieter ventured upstairs. Amara was out to lunch, so Pieter left a message for him to call when he returned. Next, he went to see the IT manager.

Dirk was in and welcomed Pieter into his small office. But the director's rapid-fire queries felt more like fastballs and curve balls to the baseball-loving IT manager.

"Dirk, I was reviewing the budget earlier," Pieter began. "I saw a note that you recently issued new types of phones to the agents in the Art Research and Recovery unit, along with upgraded laptop computers. Is that true?"

"Yes, sir. After you got your new phone three weeks ago, Ursula gave me the paperwork authorizing another phone for herself. Then, when she came in for a lesson on how her new phone works, she ordered phones and new laptops for Nina's team."

"Who authorized that?"

"You did. She gave me the paperwork. It was your signature."

"Excuse me. You're saying that I authorized purchasing new phones and laptops?"

Dirk gave a cursory nod.

"When?"

"Last week, once it became evident Agent von Scholz was promoted to team leader, and we learned agents Schmidt and O'Sullivan were returning as well."

"And you're saying I signed the paperwork?"

"Yes, Pieter, It was your signature."

"Was it Ursula who brought to you what I signed?"

"Yes."

"Interesting. What else did I recently approve?"

"Well, a week ago, you re-authorized surveillance of Kristofer Bronn's antique shop in Leipzig. That authorization was due to expire, but she said you wanted it renewed."

"Go on. What else?"

"She said you approved enabling the tracking software on their new smartphones."

"And what does that do?"

"It makes it easy to see where the person using a phone is located by using a GPS signal. Up to now, we've needed to triangulate a cell phone's signal using three cell towers to locate people. With these new phones, a blue dot shows where the person is."

"A blue dot where?"

"The blue dot is on the phone."

Pieter pulled out his phone and turned it several times in his hand.

"Dirk, I'm not seeing any blue dots."

"Uh, let me explain."

"Please do."

"Here's how it works. When one phone links to another, the first phone can see where the other phone is located. It shows up as a blue dot on the first phone's screen. When the person carrying the phone moves from one location place to another, he or she can be followed."

"Interesting. And you're saying Ursula told you I asked to be linked to Nina, Brian, and Erick's phones so they could be tracked in the field?"

"Yes, exactly. She asked that they appear on her new phone as well."

"Do you know why?"

"Well, Pieter, you should know."

Pieter's brow furrowed in confusion. "Know what?"

"Ursula said you want the three of them surveilled because Agent

O'Sullivan is involved in criminal activity, and as part of the internal investigation, you need to track him at all times."

"She told you I said that?"

Dirk shrugged. "You signed the paperwork for all of it – their laptops and phones – and for me to turn on and set up the tracking feature. You also approved the overtime for Nicholas and me to do the tracking and report to Ursula daily."

"Hmm. Is there anything else I should know about all this tracking stuff?"

"I think Ursula forgot to get the information where I placed it for her to retrieve online. I sent it to her inbox last night. So I printed a new report on where O'Sullivan, Schmidt, and von Scholz are this morning."

Dirk reached for the report on his desk and handed it to Pieter.

"When you came in just now, I thought you were looking for the team members' locations. Ursula texted me early this morning for an update and a printout. She said she'd come by my office to pick it up this morning, but she hasn't yet." Dirk fumbled on his desk for more paperwork. "And, uh, here are the approvals you signed. I haven't filed them yet."

Dirk got quiet, sensing something was wrong. He began wondering and then watched as Pieter clenched his teeth, scowling as he paged through the approvals. Then, he saw each team member's location this morning. Pieter's body language revealed complete unawareness on his part. He knew nothing about what was happening. And Dirk, uncomfortable with the line of questioning, felt awkward and guilty.

"Dirk, let me ask you a few more questions. Does this report show my three agents are in Settat right now?"

Dirk nodded. "Yes. You can see their dots on the map. As I said, I printed that for Ursula; she wanted it from me this morning."

Pieter nodded, taking it all in. "Okay. Before you show me where Ursula is right now, is there anything else going on that I approved? Like anything else in the last month or two, we haven't just discussed that I should know, but perhaps I don't know about?

Dirk shifted uncomfortably from foot to foot. "Perhaps."

CHAPTER FORTY-FIVE

Access

On the drive back to the hotel, Brian stopped at a pharmacy, hoping to find something to relieve the indigestion bothering him after almost every meal lately.

When he returned to the hotel, he found Erick and Solie at the table in the far corner of the large dining room. He joined them and began to share Ahmad's story. Both expressed amazement as he described Ahmad's family history and his detailed description of the plane crash.

Upon learning the caravan story, how the camels carried and towed the gold on carts, and the sheer volume of the stolen goods, they agreed a large box truck or a small tractor-trailer would be needed to haul the hidden booty.

"Did you get any hints about where the bounty is located?"

"Not yet, but the old man said he'd give Nina the location, then drive her back here."

"Brian, I screwed up on the way back here. I called Pieter but I let it slip that Nina was with the man who saw the plane crash. I also told him we suspect that something's up with Ursula. He sounded surprised."

"Well, there's little doubt our office has been compromised," Erick said. "I suspect the Russians may be sending more agents here besides the two who arrived last night. We need more help as soon as possible. Solie, can you reach Pattison again?"

"I'll try him now."

When she got his voicemail, she left a message, only saying she called.

* * *

The meeting with Ahmad ended. Nina bowed slightly while thanking Samira for her hospitality. She thanked Ahmad for the bounty's location and keys. She promised to keep him informed and gave him a polite two-cheek kiss. She walked to the doorway and, looking back, saw them holding each other's hands. Nina said, "Shalom."

Nina climbed into Abraham's waiting car, and they headed to the hotel. Along the way, he suggested he drive her and the other agents to the mosque in Labrikiyéne.

She thought his assistance would be helpful, but she didn't want to commit to anything without consulting the others. He continued chatting with her, trying to convince her of his good intentions.

When they arrived, Nina asked Abraham to park and come inside before she closed the car door. It was a last-minute decision.

Nina waited for Abraham in the lobby. A shiver went up her spine. It felt odd knowing that only yesterday, she'd arrived in the same spot, hunted by a stranger, and now she was inviting him in. The shiver subsided as she and Abraham went to the dining room, where she spotted the others in the corner. They'd just begun eating lunch.

"Abraham, meet Erick and Solie. You already know Brian."

Brian stood to welcome the unexpected guest and shook his hand. He instinctively knew Nina must have had a plan for the young man to assist them in pursuing the treasure. "Come sit. We were discussing your ride into the desert and where it might lead us next."

"Abraham and I spoke on the way here. He's offered to go with us to the site," Nina explained. "He says it's just over an hour by car."

"And how long by camel?" Erick joked.

Ignoring him, Nina told the team briefly about her camel ride, then explained how they'd have to access the art and gold concealed in the lower basement of a mosque in a tiny village located further south called Labrikiyéne. Then Nina reached into her bra and pulled out two keys.

"This one gets us into the mosque. The other opens a steel door hidden behind a decorative wood panel. Behind the steel door is something terrible. It's a spiral staircase called the 'stairway of death.' It's a tight fit for a man who would get stuck as he descends narrowing stairs. Only a small woman has a chance to get to the bottom. What's worse is that after so many steps down, a man or a small woman carrying too much gold on the stairs will trigger a mechanism, causing swords to suddenly jut out across the stairs. The swords would prevent a return to the top, and he would be there for so long that the person eventually dies. He spoke of another, in his words, 'horrifying scenario' but stopped short of describing what could happen."

Ahmad also said the stairway's so small that we won't be able to bring any art back up.

Erick nearly choked on his food upon hearing the circular stairway's description and the swords trapping men and offering no exit.

Nina continued. "Access to the secret lower level is by a ramp from outside the building. Ahmad said, 'You'll need a backhoe to move rocks and a large trailer to haul away the goods."

Then Abraham spoke up. "Madame, a forklift will be necessary to move the gold sitting on pallets."

"Thanks, Abraham. Have you been in the lower level at some point?"

"Yes, Grandfather took me when I turned eight and twice after that. I still was small and skinny. But even then, I remember the staircase to the lower level was narrow. He asked me to retrieve one gold bar. A few years later, I could no longer go down those steps."

"So we'll need a truck?"

"Oh yes. A strong truck to carry what's there. Grandfather says gold is much heavier than it looks."

When Erick and Brian asked the teen more questions, he answered forthrightly, never hesitating. They all felt he was trustworthy and felt better about his being on the case with them.

Listening to the conversation, Solie sensed it was time to try Pattison again.

CHAPTER FORTY-SIX

Where is Ursula?

Pieter was annoyed at Dirk for the snippy answer. He shook his head. *"Perhaps? Perhaps what?"*

"I'm sorry, Pieter. I prefer to wait for Ursula to return, and she can answer your question."

What Dirk was referring to in response to Pieter's question was a situation several months earlier, when Wilhelm was still alive. Ursula had Dirk install an audio bug in the hotel suite assigned to visiting Interpol employees coming into town. She told Dirk it was due to Agent O'Sullivan's illegal activities, so he gave her the small recording device.

Unbeknownst to Dirk, Ursula, seeing how it was done, had returned to the hotel with Olga after Wilhelm died and placed several additional audio bugs in the same suite's bedroom. When Ursula and Pieter started sleeping with each other, they'd use the 'paid for' company suite. Olga would listen to recordings of Ursula asking Pieter questions beyond the scope of her day-to-day work. It gave Ursula a way of proving to Olga, her first-level handler, that she had successfully infiltrated Interpol. And Ursula knew how much Olga enjoyed listening to their playful romps in bed.

Pieter looked at his watch. It was noon. Now, he was angry at Ursula's absence.

"Dirk, before I leave, you said Ursula has one of those new smartphones, right?"

Dirk nodded. "I set it up and gave it to her."

"She turned in her old flip phone?"

"That's protocol."

"Can you tell me where she is? You know, can you show me where she is by using that little blue dot you told me about?"

"Give me your phone. I'll show you how to look."

"She's supposed to be at the beauty parlor, but she's over an hour late. *Much later than her regular ten to twenty minutes.*

Dirk grimaced. "Hmm. This is odd. The blue dot is on the highway heading east. Why would Ursula be heading toward Amsterdam? She was supposed to meet me here earlier."

* * *

Less than six miles away, Dmitri was driving east on the A-4 after completing their dastardly deed. Beside him, Katya recalled seeing Ursula's strangled body slumped while seated in the beauty parlor's chair. Then she replayed Olga, getting nasty with Dmitri, demanding he hurry to remove Ursula's body since another customer was due soon. Then Dmitri pulled his gun and shot Olga in the chest. Katya couldn't get over Olga's disbelieving look and horrified grimace as she fell backward against Ursula's legs and slumped to the floor like a limp ragdoll. Katya cringed at the memory. What a mess it was, with blood splattered everywhere! Katya had thrown up moments after seeing it happen, and then Dmitri began yelling that it was time to leave.

She then remembered grabbing Ursula and Olga's fancy pocketbooks as they left through the back door and throwing them into the car's back seat as they drove away. With that last thought in mind, Katya turned and, reaching back, grabbed the handles of the two pocketbooks. With a massive tug, she yanked them forward, clobbering Dimitri on the side of his head, badly slicing his flat, disfigured ear in the process.

"God damn it, woman. Can't you be more careful? My ear! Damn you – it's bleeding."

"You're such a jerk. That's her blood splattered on your face."

"No, it's not. Damn you, Katya. You just slashed my ear. Find a cloth of some kind. The blood is trickling down my neck. I need to stop the bleeding."

She reached into Olga's pocketbook, looking for a tissue. Instead, she pulled out an item she never expected to find. "Wow! Look at this! Olga must have been into pleasing herself. I never carry mine in my pocketbook. And look... a leather rope."

"She was a dominatrix."

"A what?"

"A dominatrix – someone who takes the lead in weird bondage sex with ropes and whips and crazy things like that. Katya, get me a rag or something for my ear."

"Well, that's not my style. Oh! Look at this. Ursula has, or should I say she had, one of those new fancy phones. Look at all these cute little pictures on the screen."

"Get rid of that," Dmitri ordered. "Throw it out the window."

Katya held it out of his grasp. "No! Let me try this little picture thingy. It says, 'Find Them.'" She watched the screen intently. "It's doing something. Wow! It looks like Ursula's boss is looking for her. And he's left her a text message. Ha! She's late, and he's wondering where she is. He doesn't know it, but he'll wait forever before she shows up!"

"Katya, I told you to toss that phone out the window. Do it now." He reached for the phone.

"No. I want to keep it."

"Damn it, Katya! Here, give me that ... let go of it, damn it, bitch! Let go!" He leaned his arm on her chest as he reached even further.

"Dimitri! You're hurting me. Dmitri, watch the ... No! Ahhh!!!"

Straining to reach across Katya to grab Ursula's cell phone from her hand, his left hand suddenly pulled on the steering wheel. The car, traveling at a high speed, jerked hard and veered off the highway, smashing head-on into a concrete overpass.

The impact snapped Dimitri's neck. He died instantly. Katya also suffered a broken neck and several broken ribs punctured and penetrated deeply into several internal organs, causing severe internal bleeding. She was bleeding severely and was barely alive, with only minutes or less to live.

Remarkably, while holding Ursula's phone during the crash, Katya's fingers inadvertently made a call.

* * *

Miles away in the IT office, the conversation with Pieter continued.

"Why is she on the highway heading to Amsterdam?"

Just then, Pieter's cell phone rang.

"Wow! What a coincidence, Pieter! She's calling you."

Pieter grabbed the phone, unintentionally hitting the speaker button. "Ursula, where in God's name are you, and what the hell is going on?"

"Help. Please help me. He's dead."

"Ursula? Ursula?"

"Help… me. Help…"

"Who is this?" Pieter demanded.

"Call Sokolov… tell Ivan I—" With her last breath, Katya died – still gripping Ursula's phone.

"Who is this? Are you okay? Hello? Are you there?" Pieter looked at Dirk, who seemed equally stunned by the exchange. "What the hell just happened? That wasn't Ursula calling, was it?"

"It was her phone, but the woman at the other end – she sounded Russian."

"And she was asking for—" *Oh God! She was asking for Ivan Sokolov.* Pieter gasped at hearing Sokolov's name. The bits and pieces of information he received in the last few hours suddenly connected like dots in a child's puzzle book, forming a picture. Pieter understood as his mind flashed back to a meeting at an art convention in Moscow years earlier – and it wasn't a good meeting. Suddenly realizing the depth and complexity of what was happening, he turned and left the room, heading back to his office and deciding what to do next.

Dirk was left wondering. *What is going on?*

* * *

Less than an hour passed when authorities called the Russian embassy in The Hague, advising them of the crash on a nearby highway and the deaths of two Russian nationals. Within minutes, a Russian fixing team responded to the scene. It was the same two comrades who, thirty minutes earlier, cleaned the mess at the beauty parlor and set it ablaze. When they arrived, a tow truck was still present, and the two bodies found in the car crash were just being moved to the morgue. The local Dutch authorities on the scene handed over three pocketbooks and four cell phones. One phone was reported to have been found by the first responders gripped so tightly in the hand of the deceased woman that all her fingers needed to be forced open to release the device from her hand.

The fixing team returned to the embassy, bringing the blood-covered purses and phones. Once inside, they went to Sokolov, who was waiting in his highly decorated office, sporting several masterpieces, including a famous Caravaggio, missing and unaccounted for since WWII. "Well?"

"As we suspected, it was Dmitri and Katya. Both were killed instantly."

They dumped the contents of three pocketbooks onto a table.

"Ivan, we think Katya grabbed Olga and Ursula's purses as she and Dmitri left the beauty parlor earlier. The police were curious. I lied, saying that two women had left their pocketbooks at a party at the embassy last night and were being returned to them by the couple in the car."

"Ha! Look at this! No doubt it was Olga's. She loved to tie people up," Sokolov said with a barking laugh. He picked up the new-style cell phone. "Who did this belong to?"

"We think it was Ursula's. We were told it was in Katya's hand when they hit the wall. They had to pry it from her fingers."

"I like this. It feels better than my Blackberry. The glass has a little crack but looks like it's working."

"There's a new feature in that phone. It lets you know where your friends are."

"How is that?"

Sokolov got the same lesson, almost word for word, as Pieter had gotten from Dirk an hour earlier and two miles away.

"Hmm. So, if this is Ursula's phone, is it linked to anyone else in her office? Do you know how to check?"

"I toyed with it on the way back. Look here. I think it is Ursula's phone, and it's been linked to three, uh, no, four other phones. Do you see the blue dots?"

"Yes. You said a moment ago that the blue dots are people. Right?"

"Well, the dots are other phones, and we would assume each person is carrying a phone."

"Can you tell who they are? Or, better yet, *can you tell me where* they are?"

"We already checked that. Ursula is linked to a phone in The Hague and to three phones in Morocco right now."

"Incredible! Uh, don't tell me – let me guess. Are they in Settat?"

"How did you know?"

Sokolov smirked. "I'm always a step ahead. It's why I'm the boss. Can you tell me where in Settat?"

"It looks like they're in the center of town – someplace on the main street."

"Are names associated with the blue dots?"

Yes. One for each dot. Von Scholz, Schmidt and O'Sullivan."

Sokolov rubbed his chin and quickly assessed the situation. *Hmm. O'Sullivan is in the field and in the middle of things again. Years ago, I had a perfect arrangement with Klaus and Paolo. It was good for them and good for me. But Wilhelm and O'Sullivan messed things up. I know exactly what to do. And that other fellow. I remember him.*

"Okay. Giorgi, call downstairs and have them get the embassy's chopper ready. We need to get to Schiphol immediately. Call and charter a private jet from Schiphol to Settat. Have them file a flight plan to take off at 2:25. Yuri, pack three automatic rifles, protective vests, and night-vision goggles from the safe room. We might be seeing a little action. And while you're both getting things ready, I need to make a call. We have a bus full of cadets posing as archeology students heading in the wrong direction to an ancient oasis. They need to turn around and head to Settat. My watch says 1:28. I'll see you both downstairs in ten minutes. Bring Ursula's phone with you. And did you see a charger for her phone in her pocketbook? We're going to need that."

"Do you want anyone else to join us? Perhaps one or two marksmen from the embassy's swat team?"

"I don't think so. Now hurry."

<u>**CHAPTER FORTY-SEVEN**</u>

Solie Calls Pattison

Solie stepped away from the table and called Pattison again. It was 1:40 in Settat and morning in Virginia. Pattison was drying off from his morning shower when his phone rang.

"Good morning, Bill. I can confirm that the Interpol team's leader, Nina von Scholz, and Brian O'Sullivan met this morning with an elderly man who claims he witnessed a German Junker go down in late August 1944. The individual was a youngster who, at the time, was traveling from his grandfather's house in Settat to his home in Marrakesh.

"He cited extensive details about the event, likely a Junker 290 plane crash landing on a narrow desert road. He mentioned Nazi officers being on the plane, then being picked up and flown away in small prop planes. He said the gold and art were moved to the sub-basement of a mosque, which remains locked up tight in a small town due west of Ben Guerir.

"Bill, we'll need the air transport from Malaga you mentioned down here in Ben Guerir. We'll also require a large forklift to move rocks from a hidden entrance. Are things set with the Moroccan Royal Air Force base commander?"

"I can get a C-5 Galaxy from Malaga into Ben Guerir overnight tonight. Its nose folds down and opens wide enough for a tractor-trailer to drive into the fuselage. Don't worry about the weight. I spoke to the base commander at Ben Guerir and gave him a general overview of what's been happening. I said we'd be moving a few art pieces and returning them to folks in Amsterdam. He says he's happy to assist with the retrieval efforts if needed. I already told him we'd need a forklift to move a pallet or two. If you say rocks need to be lifted, I'll need to get back to him on the size of the forklift. When we spoke, I didn't mention the gold. Oh, and I've alerted our ambassador to Morocco and given him deeper insight into the case. I think we're good, but it could get dicey if local politicians show up and see us pulling gold from the basement. I'm not sure taking a bunch of gold bars from their country will go over very well."

"Bring a lot of tarps to use as covers," Solie advised. "And it'll probably be far more than a pallet or two. The older man couldn't remember how many there were, but I understand the gold is sitting on a *lot* of pallets."

"I'll have a team of fully armed agents on the plane to help. They'll arrive overnight at the base and can be at your location by seven tomorrow morning. You should arrive by five and send us the building's GPS coordinates. I want your group to hold off going to that mosque today. There's no need to expose the location or stir up any locals. Just keep it all under wraps until early tomorrow.

"Oh, Solie, one other thing. I just got a quick blip from our agent embedded with the Belarus cadets. Five minutes ago, the bus that left Marrakesh this morning for Ksar Tamentit stopped after driving several hours into the Algerian desert and turned around. Our guy said it was now heading toward Settat. We have no idea how that bus loaded with cadets would know to stop and start heading back toward your position. Information about your Interpol team's location is being leaked over there. Watch your back. One of them isn't legit."

"Thanks, Bill. Later."

Solie left the conversation feeling uneasy. She knew telling the others they needed to sit tight and wait until tomorrow morning wouldn't go well. She was also concerned about a leak and returned to the table, wearing a frown.

"Why the gloomy face?"

"I have information to share. Please don't take this the wrong way, but we need to stand down until morning. Pattison told me the CIA is overnighting a big transport with a CIA team to help us move everything, and he's arranged for heavy equipment to move the stones covering the access. I have to agree because if what Ahmad told you is accurate, there's no way we can remove what we find in the lower level."

Recognizing the logic, and wanting to sway a negative response from Erick, Nina responded first. "I agree. What Bill said sounds like a good plan. Have you heard anything about the group headed to Ksar Tamentit? God willing, they're still driving in the wrong direction."

Solie hedged. "Well, here's where it gets sticky."

Nina paled. "What do you mean?"

"Pattison told me the bus just stopped ten minutes ago. Our embedded agent said it was turning around and heading to Settat."

"Oh my God," she gasped. "If they find us, we'll be outnumbered."

"You're overthinking this, Nina," Erick said. "What can a bunch of kids on a bus do?"

"We don't know the background of these so-called Russian students. We only have a problem if they're all from a military academy."

Solie sheepishly spoke up.

"Pattison just shared they are."

"Are what?"

"They're cadets, first-year plebes from a military academy in Belarus. It's like West Point. That's how our agent infiltrated the group."

"Damn it! This is crap," Erick barked. His eyes narrowed as he grimaced in worry. "We should have known what we were up against sooner. Solie, what's happening with the CIA that we only got part of the story?"

Nina intervened. "Erick, please. It's not her fault. Sorry, Solie."

Solie shrugged. "I'm sorry, too. I didn't know they were military until a few minutes ago."

"Let's think for a moment," Brian suggested. "According to Abraham, the mosque is over an hour away. But since he's with us and offered to help, I think we should go there now and scope out the town and the mosque."

A discussion ensued.

Nina took a sheet of paper and drew a line down the center of the page. "Let's do a 'Ben Franklin.' Reasons to leave now on the left and wait until morning on the right."

Erick smirked at the suggestion. "Let's *not* do a silly Ben whatever. Let's just go. We'll look and not go in. Then we'll come back and get a good night's sleep. Is that okay for you, BJ?"

Bria held off responding.

So Erick continued bolstering his position in favor of going. "While we're there, we can make sure the front door key works. It'd be pretty awkward if we arrived in the morning and couldn't even get in. Is everyone okay with that?"

"That's not a bad approach," Brian conceded with a sigh. "And Erick does have a point about making sure we can get in."

Nina, looking for consensus, turned to Solie. "How about you? You haven't said anything."

"I can go along with a quick stop to check the door key. But we shouldn't linger for more than a few minutes. We certainly don't want to draw a crowd. I'll let Pattison know we'll be scoping out the town and checking the key to the mosque."

"Nina, should you be calling Pieter to let him know?" Erick asked. "Or Amara?"

She referred the question to Brian. "What do you think?"

He shrugged. "Calling either of them right now does nothing for us with this decision. Let's go and make it a quick visit like we just agreed. We'll let young Abraham try the key on the door to make sure it works. He's dressed like a local.

"Pattison asked me to get the mosque's geo-coordinates," Solie added. "We can do it while we're there."

Nina stood. "Okay. It's 1:45. Let's meet back here at two. Erick, keep Abraham with you 'til we leave."

"Okay, boss."

Fifteen minutes later, Nina's team and Abraham were in the two rental cars, heading toward Ben Guerir and Labrikiyéne's mosque.

* * *

At Amsterdam's Schiphol airport, Ivan Sokolov was arriving with his posse by helicopter. It set down twenty yards from the private Lear jet. A quarter mile away, armed airport guards waved the Russian embassy's bulletproof BMW X-7 with darkened windows and diplomat plates through the security gate and sped toward the private jet. The timing of its arrival was perfect as it pulled up just beside the plane and Sokolov, standing on the tarmac.

Ivan made two brief calls as his posse moved several bags from the helicopter and BMW onto the plane.

Standing beside the jet's stairway, with one hand on the handrail Sokolov, he removed his sunglasses and called out to Giorgi and Yuri, who had just finished loading the bags.

"Come take another look at Ursula's phone. Can you tell me now what's happening?"

"Ivan, see those blue dots. They're moving. They're heading south from Settat."

Sokolov nodded. "Interesting."

"Ivan, do you want me to get a map?"

"No need. Giorgi, tell the pilot we need to revise our flight plan. Instead of landing in Settat, we need to fly to Marrakesh. Yuri, get our Russian embassy in Rabat on the phone. Tell them I'm coming to Marrakesh by private jet. We'll arrive in under three hours, and I'll need a full-size SUV to meet us at the airport. And now, before we take off, I need to call that damn bus again and get them headed to Marrakesh, not Settat."

He made the call, and as he finished, Giorgi approached him. "Ivan, the pilot says he'll need ten minutes to revise the flight. I told him that was okay."

Sokolov gave the closest he could to a smile. "Well done, Giorgi. You and Yuri will get a Red Star when we return for today's clean-up and for finding that phone with the blue dots."

Ivan was walking up the stairway when his phone rang.

CHAPTER FORTY-EIGHT

Pieter's Call

After finishing with Dirk, Pieter returned to his office, overwhelmed. So much was in flux, along with all his other Interpol responsibilities. It was now 2:20. Ursula's lengthy absence verified what he feared most – that she was a spy. With his suspicions confirmed, he knew it was time. He didn't expect he'd ever have to do this. Taking a deep breath and reached for his Rolodex. His mind mumbled as he flipped through the lettered indices: *M, N, O, P, Q, R.* Then, arriving at S, he picked at individual cards: *Santorella, Scata, Schierenbeck, Sclafani, Semler, Smith, Sniffin. Here it is.*

He picked up his phone and made the call. The ringtone sounded different.

"*Dah.*"

"Is this Ivan Sokolov?"

"*Dah.*"

"Ivan, it's Pieter Van Deusen."

Sudden recognition. "Ah, yes! Pieter, the art lover with Interpol. It's been a long time."

"Eleven years," Pieter acknowledged.

"How can I help you, or should I ask, how can I possibly help Interpol?"

"I'll get right to the point. You've been meddling in our work. You need to back off."

"Oh my. Pieter, is that what this call is about?"

"That's half of it."

"And the other half?"

"You know what I mean. You have plenty to do in your Russian sandbox. Make sure you stay there, we agreed when we spoke eleven years ago."

"Pieter, Pieter! You sound upset – as if your toes have been stepped on. Is that it?"

"You're on thin ice, Sokolov. Get your ass back to Moscow and St. Petersburg. You have enough stolen World War Two-era art sitting in your basements to fit out all the yachts of your corrupt oligarchs and still have paintings and sculptures to sell to the Saudis and Chinese."

"You're sounding upset, Pieter. Oh! Are you missing someone? Ah! Yes! That must be why you're upset! You're missing Ursula, aren't you? Your warm sex kitten has left your bed. Ha, ha! Don't plan on seeing her anytime soon." Ivan snorted an evil laugh. "I need to fly, Pieter Van Deusen. Goodbye."

Pieter slammed down the phone's handset, even more upset now, knowing he'd probably never see Ursula again. *That bastard should rot in hell. Only the devil knows what he's done to her.*

Considering his next steps, Pieter left his office and returned to IT. As he entered the doorway, he watched Dirk, who was overweight, devouring a sandwich at his desk. He watched as he picked a piece of tomato and a glob of mayonnaise from the front of his shirt and stuck it in his mouth. Pieter held back and watched Dirk lick his fingers clean and then take a lick at the fabric. Pieter rolled his eyes in disgust, pretending and wishing he hadn't seen that, then gave a slight cough to announce his presence.

"Dirk, I need you to show me how to locate Nina and her team again."

Dirk put aside what remained of his lunch. "Sure."

He thoroughly licked his fingers and, after wiping them on his shirt, began looking. "They're still in Settat. No. Wait. Hmm. It looks like they're moving."

"Which way?"

"South."

"Thanks. I'll take it from here. A few more things: Stop surveilling Kristofer Bronn's shop, sweep my apartment for bugs, and sweep the hotel suite where guests stay. Let me know if you find anything."

"Got it."

"I'm going to Amara's office to review a few things. I'll be there if you need me."

* * *

South of Settat, Nina's team was finally on its way, heading to the mosque, but was still within cell range. Brian's phone rang. Not expecting a call, he managed to steer with one hand, and answered the call with the other.

"*Pronto, pronto! Professore* O'Sullivan?"

"Yes, uh, *Si.*"

"*Questo è Monsignore Borrelli. Monsignore Borrelli in Vaticano.*"

"*Ciao!* What can I do for you, Monsignor?"

"*Professore,* uh, please excuse my poor English. I will go slow. I have *importante e interessante* news about the scrolls you brought here. We have – how you say? – done tests. We have found the scrolls, uh, authentic. Yes. This is good. This is very good!"

"*Fantastico! Grazie, Monsignore!* Thank you so much."

"Uh, yes, and now you must return to the Vatican. You must sign papers, release papers. When, uh, how soon can you return?"

Brian's brow furrowed. "I already signed everything you gave me to sign."

"*Professore* O'Sullivan, let me speak slow – that was before we knew the scrolls were authentic. Padre Grajales and Padre Fioretti, our scientists in the *laboratorio del Vaticano* – uh, they are ready to move forward. The scrolls now must be, how you say, unfurled and read. When can you be here?"

"I can't promise a specific date, Monsignor, but hopefully soon. Let me call you back in a few days. *Va bene?*"

"*Si. Grazie!* Please. Soon. Very soon. *Ciao, professore!*"

He ended the call and shook his head.

Nina turned to him. "Was that the priest at the Vatican?"

Brian nodded.

"What does he want?"

Before answering, and despite the air conditioning being on full blast, Brian suddenly felt a sensation of warm stuffiness. He opened his window for some fresh air and a breeze.

"He wants me back at the Vatican. The scrolls we found in Katrina's basement are age-authentic, and now he needs me to sign papers permitting the Vatican's lab to take that next step of unfurling and reading them."

Nina's eyes widened. "Wow! If the scrolls are real, I bet they're worth a fortune."

"Yes, but they'll be donated to the Church."

"That's very generous of you, Brian. By the way, you mentioned at dinner the other night your twin sisters' birthdays were coming up. Did you remember to call them yesterday or at least text them when you were in Rome?"

Brian shook his head. "No. With everything going on, it slipped my mind. I need to be better."

"You really should, Brian. You need to stay in touch with them. Just leave a simple voicemail. How about Shawn? Have you called her?"

"No."

"And when you stopped in Malta, did you remember to leave money at your mother's house – the money you promised Carlo? It's been months since he's been paid."

His shoulders slumped. "No. I forgot that, too."

"And Massimo. Did you—"

"Nina, please stop! Not now. I'm not feeling well."

Brian had begun feeling dizzy and nauseous, even before Nina's interrogation. Her line of questions felt like a throwback to old times with Grace from years earlier. It made him feel worse and caused his blood pressure to rise. He pulled off to the side of the road, turned off the ignition, and opened his door. He just sat for a moment, his head in his hands against the steering wheel.

Following in the car behind them with Solie and Abraham, Erick pulled alongside and rolled down their window. "BJ, is everything alright?

"It's my heart. It's racing again, and I'm dizzy. It's the damn A-fib thing. My mind and my feelings are overloaded, and I have a monster headache. I'm anxious and feeling sick to my stomach. I need a minute to pause, breathe, and pray a Hail Mary. If I do that, most times I can get my heartbeat to slow down and get back to a normal rhythm."

Getting out of the car, Solie and Erick approached Nina and called her aside.

"Is he alright? BJ looks as pale as a ghost."

"He just had a call, and then I asked him some questions. I think I upset him, and he said he didn't feel good after that."

They stood motionless as Brian took a short walk. The sunshine was bright; its intense heat made them all uncomfortable. Still in the car, Abraham wondered what was happening.

Brian returned with a small smile and looked relieved. "Sorry, guys. I'm feeling better. Erick, you, Nina, and Abraham should be the lead car when we leave since he knows his way to the mosque. Pick his brain about the surroundings as we get closer to town. Solie and I will follow you three."

Erick nodded. "Sure. Makes sense."

Concerned about her lover's condition, Nina was hurt by Brian's suggestion of riding with Solie. She realized how she asked her questions bothered him. *He's still delicate. I have to be careful.*

They had just resumed driving when a call came in on Solie's satellite phone. Solie, driving to give Brian a break, asked him to accept the call. He did and handed her the phone.

"I have a couple of updates for you, Solie. The transport plane in Malaga will be delayed a day. I was originally told it was available and ready to go anytime. But they're doing maintenance on a flight-control module. It's a four-hour fix, but then the plane needs to be test-flown for safety, so it becomes a twenty-four-hour delay. Instead of arriving early tomorrow, it'll be the next morning. That shouldn't cause any issues there. Right?"

"It shouldn't, but the Interpol team is anxious, and they've decided to ride down to the little town where the mosque is. I'm along for the ride, so we stay together as a group. They want to scope out the location and get a general view of where everything is supposed to be stashed. Plus, they want to make sure the key to the front door works." She paused. "You said you had updates – plural. What else have you got?"

"The group on the bus. They've stopped for fuel and were told they're now heading to Marrakesh. Our guy says they'll arrive late afternoon or early this evening."

"Got it. Thanks, Bill. We'll talk again later."

She disconnected from the call.

"Pattison, right?" Brian asked.

Solie nodded, remaining intent on following Erick. "The plane out of Malaga has been delayed twenty-four hours for a repair."

Just then, Brian's phone rang.

"Brian, it's Van Deusen."

"Hi, Pieter, what's going on?"

"A lot. Brian, I need to tell you… the phones…"

"Pieter, you're breaking up…"

"… track you, and she…"

"Hello, Pieter… Pieter?"

"Bri— … can you … me…"

The call dropped. Brian hung up and turned to Solie. "We're too far south. I've lost the connection to the cell tower in Settat."

"Do you want to use the satellite phone?"

"No, but thank you. He'll leave a voice message or try again later."

Brian sat back, glad he'd let Solie drive. He closed his eyes, and as his anxiety slipped away, his heart finally settled into its proper rhythm.

Their fifty-plus-mile drive along the N9 route south continued with more traffic than usual. They encountered road construction every ten miles, which backed up traffic at least two miles each time. Nevertheless, they continued, and as they were twenty miles north of Ben Guerir, traffic ground to a complete halt. While they waited, Abraham told Erick and Nina the town's main intersection was ahead. It'd be where they'd turn west onto a small highway called Route 2101 and travel another eight miles to Labrikiyéne. There, they'd turn north for a mile and see the mosque.

It was 3:45, and they should have been in Ben Guerir already, but now their arrival time was anyone's guess, given the roadwork. A few more minutes passed when Abraham asked if they could stop soon so he could use the bathroom. He told them an American hamburger restaurant – 'the one with yellow arches' – was just ahead.

Erick and Nina understood and smiled, hearing his request.

Another fifteen minutes passed when they finally caught sight of the arches. Erick pulled into the parking lot. Brian and Solie followed. The women left the cars in a flash and ran inside; Abraham followed.

* * *

In The Hague, Pieter arrived at the open door to the regional manager's office and found Amara on the phone. Acknowledging his presence, Amara waved him in and pointed to a chair, but Pieter remained standing.

When Amara finished the call, Pieter began sharing the sequence of events of the last few days while pacing back and forth across the room. But Pieter withheld the odd phone call he received from the Russian woman speaking broken English and that he called Sokolov.

"Here's the bottom line: Ursula's been missing all morning. But worse, Erick called earlier, saying their team believes she could be an FSB spy."

Amara frowned at hearing the FSB might have penetrated their offices in The Hague. "What do you need, Pieter? Felix and Ladasha were headed to Casablanca to support canvassing the area. But now that Nina and her team have a lead, I can redirect them to Settat."

Pieter nodded. "Get them to Settat as soon as possible. They'll be needed."

"Anything else?"

"Not right now."

Pieter returned to his office, looking at his phone again to see the blue dots. This time, he noticed they'd moved further south toward Ben Guerir. He suddenly remembered the Russian woman's voice, and it dawned on him! *Ursula's phone could be in the hands of the FSB. Maybe the team is being tracked right now!*

He tried again to call all three to warn them, but each of his calls went right to voicemail.

CHAPTER FORTY-NINE

The Burger Stop

Oleg Grechko, whose parents were post-WWII Ukrainian immigrants to New York City, grew up just off Ocean Terrace, a wealthy area on Staten Island. Interested in law enforcement, he graduated from John Jay College with a double major in forensic psychology and criminology. He went on to earn a master's degree in criminal justice from St. John's University.

Six months before 'Ollie' graduated *summa cum laude*, he applied for work with the FBI. His professor, a former FBI agent, suggested that his English, Russian, and Ukrainian language abilities would make him valuable to the Agency. Little did Ollie know his linguistic skills would soon vault his application past the FBI and directly into the CIA.

After graduation, thorough vetting, and two years of special-agent training, Ollie found himself in Ukraine with recently issued papers supporting his new foreign identity. Not long afterward, he was repositioned into eastern Belarus and was accepted as an engineering student at Minsk Higher Military Engineering School, a division of the Military Academy of the Republic of Belarus.

During his spy activities at the Minsk academy, he regularly provided insight into activities to his upline supervisor, Bill Pattison. Ollie had been in place six months when a Russian spy deep within Langley leaked images from the new American satellites to his FSB handlers. That leak stirred up old rumors of gold stashed in Grand Canary Island's caves. The belief reached a crescendo among senior FSB agents, who'd heard similar stories from now-retired, post-WWII 'cold-war' supervisors.

Within weeks, the FSB requested a cohort of first-year cadets from Minsk Military Engineering School to search the hills and caves of the Canary Islands. Ollie was among the two dozen students selected.

It also turned out that this entire Grand Canary Islands case, on which Pattison sought Pieter Van Deusen's help, was for Pattison to secure insight into the source of the leak within Langley. He was, without doubt, far more interested in the spying issue inside his house than concerns of following an old WWII rumor. Thus, it became the thrust of his effort to recruit Van Deusen's Interpol team and let them do the groundwork and hopefully reveal the in-house FSB spy.

Late in the afternoon, the bus filled with cadets headed back toward Marrakesh. Their rumblings and growls on the bus had reached a peak of frustration as the cadets grew hot, thirsty, and hungry, feeling as if they were being driven all over the place without purpose. Overhearing the complaints of those seated behind him, the bus driver decided to defuse the situation. Familiar with the area they were approaching, he called out to them to quiet down and be patient, promising a surprise with a stop in the next few minutes in the next small town.

* * *

As Nina and Solie left the ladies' room, they spotted Abraham and Erick waiting in line for burgers and went over to join them. It made them both laugh, and Erick saw them snickering and giggling like a couple of schoolgirls.

"Hey, I'm treating the kid, and it's been a while since I've had a burger," he said. "You two want anything? A milkshake or an iced tea?"

Nina smiled. "I'd love a soft ice cream cone. Vanilla, please."

"I'll have an iced tea," Solie said.

Brian was already at a table when the women came over to join him. "We're way behind schedule," he grumbled. "This was supposed to be a quick visit, but at this pace, we won't get back to our hotel in Settat until after dark, especially with all that construction traffic we just went through."

Nina, still uncomfortable, excused herself to return to the ladies' room. As she left the table, a large bus pulled up outside. Within moments, the restaurant's front door flew open, and two dozen young men in camo-colored khakis and various branded tee shirts pushed each other, rushing to the counter to order food, drinks, and ice cream.

Just then, Solie's phone rang. "It's Pattison. I need to take this outside."

Erick and Abraham, carrying their orders on trays, barely escaped the mob's rush as they returned to sit with Brian.

With a mouthful of partially chewed burger, Erick asked, "Are you seeing this?"

Brian nodded. "Yep."

"Is it possible? Could it be them?"

"Sure looks that way."

"Did you catch the school name on some of their t-shirts?

Brian nodded with raised eyebrows while Erick shoved the rest of the burger in his mouth, chewed, and swallowed. "Wow! So it is."

Abraham spoke up. "What are you talking about?"

Erick and Brian exchanged a look.

"C'mon, when you finish up, we'll tell you outside," Brian told him. "You guys ready?"

"Nina's still in the bathroom. I hope she's okay. Maybe you should send Solie in to check on her."

Minutes later, when they stepped outside, Solie finished her call with Pattison and turned to Brian and Erick.

"It's them. They're the students who were searching Grand Canary Island. Pattison said the one wearing the navy-blue baseball cap with the 'NY' logo is our guy."

"Did you see him inside?"

Solie nodded. "I did. The logo's what caught my eye."

"Did he see you?"

She shrugged. "He looked our way but didn't acknowledge me in any way."

"Can you please go back inside and check on Nina?" Brian asked. "She might not be feeling well."

"Of course. I'll be right back. Pattison said he'd send him a signal saying we're here."

The group of cadets was making Erick uncomfortable. He nudged up beside Brian and whispered, "It's unbelievable, BJ. The coincidence of their arrival at this burger place with us here… well, it's just spooky. It's what happens in books and movies, but not in real life."

"It's indeed a twist of fate. My sister Shawn calls events like this 'divine appointments.' She says God and the angels steer us into these situations more than we think."

"Look, they're starting to come back out," Erick said. "There's a guy with a blue cap and an NY on it. I think he might see us."

Brian's mouth tightened into a thin line. "Well, don't make any gestures toward him. His cap's the wrong shade of blue. Another kid's coming out now, walking behind Solie and Nina."

Brian shook his head. "Erick, we're seeing military students from Belarus wearing Yankee and Met hats at a hamburger joint in Morocco! My nieces and nephews would be laughing, saying that it was crazy.

The students remained inside the restaurant while Nina and Solie rejoined the guys.

Brian asked Nina, "Are you okay?"

"Yeah. Just some discomfort. I'm feeling better now. We should get going to the mosque. Let's travel again in the cars as we were. Erick and I'll lead the way with Abraham's guidance."

Solie whispered to the three, "Pattison just told me these kids have just been redirected to Marrakesh. It gets them further away from us for now."

"Thank goodness."

The cadet with the white NY logo on his hat approached them. He purposely bumped into Nina, thinking it was Solie. Trying to protect her, Erick pushed him. The guy in the NY cap pushed back, cursing at him in Russian as Erick shoved him again.

"Brian, please break it up," Nina implored.

A few cadets came over and broke up the skirmish.

Solie said to Brian, "That's our guy."

"How do you know?"

"Besides his NY logo hat, his navy blue shirt has the number seven on the back. I'm not sure what that means, but he told Pattison days ago what he'd be wearing if we came across him in the caves."

With the skirmish petered out, the cadets returned to their bus and boarded. As they did, Ollie looked back and winked at Nina and Solie. Then, as the bus lumbered from the parking lot, he smiled and gave a thumbs-up to the girls through the window.

They watched as the bus left Ben Guerir and headed due south toward Marrakesh.

Brian looked at his watch. It was already 5:15. They'd stayed in the restaurant longer than he expected. He knew there'd be plenty of daylight because it was summertime, but he again worried about how late it might be before they'd arrive back in Settat.

The art-recovery team's cars turned onto a small westbound highway. Young Abraham rode in the lead vehicle again. The ride to Labrikiyéne was another eight miles.

Brian thought again about meeting up with the military students.

What the heck is keeping them on our trail? I'll have to tell Shawn it sure as hell didn't seem like a divine appointment, crossing paths with a bus loaded with military adversaries. And those two FSB agents who were in the hotel that night. I'm still finding it hard to believe Ursula's a spy. But she didn't know about Moneypenny. Hmm.

CHAPTER FIFTY

The Mosque

Growth in and around Ben Guerir since the 1990s had been strong, and the community was finally catching up with infrastructure improvements. Construction of widened lanes and the installation of new communications lines and new cell towers were underway along every major road leading into and out of town. As a result, what should have been an easy final eight miles turned out to be more stop-and-go traffic as they continued to move at a snail's pace.

The team arrived on the edge of Labrikiyéne at 6:35. The town was more like a tiny village. Abraham sat up straighter as they neared the mosque and told Erick and Nina he used to play soccer with some of the boys in the village on prior visits with his grandfather.

Although Nina had the street map in mind, Abraham's directions to the mosque were perfect, and he guided them to make the final left- and right-hand turns. Upon making the last turn, they saw the building ahead of them. Unlike more decorative mosques, this building was plain-looking. Its exterior walls were about twenty feet tall and had a beige stucco exterior, which was typical for the region. Lacking very tall minarets, Youssef's mosque design featured only one modest-looking minaret standing twice as tall as the building itself. By contrast, the vast Hassan II Mosque, built in Casablanca in 1993, boasted a sixty-story tall minaret.

They pulled up outside and parked near several statues adjacent to and atop a pile of rocks. As they exited the cars, they stood momentarily, taking in their surroundings before heading to the front door of the building.

As Nina reached into her bra for the key, Brian whispered a suggestion. With a nod, she handed the key to Abraham, who took it and let them in.

It was dark inside. Their eyes slowly adjusted to the dark interior. They looked around and saw rows of vertical columns and horizontal beams supporting the mosque's flat roof over the prayer hall.

Brian turned to Nina. "Look familiar?"

"Oh my God, Brian, yes. It's similar," recalling the ornate interior of the Mezquita mosque in Cordoba, where they discovered paintings' hiding place earlier this year.

As they looked around, admiring the mosque's interior, Abraham disappeared. Moments later, a small group of lights turned on, and he proudly returned to the group. "Madame, I'm happy to let you see how beautiful the inside is."

"Thank you!"

Eyes adjusted to the scanty few lights, they admired the artisans' work as they walked around, looking at the interior and its sixteen-foot-high ceiling.

Brian watched Erick's curious look as he scanned the interior.

"This is a hypostyle mosque," he explained. "It's an Arabian style. The rows of vertical support beams create that wide, open prayer hall where the faithful gather to kneel toward Mecca."

"It's beautiful," Erick acknowledged as he panned the ceiling and other integrated designs.

"You weren't with us back in Cordoba when we found the two paintings von Richter hid inside the mosque called the Mezquita. It had eight hundred fifty-six columns of polished marble, granite, and jasper columns — holding up the flat roof. By comparison, I count sixty-four columns holding up the flat roof in this mosque. And these columns are stacked concrete blocks covered in stucco, just like the building's exterior walls."

Erick nodded. "The woodcarvings and stucco moldings are impressive designs, but the colorful and intricate Moroccan zellij tile work covering the entire floor is outstanding – and certainly unexpected for what seems to be a low-budget building. But it's awfully quiet in here. I'd even say it's spooky."

"Of course you would," Nina quipped. Then she turned to Abraham.

"Do you know where the panel is, the one with the door behind it?"

"Yes, madame, it's someplace over there against that wall."

They walked to a forty-foot-long side wall with eight-foot-high panels running the entire length. Each panel was made of plain lauan wood, showing little grain. Its simplicity makes it attractive and effectively contrasts the stylistic Arabic drawings and paintings above them depicting Moorish horseshoe arches and columns.

"It's one of these, madame. I don't remember which one."

Abraham slowly walked along the wall with both hands pressed against the panels. He was trying to recall and retrace his childhood steps, but to the team, it looked like he was trying to feel the wall's heartbeat. Then he stopped. "Here. I think it's this one."

"How do we open it, Abraham?"

"I'll show you. Watch, it's easy."

Abraham pushed hard against the panel. The 'touch release lock' used in many cabinets popped open, and the half-inch thick plywood panel swung wide open, revealing the solid steel door behind it.

"Wow! Look at that! Congratulations, boss."

"We're far from being done here."

"Nina, give me the other key."

She again reached for it in her bra and handed it to Brian. He inserted it, turned it, and heard the lock click. He turned the doorknob, and the door opened.

Brian and Erick leaned forward and, shoulder to shoulder, peered in. Despite the dark, they could make out a small platform and the steps of the circular stairway. The steps were expanded steel grates welded to a vertical, center metal column. A chain-link fence wrapped around tightly, forming the exterior wall of the staircase.

They looked up and saw the circular staircase's round frame rising to the flat roof above, but no stairs were going upward. A small glass dome at the top admitted a small amount of light – just enough to let them barely see it was there.

As their eyes adjusted, they peered further down the circular staircase, but the darkness hindered their view, and they couldn't see the bottom.

"Maybe it's an optical illusion," Erick observed, "but I'm not seeing any indication the staircase's diameter gets any smaller from where we are standing right now."

"I agree, but we don't want to try it. Ahmad said this staircase was built with a spring-loaded trap with swords of some sort. The last thing we need to do is to test if he was telling us the truth."

"Anyway, we've done more than just the drive-by we originally planned. We know where the mosque is, the keys work, and we found the rock pile topped with the statues. And that all sits above the opening of the lower level's exit ramp. So we need to head back to Settat and wait until backup arrives from Malaga."

Solie spoke up. "Did you hear that?"

"What?"

"Shh! I think someone's at the front door."

Now, the noise was more noticeable. Solie and Nina drew their handguns and moved into kneeling positions while Brian and Erick moved behind the stucco columns. The silhouettes of two figures emerged from the dark.

Solie and Nina were ready.

CHAPTER FIFTY-ONE

Intruders

The front area of the mosque, where the team had entered, was still dark. The two figures moved slowly in unison as fear gripped the entire team. Then, suddenly, the intruders came into view.

"Don't shoot! Don't shoot, madame!" Abraham shouted. "Those are my old friends from childhood, the ones I used to play soccer with when I came here with my grandfather. I told you about them on the way here."

The women stood down. "Okay, everyone," Nina said, "it's okay. We can relax."

Nina and Solie holstered their guns as Abraham spoke with his friends.

They asked him who the people were and what they were doing there.

Ahmad had drilled into his grandson never to speak of the lower basement or anything in it, so Abraham said the people were friends of his grandfather who were visiting and wanted to see the mosque. Then he went outside with them, where they were joined by a third friend who was afraid to enter the mosque and found him holding a soccer ball. The teens began kicking the ball around, as they had years earlier during Abraham's last visit.

Brian and the women began discussing the ride back, anticipating hitting traffic again. They wondered if there was a better way to return. Erick closed the circular stairway door and attempted to close the wood panel by pushing it shut. But as often as he tried to get the latch to catch and remain closed, it wouldn't. He'd made several failed attempts before

Brian, smiling at his effort, came over to help. He gently touched it, and it closed.

As the latch clicked shut, Nina suddenly let out a huge scream that echoed through the prayer hall!

Two hooded men in black, wearing protective gear and wielding automatic rifles, had entered the front door. They held Abraham and another boy by their arms and other hands and pointed the weapons at the team. The two other boys, further away from the building while playing with Abraham escaped capture and ran back into their neighborhood.

Ivan Sokolov remained in the back of the SUV, listening to music while his men handled the dirty work inside. While he waited, he picked up Ursula's phone and laughed as he looked at the blue dots. *Such amazing technology!*

Inside the prayer hall, the two hooded men made their way slowly toward the team.

"What do you want?" Erick asked nervously.

The taller man responded with a strong Russian accent. "No stupid questions. You know what we want. It is why we are here. No one will get hurt. First, of course, we must tie you up. Then you tell us where the prize is, and we let you live. So, all of you, get down on the floor."

They began to tie-wrap hands and feet. Standing beside the women, Brian whispered, "Whatever's down there is not worth our lives."

One Russian approached and shoved Brian. "You. Be quiet! Stop talking with pretty women. You tell us where prize is. Otherwise, you remain quiet."

Brian responded, "I know where the prize is. Let the boys and the others go, and I'll show you where to go."

The gunman thought for a moment.

"*Nyet!* Not you. The woman, the pretty one with long hair, will help us. She knows where prize is. She will show us."

Then Solie took a bold, brave step. "No, not her. I'll show you where to go. I'll bring you there myself."

Brian looked at Nina. She nodded. Brian nodded back. *Solie's the best choice.*

Nina leaned over toward Solie. "Here's the key."

"*Dah!* Over there, little woman. Rest of you – stay down!"

While one Russian kept his gun pointed at them, the other finished securing the agents' and teens' hands behind their backs with long zip ties. He pushed Brian and Erick together, back to back. Using duct tape, he wrapped it around both their chests. Then he zip-tied their ankles and secured duct tape over their mouths, from ear to ear. He was gentler with Nina. After zip-tying her hands and feet, he left her sitting alone.

Then he told the boys to lie down. He wrapped zip ties around their ankles and hands, then wrapped several rounds of duct tape around their knees. "No running away like friends outside. Now, brave little lady with short hair, show us the prize we've come for."

Solie walked slowly to the wall and, like Abraham, gingerly pressed on a few panels.

"What are you doing?"

Then, as the Russian asked his question, the wall panel popped open. When she pulled on its edge, it swung open on its hidden hinges, revealing the steel door.

The two Russians smiled. One laughed. "Yuri, on American television, there is a show. You guess door, and you win prize. Now, I guess. I guess door number one."

Giorgi wasn't laughing. Solie took the key from her pocket and opened the steel door. "The prize is down there," she said. "Go down the stairs. What you want is at the bottom."

"*Nyet,* little lady. You show us the way. You go first."

Solie was nervous but remembered what Nina told her Ahmad said about the stairway. She prayed that she could make it down the circular stairway, given her slight frame and weight. She looked back at the team. Nina looked at her and nodded. She tentatively stepped into the dark stairwell – her eyes adjusting to the dark as she gingerly took each step.

Yuri followed first, stepping into the circular stairway, and Giorgi trailed. After nine steps down, Yuri began feeling the need to hold his weapon close to his body. After another two steps, he told Giorgi to do the same. She continued down, and as Yuri and Giorgi continued a few more steps, they began struggling.

"Giorgi, it's tight down here. I'm getting stuck."

"You must keep going down, Yuri. Follow the woman." Giorgi, the bigger, heavier comrade, then stepped on Yuri's head.

"I can't, Giorgi. Listen to me. I'm telling you, I can't go any further."

"You must, Yuri. Keep going."

Solie continued moving slowly ahead of them, and then, in what seemed impossible, Yuri caught a glimpse of her slipping further down the metal steps.

"She's moving, but I can't. I'm— I'm stuck."

"Yuri, keep pushing, keep pushing down."

In a last-ditch effort, Yuri twisted his body and took another step. His weight triggered a latch and sprang the two swords several feet above him. Meant to cross above and trap him from returning up the stairs, one sword hit Giorgi's head, the point driving hard directly into the side of his skull. The other sliced through his jugular and larynx. The blood gushed, and his body immediately slumped.

"God damn it! Giorgi, get your fucking foot off my head! We must go back up."

Yuri waited for a response when suddenly a shot rang out, echoing loudly in the small stairwell. Then another shot. And another, and another. Then there was silence.

CIA Agent Solie Van de Berg's four shots, taken straight up from the floor of the dark lower level, hit both men squarely under their body armor. Yuri was hit in the foot and torso. With his good foot, he struggled to step up. Suddenly, another spring-loaded trap Ahmad had failed to warn about sprang. It slashed through Yuri's thigh, causing him to bleed out immediately. Solie's return path was blocked.

Meanwhile, Nina, Brian, Erick, Abraham, and his friend were wiggling about like worms on the prayer hall's beautiful tile floor, hoping to free themselves when they heard the shots.

Nina, who managed to loosen the duct tape on her mouth, turned to Brian and Erick. "That's how my gun sounds. I think she's okay but may be stuck at the bottom."

They all continued to wiggle, attempting to free themselves. Nina, who kept a six-inch knife strapped to her ankle, told Abraham and his friend to try and work his way over to her. It wasn't easy, but he finally made it. He rolled his back to her leg, pulled the knife, and managed to cut the zip tie around her ankles, and then, wiggling some more, he cut the zip tie around her wrists. Once Nina was free, she stood and walked to Brian and Erick.

Outside, Sokolov looked at his watch. It was 8:31 and getting dark. He wondered about the progress his fixers were making inside. He told the driver to wait as he stepped from the SUV. He looked around, saw no one, then walked to the mosque's front door with his automatic rifle. The boys who had run off continued to watch and whispered to each other from hiding spots in the distance. "Something bad will happen if he goes inside."

Sokolov slowly opened the door and listened. He heard the team's chatter as they feverishly tried to unbind themselves. As he made his way in, he saw Nina bend over and begin to cut the duct tape binding Brian and Erick while Abraham and his friend unwrapped themselves. He laughed to himself, seeing them in various positions on the ground.

Assessing the situation, he straightened and walked toward them, training the AR on the group. "Well, well. Good evening, all of you Interpol art lovers."

Nina turned, startled by this new gun-wielding intruder. Brian and Erick were shocked at Sokolov's sudden appearance. Nina stepped behind Brian while his mind flashed to the recent drive-by in the Hague. *Jesus! It was him. How in God's name is he here now, following me again?*

"Ah! Professor O'Sullivan. Has it really been twenty years? And look who else is here! Sweet Mr. Schmidt… do you remember me winking at you at the art show?"

Sokolov continued pointing the automatic rifle as he circled them.

"And I presume this is the young lady who's your new team leader,

Miss Nina von Scholz. Am I correct?"

Nina cringed that he knew who she was.

Irritated by his comment to Nina, Brian asked, "What do you want, Sokolov?"

"You know exactly what I want, professor. I'm here for the prize. But I would be remiss if I didn't take this moment to congratulate your very attractive Ms. von Scholz on her brilliant discovery work. Young lady, you've done what hundreds failed to do for decades. I believe you've solved a seventy-year-old mystery."

Nina eyed him with contempt.

"Ha! And now, what do we have here? I see an open door, and I presume my men are downstairs, assessing the prize. But before I check on their work, I am compelled to tell you how effective Tamara Ehrlich – whom all of you knew as Ursula Bloom – was for our cause. Over the past dozen years, Tamara's given the KGB and the FSB insight into dozens of cases that helped Mother Russia advance itself. And for me, Tamara and your former associates, Paolo Luzzi and Klaus Mueller, helped put a lot of money in my pocket and my friend Vlad's pocket.

"And professor, speaking of Luzzi, he was my friend. He lost his life trying to keep you from stealing the money that rightfully belonged to him. I also have some bad news about your little old friend in Leipzig. I've been advised Kristofer Bronn was unwilling to help me gain access to your Swiss account. But I have other plans for that.

The team was shocked at Sokolov's deep tentacles in their art-recovery team.

Despite Nina's attempts to be brave as he continued, she couldn't help but cry.

Sokolov tauntingly wiped a tear from her cheek. "Now, now, young lady. You're so sweet… and, I must say, quite beautiful and voluptuous. Ursula shared that you and the professor here have something going on. Yes, there's very little I don't know. But soon, I will have the professor's money, and he will be useless to you. You will simply put him out of your life. You'll be free to find a younger man your age – to raise your child. Yes, as I said, Ursula had eyes and ears in many places. She even tracked your visits to your doctors, not only for the injury to your leg but to the doctor who confirmed your pregnancy. Ursula reviewed and approved payments for all those doctor visits you made using the socialized medicine programs.

"One more comment. I'm surprised to see you alive, Schmidt. You were left for dead on the road to Malaga. I don't know how you survived, but you did. But now is a different story." Sokolov offered them a sneering smile. "But before I say goodbye to Schmidt and the professor, I want to see the prize we've all been waiting for."

CHAPTER FIFTY-TWO

The Climb

Minutes earlier, in the lower-level basement, Solie searched for a way out. She moved slowly in the dark, and with a hint of light coming down the stairwell shaft, her eyes caught a glimpse of the pallets stacked with gold bullion and crates covered with tarps. She was amazed the treasure sat there before her. *It's real!*

She continued looking for an escape passage. She turned back to the circular stairway and noticed tiny pieces of metal, like miniature steps, welded to the exterior of the stairway's fence-like frame. Looking more carefully, she realized she could climb her way back up to the top, but it would have to be done on what was now nothing more than a circular metal cage with dead bodies trapped inside.

Unaware Sokolov had entered the building, she placed a foot on the first piece of metal and reached up to grab the second. Then, stepping and pulling herself up, she grabbed another piece of metal and again pulled herself up. She repeated this and continued upward, carefully keeping her grip and footing on the pieces of angle iron meant for such a climb. It was slow going. She feared a slip would send her plunging backward to the concrete floor below. Nevertheless, she continued and was only one more reach-and-pull-and-step from reaching the main level, where she'd entered ten minutes earlier.

As Solie arrived, she held on tightly and looked for a way to get back inside the circular staircase cage and exit through the steel door to the prayer hall.

Just then, she heard talking outside. And then a creaking sound. The steel door was opening. Solie suddenly found herself face-to-face with an older man sporting a white van dyke. The light directly behind him mostly obscured her vision, but she saw him reaching to lift a gun. Terrified, while holding on to the cage tightly with one hand, she reached for her holstered gun with the other.

Solie yanked it out quickly, pointed, and fired. The metal cage deflected the first bullet from its mark. But she then intuitively shoved her gun's muzzle through the opening of the cage's wire frame and took the second shot. The bullet hit Sokolov above his heart and below his shoulder, knocking him backward. He landed on his back on the floor. The bullet pierced the top of his lung and made a clean exit. Solie attempted a third shot, but her clip was empty.

Despite his severe wound, Sokolov struggled to right himself. Hardly balanced, he was about to lift the weapon again when he collapsed, again falling backward to the floor into his pool of blood.

Brian freed himself from the restraints after Solie's second shot put Sokolov on the floor. He ran to grab Nina's gun, earlier kicked to the side and ran toward Sokolov. He was aiming and about to shoot Sokolov in the back when he again fell to the floor. Brian kicked the rifle to the side, out of Sokolov's reach, then bending over, pressed Nina's handgun to Sokolov's chest. Brian saw Sokolov struggling with his breathing and blood spreading across the floor.

"The easy way out of this mess for a bastard like you, Sokolov, is for me to kill you right now. But I'm not going to let that happen. You're going to come with us. You'll be turned over to the CIA, and you'll have a taste of the American justice system."

A few feet away, Nina's emotions were in shambles. Several months pregnant, her hormones were raging, and she burst into tears.

Erick was equally distraught from the extreme tension of the last thirty minutes. But this was no time for crying. "Erick, get it together!" Brian shouted at him. "I think the bullet went right through him. We need to plug the wounds in his chest so he can breathe. Grab something, anything."

Nearby, the two boys were wide-eyed at what they'd just witnessed. Free of his restraints, Abraham went to the lighting panel to turn on more lights. One of the switches illuminated the entire stairwell and the circular stairway. As they all turned, they saw and understood Solie's predicament.

"Hey, everyone! I need your help. My fingers are tired of holding on to this wire cage, and my feet are killing me. I need to find a way to get back in there before I slip and fall two floors to the concrete floor down below."

Erick tore his shirt, made two small plugs of cloth, and, with Brian's help, rolled Sokolov onto his stomach and stuffed one into the bloody bullet wound. They rolled him back over again, and Brian pushed the other into the hole at the top of his chest to halt the bleeding.

"Nina, watch that he doesn't try to get up again," Brian directed.

He and Erick walked to the stairway to help Solie, still holding onto the wire of the caged circular stairway. Erick expressed gratitude for her bravery – and her sharpshooting skills.

"Erick, you can thank me afterward. Brian, with the light on, I see two hinges and what seems to be the outline of a door. It's five feet further up from where I'm standing now. It looks like it'll swing open and allow me to climb back in."

"We see it. It'll take a bit of acrobatics because the door is small. But you shouldn't have any problem."

Solie took a deep breath. "I'm ready to try."

She carefully navigated the additional short climb up the cage's exterior, opened the metal door and, contorting her body, made her way through. Then, with nothing to aid her, she gripped the wire with her fingers, pushed the tips of her shoes into the openings in the wire cage, and gingerly climbed down. As she reached the landing, her fingers raw, blistered, and bloody, she was greeted with hugs from Erick.

Brian returned to assist Nina. Sokolov seemed to be breathing better, but he lay in a pool of blood.

Outside, members of the tiny community had gathered at the front door. They had heard the shots, and the boys who had run away gave everyone an insight into 'bad men and good people' inside the mosque. The SUV that had brought Sokolov and his fixers was long gone.

Several local men entered to see what had happened. They were greeted by Abraham and his friend, who quickly explained the tragic scene. One man, seeing Sokolov in a pool of blood, offered to help. He said he was a doctor who worked at the small hospital in Ben Guerir and offered to stabilize him temporarily. He made a call and was told a well-equipped ambulance with a team of EMTs would arrive at the mosque within fifteen minutes.

After resting briefly, Solie went to the car and called Pattison using her satellite phone. She gave him a thirty-second briefing on what happened. He promised to send an entire team by 6 in the morning to retrieve the two bodies, clean the floor, and extract the gold and art from the lower level. Solie returned inside and told Brian the plan for the morning.

A few minutes later, the team gathered and discussed their return to Settat. In less than a minute, they agreed that with Sokolov's life-or-death situation, returning to Ben Guerir was the better choice. They decided to wait for the ambulance and follow it to the hospital.

Minutes later, the ambulance arrived, and the EMTs went to work on Sokolov. Several tense minutes later, they indicated the patient would survive. As they prepared to move Sokolov, Brian locked the steel door and closed the luan panel. With both keys in hand, he asked Abraham to shut off the lights. As they left the building, he let Abraham lock the door to the mosque.

CHAPTER FIFTY-THREE

The Cavalry

Later that night, as the team and Abraham sat together in the hospital's cafeteria, Solie made a lengthy call to Bill Pattison. This time, she told him where they were and shared more details of their harrowing experience.

Amazed to hear more details of the confrontation, he congratulated her for her bravery. Pattison told her that based on her earlier call, he requisitioned a different transport plane for them. Ironically, it had just made a stop on Grand Canary Island. He rerouted it to Ben Guerir, and it would arrive within the hour. The CIA agents he intended to send from Malaga were on their way in a Gulfstream G550, due to land at the Ben Guerir airbase at 2 a.m. He told her he'd found the coordinates for the mosque in Labrikiyéne on an internal Company website, and a team of agents and all necessary equipment to move the rocks and secure the bounty would arrive there at 6 a.m.

Pattison went on to share that Ollie had messaged, saying, "Arrived in Marrakesh then sent back to Ben Guerir. Now waiting on what to do and where to go next. It seems we have suddenly lost our purpose, but the hamburgers are good."

Solie laughed heartily at that comment.

"I called and spoke with Van Deusen after you called. We discussed many things," Pattison continued. "Pieter was quite distraught. He said he'd begun to suspect something was up with Ursula when her behavior at the office grew erratic. But he couldn't accept she was an undercover FSB spy and would do what she'd done. I could tell he was nearly in tears as we spoke. He also told me he called Sokolov just yesterday and told him to back off, but I guess he didn't."

"Guy should have taken Pieter's advice," Solie remarked.

"Seriously. Then he said he tried reaching O'Sullivan, but the call went dead. He tried calling Erick and Nina several times. He wanted to tell them their positions had been compromised because the cell phones they had recently been given were giving away their locations."

"How?"

"He said Ursula had their IT manager link all their phones to hers and Pieter's. But when Ursula never returned to the office, Pieter figured Ursula had given her phone to someone working for Sokolov."

"Nina told me the team's phone batteries are all dead. It's a pain, but I'm sure glad I carry extra batteries."

Solie told him about seeing the gold and the art. "Bill, it's incredible. The room where everything is being held looks like a separate bunker, built off to the side, adjacent to the mosque's foundation. The stairway was the only connection between them. I could see the gold bars were stacked perfectly on a dozen pallets in two rows. We'll need a good-sized double-axle box truck to carry what's there. There might be fifty art pieces sitting together under tarps on another four or five pallets; we'll need a lighter truck for that."

Pattison jotted notes as Solie spoke.

"I'm amazed how all of it's been hidden there all these years. I didn't tell you before, but Nina said the man who witnessed the crash told her his family was Jewish, and they were sympathetic to the plight the Jews faced during the war. They felt obliged to see the gold and art returned to their rightful owners."

"Jewish, and they built a mosque?"

"Yes."

"Interesting. So, what's next on the agenda down there?"

"We're at the hospital. Sokolov lost a lot of blood, but he's stable. We zip-tied his feet and arms to the bed's side rails. I'll stay here overnight with O'Sullivan and Schmidt to guard him. We'll take turns watching him overnight. We chuckled among ourselves earlier as we tied him to the bed. Ironically, his guys used the same long black zip ties on us. The hospital has a huge stash of them for unruly patients. Even the ambulance carries them.”

“When the first CIA team lands at 2 a.m., two of them will go directly to the hospital to relieve all of you.”

“Thanks. Erick and I will guard him until then. Nina needs sleep. She was offered – and accepted – a bed in an unused room. Brian will sleep here, too. He and I will go back to the mosque, meet the moving team, and oversee the process of getting everything out. I believe the CIA will control the gold, but we’re leaving it up to the Interpol team to decide how they want to handle the art. Is that how it’s been agreed to with Pieter?”

“Yes. That’s exactly what he and I discussed.”

“Then we need to deal with Sokolov.”

“Sokolov will be flown to Langley or Guantanamo to be interrogated after the CIA takes over tomorrow. I think we unexpectedly caught a big FSB fish in this case. The White House may want to hear about it. His immediate move Stateside tops our “To Do” list. Solie, what will you do once everything’s been moved?”

“We still have the old man’s grandson with us. He’s asleep now as well. We need to get him back to his grandfather’s in the morning. I can use your help since the CIA will have more people here come morning.”

“I’ll call Pieter after this and fill him in, but we can handle the kid. What else? Or what’s next after that?”

“Well, shouldn’t I be asking you, Bill, ‘What’s next for me?’”

“I want you to take a month off, Solie. Head back to your place in Amsterdam to rest. If you need a vacation, go. You’re off the hook for now. I don’t need to hear from you again for – uh, let’s make it six weeks. How’s that sound?”

“Good, maybe even boring. Did you ever figure out anything about the leak in Langley?”

“We did. It’s been fixed. You can stop worrying about that.”

"Okay. I'll fly back to Amsterdam with the others and let you know what I decide."

"I've told Pieter that you and the other will use the jet the Malaga team flew down in to return to Schiphol. Thanks, Solie, great job. I'll see you get a salary bump for your good work on this."

"That's always nice to hear!"

Solie headed back inside. She shared with Brian and Erick everything that Pieter told Pattison, including how their phones were used to track them from place to place. They agreed with Solie's plans to remove the treasures the next morning and thanked her for taking leadership. They all felt immensely relieved by the CIA's involvement.

"Solie, I never knew the kind little woman who lived next door to me was so brave," Erick said admiringly. "At one point tonight, I thought we all were going to die. But you saved us. You didn't know what lay in front of you as you headed down those stairs. I'm tearing up thinking about what you did. You are an incredible woman!"

He paused to brush away the mist from his eyes while collecting his thoughts. "I've been thinking. After these last two cases, I don't know if I can stand this drama anymore. I think I'll leave this art-recovery business and work as a florist or something equally safe. And while I'm thinking about it, can I have Leo back?"

Solie grinned. "Of course, Erick. But remember, Leo is a girl cat, and her new name is Bashful."

Erick hugged his friend. "Thank you. Thank you so much."

Exhausted physically and emotionally, Brian went to the room where Nina was lying down.

She heard the door open and saw him silhouetted in the light from the hall. He crossed the room and went to sit on the bed.

"Remember last night when those two FSB agents left the hotel in the middle of the night?" Nina asked. "When Erick came to tell us, and I told you I felt the baby move? After that moment, I felt different about my job. Can we do something about that?"

Brian nodded, though she couldn't see him in the darkened room. "We can look into it. I'm obliged for another two years, but with the unusual circumstances surrounding our unit – especially with Ursula being a spy – they might want to disband us."

Sitting up, Nina sighed. "I hope so."

Brian slid an arm around her. "There are still a few things I need to deal with – the scrolls in the Vatican and Massimo's missing art."

With her eyes closed, she looked toward the sound of his voice and then hesitated, not sure how he would react to her following question. "Sorry to ask, but you never told me if you sent the money to Massimo."

"I did. After I visited Monsignor Borrelli at the Vatican, I stopped in the law office in Rome, scratched out a letter, got it notarized, and sent it to my sisters. In it, I gave my two brothers-in-law, who manage money for a living, full access to my Swiss account with authorization to move the money to the U.S. and invest it as they saw fit. I also directed them to send two million to Massimo if he would sign a Promissory note the law firm drafted for me. The loan would be forgiven if we found the art he intended to sell me or gave me a registered first-purchase option on his home. The loan's value will be applied to the price of his house if he decides to sell it. So, my dear Nina, please stop thinking and now go to sleep. We can go over it again in the morning if necessary."

Not getting a response, he looked at Nina and saw she was sound asleep. Getting to his feet, he gently laid her against the pillow. Adjusting the covers over her, he kissed her and tiptoed from the room.

CHAPTER FIFTY-FOUR

Elsa's Visit

The extraction of the gold and art was completed the next morning before nine o'clock. The CIA team used borrowed forklifts to move and then reposition the stones and statues just as they had been for the last sixty-plus years. The truck carried everything back to the Ben Guerir Air Force Base. The gold was driven on a truck into the open nose of the Galaxy while the crates of art were loaded on a smaller transport and flown back to Amsterdam. Six CIA agents accompanied gold, and two accompanied the art. Sokolov was flown along with the shipment of gold to Langley Air Force Base in Hampton, Virginia. He rode in the back of the plane on a gurney, ironically, just feet away from swastika-embossed gold bullion worth over six hundred million dollars.

Upon returning to Amsterdam, Nina and Brian took two weeks off to adjust to their new lives as a couple deeply in love. They took long walks in Vondelpark and felt fulfilled living together. With the baby coming, Nina couldn't be happier. And Brian – living his new chapter as Massimo suggested – felt lucky to have made it past his antagonist and the anxious moments he caused.

In those two weeks, since they were back, Pieter Van Deusen never came to visit them, and the two conversations Pieter and Nina shared were vastly different from their prior talks. His strong authoritarian tone had diminished, and his approach softened. He seemed much less controlling than just weeks earlier. In one call, Pieter said both she and Brian could have their employment contracts voided. It was their choice. Only a letter stating their wishes to leave was required for each.

Then, a week ago, while Brian was away, Dirk called Nina to share the gossip about the in-house announcement. Pieter Van Deusen was retiring. Dirk also said Pieter was emotionally crushed by Ursula's betrayal and her apparent but unconfirmed death. Everyone in the Agency throughout Europe who knew Pieter and Ursula understood the impact of what had happened.

Brian had flown to Rome to meet again with the Fellini law firm to finalize some financial plans and his will. Then, he went to the Vatican to meet with Monsignor Borrelli and sign papers authorizing the lab to continue its work. When he arrived, the monsignor confessed that, in his excitement, he'd already approved the lab to proceed. Despite hearing what he had done in the first uneasy moments, the meeting was terrific as the monsignor reported that after the lab had unfurled the two scrolls – one parchment and the other leather – the scientists could read them. Both were written in Greek.

The scrolls, it turned out, appeared to be a letter from St. Paul to Timothy and the Ephesians – the early Christians who lived in Ephesus – the abandoned ancient city south of Izmir, Turkey. This letter by Paul had never been seen before, and the document had been sent to scholars in the Vatican Library for an official review. It mentioned how Mary, the mother of Jesus, had moved to a small house in a community just south of Ephesus. Monsignor Borrelli also said the cup that Brian brought to the Vatican had been carbon date tested and fell in line with being made from materials found around Jerusalem sometime between one and 10 A.D. So, as the note found inside the cup implied, it might have been used at the Last Supper, but there was no way to confirm it.

Brian was pleased with what he had learned, then returned to the Fellini law firm, this time near their office close to Ciampino airport. He sat for two hours reviewing his holdings – the houses Luca initially owned and those acquired by the youngest Fellini attorney, the family real estate investor. Then, he signed the will they prepared for him.

As Brian left their office, he felt good except for one open situation. For that, he bypassed Pieter, now a short-timer with Interpol, and called Bill Pattison, having been given the number by Solie.

Pattison took the call right away and was able to share that the CIA, in cooperation with Interpol, implemented a sting operation in Malta a day earlier. Sebi, the local who supported FSB activities in Malta and who served several other capos there – including Knights of Malta's Grand Master Tony Costa, had been captured while sunning himself on the roof of his home near the airport. The Templar knight's armor, sword, tunic, and flag, once hidden in the hillside at the DiBotticino family quarry, were finally delivered to the Order of the Knights of Malta, and the promises made by Luca Luciano were finally honored.

However, Pattison said, the CIA couldn't give him any news on Massimo's missing art. Bill speculated it had already been dispersed among several oligarchs and was on display in the living rooms of their super yachts. He said the Agency would keep this situation open.

Brian returned to Amsterdam the following day. On his way home, he considered leaving the agency to enjoy his life with Nina. She was such a loving young woman; he felt blessed. He wondered about being a father and raising a child. Would they remain in the Netherlands? Would they move to New Jersey, where his sisters lived? He wondered about a hobby. Painting? More art research? Would spending time again as an adjunct art history professor at a major university be the path? Or would he relive the stories and write about the many adventures of his career in a memoir?

A thought occurred to him. *Maybe it would be easier to change Erick's mind about working as a florist assembling wreaths, and we could re-engage in our detective work looking for lost and stolen WWII art. After all, except for the recent murders and killings in the last year, researching lost art was, well... fun.*

He arrived at Nina's house just before noon. After putting his travel bag and clothing away, he returned downstairs. After hugs and kisses, Nina reminded him that his half-sister, Elsa, who was Karl von Richter and Sweet Hilda's daughter, would be visiting today. She asked him to run to the local Albert Heijn grocery store to pick up a short list of items. He was happy to run the errand and enjoyed the short walk through the neighborhood.

Shortly after 11, Elsa arrived in town from Leipzig by train. After a long walk to the front of Amsterdam's central train station, she took an Uber to Nina's house. The ride was only about twenty minutes, but when she arrived, she felt exhausted from her long train trip, which had begun at dawn. She felt anxious as she knocked at the front door, not knowing exactly how the visit would go.

"Welcome, Elsa!" Nina greeted her. "Here, let me take your bag. I'm so glad you accepted our invitation to stay the night. Follow me to the guest room. Brian's so excited about meeting you! He's at the store now but will be right back. Would you like to freshen up?"

"*Bitte,* uh, please, *und danke.*"

"*Gern geschehen.*"

Nina showed Elsa to the guest bathroom, then returned to the kitchen to boil a pot of water. She put out a plate of the iced ricotta cookies she had learned to make because she knew they were Brian's favorite.

When Elsa returned a few minutes later, Nina offered her tea. "Do you have a preference?"

"Earl Grey, please, if you have it."

"I do, and I have enough to make a pot for both of us."

Minutes later, the two women carried their teacups into the living room and sat on the couch, engaging in pleasant conversation. Although Nina was fluent in German, she spoke to Elsa in English because Brian would be returning momentarily, and she thought it would be nice to have Elsa greet him in his native language.

"Thank you for inviting me. I can't believe I have a half-brother who lives in America."

"Well, Elsa, it's been quite a story since you brought your father's diary into the antique store to be evaluated."

"Yes. My mother kept it among her private things for many years. I never knew about it until she was dying. A few days before she passed, she revealed it to me. She told me it might be worth something and suggested I sell it. That's when I went to see Mr. Bronn. I hope it hasn't caused any problems. Uh, maybe it was helpful, too?"

"Oh, Elsa, you wouldn't believe its impact on Brian's life." *If she only knew!*

As the conversation continued, Nina observed the pretty woman's facial expressions as she spoke and soon noted minor similarities to Brian's mannerisms and looks. Nina did some math and estimated Elsa to be about eighteen months younger than Brian.

Their exchange was robust. Nina thoroughly enjoyed her openness. Elsa then revealed that she had brought several dozen photos to share with Brian. Nina apologized that he was taking longer than expected to return but encouraged her to share them. Elsa reached beside her, opened an envelope, and laid the old black and white photos on the coffee table. A minute into the photo review, Elsa surprised Nina.

"I was a twin. When I was born, my mother had a baby boy as well. He was a few minutes older than me. Unfortunately, a few weeks after I was born, the Russians were getting ready to leave the Bendlerblock building in Berlin, where my mother worked. The Russian commander, whom my mother worked for, took my brother away."

Nina looked shocked. "God, why would he do that?"

"The commander believed he was the one who had gotten my mother pregnant, and he thought we were his children." Elsa shook her head — the sadness in her heart filled her eyes as it had many times before. "But he was wrong. My mother told me she knew she was already several weeks pregnant by a Nazi soldier named Karl von Richter. When the Russian commander finally left the Bendlerblock building, he took my twin brother, left me there with my mother, and returned to Moscow."

"Oh, my God. What a terrible story. It no doubt crushed your mother. Did you ever get to meet him – I mean, meet your twin?"

"Only once. He visited my mother when I was in my early twenties. He was barely nice to her, but his behavior toward me was cold and rotten. He didn't care for a moment that I was his twin. I'm not sure how he found my mother, but he never visited us again, and I know he never wrote to her."

"I'm so sorry to hear that. I'm sure it made your mother sad for many years."

Elsa began to cry. As she composed herself, she said, "It did. And it made me sad, too."

Nearby, as Brian left the supermarket, a call from Monsignor Borrelli came in. He stopped to take it, wondering what the friendly priest had to say. At first, he was hard to understand as he bubbled enthusiastically.

"It's true, Brian. The Biblical scholars here in the Vatican agree! They say the Greek written on the scrolls is 'Vox Paulus.' It means 'Paul's voice.' They say there's no doubt the letter was written to the Ephesians, and its words had never been seen before. It's a miracle to have found this."

"That's fantastic news, Monsignor, but I'm afraid I can't talk now. I'll have to call you tomorrow. *Ciao!*"

In the living room, Nina and Elsa continued flipping through the curly-edged black-and-white photos when one person's face – especially his eyes – suddenly caught Nina's attention.

"Who's this?" she asked with alarm in her voice.

"Oh, that's him – my twin brother standing beside me. It was taken the day he visited. We were in our twenties."

Thinking he looked familiar but not quite able to place him, Nina asked, "What's his name?"

"My mother called him Karl. But the name given to him by the Russian commander was Ivan. Ivan Sokolov."

Nina leaned back on the couch, stunned by what she heard. Her insides turned.

At that moment, she heard Brian come through the front door and his phone ringing. She excused herself from Elsa and went to the kitchen. Brian put the groceries down and began pacing around the kitchen.

She heard him saying, "How could they do that? No way! It's way too soon."

The call ended.

Pale and in shock, Brian repeated aloud what he'd just said to Pieter. "How could they? How could they do that so soon?"

She was putting the milk into the refrigerator. "Who was that, Brian? What's going on?"

"It was Pieter. He called as I was coming in the house."

Her eyebrows rose. "Pieter? About what?"

"He called to tell me Pattison just sent an email. Late last night, the CIA completed a high-level prisoner exchange with the Russians. Ivan Sokolov and another FSB spy caught two years ago were flown to the Kremlin this morning in exchange for two American agents who were being held in Moscow."

She grasped his arm. "Oh, my God! Brian! How could they do that so quickly? I mean, he was just caught!"

"Do you know what freeing Ivan Sokolov means? It could have a horrible impact on our lives!"

Nina's face paled. Her eyes widened. "Oh, my God, Brian. You don't know what I just learned from Elsa. You should sit. She has a twin. She showed me a picture. Her twin brother is Ivan Sokolov. It means—"

Suddenly, Brian felt a severe sting run up his arm. He reached toward Nina as the unbearable pain continued to his chest, crushing him like he was under the foot of an elephant.

Brian collapsed to the floor.

"No! Oh, my God! No! Brian! Brian! Stay with me! Brian! Not now. You can't…"

THE END (Or is it?)

Map of Key Locations

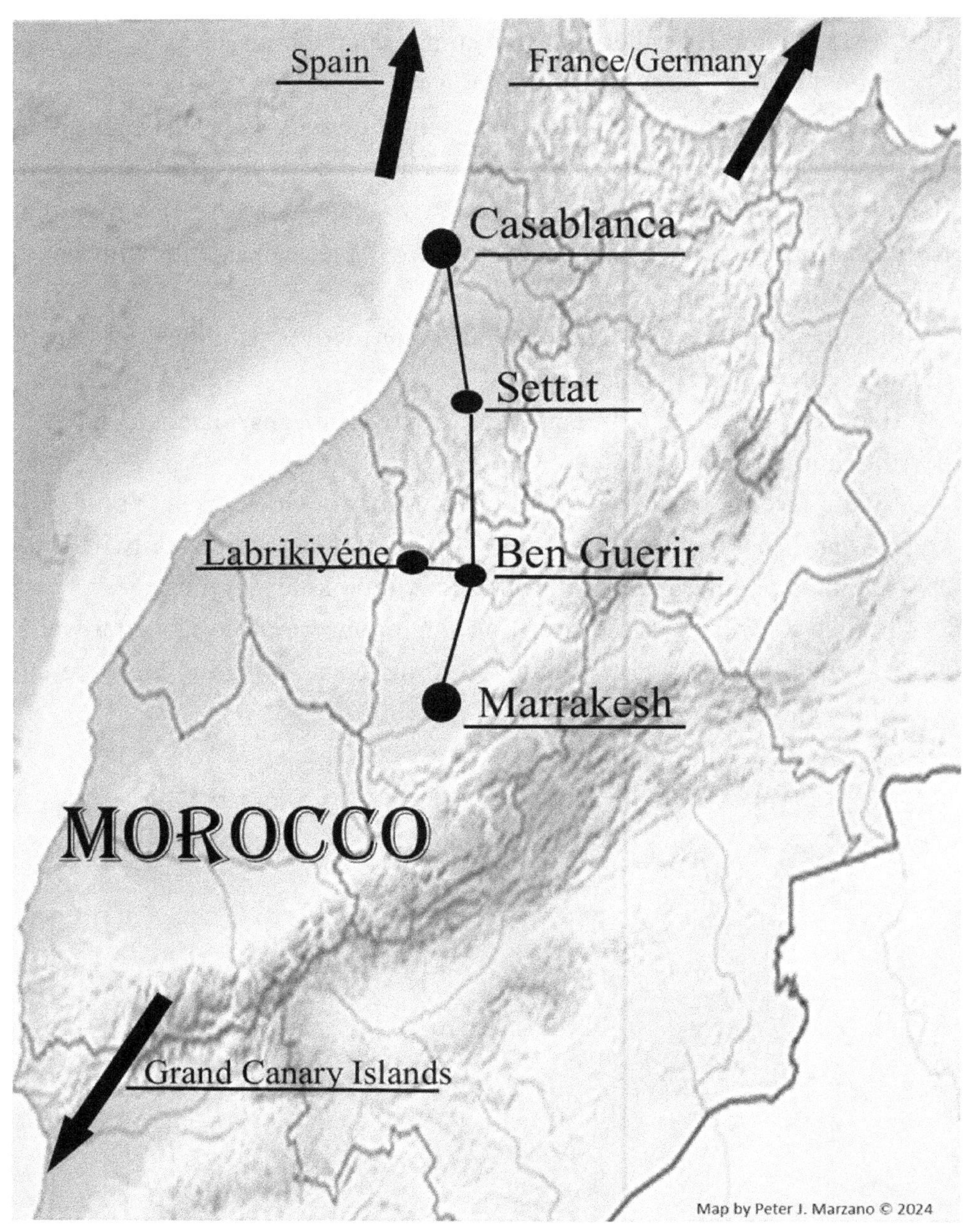

Fictitious Characters (Alphabetically by First Name)

Abraham (1)	The twins' grandfather led the camel train to secure the contents of the crashed airplane and bring it back to his home.
Abraham (2)	Ahmad's grandson when Ahmad is elderly. Abraham finds Nina and brings her to his grandfather, Ahmad, who witnessed the plane crash.
Ahmad	Twin brother of Chadu, he saw the crash of the Junker -290 plane carrying Göring's gold and art. He meets
Amare Chikere	Interpol's regional ops manager for Western and North Africa. He is called Chick by his associates.
Argyle	A young artist in Greenwich Village, NY, and a riend of Massimo Marini.
Brian O'Sullivan	Natural-born son of Katrina Amorino and Karl von Richter is an art history professor at Rutgers in NJ. He's an agent in Interpol's Art Research & Recovery Unit, searching for lost art stolen by the Gestapo and
Carlo Vieneri	Groundkeeper for Katrina and Luca's house. He also kept the house for Brian after Katrina's passing.
Chadu	Along with his twin brother Ahmad, he saw the crash of the Junker -290 plane carrying Hermann Göring's gold and art.
David Smith	CIA agent reporting to Bill Pattison.
Dmitri	Russian FSB agent who reported to Ivan Sokolov and managed FSB agent Olga.
Elsa	Sweet Hilda's daughter. She was given Karl von Richter's diary by her mother and brought it to Kristofer Bronn's antique shop to sell it.
Erick Schmidt	Interpol agent who is part of the Interpol team with Brian and Nina searching for lost art stolen by the Nazis in World War II.
Felix Freeman	Interpol agent reporting to Amare Chikere. From Liberia, the country started by American slaves who
Ivan Sokolov	FSB head agent. He managed art taken by Russians from Germany after WWII. He was Putin's friend and was in Putin's social circle.
Jay Stemmler	CIA agent reporting to Bill Pattison.

Youssef	The twins' (Ahmad and Chadu) father and Abraham's (1) son. He built the mosque in Labrikiyéne.
Katrina Amorino-Luciano	Brian's natural mother.
Katya	Russian woman, new at being an FSB agent.
Klaus Mueller	Former director of the Interpol Art Research unit and father of Wilhelm Mueller.
Kristofer Bronn	Retired Interpol agent who searched for art stolen by the Nazis in WW II. He owns an antique shop in Leipzig, where the Karl von Richter diary was brought.
KvR (Karl von Richter)	Brian O'Sullivan's biological father. German SS soldier who misplaced his diary that has information about the plane crash upon which the story is based.
Ladasha Daddah	Interpol agent reporting to Amare Chikere.
Luca Luciano	The former priest who marries Katrina. Adopted Paolo Luzzi. Opened wine export business. Brother to Dominick and Stefano Luciano, Sr. Uncle to Dominick and Stefano.
Luciano cousins	Luca's nephews, Dominick and Stefano, ran the Luciano family bank in Rome.
Massimo Marini	Brian's friend, who lived in Greenwich Village, NY, when he and Brian went to college.
Monsignor Giorgio Borrelli	Located in the Vatican, he manages the art collection.
Nina von Scholz	Interpol agent, part of the Interpol team, with Brian and Erick searching for lost art stolen by the Nazis in World War II.
Olga	Russian FSB agent who owned and ran a beauty parlor. She reported to Dmitri and managed FSB undercover spy Ursula Bloom.
Paolo Luzzi-Luciano	Katrina and Luca's adopted son. He is employed by Interpol.
Solmaz Van de Berg, called Solie	A neighbor of Nina von Scholz. She is a CIA agent who reports to Bill Pattison.
Sweet Hilda	Cook in Berlin during World War II. She discovered Karl von Richter's diary and gave it to her daughter, Elsa.
Tony Costa	Grand Master of the Order of the Knights of Malta

Tricia, Kathy, and Shawn	Brian O'Sullivan's sisters through his adoption.
Ursula Bloom	Secretary to Wilhelm Mueller, then Pieter Van Deusen. She was an undercover FSB spy who reported to Olga. Born Tamara Ehrlich in East Germany.
Wilhelm Mueller	Director of Interpol Art Research unit. Son of Klaus Mueller. Managed Art Research and Recovery team.

Real Historical Characters

Andrei Konstantinov	A WWII Russian war veteran and curator of all the art initially stolen by the Germans during WWII and then moved to Russia by the Soviet Trophy Brigades.
Hermann Göring	Germany's World War I fighter pilot ace and convicted WWII criminal who died by suicide. One of the most powerful men in the Nazi Party, commanded the Luftwaffe, president of the Reichstag,-headed Gestapo, head liquidator of confiscated estates, Hitler's chosen successor.
Hans-Joachim Pancherz	15 April 1914 – 4 May 2008. He was a German aviator and a test pilot.
Soviet Trophy Brigades	Soviet soldiers who, in WWII, were directed to retrieve art from Germany and bring it to the Soviet Union, where it was hidden and stored indefinitely.

Locations and Events of Interest

Ben Guerir	A city north of Marrakesh. Former location of a US Air Force Strategic B-52 bomber base.
Casablanca	A city in northwestern Morocco.
Casablanca's Jewish Ghetto	The poor Jewish community is located in Casablanca's inner city.
Ksar Tamentit	Located in Algeria. Built at an oasis in Tamentit.
Ksar Draa	Located in Algeria. Built by Jews in a location in the desert where there was once water.

Labrikiyéne	A small village west of Ben Guerir.
Marrakesh	A city in northwestern Morocco.
Settat	A city in northwestern Morocco, south of Casablanca.
Timimoun	Located in Algeria. A small village near the Ksar Draa.
Templar Knights	A wealthy Catholic military order founded in 1,119 A.D., headquartered in Jerusalem. The Order existed for two centuries during the Middle Ages.
Templar Trials	Trials against the Knights Templar in 1308. A document of the events written in Latin was rediscovered in 2001 and is now in the Vatican Secret Archives.

Sources

1. Wikipedia Commons; http://en.m.wikipedia.org/wiki/Wikipedia:Copyrights
2. Laura Holsomback Zelman, Master's Thesis; Looting and Restitution during World War II: A Comparison Between the Soviet Union Trophy Commission and the Western Allies Monuments, Fine Arts, and Archives Commission (unt.edu)
3. Wikipedia: Definitions of GPR and LiDAR
4. Wikipedia: Berlin Conference of 1884–85, Britain, France, Germany, and Portugal divided West Africa and made colonies. The territory that remained independent was Liberia, which had been established by the American Colonization Society, which declared its independence in 1847.
5. Wikipedia: Moktar Ould Daddah - Mauritania's first Prime Minister from 1957 to 1961 and then served as its first President of Mauritania, from 1960 until 1978, when he was deposed in a military coup d'etat.
6. Amara means "grace" in Igbo, Western Africa; Chikere means "God created" in Igbo, Western Africa.
7. Wikipedia: Wikipedia.org/wiki/List of claims for restitution for Nazi-looted art

About the Author

Peter J. Marzano is the son of an Italian and Irish family. His father arrived in New York City in 1908 from Calabria, and his mother came in 1928 from Cork. Born in Manhattan's Greenwich Village, he grew up on Staten Island, where he attended Staten Island Community College. Marzano served a construction apprenticeship and then began a sales and sales management career with divisions of General Dynamics, United Technologies, AT&T, and Air Liquid. His broad business experience spanned 45 years, allowing him to travel nationally and internationally in Europe for work and pleasure while living in Staten Island, Atlanta, Orlando, Hartford, and Wilmington, North Carolina. Marzano's knowledge and technical experience allowed him to help customers in various industrial settings.

Marzano dated his high-school sweetheart, Kathleen Coyle, for five years before marrying in 1972. Now married for fifty-two years, they have four children and eleven grandchildren. Besides designing and general contracting three of his homes, he is an avid photographer and loves capturing images of family, friends, outdoor scenery, and wildlife.

Marzano and his wife currently reside in Connecticut.

Taken from Carinhall is his third novel and third in the series, along with ***Litany of Sorrows** and **Search and Deception.***